ONE DARK SUMMER

SASKIA SARGINSON

Boldwood

First published in Great Britain in 2025 by Boldwood Books Ltd.

Copyright © Saskia Sarginson, 2025

Cover Design by Jane Dixon-Smith

Cover Images: Shutterstock

A CIP catalogue record for this book is available from the British Library.

Paperback ISBN 978-1-83603-017-1

Large Print ISBN 978-1-83603-018-8

Hardback ISBN 978-1-83603-016-4

Ebook ISBN 978-1-83603-019-5

Kindle ISBN 978-1-83603-020-1

Audio CD ISBN 978-1-83603-011-9

MP3 CD ISBN 978-1-83603-012-6

Digital audio download ISBN 978-1-83603-014-0

This book is printed on certified sustainable paper. Boldwood Books is dedicated to putting sustainability at the heart of our business. For more information please visit https://www.boldwoodbooks.com/about-us/sustainability/

Boldwood Books Ltd, 23 Bowerdean Street, London, SW6 3TN

www.boldwoodbooks.com

A riddle: Who chooses me must give and hazard all he has.

— *THE MERCHANT OF VENICE*

PROLOGUE

My fists hurt from beating them against the side of the
container. My throat is raw from screaming. Out there, in the
world, people are rushing home from work to make tea and
catch the next episode of their soap opera. They don't know
how lucky they are, how privileged. I'd do anything to be like
them. To be safe in my ordinary, mundane existence, knowing
who I love and where I belong.

I used to be one of the lucky ones. But not any more. I've
made the biggest mistake of my life and it's too late to go back. I
hug myself, cradling my aching hands. Fiery pain shoots
through the muscles in my thighs and spine. I can hardly turn
around in here. There's only just enough space to sit huddled
over with my legs bent; when I can't stay in that position any
longer, I shift with difficulty onto my knees, the crown of my
head pressing against the container. Panic is a pressure on my
chest. There's not enough room, not enough air, not enough
breath in my lungs.

I don't know if he's going to let me out, or what he'll do to me if he does. Nobody else knows where I am, except one person. And there's no way she'll help me. Not after what I did.

My body convulses with shivering. I can't stop. I lean my head against the side of my velvet-lined prison, hard, dry sobs sticking in my throat. I should never have come here. I should have left the past alone.

It's black as the grave. The air is stale. Shouting has made me light-headed. Oh, God, I don't want to die, locked in a metal box, trapped and helpless in the dark.

PART I

1

MEG

Now, 2008

This is what I remember: a lot of blood, a sudden red spurt, sticky in his hair, shocking against his skin. And water, a weight of dark water sucking him down. Then he was gone. Nothing else comes back to me, but I can't shake off the feeling of guilt, the feeling that it was me, that I did something bad. People say going back to the place where it happened will jog lost memories, allow neurons to make connections, firing up the past, spitting out the truth.

It's been fifteen years since I was last in the house where it all went wrong, where even as a child I sensed secrets clogging the air.

That changes today.

My taxi pulls up outside Deben Manor. The driver cuts the engine, and the wipers stop mid-wipe. Rain speckles the windscreen. 'That'll be five pounds, love,' he says over his shoulder. I fumble inside my purse for the fare, pressing it into his outstretched palm, and take my first proper look at the place.

Through the distortion of raindrops on glass, the Georgian house holds no sign of the darkness I unleashed the last time I was here, no trace of the tragedy I caused. Its stone facade is stalwart, its large, lighted windows promising warmth inside its sheltering walls.

As I get out of the cab, the front door of the house is flung open, and a statuesque, blonde woman strides out into the drizzly morning. My breath catches in my throat. The cab has already driven off, disappearing down the drive. I glance at its retreating shape. I should have told him to wait. What if I need to make a quick exit?

The blonde woman looks at me, and as her gaze travels over my face, the muscles in my shoulders tense. My jaw is clenched so hard, my teeth hurt. I'm wearing a purposefully unexceptional outfit of white shirt, black V-neck jumper, straight-cut clean jeans and cheap trainers. I withstand her scrutiny without blinking, as if I'm in a police line-up, and I'm the suspect.

It feels like an eternity, but it's probably only seconds before she steps forward with her hand outstretched. 'Margaret Danby?' she grins. 'You have no idea how much I've been looking forward to your arrival!'

'Mrs Manners?' We shake. 'Pleased to meet you.'

A large ring on her finger digs into my flesh as she squeezes. 'If I'd had to spend one more minute without help... well, let's just say, the corkscrew was already in my hands!' She laughs, her generous mouth pulling back to expose perfect, white teeth.

She doesn't have a clue who I am. Relief. Triumph. But a tiny part of me smarts at this proof of how little she ever knew or cared about me, how unnoticeable I was all those years ago, and still am now. And yet, of course, it's what I've been counting on.

Two flaxen-haired children tumble out of the house behind their mother. They are wild-eyed and barefoot, faces smeared with what looks like strawberry jam. The youngest has his trousers on inside out, his curls flopping in an unruly tangle over his forehead. 'These are the rug rats,' she says, pointing at them in turn, 'Kit is three. And this is Artemis. She's five.'

'Hello.' I bend down to smile at them, hoping they can't smell my fear. 'I'm Margaret. It's lovely to meet you.' I stop myself on remarking on their shoeless state. It will sound like a criticism of their mother.

'Do we call you anything for short?' the woman's asking.

'No,' I say quickly, straightening up. 'Just Margaret.'

For all her gushing enthusiasm, she's distracted, impatient to get this meet-and-greet over and done with. It gives me a chance to notice the small frown lines etched between her immaculate eyebrows and her nervy mannerisms. She's dressed in a pale pink cashmere sweatshirt and matching joggers with caramel Ugg boots, and her wrists jangle with bracelets. 'Call me Ophelia,' she says. 'We don't stand on ceremony here.' She turns, tripping over the little boy, and tuts, 'God, Kit. You're always in the wrong place. Anyway, come in, come in,' she continues, beckoning. 'Let's get out of this weather.' She shivers. 'God, doesn't January just want to make you slit your throat?'

Picking up my case, I follow her into a spacious hall, getting a fleeting impression of wine-coloured wallpaper and gilt mirrors, instead of familiar forest-green walls hung with paintings and drawings and animal heads. But there's the wide staircase I remember, and the stone-flagged floor, and I glimpse half-glazed double doors that lead into the sitting room, and a passageway towards the kitchen. I was expecting a clutter of tennis racquets, life jackets, hockey sticks, a basket of kittens, but of course, they're not here any more.

I follow her towards the glazed doors and stop dead, as if I've run into a barrier. At the end of the hall, a bigger than life-size portrait of a middle-aged man stares down at me, a slight half-smile at his lips, eyes blue as a kingfisher's wings. It's the first time I've seen his face in fifteen years. I raise a hand to cover my mouth and force myself to walk on. Ophelia is hurrying ahead as if we're on a tight schedule, gesturing left and right as she walks briskly past closed doors. 'The cloak-room. The utility room. Then that's my husband's study. He works in London.' She glances over her shoulder. 'He's away on a business trip at the moment. Makes the house feel quieter. Though my sisters are coming over tomorrow.'

I swallow my gasp. Thea and Clem. I didn't think I'd have to meet them so soon. I glance behind at the front door, my instinct to bolt back through it and run down the gravel drive, but I take a deep breath and follow her further into the house. The three sisters were always inseparable. When I'd done an internet search, Thea had come up as a fashion designer, working locally, and Clem an actress, based in Suffolk. Predictable glamorous career choices, although I'd imagined they'd be living in far-flung places by now, rather than staying close to where they'd grown up.

We're in a large, light-filled room with two French windows leading onto the garden. Ophelia has completely redecorated in here too. Three squashy sofas covered in bright cushions are arranged around a coffee table piled with art books; there are fat-bottomed glass lamps on side tables, and the floor is an expanse of nubbly sisal carpet. The colour of the walls and floor-length linen curtains are shades of cream, probably from some fancy company, each one called something like Pale Clay or Mushroom or Old Paper. It could be featured in any one of the glossy interior magazines I've flipped through in the dentist's waiting room. I wasn't expecting the makeover. It jars, this facelift to the old place.

But not everything has gone. I turn to examine three large oil paintings on the wall, portraits of young women with long hair and dreamy eyes. 'My sisters and I,' Ophelia explains. 'My mother's an artist. She painted my father, too,' she gestures towards the hall, and the portrait of the blue-eyed man. 'Sadly, he's no longer with us.'

'I'm sorry to hear that,' I mutter.

I study the pictures of the girls. I've seen them in my dreams, recreated them in my mind many times, and here they are, in tangible swirls of oil, within touching distance, exactly where they'd hung all those years ago. The paintings have the feel of a John Singer Sargent. Each girl is wearing a silk dressing gown with a Chinese design, and languishes in a velvety armchair, with her chin tilted, long bare legs sprawled. I examine them in turn. As I'm looking at a white-haired girl, rounder cheeked and more languorous than the honed and tense goddess in front of me, I turn to her. 'Oh,' I say, as if I've just twigged the resemblance. 'It's you.'

My gaze travels back across the portraits, resting on the pendants each subject wears on a chain around her neck, a gleam of gold at their breastbones.

Ophelia is grimacing, 'Nice to have a memory of youth. I'm an old hag now,' she says in the cheerful tone of the disingenuous. 'Worn out by these two,' she glances at the children, who've climbed on one of the sofas and are dangling headfirst over the back. 'I don't usually let them mess around in here,' she says, frowning, 'there's a playroom.'

I rescue Kit from falling on his skull, hoisting him under my arm. 'It's a lovely house.' I set the toddler down on his feet, whereupon he rushes straight back to clamber onto the cushions again.

She shrugs. 'It's been in the family for years. We lived here as children. And it's lucky me that gets to live here now. One day my sisters and I will inherit and then I guess we'll have to make a decision, you know, about whether to sell or not.'

'Your mother's still alive, then?'

She nods, the lines deepening between her eyebrows. 'She's retired to France. Anyway,' she says, giving me a dazzling smile, 'I'll show you to your room, shall I? And then maybe you could dive straight in and give the kids their lunch.'

My attention is caught by a framed engraving over the mantelpiece. I go over and gaze at it: a horse rearing on its hind legs, a hare crouching underneath, an unravelling scroll between its paws. It's the exact design on the pendants. My stomach contracts.

'The Aldredge family crest,' she says. 'My father's side of the family. The design goes back hundreds of years.' She shrugs. 'I found it in his things. Thought it deserved framing.'

She's standing by the door, tapping her toes with impatience. 'Shall we?' She's already heading into the hall, and I have no choice but to trot after her, case in hand. The children following behind.

Nothing strange about three sisters owning pendants engraved with the Aldredge family crest. Precious heirlooms passed down. Except I've recently discovered a Polaroid of another woman with the same necklace around her neck. A fourth pendant. I can't ask her where she got it from or why she's wearing it, because she's my mum and she's been missing for the last fifteen years.

Everyone has given up on finding her, except me, and now that I have the Polaroid, the place to start is here, even though returning to Deben Manor makes me feel like a frightened eleven-year-old again, and every corner is filled with lurking memories, one of which might reveal the truth of what I did that summer.

* * *

If I'd been a better daughter, more interesting, more helpful, more generous, then maybe Mum wouldn't have deserted us. My funny, beautiful mother, who read Tarot cards, loved seals and danced barefoot around the kitchen table; who wore Indian skirts and hennaed her hair and wasn't like anyone else's mum; but who, best of all, made me feel loved. Except, she hadn't loved me enough. Not enough to stay. She'd walked out on me and Dad one summer morning.

For years and years an echoing silence. No message, no news, no clues. She would never have abandoned me or Dad without any communication at all – no birthday cards, no telephone calls – no contact to say that she was alright. It doesn't make sense. For a long time, I couldn't sleep for trying to work it out, wondering if I'd missed something, if she'd left anything behind that might help me solve the riddle.

I'd only found the envelope behind a chest of drawers in Dad's flat because I'd pulled the drawer right out looking for the Monopoly set. The chest had come from our cottage. I'd shaken the envelope contents onto my bed, and a single Polaroid picture of my mother fell out. I thought at first Dad had taken it, but he's never owned a Polaroid camera. There Mum was, shockingly herself, smiling in slightly faded colour with the pendant around her neck. She must have moved just as the picture was taken because her right side was blurred. She was raising her hand, as if waving to me across the years.

I'd held the picture close, staring at the necklace. Blood pounded in my ears. Why was she was wearing a rare design belonging to a blue-blooded Suffolk clan? A family who had heraldic animals on shields and a family tree with roots reaching back in time? Mum always said she'd been an orphan, a child who grew up in care at the other end of the country.

And if it wasn't Dad behind the lens, pressing the button, then who?

* * *

My room is at the back of the house, so rather than the expanse of garden at the front, it faces north, with a view of outhouses and a cluster of dark trees. It's the same room I stayed in as a child. I just have time to glance around and put my case on the single bed before Ophelia is hurrying me back downstairs and into the kitchen.

It's a farmhouse-style kitchen, redone since I was last here, with fitted cream cupboards with wooden knobs, and heavy granite tops, speckled with grey. The floor is solid oak boards, and the industrial size stainless steel fridge-freezer is big enough to feed a small army.

Her mobile rings, and she picks it up. 'I'm on my way,' she says in a low voice. 'I know. I know. She's just arrived. I'll be with you soon.' She ends the call with a click and hoists Kit onto his booster seat as she gestures towards the fridge. 'Just give them whatever you think best. They're not fussy, and everything is organic.' Then she's gone, with no explanation about where to, or when she'll be back.

Neither of the children seem bothered by their mother's

departure or about being left with a stranger. I guess they're used to it. It was my agency who alerted me to the job vacancy. 'You're from Suffolk, aren't you?' my agent had asked. 'I think you'll want to apply for this one. Good money too.' When I realised where the job was, it felt like fate. I didn't even need an interview. I got the position on references alone.

I find a bag of dried pasta in one of the cupboards, some mushrooms and cheese in the fridge, and concoct a creamy sauce on the electric ring of the forest-green range while the pasta boils and bubbles. The kids have been playing a private game involving rude-sounding noises, but when I put their plates in front of them, Kit, pushes his away, bottom lip quivering. 'Sausage,' he says. It's not a question or demand, it's a statement of intent.

Artemis picks up her fork and daintily scoops up a mouthful. 'God, Kit, you're such a baby,' she says, in an uncanny impersonation of her mother. Then she looks at me. 'He only likes sausages.'

The fridge is empty of anything resembling a such a thing. I sit at the table and consider my small charge. His chubby face is flushed, and the congealed remains of strawberry jam make him look as though he's suffering from a nasty skin condition. His long, wet lashes are spangled with quivering tears. 'There are none in the fridge,' I explain, as I give his face a quick wipe with a damp cloth before he can wriggle away. 'And I don't have transport to get to the shops. We'll have to think of something else for you to eat.'

He shakes his head violently. 'I. Want. Sausage,' he gasps. I predict a full-blown tantrum in approximately one minute if I don't do something to distract him.

I rummage in the rest of the cupboards, offering different items, trying to make a joke of it, while Kit sobs and shakes his head, and his sister eats her meal with a look of smug satisfaction. Eventually, he accepts some sliced banana, a handful of salt and vinegar crisps and a couple of pickled artichokes from a jar I find at the back of a drawer and suspect might be out of date, but I remember Mum saying sell-by dates were all a con, and that the numbers were only there to make people paranoid and the manufacturers more money.

Did she ever live in this house? Is there a fourth pendant – somehow lost by the family – that she'd bought in a second-hand shop? It seems unlikely. The pendant isn't even the sort of jewellery she'd once liked. She didn't usually wear any, only her gold wedding band and a silver ring with a round opal. When her hand moved, the milky white surface of the stone flashed rose and blue, golden yellow and leaf green, the colours shining from deep inside the stone, as if coming up through water. 'It represents hope,' she told me. 'Hope, clarity and truth.'

I stand up and look out of the rain-speckled window, across the long expanse of lawn towards the bare beech trees that stand sentinel along the lane, and beyond that, only three miles away across the marshes, past the village of Charsford, is the river. If I followed it, I'd come to the cottage we once lived in. I wish I could remember my last moments with her – but all I recall is the smell of cut grass coming through the window as I ate a bowl of cereal. I didn't know I had to pin every detail into my mind.

Mum has never been reported as a missing person; she'd left home voluntarily, leaving a note saying we weren't to look for her. When I told Dad that I planned to go and ask the police to investigate the possibility that she'd been kidnapped, he'd argued at first, but realising I couldn't be dissuaded, he went to see them himself. He went alone, wearing a shirt and tie, his hair carefully plastered down. When he'd returned, he'd shaken his head. 'They won't take it seriously, love. She's over eighteen and there's no evidence of foul play. She left a note, so as far as they're concerned, she's a runaway. She would have gone off to London, to the bright lights, not stayed around here.'

But I knew differently. Mum hated the city. She belonged in the wild. She would never have left this area. She would never have chosen to desert me.

2

From the moment I planned my return to Deben Manor, I was haunted by a nightmare in which Ophelia points her manicured finger at me. 'My God,' she whispers. 'You're her, aren't you? Our cousin, Meg? Meg the Mouse?' Then she shudders, her gaze cold. 'Leave my house,' she says, voice rising. 'Get out. How dare you come back!'

But we haven't met since I was eleven. When Ophelia last saw me, I'd been short and chubby, my round face covered with freckles. My freckles faded as I put on a belated growth spurt in my teens, puppy fat melting away as I'd shot up, becoming tall and skinny like Dad. The grown-up me is a beanpole with jutting hips, my broad and angular shoulders the kind found on professional swimmers (ironic, as I'm afraid of water). After the agency confirmed I'd got the job, I dyed my mousey hair in the sink using a packet from Boots. The result is more Ploughed Field than the promised Mahogany, but the stronger shade has made the tone of my skin look pinker, which is a bonus. I've swapped my normal contact lenses for brown ones to disguise my grey eyes. And at the last minute, after a bout of nerves that I needed even more of a disguise, I went to the hairdresser and sat for hours inhaling chemical fumes to have a perm. Every time I glance in a mirror, I'm shocked by my new corkscrew curls, surprised if they tickle my face.

My efforts seem to have paid off. But what about Thea and Clem? When they turn up, will my changed appearance fool them too? Do they know what happened that morning? Dad reassured me it wasn't my fault. But when someone keeps telling you that, you know they're really suggesting the opposite. I don't know what the family think, but their silence is a clue. None of them have spoken to me since. There are gaps in my memory, repeating images that don't join up, don't make sense: a sudden flow of blood, my hand clasping something hard, panic like trapped wings in my chest.

* * *

At the end of my first day, it's a relief to go to bed and close the door. Coming here has been even more nerve-wracking than I'd expected. Not much has changed in my old room. The beige carpet is spotted with stains, there's a battered pine chest of drawers in the corner and the same checked curtains droop across the window. There are signs of a previous occupant: glittery stickers peeling on the window, a towelling dressing gown left behind, hanging from a hook on the door, and when I push my unpacked suitcase under the bed, I find a month-old women's magazine and an odd sock forgotten in the dust. They must have belonged to the nanny before me.

After Mum disappeared, Dad sent me here for the summer holidays. He said he couldn't work and look after me, and it would be nice for me to get to know my cousins. I could tell he was trying to be cheerful about it, and it was as if I heard Mum whispering *put on a brave face*. So, I tried, even though I was scared and sad.

'It's only about half an hour from our cottage,' he told me, as we drove to Deben Manor. 'You won't be far from home.'

'Why have we never visited them before,' I asked, 'if they live so close?'

'Oh, my sister's busy,' Dad said in an off-hand manner. 'With her painting and her family. We live different lives.' He gave a gruff laugh. 'She's moved up in the world. Or she thinks she has, anyway.' He'd shaken his head. 'She's even changed her name. Calls herself Calista now.' His fingers whitened on the steering wheel. 'I don't know what was wrong with Janet,' he muttered.

I didn't like the sound of my aunt. My tummy tightened, the sick feeling getting worse. 'That's it,' he said slowing the car as we drove past a wooden fence with a line of beech trees behind them. 'Deben Manor.'

I pressed my nose to the passenger window, glimpsing the house in slices between tree trunks. It looked imposing, sitting on a rise, above a long emerald lawn. The house was pale brick with tall windows and a mass of purple wisteria growing up it. 'Beautiful, isn't it?' Dad murmured. 'Georgian, I think.'

'It's huge,' I whispered, thinking of our cosy cottage, and how Mum and Dad always felt close even when I was in my own room at night.

'And they have a place in France,' Dad made a little cluck of disapproval. 'You'd think that one big house would be enough for any family.'

My aunt was like a beautiful version of Dad. The sharp nose and narrow eyes that made Dad look a bit like a hawk somehow worked on her, all her features in exactly the right place. Her slenderness gave her an ethereal look in her paint-splatted dungarees. 'I'm so sorry about Irene. It must be awful,' she said a stagey whisper to Dad, and then turned to me. 'And you must be Meg. I last saw you as a little thing – gosh, years ago.' Her voice rose, becoming overly loud and cheerful. 'You'll have such fun this summer with my girls.' She lifted her head, yelling, 'Clementine, Thea, Ophelia! Come and be nice to your cousin.' Dad had a Suffolk accent. Even when she shouted, my aunt sounded as if she was reading the news on the BBC.

I shrank in embarrassment as three older girls appeared: a dark-haired, imperious beauty, a strawberry redhead with enviable waist-skimming locks, and a tall girl with white-blonde hair. I saw myself through their eyes: a boring, plain child come to spoil their summer. In contrast, they were gorgeous and sophisticated, and towered over me. Through her open shirt and between her miniscule bikini, I caught glimpses of the blonde's flat, tanned stomach. Strings of tiny colourful beads looped her wrists, and all three had the same elaborate gold pendants at their necks. I couldn't quite make out the design.

Aunt Calista reeled off the girls' names. Then she puts her arm through Dad's and took him off into the kitchen to have a 'quick coffee,' leaving me at the mercy of the sisters.

'How old are you?' asked the dark one, yawning. Thea, I remembered.

'Eleven.'

'Aren't you small for eleven?' the blonde asked, Ophelia.

'Maybe,' I whispered, raising up onto my tiptoes.

'We should call her Mouse,' announced the redhead, Clementine.

The other two laughed. 'Meg the Mouse,' Ophelia said. 'Perfect, Clem.'

I wobbled on my toes, grabbed the back of a chair, and sank down onto flat feet; when I dared to look up, they were whispering together. I cleared my throat. 'How old are you?'

'I'm nearly twelve,' Clementine said, playing with her necklace and looking bored.

Thea sat on the arm of the sofa, her hands in her pockets. 'Fifteen,' she said, gazing out of the window.

'And I'm the oldest,' Ophelia said. 'I'm seventeen and three quarters.'

'She thinks she's grown up,' Thea added.

'Ha,' Ophelia laughed. 'You'll never be older than me.'

I was jealous of their familiarity, their easy bantering. I'd always wanted a sister or brother.

'I like your bracelets,' I told Ophelia.

'These?' She held up her wrist, loops of beads sliding down, rainbow colours glinting. 'Got them in a French market. We went to our house in France in half term.'

'We were supposed to go again for August,' Clem added. 'But Ma says we have to stay at home because of you.'

I didn't know if I should apologise for depriving them of their French holiday. I was desperately trying to think of something else to say, a comment on how close in age I was to Clem perhaps, when, as if acting on an unheard order, they turned to leave the room. I watched them go, chatting to each other in low voices.

I was alone, except for their dog, an Afghan Hound, who leant against my knee and snuffled into my hand hopefully. I fondled the animal's silky ears, and glanced up, to find three pairs of eyes gazing back at me. My cousins' portraits hung on the wall. I hadn't noticed before – there'd been so much else in the room to distract me – the pictures were almost life-size. In daubs and strokes of colour, the artist had picked out the exact details of each girl's features, the sinuous folds of their silky dressing gowns, the glint of gold around their necks. Overwhelmed by the force of those painted stares that told me that I wasn't good enough, pretty enough, or clever enough, I turned away, stripping my thumbnail down to the quick with my front teeth until I tasted blood.

3

My first night back at Deben Manor, I blink into darkness, forgetting for a second where I am. Something woke me. A door slamming. It takes me another second to orientate myself. Moonlight slants through a gap in the thin curtains. The scent of leather and cloves sends adrenaline rushing through me. My ears strain for sounds, but I can't hear anything except the click and tap of the sleeping house, old timbers, mice in the cavities, pipes creaking. I lean across and check my phone. It's 3 a.m.

The scream of my alarm shocks me out of sleep.

I remember waking last night. The slam of a door. I must have been dreaming. I sit up, shivering. The room is icy – maybe I need to bleed the radiator. Yesterday, I'd felt triumph that my disguise had worked, but now I feel sick about it; how am I going to keep it up? What if Clem or Thea recognises me today?

I pull on my clothes and stumble along the landing to the bathroom. Ophelia pointed out where the kids slept on our whirlwind tour, but with the noise they're making, I wouldn't have had any problem tracking them down. It's Saturday, and I'm not supposed to be working, but I can't ignore the racket. I push open the door to Artemis's room and find her sitting on top of her brother in a bedroom strewn with clothes and toys. She's holding his wrists by his head, shouting into his face as he writhes and screams. Both are still in their pyjamas. I haul her up under her armpits and then help Kit to his feet. 'I hate Arty!' He's sobbing, but as soon as he's free, he aims a kick at her knee. 'Pig!'

'Hey,' I pull him back. 'Come on. This isn't the way to start the day. Let's see who can get dressed first and they get to choose breakfast.'

'Can we have anything we like?' Artemis checks.

I nod. 'Except sausages. I'll get some when I go to the shops. But I'll have to ask Mummy first.'

'Mummy's in bed,' Artemis says. 'She doesn't like to be disturbed in the morning.'

I try a tickling tactic, chasing them around the bed and making them both giggle until they are too limp to resist getting into their clothes. 'Aunty Thea and Aunty Clem are coming for lunch today,' Artemis announces, as she allows me to brush her hair.

My hand falters before I find the rhythm of the brush again. 'That will be nice,' I say.

* * *

I've given the children their lunch and am in the middle of stacking plates in the dishwasher when Ophelia comes in with bulging grocery bags. I expect her to apologise for abandoning me with her offspring on my day off, but she dumps her shopping on the table without glancing in my direction. 'God, it's freezing outside,' she announces, as she unpacks luscious-looking olives, jars of humous and packets of ham and cheese wrapped in greaseproof paper that must have come from a deli in town. She's unwrapping a triangle of squishy brie when the doorbell rings.

'Could you get that?' she says, licking her fingers. 'Bring them straight through.'

Artemis bounces on her chair in excitement. 'Can I let them in?'

'Margaret will do it.' Ophelia tilts her head meaningfully in the direction of the front door. I wipe my palms over my jeans and walk into the hall, heart thumping against my ribcage. I pull it open, trying to compose my expression into innocent blankness.

A dark-haired woman and another with scarlet hair are standing on the step. Even with noses pink from the cold, they're as attractive and glamorous as I'd imagined they would be. Thea flicks back her glossy bob, her eyes bright and searching. I shrink under her scrutiny. 'Who are you?' she asks.

'The new nanny,' I mutter, unable to hold her gaze any longer. 'Margaret.'

'Oh, you know.' Clem jogs her sister's elbow. 'Didn't you help Ophelia decide on her?' She gives me a slow once-over. 'Immaculate references, I seem to remember.'

Clem must dye her hair – it wasn't such a bright red when she was a child. She's clutching a bottle of wine. She's much thinner too. I'm shocked by her hollowed cheekbones and coat-hanger shoulders.

Thea gives me a cool stare. 'Ophelia doesn't have much luck with nannies – half of them run off in tears.' She raises one eyebrow at her sister. 'The last one was completely mad, remember? She thought the house was haunted. And the one before that... well, less said about that the better.'

'Don't mind her,' Clem tells me with a tight smile. 'She's always grumpy before she eats.'

'That's so not true,' Thea is saying as they go past me.

Dead leaves whirl towards the house. I shut the door against the howling wind, taking the time to breathe deeply. It's alright. I've passed the second test. I was invisible to them when I was a child, and they have no reason to suspect the tall, gangly nanny with the shock of dark curls is really the cousin they called Mouse. The women are already marching through to the kitchen. I can hear them greeting their sister, the rustle of coats being shed, chairs being pulled out. There's the sound of children's voices, an excited giggle from Artemis.

When I reach the kitchen, the adults are sitting at the table, and Ophelia is pouring the wine. She glances up at me. 'Did they introduce themselves?' she asks, gesturing towards them. 'Thea and Clem, this is Margaret.'

Clem makes an affirmative noise in her throat as she leans forward to tickle her nephew's tummy. Artemis has climbed onto Thea's lap and is playing with a pendant hanging around her aunt's neck on a gold chain. The Aldredge pendant. The same as the one my mum wears in the Polaroid. 'Leave that,' Thea says, setting Artemis on the floor. 'Run and play.'

'Glass of wine?' Ophelia asks me.

I shake my head, because she seems to expect me to look after the children, even though my contract states I have Saturdays off. I don't want to make a fuss on my first day here, not with all three sisters in the room.

'Cheers.' She turns to the others, lifting her glass. 'How are things?'

In a low voice, I encourage a reluctant Kit and Artemis to

leave the room as the women chat, talking about Clem's upcoming audition for a new TV drama, and Thea's plans for a fashion show in Ipswich. I've just managed to persuade both children to come with me when a question from Thea jolts me into stillness.

'Have either of you heard from Ma?'

I pause at the door, holding Kit's hand, Artemis scowling up at me.

'I talked to her on the phone the other night,' Clem says.

'Did you ask her?' Thea says. 'About, you know?'

'The situation hasn't changed.'

'Maybe we should visit anyway,' Ophelia suggests. 'We should insist.'

'We can't,' Clem says. 'You know the rule. She's adamant about it. And we promised.'

'It's a stupid rule,' Thea mutters. 'It's been bloody years now. It shouldn't be held over our heads like this.'

Ophelia looks up at me. 'Was there something you wanted, Margaret?'

'No,' I say, my face stinging with heat. 'We're just going.'

As soon as I'm out in the corridor, the door to the kitchen is softly closed behind me. Something makes me hesitate and turn back. I stand with my ear to the door. The three of them are murmuring in urgent voices but I can't catch any words.

How strange, why won't Calista allow her daughters to visit?

'What are you doing?' demands Artemis loudly, and I put my finger to my lips.

'Playing a game,' I whisper, walking away before she can say anything else.

Hearing the sisters together gives me the same needy

feeling I got that summer, when I was their annoying cousin, foisted onto them for the holiday, forever the outsider, never privy to their secrets. Only, I'm not a child any more, and I'm here for a reason. I can't change the past or bring a dead man back to life – but I can try to find out the truth.

4

It's Monday morning, and I need to get the kids to school, but there's no sign of Ophelia and I have no instructions on what to do. I leave the children in the bathroom cleaning their teeth and knock on Ophelia's door. There's a muffled reply and I stick my head into a gloomy space, fuggy with last night's sleep, curtains pulled against the morning. A shape moves under the covers, raising her head from the pillow; she tweaks up one side of an eye mask. 'Yes?'

'Sorry,' I say. 'But I don't know where Artemis's school is.'

She sighs and raises herself into a sitting position. 'Damn, I should have told you yesterday.' She slips a silk dressing gown around her shoulders, pushes her feet into a pair of downy slippers and pads past me. The children must have heard her voice as they come tearing out of the bathroom, mouths whitened with toothpaste, and throw themselves at her long legs.

'Mummy!' Artemis says. 'Are you taking me to school?'

'No, darling.' Ophelia extracts fistfuls of robe from her

daughter's grasp. 'That's Margaret's job now. Mummy has other things to do.'

I wonder what things, exactly; as far as I could tell from my internet search, Ophelia Manners doesn't have a job, or work for a charity, or anything else that could take up her entire day.

With the kids settled at the breakfast table, Ophelia calls me into a little room off the kitchen that used to be a walk-in pantry. It's a cosy office now, with a laptop on a glass table, and an array of framed family photos on the windowsill, including one of the sisters together, pendants around their necks. 'Those necklaces,' I say. 'I noticed them in your portraits. How come you and your sisters have the same one?'

'They were made for our ancestors, three other Aldredge sisters,' she says. 'Our father said he always hoped for three daughters so that we could inherit them.'

'So, there isn't another one like it?'

She shoots me a puzzled look. 'No. Why?'

'No reason.' My face colours.

She sits at the desk on an ergonomic chair. 'I'll write down the address of their schools.' She scribbles on a note pad, tucking some hair behind her ear, exposing a large diamond stud. 'Arty goes in every day. She finishes at noon on Wednesdays. And Kit is in nursery three mornings a week, Monday to Wednesday. His nursery is part of her school – so it's just one place for you to go. But I want you to do all the school runs.' She glances up at me. 'I gather you have a clean licence. You can use our little run-around, the white Fiat outside.' As she hands me the keys, my eye is caught by another photo.

Lucian Aldredge stares at me, chin tilted. Clouds scud past behind him, sails in the background. He's wearing a navy sailor's cap, his distinctive reddish hair sticking out from under it. He's dishevelled by the wind, and a broad grin makes apples of his ruddy cheeks. But his smile is not for me.

His blue eyes regard me coldly. *I know who you are.*

I shudder and turn away, but Ophelia has noticed. 'My father,' she says. 'Lucian Aldredge. It's his portrait in the hall. He was killed years ago in a tragic accident.'

'I'm... I'm sorry,' I say.

She leans in to look at the photo. 'We miss him terribly.'

'What... what happened?' I force myself to ask. 'If you don't mind me asking.'

Anticipation kicks at my ribs as she seems to consider my question; then she slowly turns away from me. 'He drowned,' she says softly, facing his photo. 'He died saving someone. Our cousin. She—' she breaks off, swallows. 'She was always pestering him to give her sailing lessons. There was an accident. Nobody knows what really happened. He was a skilled sailor.' She turns back to me, and her eyes have hardened into a glassy stare. 'We took her in when she needed shelter.' She straightens her shoulders. 'If she hadn't been here... he'd still be with us.'

My mouth dries, and I take a step back. It was my fault. This is what Dad tried to protect me from knowing. It's airless and claustrophobic in the room. I can't breathe. Guilt squeezes oxygen from my body. I close my eyes against a grey wave of remembering. Blood blooms thick and bright against pale skin. The image knocks me sideways. My knees falter and I lean against the doorframe.

'Are you okay?' Ophelia is there, her nails sharp on my elbow.

I blink at her, the room swimming back into focus. 'Maybe I need to eat something. Low blood sugar.'

'Well, you'd better hurry up,' she says, doubtfully. 'It's a fifteen-minute drive to the school. And it'll take you ten minutes to get Kit into his car seat.'

She wraps her robe around her and disappears, hair swishing at her back. A pain in my hand makes me wince. Unclenching my fingers, I look down at the point of the car key digging into my flesh.

* * *

The first time I'd met Lucian, he'd come striding into the kitchen at lunchtime, a broad-shouldered giant, his hair a flame of red gold.

'Pa!' Thea jumped up.

He scooped her to his chest. 'How are my beauties?' he asked in a booming voice. 'I've missed you.'

The other two rushed to him and threw their arms around his waist, the four of them huddling together in such a tangle of joy, it hurt to look at them. I wished my own dad were there. Although he'd never behave like this. He'd never call me his beauty. He called me Squirt because I was small.

'Where have you been?' Ophelia was asking.

'In London. Pa has to work, my darling,' he said, dropping a kiss onto her silvery head. 'And who is this stranger at our table?' he looked at me with a bright gaze, but his teasing smile betrayed his question. He knew perfectly well who I was, but he was enjoying the joke.

'She's Meg,' Clem told him. 'Our cousin.'

'But we call her Mouse,' Ophelia said.

'Her mother ran away,' Thea added.

'Well, the child doesn't want to be reminded of that,' he admonished gently as he relinquished his clutch of daughters. 'I'm hungry. Who's going to make me some lunch?' He clapped his hands, as if calling an army of servants. 'An omelette. Two eggs. Lots of cheese. I'm ravenous.'

'I will!' they chorused. 'Me!'

Despite his energy, his exaggerated gestures and booming voice, there was a stillness about him. I didn't understand it completely, but I sensed a power coming from him, as if his certainty made him even bigger than he already was. While Ophelia prepared his lunch, Clem and Thea sat either side, leaning towards him, telling him how the new kittens were getting on. 'They're thriving, are they?' he said. 'And I suppose the father was that great ginger brute we see hanging around? The rascal who yowls all night.' He tutted. 'And now he's had his evil way with our lovely Lola.'

'Some of them are turning out ginger like him,' Ophelia said, putting a cup of tea in front of him. 'But some are black, and two look more like her.'

'What about your piano practice, Ophelia?' he took a sip of tea. 'I hope you've kept it up. I expect to hear that Mozart piece this weekend.'

'Yes, Pa,' she said, as she cracked eggs into a bowl. 'I've almost got it now.'

'And you, Thea,' he said. 'How was your last ballet lesson at school?'

In answer, she slipped from her chair and span around on one leg, arms held in front of her as if clutching a beachball. I didn't know much about ballet, despite having had lessons myself, but I could tell that she was elegant and poised as she did a little hop, landing on one leg and sticking the other straight out in the air behind her. I wished that I'd paid more attention in my own dance classes with Mum's friend Claire.

Their father laughed. 'You'll be starring in *Swan Lake* in no time.'

'And I've been chosen for the athletics team again, for next term,' Clementine told him, not to be outdone. 'The hurdles and the five hundred metres.'

'I was an athlete at school, too,' he said. 'I believe my records are still unbroken.' He patted her cheek. 'You take after me.'

And suddenly, his gaze was aimed at me. Something in his eyes had clouded. 'I can't say that you look much like your mother,' he said, as if talking to himself. 'Or your father, for that matter.' He winked at me. 'Are you sure you aren't a changeling?'

A hated blush boiled under my skin. 'Do you know my parents?' I managed, as I couldn't remember ever meeting this man. He wasn't someone I'd have forgotten.

'Of course,' he said. 'My wife is your father's sister. I was at your parents' wedding, and I met you when you were a baby.'

Energy emanated from him like a magnetic force. It was impossible not to feel drawn to him. When he turned his attention on me, it wasn't just my cheeks burning, I glowed inside. I wanted his smile, his approval. I wanted him to look at me in the same way he looked at his daughters, as if they were the most precious things in the world.

A woman came into the kitchen, dragging a hoover. She was wearing a blue housecoat, a floral scarf tied around her dark hair.

'Morning, Mrs K,' Lucian said. 'Or is it afternoon already? How are you?'

'Can't complain, Mr Aldredge,' she said.

'Mr Kerry's chest is better I hope,' he said. 'And how's the rest of your family? Your lovely daughters.'

'They're doing well at school,' she said. 'Karin's got it into her head that she wants to be a film director.'

'A film director? Well, that is a fine ambition.' He finished his lunch and stood up. 'We'll let you get on in here,' he said, 'Come along, girls. Let's leave Mrs K to try and tame the chaos.'

Obediently, I trailed behind the four of them, trying to think of something to say that would draw his approval, his light, towards me.

* * *

A loud yelp and a crash interrupts my reminiscing. I hurry towards the sound. In the kitchen, Artemis is standing barefoot in a mess of smashed bowl, cereal and milk, her breakfast splattered over her nightdress and the floor. 'He made me drop it,' she points an accusing finger at Kit. 'He did it on purpose!' Kit bursts into tears.

I grab a cloth from the sink. 'Don't move, either of you, till I clear this up,' I tell them as I get onto my knees. 'These broken bits are sharp. No need to cry, Kit. I'm sure it was accident,' I add.

The word 'accident' echoes inside my head. I can't unhear what Ophelia said. The sisters think it's my fault their father's dead.

Why can't I remember what I did?

5

The next day, after dropping Artemis at school, and Kit at nursery, I drive into Charsford and pick up some groceries, including several packs of sausages. The village shop hasn't changed; the woman behind the counter is the same too, just older, greyer; she continues to chat to another customer without giving me a second glance as she hands over my change.

Back in Deben Manor, there's a note on the hall table from Ophelia telling me she's gone out. With a fizz of excitement, I realise I have the place to myself. This is my opportunity to look around properly. I have no idea what I'm looking for, but I'm confident I'll know it when I see it. I'll get the shopping unpacked and put away first.

I bump the kitchen door open with my hip, arms full of bags, but nearly drop them in shock when I realise, I'm not alone. A wiry woman at the sink turns towards me, hands clad in yellow Marigolds. I recognise her. She's even wearing the same type of housecoat. Her hair has turned iron grey and it's pinned into a neat bun. She's thinner in the face, but it's Mrs K, without a doubt. It hadn't occurred to me that she'd still be working here. I cringe inside but have no choice but to brazen it out.

'Hello,' I say, putting the bags on the table. 'I'm Margaret, the new nanny.'

'I heard you were here,' she says, appraising me with pale eyes. 'The last one didn't last five minutes. Hope you're made of sterner stuff.' She seems unaware that she's met me before. I breathe a sigh of relief. If I'd passed her in the street, I might not have recognised her either; context makes a memory prompt.

'I hope so, too,' I say.

'I'm Mrs Kerry,' she says. 'You can call me Mrs K.'

'Will you be long in the kitchen?' I ask as casually as I can.

'Want to make lunch, do you?' Her voice is sharp.

'No,' I say, quickly. 'No hurry.'

'I'll be another thirty minutes, then I'm going upstairs,' she says. 'It's my day for changing the sheets.'

'I'll just unpack this lot, then,' I say. 'And I'll leave you in peace.'

She bustles around, while I put the groceries away as fast as possible, shoving packets of sausages in the fridge. I don't want to waste any of the thirty minutes I have left. I sense her giving me sideways looks, and keep my face turned away.

I decide the place to begin my search is the attic. It's furthest from the kitchen, and I may as well start at the top and work my way down. I've never seen inside it. The room was always locked. It used to hold a fascination because of it.

My first night at Deben Manor as a child, I'd woken to find myself outside that door, toes curling against cold floorboards.

I'd blinked into the gloom, too scared to move. It wasn't the first time I'd sleepwalked, but it was the first time away from home. At the cottage, Mum or Dad would guide me back to bed. I didn't know where I was. My nose itched. Funny-smelling smoke drifted from the floor. I shivered, peering around, unable to get my bearings. I put my hand out and came up against a wooden surface, feeling along it and down, locating a handle. I tried to open it, but however hard I pressed, the door refused to give. Panic shot through me.

As my blindness receded, shapes formed from shadows. I wasn't inside a room. I was outside it, standing on a narrow landing with a steep flight of stairs behind me. I must be at the top of the house. The smoke seemed to be coming from under the locked door, but there were no crackling flames, no sign of burning.

The next morning, at breakfast, I'd asked Ophelia about the room. 'It's where Pa keeps the art stuff that he's going to sell,' she'd told me. 'Inside, there's a special sealed container for paintings that need to be kept at the right temperature. We were here when he had it delivered. A metal crate.' She crunched a mouthful of toast. 'It took three men to carry it up the stairs.' She laughed. 'They were swearing and sweating. But Pa was excited.'

I was intrigued by the idea of this container. 'What kind of temperature does it have to be at?'

She swallowed and licked her lips. 'I don't know exactly,' she said. 'But paintings can't get too hot or too cold, or damp or anything, or they'll be spoiled.'

'Can I see?'

She shook her head. 'We're not allowed up there.'

Ophelia told me the smoke drifting under the door was

from her father's cigar – he kept a box of them on his desk in his study, the lid decorated with bright parrots and gold scrolls – but he often smoked in the attic while he was working. After that, when I'd woken at night to the scent of cloves and leather, I knew Lucian was in the room above, sorting through his latest acquisitions. It had been reassuring knowing he was close. I could even hear him sometimes, the creak of a floorboard as he trod across my ceiling.

* * *

I glance at my watch. I should have at least twenty minutes left for my search if I hurry. Leaving Mrs Kerry in the kitchen, I go through the hall and up the main staircase to the first floor, moving softly along the landing, then up the narrow, steep flight to the attic. The bare boards are slippery. It makes me shudder to think of myself as a child climbing them in my sleep. It's a miracle I didn't break my neck. At the top, the door is shut. Hesitantly, I push against it, turning the handle. It doesn't move. I shiver; this part of the house is freezing. A whistling draught bites at my ankles.

I step away from the door, wondering if the sealed container is still inside, and if any of Lucian's treasures remain in there. I can't think of any other reason why the door would stay locked after all this time.

As I go back down, I hear the roar of the hoover. It's too risky to start searching other rooms with Mrs Kerry on the loose. There must be a key to the attic somewhere – I'll look for it as soon as I have an opportunity.

My chance comes that evening. The kids are in bed, Mrs Kerry has gone home, and I've put the kettle on for a cup of tea when Ophelia sashays into the kitchen, red dress swirling around her knees, high heels clicking on the tiles. 'I'm nipping out,' she says. 'Saul will be home late. You don't mind babysitting, do you?'

'That's fine. I'm staying in,' I add unnecessarily. The kettle boils and I get up to pour water into my cup, pushing the teabag against the side.

'Good.' She smiles with painted lips, gazing past me at her reflection caught in the dark glass of the window. A toss of her head sends her hair swinging around her shoulders like a shampoo commercial.

After she leaves, I wait to hear the front door shut, then the sound of tyres on the gravel. I count to ten slowly, to check she's really gone before I slip into her study and begin to open drawers. I rifle through paperwork, pulling out plastic folders and phone chargers, lip balms, receipts, stubs of pencils and old diaries. There's no sign of any key. The only thing I'm uncovering are Ophelia's untidy habits. She's the kind of person who keeps pristine surfaces, but underneath, in hidden cupboards and drawers, a tangled mess lurks. I pick up a lipstick without a top, the waxy end crushed to a stump and speckled with dirt.

'Looking for something?'

I gasp and swing around. A man dressed in a suit, tie loosened around his neck, stands there, leaning against the doorframe. He's got cheekbones to cut yourself on. He pushes a hand through thick, dark hair. 'The nanny, I presume?'

I nod, warily. 'Margaret Danby.'

'Saul.' His gaze flicks over me, lingering at my waist and legs, and returning to my face. 'The husband.' His tone is ironic, eyes mocking.

I feel a blush starting at the base of my neck and turn away, not wanting him to see the blaze in my cheeks.

'You're off limits, Margaret Danby,' he says. 'What are you doing in here?'

I glance at the open drawers, the piles of paper I've dumped on the desk. My mind scrabbles for an excuse. 'The contact number for Artemis's school,' I invent. 'She may not be able to go in tomorrow.'

'Why not just ask my wife?'

'She's not here.'

'Where is she?'

'I don't know.'

I shove the mess back into the drawers while he watches. Will he tell Ophelia I've been snooping through her stuff? I want to get out of the room, but he's blocking my exit. I've worked in households with men with wandering hands. My invisible act doesn't always protect me – in fact, some men think that the plain, awkward nanny will be only too grateful for their attentions. As I try to slide past, he puts out an arm to stop me passing. 'Where are you off to in such a hurry?'

I taste his astringent cologne at the back of my throat. My insides clench. I'm alone in the house with him.

'I'm going to bed,' I say, keeping my voice steady and ducking under his arm. 'Excuse me.'

'What, you're leaving me here on my own?' His beery breath makes me wrinkle my nose. He turns to watch me as he slumps against the doorframe, seemingly amused. 'I already feel as if you don't like me very much.'

'I don't have an opinion. You and Ophelia are my employers.' I am aware of how stiff and prissy I sound, but I don't want him to know he's scaring me.

'I suppose you've met Clem and Thea by now?' His mouth tightens. 'It's those sisters you need to watch out for, not me. They work in a pack.' He follows me out of the kitchen into the corridor. 'Never cross one – because they'll all take her side.' His voice rises as I walk away. 'Don't say I didn't warn you.'

'Goodnight, Mr Manners,' I say, over my shoulder.

As I mount the stairs, I hear him laugh. Now I understand the rapid turnover of nannies in this house. If he behaves like that with all of them, no wonder they leave in a hurry.

6

I wake to the sound of raised voices. Saul and Ophelia. I can't make out words, just the force of their anger. A door slams and a bolt of adrenaline hits my heart. I'll never get back to sleep now. I fumble for my phone in the darkness and squint at it: 3 a.m. I listen for more shouting, but the house is quiet again, just a lingering tension, the backwash of their argument stirring up molecules. I turn over, plumping my pillow, and settle my cheek against cotton; I'm drifting off when another noise alerts me. A quiet scrabbling above my head. It's coming through my ceiling. Mice or rats? The attic room is directly above me. I lie down again, determined to get some sleep.

* * *

The next morning, I'm bleary from my disturbed night, and I need all my patience to cope with the children. Neither of them wants to get dressed, and then they're fractious and demanding at breakfast. Luckily, it seems Saul has already left for work, and Ophelia is in bed. I couldn't face dealing with the parents as well. Outside the window, it's wet and grey.

I drive the children to their school and nursery, hoping I'll have some time alone in the house when I get back. I want to find that key.

On the way home, dark clouds whirl across the flat landscape. The sky is alive with flailing branches and ricocheting twigs, skeleton trees tossing in the wind. Bursts of rain shatter across the windscreen and I hunch in my seat, leaning forwards, gripping the wheel; even with the wipers set to fast, the rubber blades are hardly able to clear the glass before the next wave splatters.

The summer I stayed at Deben Manor, each day seemed hotter than the last. Every morning was golden, shimmering with heat. Calista would disappear into her studio at the back of the house, discordant jazz notes seeping under her closed door. On my first Saturday, Lucian asked if I wanted to go out on the water with him and the girls. I shook my head. I couldn't swim or sail, I explained. He'd looked horrified. 'The granddaughter of a fisherman, afraid of the water?'

I stared at my shuffling feet, squirming with embarrassment.

'Time to conquer your fear,' he said, rumpling my hair as he strode past, life jackets stacked on his arm, shouting at the girls to hurry up if they wanted to catch the tide. 'We'll have you swimming and sailing by the end of the summer. Don't you worry.'

Standing on the doorstep, I nibbled anxiously at my nails as I watched them pile into the Land Rover, the girls vying for the passenger seat next to their father. The thought of getting into a dinghy terrified me, and yet, I was envious of them going off together.

The dog bounded around the Land Rover barking in hopeful excitement; they pushed him away. 'No, Matisse, you can't come.' He returned panting to my side, and we watched them drive off in a cloud of fumes, Lucian waving one hand out of the driver's window, his navy sailor's cap tilted low.

I'd never minded that I wasn't talented, or that my face wasn't considered pretty. Nobody discussed looks in our family. We were more likely to talk about birds we'd sighted in the marsh, or a book one of us had read. For the first time, I longed for pouting lips and a neat nose, hating my freckles and dish-water-coloured hair. Standing there on the gravel, breathing in the fading fumes of the Land Rover, I realised that although I couldn't magic myself into being beautiful, I could be braver. If I asked Lucian to teach me to sail, I'd spend time alone with him. He'd have to notice me then.

* * *

Back at Deben Manor, I hurry through stinging rain into the house. I'm not wearing a coat and am soaked on my dash from car to front door. I stand in the hall, shivering as I take off my boots. The bump and roar of the hoover comes from the play-room. Damn.

As soon as I'm in my room, I strip off my wet things and grab a towel to rub my hair. Crossing to the chest of drawers with the towel over my head, my foot hits an obstacle and pain shoots through my toe. I let out a yelp, hopping around the room. The corner of my suitcase is sticking out from under the bed. Odd. I'm sure I'd left it pushed right under. I sit on the mattress to cradle my throbbing toe, and that's when I notice that one of my drawers is slightly open. Inspecting its contents, I see that although I'd arranged my socks on the left-hand side of the drawer, now they're mixed up with my underwear on the right.

I sit back on the bed, darts of anxiety pricking my chest. The hunter has become the hunted. I feel sick. It must have been Ophelia. Saul must have told her about finding me in her study. I press my forehead hard, trying to think. But he would have told her last night, so why hasn't she confronted me? Maybe he hasn't told her, maybe she's been snooping in my stuff because I seem familiar, but she can't quite place me? The photo of Mum with the pendant is hidden in the side pocket of my suitcase. I check to see if it's there. It is, but did whoever-it-was discover it? I bite my nails, working out what to do. If Ophelia doesn't say anything about Saul finding me in her study or the Polaroid, then I won't complain that someone's been in my room. I don't want to leave yet. I need more time. But I should hide the Polaroid. I think of the loose floorboard in the summer house – the old secret hiding place.

Zipping on my mac, I go into the pelting rain with the envelope containing the Polaroid tucked into an inner pocket. Rooks complain from the beech trees as I make my way across the wet grass, leaving darkened footprints behind, aware that anyone looking out of the upstairs windows would have a clear view of me. Imagining a gaze on my back, I hurry on towards the cover of the shrubbery at the bottom right-hand corner of the garden, where laurel bushes and rhododendrons clump together, and the land falls away into a dip.

The old summer house is still here, hidden behind shrubbery. I thought it might have been demolished. Dead ferns grow between the stumpy stilts keeping the building off the ground. It's streaked with green, the vertical planks slimy and rotten; pointed thatch sags over windows meshed in cobwebs, panes cracked, ivy tendrils twisting their way inside.

I step gingerly up four rotten-looking wooden steps and go inside, grateful to be out of the rain. As I take my hood down and look around, there's a blur of movement behind me and I'm hit by something heavy on my upper back. Sharp needles dig into my shoulders, and I yelp, spinning in panic. The weight clings and I catch my breath. A cat. He must have been up in the rafters, and he seems reluctant to leave his new perch. With difficulty, I twist around to unpin fishhook claws from my jumper and by bending one arm up behind my back and leaning forwards, manage to haul him over my shoulder. I straighten, panting, my neck raked with scratches, an ancient-looking black cat in my arms. He has a white sock on his back foot and a star on his chest.

'Fred!' The pleasure of recognition makes me gasp. I put him down. 'You're huge! You were a kitten last time I saw you. That's some trick,' I tell him. 'You've turned into a circus cat.'

He thrusts his square head into my palm, his rattling purr intensifying. His tail coils around my left calf. His fur is scruffy and speckled with white, one ear is torn. In my fantasies, he'd been adopted by a kindly old lady and has been living a life of comfort all this time. Clearly, this is not the case. 'I abandoned you, didn't I,' I murmur. 'I'm sorry.'

I scratch under his vibrating chin, soggy with dribble, and he closes his eyes in bliss. I notice a jagged hole in a floor-board near the wall and guess it's his route in and out. I lean down to inspect a pile of old fabric on the floor covered in his hair. The Liberty of London label still sewn inside. Then I'm on my knees and feeling across bare boards, my fingers finding the loose one. I use my nails to prise it free, peering into the dusty space below. I take the envelope out of my pocket and place it in the gap, fitting the board back into place.

It was John who showed me the summer house, and the hiding place.

John, who was my best friend that summer. Yet, I never knew his surname or where he lived.

It had been a Saturday morning when I met him; Lucian and the girls were off on the river and Calista in her studio. Matisse and I were in the garden; the dog happily sniffing and stopping to cock his leg. I'd told Lucian I wanted to learn to sail, asking him to teach me, but he said we needed to wait for the perfect day, the perfect weather conditions. I'd asked him several more times, but we were still waiting.

I was bored on my own. I found an old tennis ball in the grass and threw it for the dog. It landed behind a spreading rose bush. Matisse disappeared after it; I followed, telling him he was the worst retriever ever. The words died in my mouth. The dog was greeting a stranger enthusiastically, tail wagging, jumping up with his big paws on a boy's chest. The boy was laughing. They were obviously old friends.

'Hello,' I said. 'Who are you?'

The boy startled, glancing at me from under a ragged fringe. He was about my age. He pushed Matisse down, brushing half-heartedly at the dirt on his shirt, looking over my shoulder, as if afraid someone might be lurking behind me.

'It's alright,' I said. 'If you're worried about the others, they've gone sailing. And my aunt is in her studio.'

He seemed to relax, although he still hadn't answered my question. Matisse was sitting beside him, and the boy rested a hand on his great head in a proprietorial manner. I was certain he was a trespasser, but he acted as if he owned everything.

'What's your name?' I asked again.

'What's yours?' he shot back.

I noticed cracked scabs on his elbow, rips in the knees of his jeans. I should have had the upper hand; I was entitled to be on this lawn. But I was afraid the boy might disappear if I didn't answer him.

'I'm Meg,' I said. 'A cousin. I'm staying for the holidays.'

The boy bent down and scratched Matisse's head. 'John,' he said as he straightened up.

'Do you live near here?'

'Not too far away to cycle.'

'Do you know the Aldredges?'

He shrugged. 'Not really.'

'You're trespassing?'

He looked hurt. 'I used to play in this garden when I was young. Only my dad has banned me from coming here.'

'Why?'

'He used to be the gardener – but he got sacked. The Aldredges might not want me here, either.' He gives me a steady look. 'Are you going to tell on me?'

'No,' I say.

'Promise?' He came closer and held out a grimy hand, wet with Matisse's slobber. We shook, his fingers firm around mine. He grinned. 'Alright then.' His tension fell away. 'Have you seen the summer house?' he asked, throwing the ball impressively far for the dog.

The building looked like something from a fairy tale: a round wooden house with a thatched roof. Inside, there was a table and chair, a rocking chair in the corner, and a bookcase empty of books. 'They never come here,' he said. 'But you can, if you like.'

I didn't tell him that it wasn't up to him to give permission. I wandered around, giving the rocking chair a little push, running my fingers over the dusty bookcase. I was excited by this discovery: something I could keep from the girls, instead of it being the other way around all the time. Matisse had followed us and was slumped on the floor, his head on his paws.

'And look at this,' John continued. He was kneeling, fiddling with the edge of a board, and the next minute he'd pulled it up. 'See,' he pointed down into the narrow gap beneath. 'We could leave notes for each other. If we wanted.'

My chest warmed with the knowledge that he'd like us to become friends, and he saw us leaving secret notes for each other. Up until now, I'd been an outsider. My cousins only suffered my presence, but John was already including me in a circle of two.

'Alright,' I said as casually as possible. 'But I should go back to the house now. It must be lunchtime.'

I slapped my thigh to call Matisse to me. The dog looked uncertainly between us until John pointed at me and said sternly, 'Go.'

Matisse at my heels, I turned to leave.

'I'll be here this time tomorrow,' he said, picking a scab on his elbow.

7

In the kitchen, Mrs Kerry turns from cleaning the oven. 'Just in time.' She stands up and runs water into the kettle. 'Cup of tea?' she asks. 'I'm having one.'

'Yes, please. Milk, no sugar,' I add.

'Been out in the garden?' she says. I can't deny it. The bottoms of my jeans are muddy, my perm dripping around my shoulders.

'Whatever for?' she exclaims. 'In this weather?'

'I don't mind a bit of rain,' I say. 'I wanted to explore. The grounds are huge.' It occurs to me that as we're talking about the garden, I could try and find out more about John's dad. 'Does anyone in the family have green thumbs?'

'Bless you, none of them would know a weed if it bit them!' She laughs. 'Mick Smith is the gardener.' Hearing the name makes me startle. 'He's been working here for... oh, years. Like me,' she goes on. 'We both worked for Mrs Manners's parents, the Aldredges.' She mashes the bags against the sides and ladles sugar into hers.

Mick Smith. He used to appear without warning, blank and

inscrutable. He spied on the girls out of his one good eye, watched them sunbathing in their bikinis. I'm surprised he's still here. He was a creep.

She puts two cups on the table and sits down, pulling her chair closer to mine. 'Like plants, do you?'

'Everyone does, I suppose,' I say, lamely. 'Was there a gardener here before Mick?' The words come out before I can stop them. Too much, too soon, I tell myself.

Mrs Kerry looks at me in surprise; she shrugs. 'Funny you should ask. The one before, Edward Catchpole, he got the sack by Mr Aldredge.'

'Really?' I take a sip, relieved that she seems to accept my curiosity. 'Do you know why?'

'Talk at the time was he was light-fingered. He was a quiet man. Never had him down as a criminal type, but then you never can tell, can you? He wasn't prosecuted or anything, but they moved out of Charsford sharpish after.' She takes a slurp of tea. 'So maybe there was something in the rumours.' She gives me a sideways glance. 'His wife died not long after that. Tragic, really. They had a little boy.' She narrows her eyes. 'Why do you ask?'

'No reason,' I say quickly. 'Just being nosey. So, you worked for the Aldredges when Mrs Manners was a girl?' I go on, hoping to distract her. 'What was that like?'

'They only got me in once a week. Between you and me, the place was a pigsty. Animals and mess everywhere.' She rolls her eyes. 'It wasn't easy to keep on top of it. Mr Aldredge, God rest his soul, appreciated my hard work. He was a good employer, the sort to give people second chances. But Mrs Aldredge kept herself to herself.' She tuts under her breath. 'She was a bit vague, if you know what I mean. I don't think she cared what kind of muck she lived in, just so long as she could do her paintings. But I've been cleaning for Mrs Manners since she got married, and before that. She likes things neat and tidy.' She blows on her tea.

I lower my voice. 'Mrs Manners said her father died in a sailing accident?'

She sucks in her breath. 'Terrible,' she nods. 'Terrible thing.'

'Mrs Manners mentioned something about... a girl? Their cousin?' I swallow, wondering if reminding her about me is a good idea.

Mrs Kerry shakes her head. 'Funny little thing. She was staying that summer. Her mum had gone off somewhere. Well —' She pulls her chair closer. 'Mr Aldredge took her for a sail early one morning, and the boat capsized. The family think the girl must have done something silly. Mr Aldredge was an experienced sailor, you see. He was injured in the accident. Hit his head. But he held her up, made sure she lived. Hours he struggled in the water to save her. But by the time rescue came, it was too late for him.' She hesitates, glancing at me as if she's thinking of saying something else, but takes a noisy gulp of her tea. 'It was hard on the family, knowing he'd given his life for hers.' She sighs again. 'Tragic loss of a good man. And those girls,' she sighs. 'Like orphans, they were.'

I gaze at the floor, trying to make sense of what she's just told me. No wonder my cousins hate me. She said he hit his head – so that explains the image of blood I keep having, a red welt pushing up out of broken skin. I just wish I could remember properly. Then I register what Mrs Kerry has said, and raise my gaze, frowning. 'Orphans? But their mother was still alive?'

Mrs Kerry tightens her lips. 'She took off to live in France just weeks after the accident – soon as the funeral was over, she abandoned those children. They have a house there. Well, they managed, brought themselves up, alone in this old place.' She frowns. 'Course, I did my bit. I like to think it made a difference. They felt a bit like my own daughters. I'd do anything for those girls. Mrs Manners, bless her, she wasn't married then. Luckily, I was able to keep cleaning, and keep an eye on them, too.'

'You mean, the three daughters lived here on their own?' I stare at her.

She nods, her mouth tight.

'Why do you think their mother left them?'

She leans closer, her brow furrowed. 'If you want my opinion, she didn't have any maternal instinct. Her painting was what mattered. You could see it, plain as day. She had no interest in her own children.'

'But was it legal to leave them?'

She looks at my shocked expression and her lips tighten. 'There's many a girl married with a bun in the oven at sixteen,' she says, in a seeming turn-around. 'When I was a girl of twelve, I was minding my brothers and sisters while my mum were off doing shift work. Kids nowadays don't know they're born. Everything done for them. It's made those Aldredge girls tougher for having to grow up fast. You mark my words. It hasn't done them any harm.'

'Well,' I stand up, needing to be alone with my thoughts, instinct telling me that this is just the beginning of a favourite rant. 'I should get going.'

She gets up, groaning as she straightens her knees. 'And I have the rest of the oven to finish.' She unpeels the end of a tube of mints and offers me one. When I shake my head, she pops one in her mouth, and snaps on her Marigolds.

'By the way,' I turn at the door. 'Do you clean in the attic?' I keep my voice casual. 'I've noticed the door is locked.'

'Mrs Manners don't want me cleaning up there,' she says, moving the sweet in her mouth. 'Never has. And neither did Mr Aldredge when he was alive. I think they have valuables and that in storage. And I'm not complaining. The rest of this place is big enough for me, what with my rheumatism.' She's turned her back and is already scrubbing at the surface with fierce determination.

* * *

For the first time, I know his full name. John Catchpole. In the car on the way to pick up Kit, I tell myself that now there's nothing to stop me trying to find him. He might be living close – I could bump into him at the village shop – the thought makes my stomach flip. Would he remember me? He'd remember Fred, I'm sure of that. I could tell him that the kitten has grown into a huge tomcat and is still living in the summer house. I imagine John's smile, the steady warmth of it.

John is the only other person who knows about Fred. But he wasn't there when I discovered the kitten.

* * *

Matisse was barking like a maniac next to the stream, nosing at a lumpy sack half submerged in the water. I knelt on the bank and pulled it out. The contents didn't weigh much. I struggled to undo the sodden knot, gasping as limp bodies tumbled in a heap at my feet. Lola's kittens from the house. I reeled back in horror. But under the heap of drenched fur, something moved.

I picked the mewing creature up and held him against my heart, tucking him under my T-shirt for warmth, where he curled, wet and shivering, against my skin.

I needed something to dry him, a bed and some food. I hurried back to the house, hoping everyone was out. The place seemed deserted, and I slunk into the kitchen. Using my one free hand, I grabbed a shopping basket from the hook on the pantry door, filling it with a couple of plastic bowls, some tins of cat food, an opener, and a half-finished packet of salmon-flavoured kibble. In the living room I pulled an embroidered shawl from the back of the sofa, bundling it into the basket. As I leaned over the sofa, a flash of bright fabric caught my attention. It was sticking out of the dip between the cushions. I pulled it free, unfolding it into a familiar cardigan.

My breath caught in my throat. I pressed it to my nose, inhaling patchouli and rose. Closing my eyes, I let the woollen folds give up other subtle scents: Mum's almond shampoo, the briny tang of salt marsh. It was like burying my face in her hair, feeling the warmth of her cheek against mine. There was even the darned elbow – red threads against fuchsia wool – that I remembered her mending after she'd found a hole in her sleeve.

'What have you got there?'

Calista stood in the doorway. I blushed, thinking she meant the kitten, hidden under my T-shirt, and I angled my body away. But her eyes were on the cardigan. 'It's my mum's,' I told her. 'When was she here?'

Calista crossed the room and held out her hand. I curled my fist tighter. 'Let me see,' she said, her outstretched fingers hovering. I shook my head, but she snatched it from me. 'No.' Calista's eyes were hard. 'It's mine.'

I wanted to snatch it back, but I was afraid she'd see the lump under my top, notice the way I was cradling it in my other hand. She'd take the kitten away too.

I frowned, confused. She didn't seem to notice that I'd

stolen her shopping basket and filled it with cat food or that I'd taken her embroidered shawl from the back of the sofa and stuffed it into the basket.

Back in the summer house, I made a nest on the floor of the summer house out of the shawl. It had a label saying Liberty of London. Once he was dry, I saw he was one of the black ones, the one with the white sock on his right back foot and a star on his chest.

I didn't believe Calista had the same cardigan as Mum, not with the same darned elbow. She'd lied. It meant Mum had been in the house; but Dad had said she hadn't, and I trusted him to tell me the truth. It was like the hardest maths equation. Impossible to solve.

* * *

I've always believed it was Mick Smith who drowned the kittens. I don't understand why Ophelia has kept him on as gardener; the girls called him a pervert and a creep, even back then. They'd laughed at him, despised him. So why is she employing him?

8

It's Wednesday, Artemis's half-day, and the three of us are in the playroom, building a Lego farm on the floor. Kit glances up from arranging a Lego cow on a square of green plastic. 'Margaret?' Only he can't pronounce my name properly, sounding it as Marquet. 'I'm thirsty.'

I get up from my cross-legged position, wincing at tight hamstrings. 'Artemis, can you be in charge while I nip to the kitchen?' I ask. 'I'll fetch some juice for both of you, and a biscuit.' The child gives me a serious nod. She loves to be given responsibility, especially over her brother.

As I near the kitchen, I hear voices. Ophelia is so often out, I've come to expect the house to myself. I softly push open the door and see the three sisters together around the table, heads close, talking quietly. Clem is the first to notice me; she clears her throat warningly. 'Hello, Margaret,' she says. 'How are you?'

They fall into casual chat among themselves about mundane subjects while I pour the juice and grab a couple of digestive biscuits, knocking over the sugar in my haste. I feel like a mouse in a roomful of cats. My skin prickles with their gazes.

'Margaret reminds me of someone.' Thea's voice comes from behind me, and I freeze in the middle of sweeping glittering grains into my hand, my nightmare coming true.

'Maybe an actress?' Clem suggests. 'Sigourney Weaver?'

'What, just because she's tall?' Ophelia laughs.

My heart is racing. I need to get away from their scrutiny. It feels too good to be true that they haven't recognised me so far – and now that Thea has twigged a familiarity, I could be exposed at any moment. I tip the sticky sugar into the sink, grab the juice and biscuits, and walk quickly towards the door with my head down.

'What are you going to do with the children this afternoon?' Ophelia's voice halts me.

I stop at the threshold. 'If it clears up, we can go for a walk,' I mutter. 'Maybe go to the village playground.'

'But what if it doesn't?' Thea asks, as if the weather is somehow my fault.

Before I can reply, Clem has turned to Ophelia. 'Have you still got our old dressing up box?'

I hover, holding the juice and biscuits, uncertain if this concerns me.

'God, yes.' Ophelia nods. 'Still stuffed with fairy wings and Ma's cast-off evening gowns.'

'Pirate swords,' Clem says, laughing. 'And the Peter Pan outfit. I loved that one.'

'Good idea, Clem.' Thea says. 'Well, if the rain keeps on.' She turns a searching glare in my direction. 'You could devise a game using the dressing up things. Couldn't you, Margaret?'

'Where is it?' I ask, backing away into the shadows. 'This dressing up trunk?'

'It's in the corridor, outside my bedroom,' Ophelia says. 'A big, old wooden chest.'

And with that sorted, the three of them lean across the table towards each other, their voices becoming intimate. I slip away, unnoticed, down the corridor, relieved to have escaped. But one of them will remember me, eventually.

It's ironic to think that when I was here that summer, I'd longed for them to take notice of me, to include me in their group, but the three had been an impenetrable unit of superiority, impossible to infiltrate. Calista told me I could use the red telephone on the hall table every Wednesday evening and Sunday morning to call Dad. When I made my call, I'd often heard the click of the extension being lifted, the soft breath of someone listening in. It had made me self-conscious and stilted, knowing one of the girls, perhaps all three, were gathered around the other receiver. I couldn't speak to Dad properly, and I would stutter and cut the call short, hearing his disappointment as I told him I had other things to do. 'Well, if you have to go, love... don't worry. We'll speak again soon. I'm glad you're getting on alright there.'

* * *

The rain turns to sleet, the wind howling around the house. After lunch, I lift the lid on a waft of mothballs and decaying fabrics. The children and I concoct games using the clothes and props tangled inside. Artemis chooses to be a queen in every new game we invent. She takes after her aunt Thea, I think, as I listen to her boss her brother around, giving orders as she looks down her nose.

Delving inside the chest, my fingers grasp a woollen fabric. It's soft in my hands: a fuchsia cardigan. Heart in my mouth, I check the elbow. The small square of red darning is still there. My body goes hot and then cold. I sit on the edge of the chest, bringing the cardigan to my face. It smells musty: old clothes and mothballs; can I detect the faintest trace of pachouli and rose? It can't still smell of her. But when I pull it on, it's as if I feel her arms around me.

'I'm bored,' Artemis says. 'Let's play hide-and-seek. Bagsy hiding first.'

I can't snap out of the confusion the cardigan has thrown me into. I know it belonged to Mum. Glimpses of her flash through my mind the last time I remember her wearing it; she runs ahead. Her smiling face, her teasing eyes. *Catch me if you can!*

If her cardigan is here, then she must have visited this house before she disappeared. But why had Calista lied to me? And why had Dad said Mum had never been here?

'Margaret.' Kit tugs at my elbow. 'Arty's had longer than ten counts.'

I stand up, trying to shake off the muddle in my head. 'Right,' I say. 'Let's go and find her.'

Kit trails behind me. We go into bedrooms, looking behind curtains and under beds. My fingers keep touching the softness of the wool, the extra layer of the cardigan.

I find Artemis in a wardrobe in one of the spare rooms. The one that used to belong to Thea. She giggles as I reach in and tickle her. 'Got you!'

'Where's Kit?' she asks.

I turn around. He was just behind me. 'Maybe he's gone to hide,' I say, 'Let's separate and find him.'

We look for ten minutes, calling out to each other at intervals: 'He's not behind the sofa!' 'He's not under Mummy and Daddy's bed!'

We keep shouting for him; he's not in any of the obvious places. I have a sick feeling. Could he have somehow left the house? Been stolen from under our noses? While Artemis searches the airing cupboard, I run up to the attic and bang on the locked door. 'Kit?' I call. 'You're not in there, are you?'

I stand with my ear pressed against the wood. There's a scratching sound. Very faint. It comes again, and I bang with my fist. 'Kit?' I know he can't really be in there. The door is locked. But there's the creak of floorboard, as if someone is standing just the other side. I hold my breath and press my ear against the door again. A soft cough quickly stifled. I take a step back, blood pounding inside my head.

'Margaret!' Artemis's voice. 'We've found him!'

I clatter down the stairs. Artemis is with her mother. They are standing by the dressing up box. 'Look,' Artemis says. She's laughing.

I peer down into the trunk. Kit is fast asleep, like a dormouse in a nest, curled up inside discarded evening gowns and velvet cloaks.

'The lid was down,' Ophelia says in a serious voice. 'If he'd woken, he would have been terrified.' She gives me an accusing look.

I can't meet her gaze. It's true. I've been careless, not even noticing when Kit had left my side. 'You'd better wake him,' she says. 'And next time one of my children disappears, tell me. It was Artemis who came to get me.'

I nod, chastened. 'Of course. Sorry.'

Clem comes up the stairs. 'You found the little monkey, then?' She smiles at the sight of Kit in the box. 'He had to be somewhere in the house.' She takes her sister's arm, and they go off together down the stairs.

I scoop Kit out of his nest, and he starts to cry. 'Sausages,' I say the magic word. 'You must be hungry. Shall I do them with baked beans?'

As I prepare their meal in the kitchen, I hear Ophelia and Clem talking in the sitting room. They laugh and there's the clink of glass. Their mood has changed from the serious one of earlier. I can't hear Thea, and I wonder if she's left to go back to work. She'd said that she was preparing a fashion show, and I suppose that must be time-consuming.

* * *

Clem has left, and I've just finished giving the children their tea when Ophelia comes into the kitchen. 'I'll give the kids their bath tonight,' she announces. Artemis and Kit yelp with pleasure and leap down to grab at their mother's legs. 'Come on, Mummy!' Artemis yells as she herds her brother out of the door.

'Ophelia,' I say quickly. 'I went up to the attic when I was looking for Kit, and... and there was someone there.'

'What?' She stares at me. 'Who?'

'I didn't see them. They were behind the door.'

'In the attic? Impossible.' She frowns. 'It's locked.'

'Come on, Mummy,' Artemis has reappeared and is trying to drag her away.

'I know,' I persist in a whisper, not wanting Artemis to hear. 'But someone coughed.'

Ophelia sighs and shakes her head. 'I hope it's not squirrels,' she says. 'They can do real damage, can't they?' She looks down at her daughter. 'Stop pulling me! I'm coming.' She glances around, distractedly. 'I suppose we might need to get a pest man in.' She bites her lip. 'I'd ask Mick, but I'm not sure...

or maybe he'd be the better option.' She's frowning, as if deep in puzzled thought, talking to herself.

'Mummy!' Artemis shouts. 'Come on!'

'Yes. Yes. Come along,' she holds out her hand. 'Where's Kit?' The door shuts behind them, and I listen to her scolding Kit for running off. Their voices fade.

Squirrels don't cough like humans or make floorboards creak. Is Ophelia lying? If so, she's an impressive actor. I remember the sounds I heard through my ceiling the other night. I'd presumed it was mice; now I'm not so sure. Then I realise that Ophelia wouldn't necessarily have heard anything in the attic – her room is at the other end of the house. I'd smelt cigar smoke on my first night here. But Saul doesn't smoke cigars. I shiver. Could there really be someone behind the locked door?

After the sailing accident, for years I'd had panic attacks and nightmares. I believed I'd finally outgrown them, but here in Deben Manor, my old uncertainty is coming back, as if the borders of myself are dissolving, my senses suddenly unreliable.

9

I've driven to Charsford shop with Kit, sent by Ophelia for emergency supplies of butter and milk. Kit points to the rows of sweets. 'I want that. And that. Can I have this, Margaret?' He's swept up a fistful of brightly coloured confectionary and clutches them to his chest. 'Pleeaase?'

'*No sweets,*' was Ophelia's command as we left the house this morning. I sigh. Why are all the goodies at child height? I squat in front of him. 'That's too many, Kit,' I say. 'Your teeth will hurt and so will your tummy.' His bottom lip wobbles, chubby fingers tightening around his haul. 'If you could have just one,' I say. 'Which would it be?'

He gives me a hard stare. He'd make a good poker player. 'You can choose your favourite.' His fist tightens, his bottom lip pushing out. 'That's my final offer.'

I can see his brain working it out, accepting the compromise, knowing there's a victory to be gained. Grudgingly, he decides on a Milky Way, and lets me put the others back.

I straighten, placing the chocolate in the basket on the counter; the shop bell rings as the door opens, and a woman murmurs to Kit behind me as my items are being rung up. I turn, smiling. The woman's fingers caress the top of Kit's blond curls. 'Lovely little boy,' she says. 'Is he yours?'

I shake my head. 'I'm his nanny.' She seems strangely familiar. Her freckled skin is dull, and her silver-grey eyes carry a weight of sadness. I know I've seen her before.

'Well. Goodbye.' I smile at her, taking Kit's hand in mine, the basket of shopping hooked over my elbow. We leave the shop, and it's only as I'm strapping Kit into his car seat that I remember.

* * *

We'd bought Ice Pops; blue raspberry for me, lemon and lime for John. We were sucking at the vivid crystals as we left the village shop, blinking into sunshine, John laughing at my blue mouth.

Outside, a woman was hammering a poster onto a telegraph pole. It had a blurry photo of a fat baby on it, with a sketch of an older girl next to it. Big letters underneath the pictures said: MISSING – HAVE YOU SEEN THIS GIRL?

The woman stood back from her work, the hammer dangling from her fingers. As she turned, she caught sight of me, brows drawing together over silver-grey eyes. Her face was thin, skin papery, as if she didn't get enough daylight. 'How old are you?' she asked.

I blushed at the sudden intensity of her question. 'Eleven,' I said. 'Eleven and a half.'

'Same age as my Haley would be.' Her throat rippled as she swallowed.

I was pinned under the spotlight of her scrutiny, my cheeks burning. She blinked and rubbed her forehead. She looked tired. 'Take these.' She thrust some copies of the poster into our unwilling hands. 'Give them to your friends.'

She continued down the street, skinny legs in tight, faded jeans, a red T-shirt showing the jutting points of her shoulder blades. She began to tack up another one of the posters on a tree at the corner of the junction.

'That's Alison Greenwood,' John hissed. 'She's mad. My dad says she should have watched her little girl better.'

'Her little girl? What happened to her?'

'She got taken.'

I gasped. 'Who took her?'

'No idea.' He shrugged.

'Why do you say she's mad, then?' I tilted my head in the direction of the woman.

'Everyone says she was too busy with a new boyfriend, and she liked her cans of lager too much to care about her kid, and then someone stole her, right from outside her own caravan – that would drive anyone mad, wouldn't it?'

I looked at the woman, hammering up another poster on the next telegraph pole.

'Now every year she tries to raise awareness for her kid,' John went on. 'Even though the police have given up.'

'That's awful,' I said. 'What shall we do with the posters?'

'Chuck 'em in the bin,' he said. 'Haley's been gone for over ten years. She's not going to turn up now.' He shrugs. 'Everyone else thinks she's dead.'

I'd felt a stab of guilt as we'd thrust the sheaf of papers into the bin, but then, who could I have given them to, anyway? I didn't have any friends, not at Deben Manor, only John.

* * *

I've put the shopping away and wiped the chocolate evidence from Kit's face and fingers. He's gone down for a nap, and Mrs Kerry is ironing in the kitchen. Ophelia seems to be out. I go up to the attic and try the door handle. Still locked. I press my ear close. My breath sounds loud in the silence. No scrabbling noises or other sign of life comes from the room, no muffled cough. Had I imagined it? I rap my knuckles on the wood. 'Hello?' I say quietly. 'Anyone there?'

Nothing except the beating of my heart. I step away from the door. Perhaps my memories of the attic, the mystery surrounding it when I was a child, are colouring my imagination. Perhaps coming back here was a mistake. I don't want to be ill again.

That night, I have a nightmare about water. I'm falling through fathomless depths, and Lucian is there, waiting for me: floating below the surface, his pale cadaver's face staring at me with rotting eyes, a trail of blood leaking from his head.

I wake, gasping, my body rigid with fear. In the darkness, I imagine I can smell cigar smoke and push my face into my pillow.

* * *

As a child, the smell of Lucian's cigar smoke seemed to draw me out of bed, because I'd woken a second time to find myself standing outside the attic door, a ribbon of light at the bottom and that intense, ticklish scent drifting from under the gap. I was happy because it meant Lucian was home from London. When he was at Deben Manor, the atmosphere in the house changed, became charged with a sense of expectation, everything heightened.

In the morning, Lucian and Calista's door was ajar. I heard

them speaking, and loitered on the landing, eavesdropping. I hoped he was going to be back for a few days, wondering if he was going to give me my sailing lesson at last.

'We must be kind to the poor child,' he said.

I blushed, heart pounding. Was he talking about me?

I couldn't catch what Calista said in return.

'You owed it to your brother,' he said sharply. 'Of course we had to take her in.'

'I know, darling, and I did what you wanted, didn't I, like a good aunt?' Her voice was approaching the door, and I took a step back. 'Don't worry. We're being kind to her.' Calista's soft words sounded forced. She gave a short laugh. 'It's just, it's a bit maddening, because she's like a lost puppy.'

I scurried to my bedroom, holding this knowledge like a gift: it was Lucian who'd suggested I stay for the holidays. Not Calista. A cinder of warmth ignited inside me. My uncle had told Calista I *had* to come and stay. He wanted me here.

10

John is probably on Facebook, so I should be able to contact him – but I'm afraid he'll have forgotten me, or worse, he'll remember but be polite and distant, fobbing me off with vague excuses. He made my summer here bearable. He was like an invisible friend because none of the family ever saw him. But we spent hours together – talking and laughing – exploring the countryside around Deben Manor, or lying on the floor of the summer house, playing cards. It was John who taught me how to make a tree house and how to shoot a catapult.

* * *

I watched him pull back the elastic on his homemade catapult, letting a small stone fly; it hit his target with a *thwack*; a pinecone arranged on the summer house step. He repeated the feat several times. When I tried, I struck the door, or the stone ricocheted into the ground; only when John stood beside me and held my hands steady, did I manage to hit the pinecone. 'Visualise it hitting the mark,' he said, his breath tickling my ear. The heat of his body against mine gave me a strange need to lean in, to press myself closer.

I wriggled away. 'I can do it on my own,' I said, afraid he'd see the red roaring in my cheeks.

'Have you heard anything from your mum?' he asked.

I shook my head. 'Dad says she's gone for good.'

'But how does he know that?'

I shrugged. 'He says it was what she wrote in her note. He said she wanted to find the bright lights.'

'Do you believe him?' He took the catapult from me. 'About the bright lights?'

His question took me by surprise. It was the second time I'd been made to doubt Dad's word. I thought about Mum's dreaminess, and how I'd always felt a little bit of her was absent. 'I don't know,' I admitted, digging my toe into dried earth.

'At least your mum's alive,' he said, fiddling with a stone, tipping it from one palm to the other. 'She must be, mustn't she? Or you would have heard from the police.'

'Was your mum ill, you know, before she...?'

'She was depressed,' John said. 'I've never told anyone else. But I know you won't say anything...'

'Course not,' I said quickly.

'She took pills.' He stared at the stone on his palm. 'My dad found her. I suppose I'm angry with her. For leaving us.'

'I'm sorry.' I wanted to rub his arm in sympathy. I didn't, of course. 'Mums aren't supposed to leave, are they? They're supposed to... to just be there.'

He gave a short, bitter laugh. 'Well, ours failed then, didn't they?' He raised the catapult and let the stone fly.

* * *

I need to get into the attic. It's bizarre that it's locked and nobody in the family seems curious about it or ever goes up there. I keep remembering the cough, the creaking floorboards behind the door. I'm certain they were real.

The kids are at school. No Mrs Kerry for a change. Ophelia has disappeared off on one of her mysterious outings, and Saul is in London. This is my opportunity to search for the key again, and as it wasn't in Ophelia's study, it might be in her and Saul's bedroom.

I push open their door cautiously. There are clothes heaped over the back of a chair in the corner, the wardrobe doors gaping open. A slew of glossy magazines slides across the floor; some discarded suede boots lie on their sides, heels like small weapons. It reminds me of her bedroom when she was a teenager. She hasn't got any tidier. It's only the downstairs rooms she minds about – the ones people will judge.

It's obvious which side of the bed she sleeps on. Her bedside table is littered with magazines, pills, face creams and her silk mask. Saul's side just has an alarm clock. I pull out drawers systematically, rummaging through tangles of lace and silk, checking into corners, opening jewellery boxes. I don't like touching her private things. I try not to notice items I find hidden from sight – a vibrator, a contraceptive cap – my eyes flick away, fingers burning. I slip my hand under her mattress, kneel to look under the bed. I open the drawers under her dressing table and am confronted with bags of jumbled make-up and half-empty bottles of toner and moisturiser. I open the wardrobe doors wider and push the hangers apart. On one side there are Saul's shirts and suits, racks of colourful ties, on the other, Ophelia's clothes. She used to shop in Miss Selfridge and Top Shop, but now I see she's wearing Stella McCartney and Prada.

A noise makes me stop, heart racing. Wheels on gravel, the clunk of a car door shutting. Ophelia must be back. I glance around to make sure I haven't left any clue to my presence and adjust the wardrobe doors to slightly ajar as they were before. As I hurry across the carpet, my foot becomes entangled with one of the suede boots, and I let out an oomph of surprise as I stumble forwards. Her head is emerging at the top of the stairs as I slip out of her room. She rounds the banisters and we meet on the landing, my chest heaving. She frowns, obviously puzzled as to why I'm coming from the direction of her room. But hopefully, she'll think I've just used the bathroom at that end of the house.

I walk past, giving her a polite smile. Then I slip inside my own room and shut the door with a long exhale of relief.

* * *

Seeing all Ophelia's clothes reminds me of the long-ago planned trip to Top Shop. It had felt like the most exciting thing that had ever happened to me. Up until then, my clothes had been handmade by Mum or came from C&A, and the thought of going to Top Shop in London – the mecca of all that was fashionable and exciting – made me giddy with anticipation. The four of us were to be allowed to go on our own. Calista would come with us on the train and then she'd visit an art gallery and we'd go shopping, before meeting Lucian for tea, and then catching the train home with Calista.

At breakfast, the girls were dressed in their trendiest clothes. 'Where's Pa?' Thea asked.

'He went back to London last night. He needed to be there early, for work,' Calista said.

'But he said he'd meet us on Oxford Street,' Ophelia wailed, a worried frown etching her forehead.

'He promised to pick us up in a taxi and treat us all to tea at Fortnum & Mason,' Clem added.

'He keeps his promises.' Calista held up her hands. 'He won't let you down.'

'What's Fortnum & Mason?' I asked.

'The most glamorous shop you've ever seen,' Ophelia said. 'It smells of perfume and chocolate.'

'It's famous for its teas,' Thea said. 'I can't believe you haven't heard of it.'

'Don't forget to clean your teeth,' Calista said to us. 'And be out at the car in ten minutes.'

The girls dashed upstairs. With my shorter legs, I trailed behind. Ophelia and Clem got to the pink bathroom first, and shut the door, but when I reached the green bathroom, that door was closed too. I banged on it, and Thea's voice shouted to wait just a minute. Five minutes later, she came out, smelling of minty toothpaste and her mother's bluebell scent. She dashed past me, shouting, 'Hurry up, Mouse. We don't want to miss the train.'

I gave my teeth a cursory brush. But my nerves had upset my tummy, and I needed the loo. As I sat on the wooden seat, I kept checking my watch. A minute to go. I pulled up my shorts, pressed the flush, splashed my hands with water, and ran for the stairs. 'I'm coming,' I yelled.

The drive was empty. No car, no girls, no aunt. Disbelieving, I stood in the sunshine, shading my eyes as I looked towards the lane. Light sparkled through distant leaves as the sun glanced off moving metal beyond the trees. I waited, thinking any minute they'd realise their mistake, and the car would reverse in the lane. I'd hear the engine roaring as they sped back up the drive to pick me up.

I watched the spaces between the beech trunks. There were no more flashes of metal. The lane was empty of traffic. Nothing moved beyond the trees. The sun had reached the front of the house, and even this early, heat burnt my face. Bees hummed in the wisteria flowers. I heard the pop and creak of tree fibre expanding, the soft rustle of a blackbird's feet on the gravel as it pecked at ants between the stones.

* * *

That feeling of having been forgotten. Abandoned. I'd cried all morning, wishing I could go home, needing Mum to hug me and remind me that I wasn't a mouse. I wasn't invisible.

I rub my eyes, pushing away the memories. The wind rattles my window, whistling through gaps in the old wooden sash and gooseflesh rises on my arms. I twist the knobs on the radiator, but it refuses to give any heat, so I delve through the clothes in my drawer to find Mum's cardigan. I've taken to wearing it all the time, to remind me of her – Ophelia hasn't made a comment. I don't think she even realises I took it from the dressing up box. As I unfold it, a rainbow glint in the sleeve catches my eye. Something's caught in the weave. Bringing it closer, I'm pinching a huge diamond stud between finger and thumb. I stare at it in disbelief. Then panic hits. I'm used to seeing this rock on Ophelia's lobe, giving off flashes of brilliance. With shaking fingers, I excavate my drawer and discover the other one. Ophelia's favourite earrings. Someone has tucked them under my clothes. Holding the pair in my palm, I sit heavily on the bed, struggling to work out what this means, and what to do.

If I go to Ophelia with the diamonds, explaining I'd found them in my drawer, she won't believe me. She's just seen me coming from the direction of her room. My only hope is to put them back and pretend nothing happened. I think Ophelia is still in her bedroom. I wait, hardly breathing, listening out for the shriek of horror when she discovers her diamonds are missing.

No scream comes. I linger just inside my door, watching the landing through a crack. Ophelia appears out of her room and goes down the stairs. I examine her expression. She doesn't seem angry or anxious.

When I'm sure she's reached the hall, I risk a quick dash into her room, leaving the earrings on her dressing table and then get out as fast as I can. I take a moment on the landing before going downstairs. 'I'm off now,' I call from the hall, trying to sound casual. 'Going to collect Kit.'

If she'd found them in my room, I would have been sacked. She might have called the police. Someone has tried to make trouble for me. It was obviously an attempt to frame me, get rid of me – force me out. In the car, I tap my fingers on the steering wheel. My pulse ticks at my throat as I change gear, pressing the accelerator. A horrible thought strikes me: perhaps it was Ophelia herself who planted them? But that doesn't make sense.

Who wants me gone, and why? I'll only find out if I stay. As nobody is pointing the finger at me, and Ophelia is behaving as if nothing is wrong, I should too. Play them all at their own game. *Hold your nerve*, I tell myself, turning onto the main road. The phrase *double bluff* comes to me.

Whoever planted the earrings must have looked through my stuff too. But if they suspect or know that I'm Meg and not Margaret, why haven't they called me out as an imposter, a liar? Shamed me as the cousin who's responsible for their father's death? Ordered me out of the house? Instead, someone has sneakily tried to force me to leave, as if they have something to hide, a secret to protect. Something to do with the house. I think of the cardigan, the pendant around Mum's neck. The noises in the attic. My mind stalls, unable to make sense of it all.

I wish I'd kept a diary that summer. Memories slip into my mind, triggered by being here in the house, by seeing the sisters again, but I know there are things I'm not recalling. Especially the morning of the accident. Memory is an act of the imagination. I heard that once. And it's true. But sometimes the past comes back to me so vividly, it's like watching a film in my head.

Ophelia doesn't need to plant diamonds in my room. She can just ask me to leave. But if she did put the earrings in my drawer, it's likely that whatever's going on, the sisters are all in on it. I think of them whispering together at the kitchen table the other day, how they changed the subject when I came into the room.

When I was a child, I wanted them to like me almost as much as I craved their father's approval. On the last day I ever spent with them, I'd believed my wish was coming true. I'd thought they were finally letting me into their circle.

* * *

Thea put her head around my door. 'Come on, Mouse,' she said. 'We're going to give you a makeover.'

'What?' I looked over my book.

She strode over and took it from me, putting it down, pages crumpled carelessly against the eiderdown. 'We feel bad you got left behind when we went to London,' she said. 'We thought it would be fun to dress you up.'

I was uncertain if this was a joke but followed her obediently into her sister's room. Music played loudly from the record player. Ophelia had arranged different outfits on her bed, a tumble of fabrics, twists of belts, handbags and scarfs. They persuaded me out of my shorts and T-shirt, and began holding things up in front of me, arguing about combinations and colours.

They made me sit in front of Ophelia's dressing table. 'No looking yet,' they commanded. I avoided the mirror, keeping my eyes down. One of the gold pendants was lying on the surface, next to a clutter of bangles and an open cosmetic bag. Obeying an irresistible urge, my fingers went to it, turning it over, feeling across the raised surface, examining the details of the horse and hare.

'Don't touch,' Thea said.

'Sorry,' I put it down.

'They're special, you see,' Clem said, almost apologetically. 'Pa says they're an emblem of our heritage.'

'Now,' Ophelia said, wielding a cosmetic brush with squint-eyed concentration. 'Close your eyes and don't move.'

I obeyed, until she told me to 'look up,' while she did something ticklish to the skin under my bottom lashes. Feather-like brushes whisked across my skin, and Ophelia's warm breath touched my cheeks as she leant close. Her undivided attention gave me butterflies in my tummy.

'Stand up,' Thea commanded. 'Let's have a look.'

I searched their expressions, hoping to use their faces as my mirror. But they were blank and inscrutable.

'She needs something doing with her hair,' Thea said. She picked up Ophelia's comb. My scalp jerked and smarted as she worked through my hair, applying a cloud of chemical-smelling spray and then attached some hooped clip-on earrings to my lobes.

'Yes,' Clem nodded. 'She looks...'

'Pretty,' Ophelia finished.

'Not bad,' Thea added.

They turned me in front of the full-length mirror and stood back to watch my reaction. A small part of me had been afraid that they'd made a fool of me, dressed me as a clown, drawn a moustache on my face, but I'd become an Aldredge. I looked like their cousin at last. I could even be their sister. The girl in the mirror was older, brighter, more sophisticated than me. Eyeliner and mascara made my eyes look huge, the pink on my cheeks glowed, giving me angles and shape where before there were none.

The girls paraded me downstairs. 'Shame Pa's not here to

see,' Ophelia said. I silently agreed. If he was here, he'd look at me admiringly. 'Well, well, we have four beauties in the house now,' he'd say.

'Ma,' they called. 'Ma?'

We trooped into her studio. But Calista wasn't at her easel. A blank canvas stood ready to be worked on. I looked at a finished portrait leaning against the wall: a woman with startling violet eyes, her pale face framed with a mass of dark hair. A snapshot of her was still clipped at the top of the painting for reference. There were other Polaroids of people I didn't recognise pinned up on a cork board. But the paints were in their boxes, brushes standing in jam jars of turps.

'Too hot to paint, I expect,' Clem said. It was like a greenhouse in the studio. The big Velux windows were shut, trapping the smell of paint and turps and thickened heat, and several flies who buzzed against the glass uselessly.

We left the studio and called for her through the house. Eventually, we heard her reply. Her voice came from upstairs, behind the closed door of her bedroom. There was a weekend case on the bed, opened. She was filling it with clothes.

'Look, Ma,' Ophelia said. 'We've transformed Mouse.'

Calista glanced at me, her eyes skidding across the surface of my new look. She seemed flustered. 'Very nice.'

I could tell the girls were disappointed with her response, and their interest in me dropped away as they sat on the bed, turning their attention to their mother. 'Why are you packing?' Clem demanded.

Calista's left eye twitched. 'A friend in London has asked me to stay with her for a couple of days.'

'What. Just like that?' Thea asked. 'You never go away.'

'What about us?' Clem's voice was incredulous.

'You'll be alright, darling,' Calista said in a pleading tone.

'You've got each other and this big house. You will be kind, won't you?'

'But how long are you going for?' Thea asked.

'I don't know,' Calista said. 'She's... sick. So, she needs me. I'll telephone and let you know when I can come home.'

'Have you told Pa?' Ophelia asked.

'Of course.' Calista turned away from us and rooted in her open drawer. 'Now my darlings, I need to concentrate. You know how vague I can be. I don't want to forget something.'

'But you're only going for a few days,' Thea reminded her sternly. 'You don't need much.'

'True,' Calista said, her eyes suddenly very bright.

'We'll be on our own,' Clem said. 'Pa's not here.'

'I know,' Calista said. 'But Ophelia is over seventeen, and none of you are babies. Mrs K will be in to clear up and keep an eye on you.'

She shooed us out while she finished packing; we went to say goodbye before she got into the car. Each girl kissed her, and then, to my surprise, she clasped me in an embrace. Her thin body trembled. 'Goodbye, Meg,' she said. 'I'm sorry I haven't been the best aunt. I promise to make it up to you.'

We formed a forlorn group in the shadow of the house, waving as she drove away. Calista was always around, in the kitchen or behind her easel, vague but constant. It was Lucian who went away – to his flat in London, to important meetings and to auction houses all over the country. The wood pigeons cooed, afternoon shadows lacing the lawn.

It was strange to be in the house without adults at night. Thea and Ophelia cooked pasta with a tin of tomatoes mixed in, and Clem opened a couple of bottles of Lucian's beer, and we all had sips. The bubbles stung my throat, and it tasted bitter. Ophelia put music on loud. 'But when will Pa be home?' Clem worried.

Ophelia shrugged. 'He'll be back from London tomorrow.'

'Shame it's too late to organise a party.' Thea said. 'With the whole place to ourselves.'

The beer made me burp and feel sick, and by the time I went to bed, my face was a ruin of smudged make-up. I used soap and a flannel to get rid of the greasy mess, peering into the bathroom mirror, becoming me again. As I got into bed, I realised that I'd forgotten about John. He must have waited for me in the summer house.

My last waking thoughts were of Mum. I missed her so much it hurt – I wanted to go home to our cottage, to be in my own bed in my own room, with Mum reading me *The Lion the Witch and the Wardrobe*, and kissing me goodnight, her long hair trailing my cheek as she pressed her lips to my forehead. *Please come back*, I whispered into my pillow. *Please, Mum. I need you.*

12

As Deben Manor is miles from any public transport, Ophelia
has said I can use the Fiat whenever I like, just as long as I pay
for my own petrol. It's my day off, and I'm going to visit Dad for
lunch. Before I leave, I need to feed Fred.

A weak sun glints through clouds making the garden look
less bleak. I have the place to myself as usual; none of the
family seem interested in coming out into the cold and wet.

After giving Fred his breakfast, I take the longer route back
from the summer house, along the banks of the stream. As I
walk under the beech trees near the boundary fence, the rooks'
strident cawing seems to be warning me of something. The
stream sinks underground here to pass beneath the lane, and
the boggy ground is covered in a mulch of decaying leaves. It's
shady and damp under the spreading branches. My hands are
in my pockets, shoulders hunched against the cold. I remember
how John and I had climbed to the top of the tallest beech tree,
pretending we were on a ship sailing to America.

My foot hits uneven ground, making me stumble and I
nearly fall. I grab the fence and steady myself. Below me, the

surface rises in a long mound. I kick away some of the rotting leaves, and my breath catches as I realise what I'm looking at. The sun has ducked behind clouds and shadow envelops me. Sleet is falling, hitting my face with sharp pecks of ice. I stare at the unmarked grave and pull my coat tighter around me.

A rasping cough behind me makes me jump. I turn. Mick. It's the first time I've seen him since coming back. His face is leaner, creased with lines, tanned even in the winter. One pale blue eye is fixed on me, the other has a milky haze over the iris. His thin mouth is clamped shut. He's only wearing a shirt and shapeless jacket over his baggy gardening trousers. His bare hands are swollen and red. He regards me with disapproval. My throat tightens. I gesture towards the mound of earth. 'Is... is something buried here?'

He mutters something into his chest. I can't understand what he's saying. But he's lifted the handles of his wheelbarrow and is trundling it away before I can ask him to repeat himself. I don't think I've ever heard him speak before. He still has the upright posture and strength of a younger man – I suppose manual labour has kept him fit. As I walk back to the house, I pause and turn; he's stopped too, and is staring at me.

* * *

In the house, I can't stop shivering. The way he'd looked at me – as if he hated me. He couldn't possibly have recognised me. He'd only glimpsed me occasionally that summer. I'd avoided him whenever I could. I dry my hair with the towel in the cloakroom and press myself against the little radiator, fingers tingling with heat. My mind returns to the mound under the leaves. There must be an explanation. I linger with my back to the boiling radiator until my legs are burning.

Ophelia is in the kitchen with the children and Clem. 'I'm just off,' I tell them. 'I'm taking the Fiat. You said it's okay?'

She glances up. 'Yes. Yes. Fine.' She pauses. 'Have a nice time.'

'Where are you off to?' Clem stares at me. 'Meeting someone?'

I hesitate. Better not to mention that my dad lives in Ipswich. 'No,' I say, pushing a curl from my brow. 'A bit of shopping. Lunch in a cafe.'

'Really?' Clem sounds disbelieving.

'Yes,' I say firmly. 'And just now...' I linger in the doorway. 'At the bottom of garden, I noticed a shape that looked like a kind of grave?'

The sisters look puzzled. They glance at each other, Clem raising one eyebrow. 'Grave?' Ophelia frowns.

'Yes,' I say. 'Near the fence by the lane.'

Clem makes an 'ah-ha' face. 'The dog,' she announces, as if finding the answer to a riddle. 'She's talking about Matisse.'

'Oh, yes.' Ophelia nods. 'We buried him under the beech trees.' She looks at me. 'We had an Afghan Hound when we were children.'

Matisse. His warm nose pressed into my hand. His joyful tail whacking my legs.

I must have looked relieved because Clem laughs in a mean sort of way. 'Did you think we'd been burying our victims' bodies in the garden?'

'No,' I say quickly. 'Of course not.'

'It was a joke,' Ophelia says with a frown.

* * *

In Ipswich, I park behind Dad's block of flats. I lean forward into the mirror and carefully remove my contact lenses, putting them in the plastic container. Dad might not think anything of my new hairstyle, but he'll think it weird if I turn up with brown eyes. I put my glasses on. The sleet hasn't let up. Pale flakes tumble and swirl out of a flat, grey sky, the world scrubbed of colour. I hurry through freezing puddles, past parked cars, towards the back entrance of the block. I pause to wipe my glasses on the corner of my jacket. As I step past a bundle of clothes heaped in the doorway, it moves, and a face appears. I gasp. A young girl looks up at me. 'Spare some change?'

I fumble in my purse and lean down to give it to her. Poor kid. Homeless in this weather. She snatches at the money, and now that I'm looking at her more closely, I realise with a jolt that she's not young – her cheeks are sunken hollows, a web of lines nets her eyes, and her skin is ashen – she could be anything from thirty to fifty. She huddles back into her sleeping bag.

As I push through the doors, a horrible thought occurs. Is Mum out there somewhere, begging for change in a doorway?

I pant up three flights of stairs, avoiding the claustrophobic lift. Mum would never get into one. I suppose I've caught her phobia, like Dad's terror of water. Fear can be inherited, as much as the shape of a nose or a particular laugh.

I let myself into the tiny entrance hall of our flat. Dad calls out from the kitchen, 'That you, love?'

I kick off my shoes, and pad through to find him. 'There's a homeless woman sheltering in the back entrance,' I say.

'She's been there before,' he says. 'I give her a sandwich and a hot drink if I see her.'

'Ah, that's kind of you, Dad.' I plant a kiss on his raspy cheek. 'Ouch,' I say. 'You haven't shaved today.'

He rubs a hand over grey bristles. 'Seems little point if I'm not going anywhere.' He smiles. 'But this is a treat. Having my favourite person for the afternoon.' He peers at me. 'You've done something to your hair. Very nice.'

'Smells good.' I gesture towards the stove.

I'm not wearing Mum's cardigan. Dad would recognise it, and he'd ask questions I can't answer. He'd be upset about me working at Deben Manor. After that summer, I'd asked several times if I could visit. I'd wanted to find John, or at least leave a note. But Dad had been unusually firm. I was never to go there again.

He's making chilli, and my mouth waters at aromas of ginger, garlic and cumin. I take over the job of doing the rice. When the water is boiling, I tip in pale grains. 'Perfect meal for this weather.' I smile at him. My father likes a lot of heat in his chilli, so I put plain yoghurt on the table.

Sitting at his fold-out table crammed between the oven and the kitchen cabinets, the room seems even more cramped than usual, I suppose because of the contrast with the generous spaces of Deben Manor. As we eat, Dad asks about the new job, and I answer truthfully about the children and my duties, but skip being specific about my employers or the house. I hate lying to him. I ask him about his chess club, about the woman in the downstairs flat who presses her homemade madeira cakes into his hands and drops hints about trips to the cinema. 'I'm too old for another relationship, love,' he says. 'There was always only ever one woman for me.'

After we've cleared up, with me washing and Dad drying in comfortable silence, I make us both a cup of tea and we take it into the sitting room.

'I'm sorry about that time I sent you to stay with your cousins,' he says suddenly. 'You needed to be with me after your mum left.'

I nearly spill my tea. He never talks about that summer, or Mum.

'I'll always feel guilty about it,' he goes on. 'The truth is, I was having a breakdown. I couldn't let you see me like that. I couldn't look after you. I could hardly look after myself.'

'It's not your fault, Dad,' I say. 'You were doing your best.'

'But it wasn't safe there.' Dad looks grim. 'You nearly died.'

'But I didn't.' I touch the place on my left leg where, under my trousers, a zigzag of puckered scar tissue stands out against the rest of my skin. 'Actually,' I say slowly, 'I wanted to ask you something about Deben Manor. Did Mum have any connection to the Aldredges, or the house? Besides through her marriage to you, I mean.'

He looks startled. 'Your mum? No. She only met Janet and Lucian twice. They came to our wedding and your christening. We didn't mix, as families. My sister changed after her marriage, for the worse I'm afraid.' He shakes his head. 'Calling herself Calista!' He tuts. 'Behaving as if she was ashamed of her background.' He frowns and then seems to remember the question. 'Why do you ask?'

'No reason.' I sip hot liquid and am about to suggest a game of Scrabble to distract him when he puts his tea down on the coffee table and clears his throat.

'I have something for you,' he says. 'Something I should have given you long ago.'

He heaves himself out of the sofa and goes to the bureau. He takes out a manila envelope, comes over and places it in my hands. 'I'm going to leave you to it,' he says. 'I'll be in my room when you want to talk.' His eyes are watery, and his mouth trembles.

'Dad?'

But he waves his hand towards the envelope on my knees and shuffles out of the room.

I open the unsealed top and slide out the contents. Postcards slither into my lap. I recognise the writing at once.

Meg, I need to hear from you. Even if it's just to tell me that you're angry. Please write to the PO Box. Mum.

The words stun me. I press my hand to my mouth.

Meg love, I don't blame you for not replying. I can imagine how hurt and angry you are. But remember how much I love you. I promise I can make this right. Love, Mum.

Meg, It's okay. I understand. I don't deserve your forgiveness. I thought I'd be able to see you by now. It's all taking longer than I thought. Perhaps I've been a fool. But I think of you every moment of every day, love Mum.

Meg love, I'm sorry I had to leave. It might be hard for you to understand until you're older, but I'll do my best to explain when I see you. I promise we'll see each other soon. Please write with all your news. I love you, Mum.

I shuffle the four cards, trying to make sense of them. The dates are stamped on the postmark, and I sort them according to those. Facts reel through my head: she'd written to me and left a PO Box for me to reply to, and Dad had kept this from me? She'd been waiting for me to write back. I feel sick. My stomach cramps and I clasp my knees, squeezing my eyes shut. One thing is clear, she'd left voluntarily, but she hadn't meant to leave forever, not at first anyway. Tears blur my vision, spilling down my cheeks. I take off my glasses and wipe my eyes. Putting them on again, I turn each card over to look at the address. The postmark is London.

That's why Dad was certain she'd left for good, why he'd told me she'd gone to find the bright lights. What had happened to prevent her coming back? Anger builds in my chest, shutting down my breath. How dare he keep these from me? I take my glasses off again and lean forwards, pressing my forehead into my palm. I wait until I have some control over my emotions before I go and find him.

He's sitting on the edge of his bed in his room with his back to me, looking at the swirling sleet behind the window. His balding head is speckled with age spots and his shoulders are stooped.

'Why did you keep them from me, Dad?' My voice shakes with anger.

'I'm sorry,' he says, standing and turning to face me. 'At first, I thought I was protecting you. I was scared she wouldn't follow through with her promise to see you – I thought to give you hope and then take it away would be even worse.'

My fingers twitch at my sides. I curl them into fists. 'And then?'

'I felt betrayed. Confused.' He squeezes the bridge of his nose. 'I wasn't thinking clearly. I suppose it was one of the only things in my control – keeping those cards.'

He looks old and defeated, and I remember that he's suffered from depression and anxiety ever since she left, and now he has a weak heart too. My anger drains away.

'She went to London,' I say, trying to make sense of it. 'But then... she just stopped writing and disappeared?'

He nods. 'The postcards stopped coming.'

'You don't think something happened, to stop her writing again?'

'I'm sorry, love.' He shakes his head. 'I didn't want to tell you this. She left to be with someone else. A man.'

'A man?' I echo. Why had that never occurred to me? When I was a child, my parents' relationship seemed perfect. I'd always assumed she'd been forced to leave us – I'd never thought she'd run away on purpose. But I'm an adult now. I should have guessed this possibility.

He stares down at his clenched hands. 'In the end, she made her choice.'

A choice. Pain jabs between my ribs. 'She sent you postcards as well?'

He nods, not meeting my eyes. 'Just one.'

I sink onto the bed, noticing a small picture of Mum on his bedside table. An early photo from the look of it – perhaps just after their marriage – a memory of happy times, of the woman he fell in love with.

Now I understand why he put all the other photos and memories of her away. Why he didn't want to keep searching for her. Why he was certain she'd gone for good. She's been with another man all this time. A thought slices into my mind, maybe she has a new family by now? I can't let myself imagine it. I struggle to hold another thought that comes to me: better she's alive than dead, even if she's lost to us. But that honourable glimmer is destroyed by a wave of anger and hurt, painful as if I'm a child again, wanting to know what I did wrong, why she left me. Why I wasn't good enough.

Wearily, I go over to Dad and take his hand. We face the

view of the street below, looking down on the tops of buses going past, cars with their headlights on, people hurrying under umbrellas, our fingers entwined, not speaking.

I clear my throat. 'I think I understand why you didn't give them to me,' I tell him. 'I wish you had. But it doesn't matter now.'

'I regret so much from that time,' he says quietly. 'I made some mistakes. Terrible mistakes. I wish with all my heart I could see Irene – your mum, I mean – again. I wish I could go back and do things differently.'

'Why now, though, Dad?' I ask. 'Why choose this moment to give her postcards to me?'

'I didn't want you to come across them after I've gone. I wanted to be able to apologise. Try and explain.' His voice cracks with emotion.

'What do you mean?' I turn to meet his eyes, suddenly worried. 'Has something happened? Your heart?'

'Don't fret, love.' He pats my leg. 'I'm still here. But I won't be forever. None of us will.'

I can see he's trying to reassure me. But I need to be careful. He shouldn't get too agitated and upset. 'It wasn't your fault, Dad. It was her decision.' I gesture towards the thick sleet. 'I'd better get back soon. The weather will be making the roads dangerous.'

I leave the envelope with the postcards on Dad's kitchen table.

She used to go off on her own, coming back when it was time for my bus to drop me at the end of the lane. I knew because she'd meet me with mineral-smelling skin, wet hair, and muddy toes, telling me about the day she'd spent on the marsh, showing me handfuls of samphire or sea beet she'd picked to cook for tea, or a puff ball she'd found in the field beyond our cottage. She was always in a good mood, cheeks flushed, eyes bright. I'd tried not to feel hurt that she needed time alone, apart from me and Dad. Even when she danced me around the kitchen table, or read *Narnia* books aloud to me, there was some part of her missing, as if she'd gone off in her head to a private place she couldn't share.

I feel stupid now, lying to my cousins, disguising myself, as if I'm a sleuth about to uncover some great mystery. It doesn't exist. The truth turns out to be cruel and ordinary. She left us for a lover.

PART II

13

IRENE

Fifteen Years Ago

Midnight. I can't sleep. Anxiety and excitement make my heart race and my mind skips through the plan for tomorrow. Robert snores beside me. I put out my hand and gently push his shoulder; obligingly, he turns onto his side, his breathing quietening.

I can't lie here any more. I struggle out of the sagging mattress, springs squeaking. Robert doesn't wake. I tiptoe out of the bedroom and wander through the cottage in darkness, knowing every step and turn without the need for sight, running my fingers across the crooked walls. This home with its heavy beams, low ceilings, and tilting wooden floor has been my shelter, and now I must say goodbye to it.

I go into the garden, the grass beneath my bare feet cool after the day's heat. The sky is vast and domed above me, alight with stars. I inhale the green scents coming from the marsh just beyond the hedge, the salty breath of the river, realising I'll never stand here on a summer night again.

What am I doing? I bury my face in my hands. I can still

smell Paul in the creases of my skin. He'd kissed my eyelids that afternoon. 'You're mine,' he said. 'You always have been. Tell me, Irene. Tell me you belong to me.'

It went deeper than words. I had been his long before I met Robert. Before I was a wife, before I was a mother, before I made a home by a river.

* * *

After a few hours of restless sleep on the sofa, my face in the bathroom mirror is tense. Luckily, Meg is too wrapped up in thoughts of the day ahead to notice. She's in her last term of primary school and the dreaded sports day is over. But she won the sack race and is still wearing the medal to prove it. Today is the start of her last week before the summer holidays.

'Do you want cereal,' I ask, 'or toast?'

'Cereal, please,' my daughter says, oblivious to the fact that I won't be here to make it for her tomorrow. Tears prick my eyes, and I squeeze them away. I can't allow myself to weaken. Robert will manage for a few days, and I'll see Meg again soon.

She looks up as I place the bowl in front of her, and I turn away from her trusting smile, pretending to wipe the table. I watch her eat, this daughter of mine. She is small for her age, limbs round with puppy fat, her face a starscape of freckles. Love makes me dizzy. I would do anything for her. Anything except the one thing she would ask of me – to stay here, to stay with her father.

Robert comes in, bending his neck to prevent his head bumping the ceiling. He folds his long limbs onto a stool at the round table, and rumples Meg's hair with a big hand. 'Aright, squirt?' He takes a sip of the tea I've made him. 'You were restless last night, love,' he says to me. 'Did you end up on the sofa again?'

'I did. Couldn't sleep.'

'Not my snoring, I hope?'

'Definitely nothing to do with your snoring.' I shake my head. 'You've done nothing wrong.'

He raises his gaze, sensing something off. 'You alright?'

'Yes. Ignore me. Overtired.' I force a smile. 'I've left your packed lunch on the side.' But I'm really saying: *please understand, please forgive me. It's not that I don't love you, it's just that I love him more.*

I follow them outside and watch as they get into the car, staring after them for as long as the Ford rumbles and bumps up the track toward the main road, clouds of dust mushrooming behind. I want to sprint behind and hammer on the passenger window, tell them to stop so that I can hug Meg again, hold her close to my heart. But the car has turned the corner. I go back into the house and tidy the kitchen as if it's a normal morning, except my breath is quick and shallow, nerves fluttering under my skin.

Upstairs, I pull my packed case from under the bed. I take the note I composed last night and leave it on Robert's bedside table, slotted into an envelope, sealed shut with his name on the front. I hesitate for a moment, then slip off my gold wedding band and place it on top, leaving my only other ring on my finger, the silver band with the opal.

I need to do something with the Polaroid. I take it from my bedside drawer and look at it one more time. It's blurred. I'd moved just as it was taken, and Paul had rolled his eyes, and told me to keep still for the next one. Despite the imperfection, the pendant he'd given me is visible around my neck, glinting gold, and I'm smiling broadly. He'd discarded this blurred one, and I'd slipped it into my pocket. Now, I put it in an envelope and shove it to the back of the bureau drawer in the living room, behind the board games that hardly get played. I'll retrieve it when I come back for Meg.

Sunlight catches a framed photo propped on the bureau: me and Robert, taken by a professional on our wedding day. When the photo was taken, I had no idea that I was moments away from my carefully reinvented life imploding.

We'd had a small registry office ceremony, with just my ex-flatmates and my friend, Claire, a handful of Robert's friends, his mum and his sister and her husband. When he'd told me about his sister, Janet, I'd heard the pain in his voice. 'We're not close any more,' he'd said. 'After she left art school, she met her husband, and since then...' He'd shrugged, looking wistful. 'She was my best friend when we were growing up. But after meeting him she's changed the way she speaks, even changed her name. Calls herself Calista. They live on the other side of Suffolk and have two young daughters. I've never met their kids. We have nothing in common any more. I think she's embarrassed by me – by our background, growing up in a council house, having a father who was a fisherman – but...' he'd sighed, 'she's my sister, so I've invited them.'

I wore a white jacket and long white skirt, aiming to look as cool as Bianca Jagger, although mine was off the rack, not haute couture, and I hoped my marriage would last longer than hers. I carried a small bouquet of white roses. I met Robert in the anteroom. His suit jacket was a little short at the cuffs, and his bony wrists looked vulnerable. I picked one up and kissed it. Our guests were already waiting for us in the registry office. We entered together, Robert holding my hands as we spoke the words the registrar was prompting. Tears shone in his eyes, and I wondered what I'd done to deserve such a good man.

Outside, our guests threw confetti, pastel fragments swirling in the wind, landing indiscriminately in hair, down cleavages, in the gutter. At the bottom of the steps, people came forward to congratulate us. Robert's mum was dabbing her eyes with a hankie. The photographer posed us in front of the registry office, and we'd smiled for him, dazed by the moment. Then a gap opened, letting a woman through. I knew it was his sister – they looked alike, except somehow her features added up to something beautiful. 'Irene, this is my sister, Jan— er... Calista,' he said. She was wearing a floaty purple dress, beaded necklaces, her hair loose down her back. She looked gorgeously bohemian, but there was something stiff about her manner. She gave me her hand and smiled.

'How lovely to meet you,' she said, every word carefully enunciated. 'I love your outfit.'

A large man crowded her side. 'My husband,' she went on, glancing up at him with an adoring expression. 'Lucian Aldredge.'

I'd never heard the name before, but the red-gold hair, the fleshy, handsome face. The arctic eyes. My body went rigid. It was him. But it couldn't be. He was dead. I gripped my bouquet. I'd forgotten to throw it. Something sharp pierced my finger. I felt the welling of blood and raised my hand to my mouth, tasting metal.

'Irene,' he said, without a pause. Not a blink or a tremor. 'Good to meet you. And many congratulations to you both.'

He leant forward, meeting my gaze with a fixed intensity, and took my hand, the one with the wounded finger. Instead of shaking, he squeezed hard. My bones concertinaed inwards. I felt a brief pain, and he released his grip.

Everything around me fell away, tilting into oblivion. All

that existed was the two of us, memories flashing past, his mouth over mine, our naked bodies welded together.

'Irene?' Someone else was saying my name.

I snapped back into the moment. The world rushed in. Paul was looking at me with curiosity, the cerulean blue of his eyes unfathomable.

I wanted to scream, to throw my arms around him, to slap his face. I did nothing.

'Irene?' Robert repeated, his face creased in concern. 'Are you alright, love? You look pale.'

A hum was building inside my chest, pressure, a weight on my heart, but I managed to nod. I couldn't trust my voice. Robert tightened his arm around me. 'Are you coming to the pub?' he asked them. 'There's food.'

'Sorry.' Calista shook her head. 'We can't stay. We've left the girls with a sitter.'

Lucian slapped Robert on the shoulder. 'Well done, Rob. We thought you were destined to be an old bachelor.' He didn't look at me as he took his wife's arm, and they walked away through the small crowd. An elegant couple. People gave them space, stepping to the side.

I stared after them. It couldn't be him. It must be his double, a doppelganger.

My stomach lurched. If it really was Paul, my Paul, he would have recognised me. Yet he'd given no indication we'd even met before. Why hadn't he let me know he was alright? All these years, I'd been afraid they'd killed him.

The thorn had gone deep into my finger. Blood dripped onto my skirt, and when I tried to wipe the mark away, it stained the fabric.

That night, the first night of my honeymoon, I was thinking of Paul. It was him I pictured as I slipped out of my ruined skirt, him I thought of as Robert pulled back the sheets for me. To get his telephone number, I'd have to ask Robert, and he'd want to know why I needed to speak to his brother-in-law, someone who was supposed to be a stranger to me. I had no way of communicating with him, of asking him what the hell was going on.

Now, years later, he is waiting for me at the end of the track. I leave another note, flattened out on the kitchen table for Meg, telling her I won't be back for tea. I've left her something to eat in the fridge. A tomato quiche, her favourite. I glance at the drawings stuck to the wall that Meg did when she was younger; stick figure parents swinging their smiling child between them, carefully drawn under a yellow sun, life simplified in crayon. My guts roil and clench. But she will understand, in time.

I close the front door and hurry along the rutted track with my case. The sky is a sweep of blue, seagulls wheeling overhead. Paul's car is parked near the church, as arranged. He gets out and holds his arms open, and I go into them.

'My darling,' he says, enveloping me in one of his bear hugs. 'My brave darling.'

He holds me tight, and I press my nose into crisp folds of shirt, wanting to bury myself inside his arms. But he releases me and smiles down. 'And now you can wear this again.' He takes something from his trouser pocket.

The cold slither of a chain looping my neck, the heavy gold pendant resting against my breastbone. My fingers go to it. 'I love it,' I say. 'Where did it come from?'

'I told you before,' he says, raising one eyebrow. 'It's the Aldredge crest. A family heirloom.'

I don't contradict him or call him out on it, the boundaries between truth and lies blur when I'm with him; it's part of the magic that happens when we're together. Anything seems possible.

'It's perfect on you.' He leans forward and traces the lines of the pendant, then his fingertips are swirling across my collarbone, my throat, slipping around my neck, his fingers flexing into my hair at the back of my head; the pleasure makes me gasp.

'Let's go,' he says. 'Before someone sees us. You left the note for Robert? You wrote what I told you to say?'

'Yes.'

He takes my case and puts it in the boot as I slip into the passenger seat. The boot clunks shut, and he gets in beside me.

'I told him not to look for me,' I add, wanting him to know I followed his instructions to the letter. 'I said I'd be in touch. That I was safe.'

He smiles as he turns the ignition key. 'Well,' he says, grasping the gear stick. 'This is it, princess.' He picks up my fingers and kisses them. 'Our new beginning.'

I don't look back at the Norman church, the twist of track leading to the cottage, the glitter of the river. Although my heart is weeping, I look ahead through the windscreen towards London, and the future.

14

Paul's London flat is on the third floor of a Victorian mansion block in Fulham. He carries my case for me as we go in through grand double doors into a fusty entrance with an old-fashioned metal box lift. Paul sets off up the stairs; he knows my claustrophobia means I'd rather climb umpteen flights than get into an elevator.

'Here we are,' he unlocks a door, and ushers me inside. I step in before him, breathing heavily from walking up three floors in the stuffy stairwell.

'One bedroom,' he says. 'It's small, but it suits my needs. It's just a place to crash when I'm up in town. And I can do business out of it.'

I look down a narrow passage, carpeted and painted in grey. My nostrils prickle at the spike of bleach in the stale air. He shows me the bedroom; it's sparsely furnished, the double bed covered in a shiny grey coverlet, fitted white wardrobes flush along one wall. It looks like a functional, plain hotel room, somewhere you'd expect to find a Gideon Bible and a cheap hairdryer stashed away. It's not what I was expecting. He opens a couple of drawers and tells me I can use them for my things.

'I'm so glad you're here,' he says, pulling me in for a hug. 'At last, I've got you all to myself.' I breathe him in: salty, warm. I tell myself that it doesn't matter what the flat looks like; if Paul is here, it's home.

When we disentangle, I look out of the bedroom window at a row of shops opposite, and I'm guessing there are flats above. Through grubby glass, I see a queue of people at a bus stop below, orange plastic barricades around some roadworks and three men in hard hats staring into a hole in the tarmac. The roadworks have closed off half the street, causing a jam of cars and vans, bikes and motorbike couriers weaving in and out of the traffic.

I am suddenly dizzy with the switch from one life into another. I need air. I try to open the catch but it's behind another pane. Paul comes up behind me and wraps his arms around my stomach. 'It doesn't open,' he says. 'Double-glazed.'

He folds my fingers inside his. 'Come and see the rest of it.' He leads me into a small, white kitchen, with matching mugs on a shelf, a row of knives glinting on a magnetic strip, a silver electric kettle; and then, down a narrow passage into a windowless tiled bathroom with grey towels, the hum of a fan as he flicks on the light. There are no family snaps, no sign of his life as a father, an art collector, a sailor. He waves towards a closed door. 'That's my office and storage room.'

He takes me back to the kitchen and opens the fridge, producing a bottle of champagne with a flourish. 'Time for a toast,' he says, popping the cork, and pouring fizzing liquid into two crystal flutes.

He dominates the room, standing with his feet planted apart on the lino floor, his broad, muscular shoulders defined under his fine cotton shirt. A triangle of freckled, ruddy skin is visible between the open top buttons. I know the smell of that skin so well, the scent of his cologne; thyme and leather and tobacco. A man's smell. I don't know another male who epitomises the old-fashioned idea of what a man should be – every fibre of his being says hunter, protector, warrior.

The florescent strip lighting is giving me a headache. I hold my glass up and try to enjoy the ritual, to feel the weight of the occasion, the joy of finally being together properly – I remind myself that we'll sleep the whole night in a bed and wake in each other's arms. I should be excited. But instead, I'm thinking of Meg returning to the cottage and finding me gone.

'No tears.' Paul's eyes hold mine as we clink glasses, reading my thoughts. 'You've done the right thing.' He takes a sip. 'Robert doesn't know who you are, not like me.' He kisses me hard on the lips. 'I know you, Irene, through and through. There's no hiding from me.'

Bubbles catch in my throat. I focus on him, drawing strength from his certainty. There's safety in our shared history – in our plans for a life together, a future that was always supposed to exist before it was stolen from us. We will have our own house in Suffolk, and Meg will live with us; her cousins will stay over when they're not with their mother; they'll be like the sisters Meg never had.

* * *

I wake with a sour taste in my mouth. The bedroom is stuffy and dark. I reach for Paul, but his side of the bed is empty, his pillow warm. I sit up, pulling the slippery cover around my naked shoulders. 'Paul?' The blind cuts out all light. I have no idea what time it is. I peer across at the luminous numbers on the alarm clock on his side. Eight o'clock.

The buzz of an electric toothbrush sounds through the quiet, and I slip out of bed, pulling on his shirt from the day we arrived, enjoying the faint tang of his sweat. My feet sink into the soft embrace of carpet. The bathroom door is open. Paul is at the sink, running a razor over his chin, a towel wrapped around his waist. He's broadened with age, but his body is as taut as it was when I first met him; his skin holds a tawny sheen, the gloss of health. A knot of longing unfurls inside me.

We've spent the last two days in bed, making love, sleeping in each other's arms, only getting up to fetch food and drink, to take showers together. The intensity of it has helped quell my anxiety. My body is alive with the memory of sex, my skin sensitised, nipples sore. But it was a holiday, and now we need to face the music. Paul said we'd tell Robert and Calista that our marriages are over, and he and I are going to be together.

'You're up early,' I say. 'Are you going somewhere?'

He screws up his face in apology. 'Sorry, princess. Work. A meeting with a client.'

'Oh.' Disappointment falls like a stone. 'When will you be back?'

'I'm not sure,' he says. 'I'll keep in touch.'

'What about Calista?' I ask. 'When will you talk to her?'

He puts the razor down with a clink on the side of the sink, pats his face with a towel and looks at me. 'She's delicate,' he says. 'I must tread carefully. And there are things I need to put in place, financial things. That's what this meeting is about.'

'But we said we'd deal with it today. Shouldn't I phone Robert and break the news to him, about us?'

'We need a bit more time,' Paul says as he passes me in the doorway, grabbing my bottom with both hands and pulling me to him. Our bodies collide, his mouth on my neck. 'God, you're gorgeous,' he whispers. 'You know that, don't you?'

There's a moment of disconnect – I'd taken it for granted he'd be like me and want to sort things out as soon as possible. 'But we'll tell them soon? Paul?' I follow him back to the bedroom and watch him get dressed. 'It's not fair to keep Robert in the dark for much longer.'

'Call me Lucian,' he says. 'Otherwise, you'll accidentally call me Paul in front of other people.' He's buttoning up a shirt he's slipped from a hanger. 'Would you like to see what I've bought you?' he says. 'That should cheer you up.'

He throws open the other side of the wardrobe with a flourish, as if he's a magician. *Abracadabra! For your amazement, the severed halves of my assistant in two separate boxes!*

I don't know why that sentence pops into my head. The image makes me shiver as I look at the clothes he's revealed, night things by the look of them, feminine. Expensive.

'Do you like them?' he asks, looking almost coy. 'You never dress up, always in the same old things. Thought it would be fun for you.'

I run my hands over the softness of silk, the slip of satin. Colours leap at me: ruby red, damson, chocolate, electric blue.

'I'm looking forward to seeing you in them when I get back.' He nods towards the kitchen. 'You shouldn't go out, but in case of an emergency, I've left some cash. I've taken your credit card.'

'You... what?' I startle.

'Just for now,' he smiles. 'In case you forget and use it. In case Robert tries to find you.'

He drinks half a cup of black coffee and kisses me on the mouth. 'What's my name?' he asks in a teasing voice.

'Lucian.'

'That's my girl.' He kisses me again and I taste the acidic tang of caffeine on his breath. The front door closes. Silence washes around me. From the street outside, the muffled shriek of a drill cuts through the double glazing.

The grey walls of the flat close in on me. To distract myself, I open the wardrobe and slip one of the dresses from its hanger. A long, slim tube of blood red with a plunging neckline dangles from my fingers, fragile as a handful of poppies. I hook another out. Chocolate satin, short, flared, with coffee coloured lace at the hem and shoestring straps. I've never owned anything like them, never wanted to. They're impractical for anything other than lounging on a leopard skin rug. But he's a typical man. Getting female shopping wrong. In a way, it's sweet. Touching. I put the slips back on their padded silk hangers and close the wardrobe.

I can't stay in the flat. I need to find a way of contacting Meg. I'll be careful, but it's unlikely that anyone who knows me will be in Fulham. I get dressed in my usual wraparound skirt in Indian cotton and an old T-shirt, push my feet into flip-flops, pick up the twenty-pound note he's left me, and the spare key. In the street, I'm assaulted by a stench of fumes, the roar of engines, tyres on tarmac, the unmuffled scream of the drill. I press my hands over my ears. It sounds as though the whole world is screaming.

Robert will have read the note by now and told Meg that I've gone away for a while. I blink into the harsh light, walking until I find a post office, where I buy plain white cards and stamps. I arrange for a PO Box address. Standing at a table littered with off-cuts from stamps, I write a card:

Meg love, I'm sorry I had to leave. It might be hard for you to understand until you're older, but I'll do my best to explain

when I see you. I promise we'll see each other soon. Please
write with all your news. I love you, Mum.

Then I compose a short note to my friend, Claire, and drop
them both in the postbox on my way out.

I wander the streets, trying to get my bearings. I don't know
London, have never lived here. I think about Claire. I feel bad
for leaving without telling her.

We'd met at college when I was taking a night course in
Creative Writing, and she'd been the model for the life drawing
class. She'd explained that she wanted to be a dancer, have her
own academy one day and teach little girls the love of movement. She doesn't know about Paul. I promised I wouldn't tell
anybody about us, even though I was burning to let it out to
someone, to her, the only real friend I had in Suffolk, apart
from Robert.

I miss her. If she was here, we could explore the city
together, try on clothes we have no intention of buying, people-
watch over coffees at a pavement cafe, eat ice creams in the
park. My stomach rumbles. I haven't eaten since yesterday. I
buy a bunch of bananas from the fruit and vegetable stall in
Paul's street; the wiry man winks at me as he gives me my
change. 'Far from home, are you, love?'

I stare at him.

'Can't place your accent,' he explains, 'but I'd put my
money on you being a country girl.' He taps the side of his
nose. 'It's the rosy cheeks.'

'I'm from the North, originally,' I tell him, turning away,
peeling a banana.

People can never place me. My accent still has a
Mancunian burr, but it's all over the place, a blend of intona-
tions, a slip-sliding way of pronouncing vowels and conso-

nants, picked up from all the different families and institutions I've lived in, TV programmes probably, too.

I can't finish the fruit. My stomach has shrunk with the pain of missing Meg. I drop it into a bin, tucking the rest of the bunch under my arm.

In the flat, I pace up and down the narrow corridor, around the small rooms, leaving tracks in the carpet pile. I wait for the phone to ring. Out of boredom and curiosity, I turn the handle of the door to his office. But it's locked. I think about trying on the things in the wardrobe just for something to do; but I don't have the energy or the heart. What do I care about new clothes when I'm separated from Meg? All I can think about is when I can see her again, and how I'm going to tell Robert I want a divorce.

When Paul calls, later that afternoon, I know from the tone of his voice what he's going to say. 'I won't be back tonight. I'm so sorry, princess.'

I hold the receiver close and try to control my breathing. 'Tomorrow?' I manage.

'Of course,' he says. 'Miss you.'

15

When Paul suggested this plan, I'd understood we'd let our partners know almost immediately. After that, Deben Manor would be put up for sale, and we'd start looking for our own place. As soon as possible, Meg would come and stay in London for the summer holiday. We'd go to museums and art galleries and feed the ducks in Hyde Park.

I'd been unhappy about the idea of running away. I'd wanted to be honest with Robert straight away. But Paul hadn't agreed. 'You're too soft-hearted,' he'd said. 'You won't be able to go through with it. He'll act the victim and you'll capitulate. I know you, princess.' He'd cupped my cheeks between his hands. 'A clean break is the best thing. Leave a note. Give him some time to adjust to the situation.'

'I don't know,' I'd said, chewing my lip. 'It doesn't feel right.'

'He hasn't made you happy,' he'd said. 'If he had, do you think you'd have spent the last three years lying to him?' And it was true. I'd already betrayed Robert. Paul and I had started to see each other when Meg was eight. We'd made love while she was at school and Robert was at work. It started after Paul had paid me a surprise visit at the cottage one weekday morning. I belonged to him, always had.

Shame fills me. Robert is better off without me.

Without Paul here, my thoughts turn on me. *You're worthless,* they murmur softly, *worthless and stupid. You've abandoned your daughter.* I sit up, feeling nauseous, scribbling out another card to Meg to post tomorrow. I blow my nose on a tissue, plucked from the box by the bed. Perhaps there'll be a reply to my first one waiting for me.

It was Paul who gave me the confidence to believe I could become someone else. The only reason I'd made Suffolk my destination was a chance remark he once made before we were separated. Because of him I got away from my past, taking coaches, sleeping in their fusty warmth, jerking awake as the vehicle lurched around corners. I'd noticed the countryside changing, becoming different from the dark hills and jagged stone outcrops I was used to. The flatness of the land, the watery nature of it, the wide, open skies: it all felt manageable, clean, pure. I could spot trouble coming; there was no way anyone or anything could creep up on me in all this flat space.

When I was settled in a new town, amongst strangers, I set out to be the woman I told myself I would have been if I'd had parents to love me, if I hadn't grown up in a children's home and been moved from one foster placement to another. I thought I could outrun the whispers in my head, the memories of rough fingers, sour breath, voices telling me I was nothing, that nobody would believe me.

I'd slipped a notebook and pen into my bag before I left, intending to write poetry while I was here, conjuring lines about love. Instead, I want to put down how it happened, pin it onto the page – how I met Paul – our story. Maybe one day, I'll give it to Meg to read and she'll understand why I'm doing this.

I pull the notebook from my case and turn its virgin pages. I tap the end of the pen against my front teeth and start to write.

I was eighteen when I moved out of my last foster parents, Sue and Pete's, into a studio flat at the top of an old building. I went around touching the walls, the scratched surfaces, the old armchair in the corner with the stuffing coming out – my own home – it felt too good to be true. The other tenants in the block were ex-care like me, or kids fresh from remand school. One night, my buzzer rang just after midnight.

After I let him in, Luke behaved like a cornered animal; fidgeting, eyes wide, pacing my flat, looking out into the street. He said he'd done something stupid, and now he needed to lie low. I didn't want to know the details, and he didn't offer them. 'What about Sue and Pete?' I asked him. 'Do they know where you are?'

He looked away, and I held his chin in my hand and forced him to confront me. His large, black eyes were sheeted, unreadable. He shook his head. 'They threw me out.'

My foster brother, Luke, was my family back then, my only family. We weren't related by blood, but we'd been in the same children's home and then two foster homes. That kind of shared experience forms a bond. I knew something was going on, he'd been evasive for a while, disappearing for days, and he had more money than he should. He'd tried to give me a gold bracelet. I'd told him I didn't want it if he couldn't explain where he got the cash to buy it.

I said he could stay one night and no longer. I didn't want to risk losing the flat, getting into trouble with my care worker, or the police. 'Isn't there anyone who could help you?'

'There's someone,' he said, hesitantly. 'I don't know. Maybe.' He twisted his hands together.

'Who?'

'Some people call him The Governor. But his name is Paul.'

'Can you contact him?'

He went down to the pay phone in the hall. Afterwards, he seemed a little calmer. He said Paul had promised to come.

Luke slept on my floor, curled on the moth-eaten carpet with one of my blankets over him. He whimpered in his sleep, throwing out an arm. I woke him and told him he could get in with me. We shared my single bed, his head heavy on my shoulder. He was only seventeen. He smelt like a boy – ripe and musty – a fug of unwashed clothes and dried sweat and hormones. The bell rang early the next morning before dawn.

I ran downstairs before anyone else could get there, wrapping my dressing gown around me. Instead of the thug I'd been expecting, a tall young man stood on the doorstep with piercing blue eyes, red-gold hair, and a wide mouth. He glanced behind him, before slipping past into the hall, a finger to his lips. Inside the flat, he ruffled Luke's hair, said he was an idiot. 'I'll get him out of the area,' he told me. 'Fix him up with some people I know in London. He'll be alright. But he needs to break contact with you and everyone else here.' I was surprised by how middle class he sounded. 'I'll let you know when he's safe,' he said. 'Meanwhile, don't speak to anyone about me, or him. You never saw me. Luke was never here. Right?'

He discreetly turned away while Luke and I hugged.

'We'll see each other again,' Luke whispered, sinewy arms tight around my shoulders. Through his thin chest, his breath came shallow and fast. I could tell he was struggling to hold back tears.

'I know,' I told him. 'We will.'

'Let's go.' Paul's voice came from behind us. When he passed me, he touched my wrist, his fingers trailing my skin. He turned at the door as he pushed Luke in front of him. 'Don't worry,' he said. 'I'll keep him safe for you.'

* * *

I feel winded, as if someone has landed a punch in my guts. My PO Box is empty. I'd been depending on getting a message. But it's only been five days. Finding me gone will have been a shock. She'll be upset and angry. I bite down on my lip until it hurts. How am I going to make this up to her? How is she going to trust me again? When I'm with Paul, I see the world in the way he explains it. Without him, all that certainty falls away.

I post my other card to her. It doesn't say much, a variation on my others. The words seem hollow and repetitive. I make my way past the queue of shuffling people and push out into the street.

Back in the flat, I want to fling the sealed windows open, fill the place with music and flowers and the smell of cooking. I pick up the phone from the table by the front door. School has finished. Meg might be sitting in the kitchen having her lunch or lying in the garden with a book. Paul told me not to contact her, but I need to hear her voice. I dial the number for the cottage, heart thumping, listening to the ringtone. I imagine how it will sound in the cottage, the dust motes turning in the sunbeams. After a few minutes, I put it down.

As I turn away, the phone vibrates, the sound startling between the narrow walls of the corridor. I grab it, breathless. 'Love?' She's pressed ring-back, I think.

But it's Paul's voice.

'Where are you?' I ask, unable to conceal my need. 'When will you be back?'

'I'm in Suffolk,' he says. 'I'm going to spend the weekend here. Don't be upset.'

I am, I am upset, I want to shout into the receiver. I swallow hard.

'I'm going to talk to Calista,' he says, his voice dropping. 'I'll get the ball rolling. She's not going to like the idea of selling the house.'

'Are you going to tell her about me?'

He hesitates. 'Not yet,' he says. 'Because of Robert. We should stick to the plan and wait until things are progressing before we reveal the truth to them both.'

'A whole weekend without you?'

'I'll be there on Monday,' he says. 'I'm longing for you.'

'Has Calista heard from Robert? Does she know I've left?'

'Yes,' he says. 'In fact, Meg is here, at Deben Manor.'

'What?' My legs give way, my shoulders sliding down the wall until I'm sitting on the floor.

'Robert couldn't manage – it's the school holidays and he has to work.'

I have a weird, out-of-body sensation. Things are spooling out of my control. I didn't know where my child was sleeping, who was feeding her, who she was with. There's a glitch in time. I can't speak.

'Think about it, princess,' he's saying, his tone soothing. 'It's for the good. Meg is getting to know her cousins. It will make it easier for all of them if they can make friends.'

'Are they getting on?' My voice falters.

'Famously,' he says. 'Have you been wearing your new clothes?'

I bite the edge of one finger. I don't want to disappoint him. But he'll know if I'm lying. 'Not yet,' I say.

'Can't wait to see you in them,' he says, his voice breathy. 'Must go.'

'Love you,' I say, but he's put the phone down.

My fingers are welded around the receiver. I'd been thinking of her with her father in the cottage, imagining her finding comfort in the marsh, going to our favourite places to watch the seals on the mud flats. It frightens me that I'd got it so wrong. That I hadn't somehow known. Another thought: my postcards will be dropping onto the doormat at the cottage. I'll have to trust that Robert will give them to her. I replace the receiver in its cradle. It's not for long, I think. A couple more days.

I open the wardrobe, catching a whiff of department stores. I shrug off my clothes and select the red tube. It slides over my naked skin like cool hands enveloping me. The fabric shimmers in the overhead light. The pendant is lying on the chest of drawers. I pick it up and feel the weight of it in my palm, put the gold chain around my neck, fingering the heavy disc, the raised surface. I wonder where he really got it from.

In the mirror on the back of the wardrobe door, a stranger is reflected in the glass. I can't make up my mind if I look more like an actress in a high-end porn film or a screen siren from the forties. It's an act, I tell myself, a bit of fun, dressing up, pretending to be someone else. He doesn't really see me like this. It's a fantasy – but his fantasy, or yours?

I can't afford doubt. I need something to focus on. I take out my notebook and pen and settle at the kitchen table, folds of red slipping over my thighs, the pendant snug against my breastbone. Writing eats up time, and I have two days to fill.

* * *

After the wedding, I didn't see Paul again until Meg's christening. Meg was nine months before we got around to christening her. A friend of Robert's was to be godfather, and Claire was godmother. Lucian and Calista had moved to the Norfolk coast by then, but they came down for the ceremony.

This time, I was prepared; when Lucian arrived, I observed him carefully. There was the teardrop-shaped scar on his right cheek, the mole above his left eyebrow, and he still had the mannerism of running his tongue across his front teeth, pushing his top lip out. 'Paul,' I whispered under my breath. But he gave no indication he'd recognised me.

They came without their children. Calista had had a daughter called Clementine ten months before, but you'd never know it from her perfect figure. I was still carrying extra weight, still feeding Meg, revelling in those intimate, milky moments. Calista confided that she couldn't breastfeed, and had been ill throughout her pregnancy, confined to bed. 'It's the last one,' she said. 'No more children for me.'

I'd asked her if it had been a difficult birth, and she'd given me an odd look. 'No,' she said. 'Not really. I suppose the hard part begins after they arrive.' I thought she was telling me she had postnatal depression and I wanted to hug her. But she held herself aloof, and I knew it wouldn't be welcome. There was something brittle about her.

Lucian said he'd been down to Suffolk a lot, looking for the perfect house for the family while he visited auction houses and galleries in the area, staying over in hotels and pubs.

'I've found it,' he said. 'A place called Deben Manor. Near the river, close to a village. We'll be moving in a couple of months. The girls will love it. It has a huge garden.' There was no trace of Manchester left in his vowels. But he'd always had a knack for accents. 'After all, Suffolk is where my family are

originally from,' he added. 'It feels good to be coming home.'
He looked right at me when he said it, his eyes holding a
challenge.

'The garden is enormous. We're going to need a gardener,'
Calista said, frowning.

'Leave it to me, darling. I have a contact,' he said. 'A reliable
sort, apparently.'

'It will be nice to be finally settled somewhere,' Calista said.
'We've been moving around a lot for the last few years. I can
have a proper studio at last.'

'Meg and your youngest will be similar ages,' I said. 'Perhaps the cousins could see each other, once you're in Suffolk.'

Lucian and Calista both made polite agreeing noises, but I
could see from their removed gazes and Robert's doubtful
expression that this wasn't going to happen.

I kept expecting Paul to wink at me, any signal that he knew
me, an acknowledgement of our situation, our past, something
to let me in on the lies he was telling. But there was nothing. I
began to think he wasn't Paul, just an uncanny look-alike.

It was years before he came for me. I suppose I'd been waiting. I knew our history tied us together more than our vows to
Robert and Calista. Golden rings and pieces of paper meant
nothing compared to the weight of the past.

16

From the kitchen window I can see bunches of roses outside the supermarket across the road. It only takes five minutes to nip out and buy a bunch. Who says the flat can't have some life and colour in it? The blooms are a beacon of hope. I have to keep believing that I'm doing the right thing, and everything is going to turn out like I'd imagined.

Back in the kitchen, I unwrap the roses from crisp folds of plastic and snip the ends of the thin stalks. I find a vase under the sink and decide the flowers should go in the bedroom. My foot catches on the drape of coverlet, and I stumble, spilling water. The grey carpet darkens, the thick pile soaking up the liquid. I go back to the kitchen and fetch a cloth, getting down on my knees to mop it up. Sitting back on my heels, I notice some faint scratches above the skirting board next to the chest of drawers. I lean forwards and touch the marks, realising they're letters. I make out a *K* and an *L* and beside the letters, a badly drawn heart.

I can't understand what they mean, or why they're here, hidden and faint, as if the writer hadn't wanted them to be seen. I stand up and place the roses on the chest of drawers, their orange petals glowing.

I get into bed, thinking about the carved letters, the childish heart. I throw off the covers and toss and turn in the hot, stuffy air. My fingers go to the place where my wedding band used to sit, the slight indentation, the paler line of skin. Robert must have been desperate to ask his sister for help. Why hadn't I realised he couldn't leave Meg alone in the school holidays? Living a double life has made me selfish.

I fall asleep holding my right hand, fingering my silver and opal ring for reassurance. It was left to me by my own mother. She abandoned me as a baby but left me this one personal token, a secret message telling me she loved me.

* * *

I ignore the scratched letters above the skirting board. I can't see them unless I get down on my hands and knees and put my face inches from the wall, so it's easy to pretend they don't exist. All day, I hear the hesitant creak and groan of the lift as it travels up and down the centre of the building, the squeak and slam of the doors as people get in and out. Pipes gurgle and belch, the plumbing like the furred arteries of an old man.

I am bored and restless on my own. I clean the whole flat until there isn't a speck of dirt anywhere, the taps shine and the paintwork gleams. Paul's office is locked, so I can't get in there, otherwise I'd have given that a going over too. I scour the windows, but the outer panes remain grubby, a layer of grease between me and the world. I run my fingers over Paul's starched shirts hanging in the other half of the wardrobe, six white and six plain blue, a couple of suits. I look at the labels. Handmade by a tailor in Jermyn Street. I find a thick wad of cash in the drawer of his bedside table. I pick it up and flick the notes, twanging the elastic band. There must be thousands here, I think, putting it back. Paul might be Lucian now, but I know the old Paul, and who he mixed with, and I wonder about the legitimacy of his art business. I have a sudden lurch of fear. I've put all my trust in him. But there are things he's not telling me.

If Meg was at home, I would have tried to phone her again. But I can't call her at Deben Manor. I remember my one visit to the gracious Georgian manor house, the high ceilings and light-filled rooms, and I try and place Meg amongst the eccentric clutter, the paintings and her cousins. She feels out of reach.

I wish Paul were here – he'd reassure me, belittle my fears, make me believe that this is all going to work out for the best. I go back to the drawer with the roll of money and pick it up again, wondering whether I should take some, just in case. It feels odd not to have access to any money. But if I take even one note, it will prove something, something I can't afford to admit to myself. I can't allow myself any doubt.

I only leave the flat to post another card to Meg. On the street, I feel exposed, and suddenly frightened, as if everyone knows who I am and what I'm doing. Every passing stranger seems to be sneering at me. The voices are back in my head, and I recognise them all: the care worker with the nasal whine, the foster father with the Northern Irish accent, the teacher with the lisp. *Stupid girl. What are you crying about? You know you like it really.*

In the flat, I open the notebook to get back to the story of me and Paul. He was the one who told me I had value, who made me feel I was worth more. I flick past lines covered in my scrawl and turn to a new page and chew the end of my pen. I suppose it could have ended that morning – with Paul taking Luke away to safety – I didn't expect to see him again, even though I'd thought about him every day.

* * *

I wanted to be a writer. I didn't tell anyone; they would have laughed. Kids like me didn't grow up to be authors or poets. I was doing A levels at the local college, juggling a weekend job stacking shelves and working in the Stag's Head three nights a week.

One evening, as I left the pub to go home, a figure peeled away from the car park wall opposite. I tensed, fingers fumbling for the keys in my pocket, holding them with the serrated point ready to stab. I walked quickly, staying in the middle of the street. My heart lurched sideways when I heard the confident slap of shoes hitting wet tarmac close behind me.

I stopped and spun around, arm straight out, holding the point of the key. 'Whoever you are. Fuck off. I don't need this. Alright?'

'Whoa!' The backlit figure was only about two feet away; he nearly ran into me. His hand closed over mine, trapping the key inside my palm. His grip was tight. 'Don't show your weapon until you're ready to use it.' He let go of my hand.

'Paul?' I rubbed my crushed knuckles.

'Ah, so you do remember me?'

'People don't usually introduce themselves by following other people home in the dark.' I meant it as a joke, to show him I didn't really care. But there was something about his broad-shouldered height, the coiled way he held himself, that made my mouth dry up and the words came out as a squeak.

'I wanted to check you were alone,' he said. 'Sorry if I gave you a fright.' His voice sounded different from when we first met: it had the nasal, twangy sound of the local accent.

'No worries.'

'Want to go for a walk?'

I thought of my reading still to do for the essay I had to write the next day. I thought of how tired I was. 'Alright.'

We went down gleaming streets, past shapes bedded down in doorways and cats slinking under cars. Sometimes a group of drunks lurched past, rowdy and uncoordinated, smashing bottles on the pavement, but I felt safe with him. He walked as if he owned the city. He made me laugh, teasing me. We went along the canal, and I breathed in the mossy, muddy smells. Under bridges, sleeping figures stirred as we went past. A face peered at us from under a hood. I stepped closer to Paul.

'Is Luke alright?' I asked. 'Can you tell me where he is?'

Paul stopped, cocking his head as if listening. He glanced up and down the dark canal. 'Don't mention his name. Don't tell anyone you know him. Understand?'

We went up some steps onto another street. He stopped outside a building and knocked on the closed door. A peephole slid open, and Paul murmured something into it. A bolt was drawn back. We entered, and he took my hand and led me along a narrow passage, through another door and down some steps. We were hit by a wall of sound: a gabble of voices, clink of glass, a woman's voice singing and the smell of hot bodies, cigarette smoke, sweat and boozy breath. We were in a kind of cellar. Faces leered out of the gloom; the lightened ends of cigarettes danced like fireflies. The only way to get anywhere was to squeeze into the gaps between shoulders and push. But people moved for Paul – I noticed they were respectful. He spoke to people in his new voice, the one that echoed theirs, shaking hands and clapping shoulders as we made our way to the bar.

A black woman was singing on a small stage, her words full of yearning. There was nowhere to sit, but someone got up for Paul, and he pulled me onto his lap. I folded into his broad chest, listening to the singer, and her longing became mine. When we left the club, Paul pressed me up against the dank wall and kissed me, then he whispered, 'Luke is safe. I can't tell you where he is, but he told me to tell you not to worry. He's sorry for the trouble he caused.'

Tears of gratitude leaked through my eyelashes, and Paul kissed the wet from my cheeks. We walked on, arm in arm. 'When you came to the flat,' I said. 'You sounded... different.'

'Middle class, you mean?' He winked. 'I needed you to trust me. And usually, people think the Queen's English is more trustworthy.' He'd slipped back into that way of speaking, illustrating his point. I was impressed. 'You could be an actor,' I told him.

He took me home, leaving me at the communal front door. 'Tomorrow, then,' he said, as if we'd made an arrangement.

17

I wake, sleepy, half-dreaming. He's here, his weight over me, crushing me, his hands tangled in my hair, and I'm moving with him, as he pulls my nightdress over my head, his mouth by my ear. 'Good morning, beautiful,' he murmurs. He smells of the sea, warm pebbles, the tang of seaweed. He only ever speaks the Queen's English now.

'I missed you,' I whisper, my hands clasping his broad back. 'You abandoned me.'

He seals my mouth with his own. And I'm lost in the kiss, the push of his tongue, the warmth of his body, the demands it makes of me. Tears and sweat mingle, salty on my tongue.

He brings me breakfast in bed and watches me eat. Bagels with salmon and cream cheese, milky coffee, a ripe, furred peach. He cuts it into slivers and feeds me, the juice running down his fingers, spilling over my lips.

'You're not wearing one of the negligées I bought you,' he says, his expression a little hurt.

The word negligée is the kind of thing a fifties housewife

might wear. I suppress a smile. 'I wasn't expecting you this early,' I say, wiping peach juice from my mouth.

'I'll forgive you. This time.' His tone is playful. 'What have you been doing with yourself?' he asks, massaging my knees through the bed clothes.

'Not a lot. Worrying about everything.' I swallow a gulp of coffee. 'A bit of writing.' I push the tray across the bed. 'Tell me, how did Calista take it?'

He takes a deep breath. 'Not well,' he says. 'She's understandably upset. But she knows I'm serious.'

'So, she's agreed? To the divorce, to selling the house?'

He nods. Relief fills me. 'Then I should phone Robert and explain everything to him.'

He stands up with the tray. 'Yes,' he says. 'Soon.'

'Why not now?'

A muscle twitches in his jaw. 'She doesn't know it's you I'm leaving her for.' He hesitates at the doorway, holding the tray. 'We don't want them talking to each other, exchanging notes. Let me get the house on the market. Give Calista a bit more time to adjust. If they find out, they could turn nasty. Make things difficult.'

When I get up, the door to the locked room stands open. I'm curious to see inside it, and rap lightly with my knuckles. 'Come in,' he says. 'I want to show you something.'

The room is square and ordinary. Grey like the rest of the flat. A venetian blind is lowered at the window. There's a dark wooden desk and office chair. He's standing beside a stainless steel crate in the middle of the room. 'I've just had it installed,' he says. 'Bit of a bugger to get it up here, but worth it.'

I wait behind him while he bends to unlock it, tapping numbers into a keypad to open the door, as if it were a safety deposit box. He stands back so that I can peer inside; through the velvet-lined gloom I see stacked paintings. The container is big enough to climb inside if you were to get onto your knees. I touch the thick metal side. 'This must have cost a bomb.'

'You have to spend money to make money.' He's got his serious voice on, the one I know I must pay attention to. 'The cost pays its way tenfold. You see' – he touches the dials on the outside – 'climate-controlled storage is the only safe way to ensure that anything precious is kept safe. The temperature must be between 16 and 23 degrees centigrade. Any sudden drops or surges could be a disaster. Mould could thrive.' He touches another dial. 'I keep it at 50 per cent humidity. Ultraviolet light is a disaster. Sunlight can damage paper, paint, leather. It's completely sealed. Nothing can get in or out, not even an insect.' He grins, lecture over. He reaches inside and wipes a finger over the interior wall, showing it to me. 'See.' He brings his fingertip close, touches it to the end of my nose. 'Not even a grain of dust.'

I compose my face into something suitably impressed. But the container is my idea of hell, and I edge away from the opening. 'Given you the heebie-jeebies, has it?' He lets out a laugh. 'Silly girl.' He kisses me, and my body softens inside his embrace: the power of his broad shoulders, the way his arms wrap around me, one firm hand holding the back of my head, the other on the small of my spine, long fingers splayed against me.

'By the way,' he says. 'You called the cottage, didn't you?'

I look at him, mouth gaping.

'You promised you wouldn't,' he says, looking disappointed. 'You need to trust me.'

'I... I just got desperate to hear her voice.'

He sighs. 'Have you been writing to her, too?'

I swallow and nod.

'You know she won't get any mail,' he says. 'Not when she's at Deben Manor.' He releases me. 'You need to listen to me, princess. Just a few more days and we can all be together. Now, I have work to do. Need to catalogue these paintings.' He gives my bottom a pat, then a little push, propelling me away. 'Why don't you have a bath? We can go out and get some lunch later.'

I have a bath because I can't think of anything else to do, and it will please him. When I soap my arms, they don't seem to belong to me. My body feels as if it's disappearing. I get out of the water and pull the plug, watching the gurgle and rush of water as it swirls away. My head hurts, and I rummage in the bathroom cabinet for a packet of paracetamol. As I reach behind a bottle of mouthwash, a comb falls out, long golden hair caught between the teeth. I turn it over in my hands, the silvery hairs wafting like tentacles. I push it back out of sight. One of his daughters is blonde, isn't she?

I put on a summer dress and fasten the necklace around my throat. The pendant presses against my breastbone. Paul lets out a low whistle. 'You look stunning.'

He says there's a great little Italian bistro a couple of streets' walk away from the flat. We stroll together in the sunshine, arm in arm. As we pass the fruit and veg man, he tilts his cap at me, and Paul frowns. 'Do you know him?'

'No,' I say. 'I bought some bananas, that's all.'

'I hope you haven't been going out of the flat. I did say only if it's necessary,' he says. 'There's plenty of food in the fridge.'

I swallow. Did he really expect me to stay in the flat, alone, for days on end? I'm not sure if he's joking, and confusion envelops me like a fog, making me stumble. His arm grips me, bicep flexing, stopping me from falling.

In the restaurant, the waiter flaps a linen napkin over my

lap, and fawns over Paul. He orders some sparkling water and a Chablis and suggests that I have the dover sole. 'It's always fresh here,' he says, giving the order.

We have a table on the pavement under a green awning, opposite me, Paul's face is tinted in forest shades. He is as handsome as a film star, and I push away the unease his remarks created, and let a wave of happiness fill me. This is what we've been denied for three years. We've existed on stolen hours and secret assignations. 'How is Meg?' I ask, as the waiter pours the wine and Paul tries it, nodding his approval.

'She's fine,' he says. 'Enjoying the garden. She loves the dog. You don't have to worry.'

'Has she asked about me? Has she said anything about me?'

He reaches across and takes my hand. 'She doesn't know I'm here with you,' he reminds me gently. 'She's not exactly moping. Kids are adaptable, aren't they? They live in the moment.'

I look down at my fingers enclosed by his. He has beautiful hands, broad and strong with well-shaped fingers and clean, pink nails. The skin on the back is dusted with golden hairs. I've put myself into those hands. The thought slips into my mind, as his grip tightens, fingers squeezing mine.

'I suppose it's useful that she's getting to know the girls, and you.' I take a sip of wine when he relinquishes his grasp. 'I mean, you'll be her stepfather soon.'

'You're happy?' He raises his glass to me. 'You don't miss your old life?'

He's looking at me expectantly. 'This is what I want.' I nod. 'To be with you.'

He rewards me with one of this wide grins. 'By the way,' he says, 'I left some money in my bedside drawer.'

My fingers tremble around the glass stem, and I grip it more firmly, keeping my expression neutral.

'I just checked,' he says slowly, 'and it's all there. I knew it would be. I knew I could trust you.'

I force a little laugh. 'You mean it was a test?'

'A sort of game, I suppose.'

'But I've left my life for you!' I allow myself to be indignant, after all, I've risked everything for him. 'Of course, I'm not going to steal your money!'

He holds up his hands. 'It was a joke.'

But it's spoilt the lunch. I have a pang of homesickness so strong it's like a punch to my stomach. As I'm picking through the bones of my fish, I pause. 'I wondered if Luke is still in London?'

Paul tilts his head to the side, forehead knotting.

'My foster brother,' I remind him. 'You said he was in London.'

He opens his eyes in amazement. 'My God, Irene, that was years ago.'

'But I haven't forgotten him. I always hoped I'd see him again.'

'The last I heard, he'd gone abroad,' he says.

'Abroad? Where?'

'I don't know.' A flash of impatience crosses his face and then his expression softens. 'But if it's important to you, I'll find out. Ask around.' He smiles. 'Don't let that be another worry. Luke will be just fine. That boy is a survivor.'

'He'll be a man, now.'

'Of course.'

Disappointment sits in my throat like a pebble. It's hard to swallow the chocolate mousse Paul orders for me; it's rich and cloying. Heat makes the road shimmer, light glancing off car bonnets like spears. I gulp down sparkling water, and the fizz burns my tongue. He reaches across the white linen tablecloth, over the empty wine glasses and crumbs, and caresses my cheek. 'You're still thinking about him, aren't you?' He sighs. 'I'll find out where he is. Promise.'

As we leave, he slips his arm around my waist. 'Paul,' I murmur, leaning my head against his shoulder. 'Sorry. Lucian. I can't go much longer without seeing Meg. I miss her so much.'

I feel him stiffen, and he steps away from me.

'I'm sorry,' I whisper.

'It's alright, my darling.' His arm goes round me again. 'I understand. But she's in good hands. She's happy. Hold on to that. I have to go to Suffolk tomorrow,' he murmurs. 'But not for long. Just need to make sure everything is alright at home and take care of some business.'

I notice a couple of homeless men under a bridge, sprawled on pieces of cardboard. They stare into the distance, their eyes glazed, reddened hands clasping beer cans. It frightens me, how easy it is to lose your way, to slip through the cracks of your life and find yourself falling.

* * *

I can't find the pendant. It's not on my bedside table where I left it. Paul is going to be devastated. In a panic, I get down on my knees, scrabbling under the bed. I check inside my drawers amongst my clothes, look in the bathroom on the shelf where my face cream sits. I've lost it – the one thing I had to look after – and I've lost it. A bloody heirloom. What's wrong with me? Did I take it out of the flat by mistake? Did it slip from my neck when I was in the street? A familiar feeling sucks me in – a dark, fragmenting despair at myself. I slap my cheek hard. The flesh stings and throbs. *Stupid girl. Stupid girl. You can't do anything right.*

When Paul comes back from Suffolk, my legs are trembling. He's in the kitchen, making tea. The kettle boils with a shriek. I clasp my hands to keep them still. 'It's gone,' I say, my chest hollow with shame. 'I'm sorry. I don't understand how it happened.'

I expect his upset, his anger, but he just gives me a fond smile. 'Darling, don't you remember? I told you.'

'Told me what?'

'That I was taking it to put in the safe at home.'

'At home,' I frown, puzzled. 'Deben Manor, you mean?'

He nods. 'You know how valuable it is. I thought it would be a good idea to put it away until we're settled in our new house. Then you can wear it whenever you like.'

His reasoning doesn't make sense. Who would steal it from the flat? My head pounds. I've had a headache for days. It's the lack of fresh air. He didn't tell me. I'm sure he didn't. But then, I could have forgotten.

When he leaves the next morning, I can't find the spare key he usually leaves on the hall table. He must have taken it with him by mistake.

* * *

When it was hot, we made love in the marsh, on a rug Paul brought from the car, or he'd drive me to out-of-the-way pubs and hotels and we'd rent a room. But then one morning, he turned the car up a gravel drive towards a house I'd never been inside before.

'What are you doing?' I said, gripping my seat. 'Why are we here?'

'Relax. They're not at home,' he said, turning off the engine. 'It's half term. Calista's taken the girls to the house in France.'

It felt strange going into the house, his arm around my shoulder. The clutter of family life lay sprawled around us. 'Those are my girls,' he said, pointing to three large oil paintings on the sitting room wall. 'My beauties.' I couldn't look at them. A flush of shame burnt my face. A large, hairy dog came bounding out of the kitchen and licked my hand. 'Matisse,' Paul said. 'Calista named him.'

He showed me around the house. When he opened the door to the master bedroom, I turned my head away again. 'I can't go in,' I said, 'it doesn't feel right.'

'Bit late to take the moral high ground, princess,' he laughed. 'We'll go downstairs, then.'

As we passed a narrow staircase leading up from the landing, I asked, 'What's up there?'

'Just the attic,' he said.

The artefacts of a family were all around me: photographs, tennis racquets, items of clothing draped over chairs. I was the scarlet woman, the mistress. I'd never understood it so starkly before. We must stop this, I thought. I'll tell him it can't go on.

'Paul,' I started to say. 'I don't think we...'

But as he led me downstairs, he was already undressing me, biting my neck, his hand between my legs. His passion was addictive, bruising, all-consuming, his lips eating mine. He made me feel alive. Robert had always been so polite in bed, so considerate and careful. I craved the feeling of being possessed by Paul. We had sex on the floor of the sitting room; he bent me over the sofa, under the pictures of his daughters.

Afterwards, stepping into my knickers, a movement caught

my attention. A man's face stared through the French windows. I let out a gasp. But he'd gone. 'Just the gardener,' Paul said, unflustered. 'Don't worry. Mick won't say anything.' He did up the buttons on his shirt. 'I'll have a word with him later.'

Paul poured us some wine and we sat in the kitchen. He looked in the fridge and pulled out a melting brie, found some crackers in a cupboard. I wasn't hungry; I knew I had to speak. I took a deep breath. 'Paul, we need to talk. We can't keep doing this.' I looked at him to see his reaction. But he'd got up, turning away from me to gaze out of the window. 'Too many people will get hurt. I think... we should end it,' I said to the back of his head, my voice squeezed tight. 'Us. The affair.'

He swung around. 'Come away with me, Irene.'

'What?' I startled.

'Let's go to London. I want you to be with me.'

I knew he had a flat there. But I was confused. 'I can't leave Meg.'

'Let me sort things out here. I want to divorce Calista. We can send for Meg later. Soon. We can be a family. I'll have access to my girls. Meg can spend time with her cousins. They'll be like sisters.'

'You actually want to divorce Calista?' I'd never been brave enough to ask, fearing what his answer might be. But I'd thought about it, dreamed about it every day. The two of us being together without any need for lies and secrecy.

'I don't love her,' he said, grabbing my hand and bringing my knuckles to his mouth. 'It's you I want. It's always been you. We belong together.' His voice cracked. 'I can't be without you, Irene.'

'Where will we live?'

'Wherever you like, princess.' He took my hands and

squeezed them between his. 'Just promise me you won't leave me.'

Before he drove me back to the cottage, he took a pair of nail scissors from his jacket pocket and snipped a lock of my hair. 'I've always wanted to do that,' he said.

It was only later, that I realised I'd left my cardigan behind. I told myself that with four women in the house, hopefully nobody would think anything of it if they found it.

18

It's been weeks in London, and the thought of Meg and Robert's confusion, the hurt I'm causing them, is unbearable. Paul comes back to the flat, his arms full of bags. He dumps them on the table. 'A good bottle of Merlot makes everything better,' he says, unpacking it, along with eggs, herbs, and a hunk of cheddar cheese. He holds my chin and tilts my face to his. 'Come on. Give me a smile,' he says. 'I'm going to make you my famous omelette. Can't have you sulking. I told you I'd need to make arrangements at home. Be patient, my little impatient one.'

He puts on music, Ella Fitzgerald, opens the wine and cracks the eggs. I sit on the edge of the fold-out table and watch him at work. He hums as he slices mushrooms.

'The house is on the market,' he says. 'And there's no point in upsetting Meg. She's safe and happy. We'll wait until we can tell her she's coming home with us.'

'Paul, I can't wait. I need to go home now,' I tell him, clenching my fingernails into my palms. 'To the cottage. I'm sorry. I can't be away this long.'

He stops chopping, looking at me in amazement. 'Don't you trust me?' he asks. 'I explained. It's not as straightforward as I thought.'

I shift uncomfortably under his gaze. 'I can't do this any more,' I whisper. 'I'm sorry. I'll get a train. But I need to leave.'

'Don't you want to be with me?' His voice breaks. 'I thought you were invested in our plan, our relationship?'

'I am. I was.' I look at him. 'It's not that. It's just... she's my child.' I open my palms. 'I mean, we can still carry on with the plan, can't we? I'll talk to Robert and tell him the truth. He needs to know what's going on. He'll be worrying about me.'

I'd sent him one postcard, telling him I'd met someone else. I felt I had to at least prepare him for the news that I wanted a divorce. But we needed to talk, properly talk about it. There were so many details to sort out.

'I see.' He sighs, looking disappointed, and then he nods, eyes bright with unshed tears. 'Alright.'

'Alright?' Relief stretches my lips wide. 'Thank you.' I slip off the table and put my arms around him. 'For understanding.'

He clears his throat, stepping away from me. 'Now, I'd better finish this or we'll never get anything to eat.'

The florescent lights hurt my eyes, and I wince, rubbing them. 'Another of your headaches?' he asks, giving me a sympathetic look.

I nod. 'Did you get any more paracetamol?'

'I can do better than that. I've got some migraine pills,' he tells me. 'Hang on.'

He goes out and comes back with a white plastic bottle. He tips some tiny tablets into my palm and hands me a glass of water. 'Here.' He watches me swallow. 'We'll see about train times after supper.'

* * *

I wake in bed, groggy and stupid with dreams. The electric blue nightdress is wrapped around my hips and my mouth is bruised. The door opens and Paul stands at the threshold, dressed in his suit. He sits on the bed and takes my hand and kisses it. 'I'm glad you changed your mind about going back,' he says softly. 'I love knowing I'm coming home to you.'

I frown, trying to lift my head from the pillow. I changed my mind? Did I? I can't remember, can't think straight. I groan and push the heels of my hands into my eyes. 'Looks like you're getting a headache again.' He picks up the bottle of pills from the bedside cupboard and tips a couple into my hand, watches while I swallow them. 'Good girl,' he says. 'You'll feel better now.'

I sleep and sleep. When I wake, he is with me, exploring my body, doing things to me that I can hardly feel. I am numb, unable to open my eyes wide. When I get out of bed, I move through treacle, stumbling and unsteady, feeling sick. I don't leave the flat. The key reappeared on the hall table, but I'm frightened of going out on my own. When I look in the mirror above the sink, I don't recognise my pale skin and empty eyes. My face is usually tanned at this time of year, my hair smelling of river and sky, my legs brown and scratched from brambles. In the bedroom, I avert my gaze from the letters on the wall, the spiky initials. But I know they're there, and the shape of them burns into the back of my eyes like a laser.

I can't always remember what day of the week it is. Minutes and hours blend into a morass of sticky time. I dream about Meg, about going home, but I can't even bring myself to open the front door, and I have no money. Except there's the roll of cash in his bedside drawer. If I dared, if I could just shake off the fog in my head, I could use some of that. It helps to know it's there.

I wake in a different colour. Ruby red. Blood red. I am stretched out, my arms taut above my head, tendons screaming. Twisting my head, I understand my hands are handcuffed to the headboard of the bed. Shocked, I struggle, trying to pull my wrists away, but the metal bites into my flesh. I am too weak to fight. The mattress tilts beneath me, tumbling me into darkness.

When I wake, Paul is next to me, lying on his back, a lit cigarette in his hand. I'm not handcuffed any more, but my wrists are raw. 'I saw a house, Irene,' he's saying. 'It's perfect for us. It's near the sea. Not far from Meg's school. I'll bring the details back next time.' He leans over and breathes smoke into my mouth. 'You'll feel better when you see it, when you can visualise our future.'

I cough, the smoke coiling inside my throat, stinging my eyes. My brain is foggy, and I can't find the words to tell him I want to leave. I hear Claire in my head. She tells me I'm an idiot. *Come home, Irene.* I pinch my skin to feel the pain, to know that I'm real. *I can't,* I tell her. *I don't know how.*

The next time Paul is with me, I'm in the chocolate night-dress. My hair tangles over my face, musty and lank. 'You look disgusting,' he says. 'Why can't you make more of an effort to look pretty when I'm doing so much for you?' I try to speak, running my tongue across mossy teeth, blinking up at his angry face. When I open my eyes, he's gone.

The orange roses are long dead, decaying heads dangle on dry stalks, brown petals curling. The water stinks. When I stagger out of bed to go to the bathroom, the carpet sucks at my feet, pulling me in, lapping me up.

* * *

Back then, in Manchester, I never knew when he'd appear, but then he'd be waiting outside college for me on a Monday afternoon. I'd sprint over and he'd sweep me off my feet before he kissed me, slow and deep. I could feel the other girls looking, their envious glances as we walked off together, his arm possessively tight around my shoulder.

When we made love, he held my face between his palms and looked at me as if I mattered, as if I counted. 'You have perfect features,' he'd say, examining them from different angles. 'Like a classical sculpture.' Nobody had ever bothered to notice me before, let alone told me I was beautiful. I craved his attention – began to see myself through his eyes.

After sex, we lay in bed, and Paul smoked, and sometimes he'd put the cigarette between my lips and watch me inhale. 'I'm going to get out of here, soon,' he said. 'Manchester is too small for me.' He'd said it like he was Humphrey Bogart in *Casablanca*.

'Take me with you,' I said.

'Yeah,' he drawled in Humphrey Bogart's voce. 'Sure thing, kid. We'll make a swell life together.'

He sat up, stubbing his cigarette out in an empty mug. 'I'm going to get into the art world,' he said, his voice suddenly English and plummy. 'I'm going to deal in beautiful things. I'm sick of the ugly shit I get my hands dirty with here.'

'What do you mean?' I asked.

'I want to be a collector, a dealer. Proper paintings. I can blag my way into that world. And I've got the money to set myself up.'

'I'm going to be a writer,' I told him. The only time I'd said it to anyone. It made my head rush with giddy excitement just saying the words out loud.

'Be whoever you want,' he said in his usual voice. 'Make it up. A lie is a key if you know how to use it.' He stroked my cheek. 'Invent yourself.'

'I didn't know you liked art,' I said.

'You don't know everything about me, princess.' He tapped his nose and laughed.

I did know he'd been to grammar school, and he could speak French. He'd grown up in the posh part of the city, but he'd chosen a different world. He said his parents were dull, and he had nothing to do with them any more. I couldn't help feeling that even dull parents would be better than none, but I didn't say so. He never spoke about what he did for a living, but I wasn't stupid: Paul always had plenty of cash on him, and he wore a knife strapped to his left leg. The people he knew looked shifty and untrustworthy. But with his handsome face and red hair and elegant way of holding himself, I told myself that Paul was different from the others.

Another time, he told me his parents had taken him on holiday to the Suffolk coast, Southwold and Aldeburgh. It was posher than Blackpool, where they usually went, but they'd fancied a change. 'It was full of these kids from boarding schools,' he said. 'Rupert this and Anabelle that.' He was talking with a plum in his mouth again, and I laughed, because it was so believable. 'I eavesdropped on their conversations when we were on the beach,' he said. 'All their talk about skiing trips and sailing and ponies. And I thought, one day I'll come back here, and I'll have some of this.' He grinned at me. 'Why should we let that lot have all the fun?' he asked in a broad Manchester accent. 'Suffolk would be a good place to be posh.' He'd swapped back to his plummy voice.

He often disappeared for days, even weeks, so I wasn't worried when I didn't see him for a fortnight. But one day, after a month of no contact, I began to get a sick feeling in my stomach. I worried that something bad had happened. I noticed a man following me to and from work. I'd got my A levels by then, and was working in the supermarket full time, writing short stories in the evenings. I pretended I didn't notice the man. He lingered on the street, and I peered down at him out of my window, from behind the curtain.

He grabbed me as I left the flat. 'We're looking for Paul Robinson,' he said.

'I don't know where he is.'

The man's fingers dug into my bicep. 'If I find out you're lying, you're going to wish you hadn't been born.' He turned and gestured with two pronged fingers towards his eyes and then at me. 'We're watching you,' he said. 'Remember.' And he made a chopping motion with the edge of his hand across his throat.

After that, there was always a man following me, and I flinched if they got too close. I hurried into buildings, stopped going out after dark, watched the street from my window.

Early one morning, the phone rang in the hall. I sprinted down the stairs in my nightie and bare feet. I knew it was him even before he said my name.

'Paul – they're looking for you, they—'

'I know,' he cut me off. 'I'm not coming back. They'll kill me. You need to leave. Get out of the city. It's not safe.'

'What? Where?'

'Just get out, Irene. Now.' And the phone went dead.

'Paul?' I whispered into the receiver. 'Paul?'

I didn't see him again for years. I thought he must be dead. And then he turned up at my wedding.

19

I think of Robert's face. Grief fills me. I have made a mistake. The worst of my life. I have to get out of here. I have to get away from Paul. The next time he gives me the pills, I pretend to swallow, pushing them behind my bottom lip with my tongue, holding them against my gum. When he isn't looking, I spit them down the loo.

Paul pushes the slippery folds of damson slip up my thighs as he pulls my hips towards him, entering me as I blink into darkness, his body arching in pleasure. But I'm awake for the first time since he gave me the pills. I want to shove him off me, but I can't let him know I'm not drugged any more. When his tongue fills my mouth, I stop myself from gagging. My heart races. I need a plan.

The next morning, he yawns and stretches, rolling over to kiss me, his breath sour with sleep. 'God, I'm knackered,' he says. 'All this driving up and down. Let's have breakfast together. I'll be out for most of the day.' His chin is rough with stubble. 'Go to the bakery on the corner, there's a good girl,' he says. 'Get us a couple of croissants. I need to have a shower.' He dips into his bedside drawer and gives me a five-pound note. He grabs my wrist as I take the money. 'Hurry back.' He squeezes hard enough to hurt.

I slip the nightdress off my shoulders, letting it puddle around my feet, and pull on my real clothes. It's the first time I've worn them for weeks, the first time he's let me out of the flat on my own. I suppose he thinks I'm still fuddled by the drugs, so I won't disobey him. It's early, and the city is quiet. I want to make a run for it, but I have nothing except the exact change for the croissants. Paul will be suspicious if I'm not back in fifteen minutes. The heat hasn't built yet, but the jaded smells of the night before linger: overflowing rubbish bins smelling of rot, disembowelled food containers dragged across the road by foxes. Delivery trucks are unloading things outside shops, awnings are being unfolded, a couple of joggers pass me on their way to the park. A woman throws a bucket of soapy water across the pavement. I jump out of the way automatically. My mind turns, making plans. I'll catch a train from Liverpool Street as soon as Paul has left today.

I'll confess everything to Robert. I'll tell him about the affair and explain about my history before I came to Suffolk. I'll beg him to let me see Meg. It's all I can think of – the life I've abandoned, and how I can apologise to the two people I've betrayed. I think of the fat wad of cash in Paul's drawer. I'll peel a couple of notes off. I should go to the police, but it will be his word against mine, and in my message to Robert, I said I was leaving of my own free will. I'd sent him a card saying I'd met someone else.

On the way back, the sweet smell of pastry wafting from the bag, I notice a headline in a newspaper on a newsstand.

Manchester Crime Graveyard, it reads. I don't have enough change left over to buy it, so I pick it up and turn the pages until I find the article, reading it standing on the street. The woman behind the stall gives me a dirty look, but she doesn't say anything. My eyes skim words.

Police... gory discovery of a hidden graveyard in Manchester... remains of bodies... gang's executions... killed with a shot to the back of the head... hands tied behind their backs... tip-off from an ex-gang member... plea bargain.

It doesn't make sense that I've never heard from Luke. Paul has always put me off with excuses. Maybe Luke never left Manchester? Was he one of these men, executed by a single shot to the back of the head, his hidden body rotting in derelict ground? Or is Luke the ex-gang member, the one negotiating for a plea bargain? Something has happened to him. He wouldn't have forgotten me.

My hands are shaking as I put the croissants on plates and pour the coffee. I try to fix a smile on my face as I carry the tray into the bedroom. I want to ask about Luke, but I'm afraid of Paul. The fear was always there, just underneath the love and desire, it had been part of my attraction to him in the first place.

His hair is damp from the shower, but he's got back into bed. He pats the pillow beside him. 'Get undressed,' he says. 'I want to see you.'

I take off my top and skirt, undo my bra, not meeting his gaze, and slip under the covers next to him, trying to remember how I moved when I was taking the pills – slowly, a little clumsily. We sit against pillows, elbow to elbow. My skin shrinks from his. He exclaims over how delicious the croissants are. I force the buttery flakes down.

Paul sighs. 'It's hard to resist you, but I need to get going.' He leans over and kisses my breasts with greasy lips. 'I'll be back.' I hold my breath to stop myself from flinching. 'Have you taken your pills?' He looks straight at me.

I nod vaguely, making my eyes blank. 'I want to see you take them,' he says, tipping two white tablets into my palm. I pretend to swallow, trying to secrete them in my mouth again, but he grasps my chin and forces my lips open to check. 'There,' he says, satisfied, as the pills slide down my throat. 'You don't know what's good for you.'

I stay under the covers and watch him dress and get his things together. My body is wound tight, every muscle tensed. He drops a kiss on my forehead. 'See you later.'

I wait for the click of the front door. Relief floods me. I go to the bathroom, and bend over the loo, retching as I throw up my breakfast and the pills. I flush, wiping my sour mouth with the back of my hand and splashing my face under the tap. In the bedroom, I put my things into my case, leaving the things Paul bought for me in the wardrobe. I pull open his bedside drawer to get some cash. The wad of notes has gone. Panicking, I open all the drawers; but I can only find loose change, some coins in the bottom of a pot on the dresser. As I'm hooking my fingers inside one of his jacket pockets, I touch something soft. Acrylic netting droops between my thumb and forefinger: a G-string in pink and lime green, with a scratchy lace trim. How many women has he kept in this flat before me?

He's been lying to me for weeks, for years. Perhaps from the first moment we met. But I can't let myself understand the depth of the betrayal. Not yet. Panic scrabbles at the edges of my mind, but I need to get out of here. I need to run. I don't have enough cash for a rail ticket to Ipswich. I'll hitch if I must.

I hurry into the corridor with my case and pull at the door handle. It doesn't budge. I twist the handle, jerking it forwards and backwards. I slam my palm against the wood. The spare key isn't on the hall table. Terror thickens my throat. I lean against the window in the bedroom and bang my fists on the glass. 'Help!' I scream. People in the street below are oblivious. Nobody looks up. Then I remember the phone. I'll call Claire. She'll know what to do. She'll help me. I pick up the phone, but it's dead. *No. No. No.* I try it again. Nothing. I bang the receiver down, my mind blank with fear. I walk into the bedroom unsteadily. My legs give way and I sit on the bed, my case at my feet.

I deserve this. I've deserted my child. I've lied to Robert and betrayed him. He's a good man – too good for me. He was steady and kind, happy with the small miracles of life. 'Little things, like talking to the robin who visits my garden,' he'd once told me. 'Feeling the breeze on my face, or warming my hands around a good, strong cup of tea on a cold day.'

Robert. I screw up my eyes, fighting tears. I knew I'd never tell him who I really was, not because I thought he'd reject me, but because I didn't want to disappoint him.

* * *

I hear the scrape of a key, the brushing noise of the front door opening over the carpet. My heart reels. I kick my suitcase under the bed, standing up quickly, smoothing my hand over my hair, then sit down again, trying to compose my expression.

Soft footsteps along the corridor. I brace myself. But it's not Paul who enters the room. Shock swallows my voice. Calista glances around. 'He's not here?' she said. 'The door was double-locked.'

'Calista... I'm so sorry... I—'

She holds up a hand. 'Save your breath, Irene. I don't want your apology. It's Robert and Meg you need to grovel to.'

'How did you know,' I ask quietly. 'About me?'

She's holding something towards me. It's the Polaroid of me in the necklace. The perfect, second one he'd taken after the one when I'd moved. I glance at it and then her, puzzled. 'You found it?'

'He gave it to me. He wanted me to paint you. Like all the others.'

'The others?'

'His collection. He likes me to paint them once he's grown bored with them.' She gives me a pitying look. 'He made you feel special, didn't he? He made you believe you were the most important person on earth.' She stands by the window and glances down into the street. 'It's not real. It's a game to him. I'm the mother of his children, his wife, his artist. I'm the only one that's real. He's already bored with you. As soon as he owns a woman, she loses her value.' She nods towards the back room. 'A woman can't compete with a picture. She grows old, gets ill, loses her looks. He prefers beauty pinned down, captured forever in paint.'

'He said he loved me. He said we'd be together, a family with Meg.' The words sound pathetic. My cheeks burn with shame. 'He was lying, wasn't he?'

'He told you what you wanted to hear. And now he knows he's more important than your own child.'

Her words are like a knife sliding into my heart. 'I met him in Manchester. He was called Paul then.' I squeeze my fingers together. 'We were lovers before I met Robert. And then again, in Suffolk.'

She looks at me coldly. 'How long has your affair been going on?'

I swallow. 'Three years.'

'It was your cardigan, wasn't it? In the sitting room?'

Memories tumble towards me: Lucian making love to me on the carpet, naked under the portraits of her daughters. I can't look at her.

'He's addicted to sex.' Her voice is hard. 'Obsessed with beautiful women.'

'He's changed since we came to London. He's been keeping me here. He drugged me.'

'He's got appetites that mean he's insatiable. He'll have been seeing other women during your affair – you won't have been the only one.' She looks at me scornfully. 'Go back to Robert – if he'll have you.' She takes some cash out of her purse.

I take the proffered note. 'Thank you.' My voice is small.

'I'm not doing this for you,' she says fiercely. 'It's the first time I've refused to paint one of his women. But I can't do this to my brother, to my niece. Meg is a sweet child – she doesn't deserve this, and neither does my brother.' She looks at me. 'Lucian can't know I was here. He thinks I'm visiting a gallery.'

'Why do you stay with him?'

'He's my husband.' Her eyes are blank. 'The other women are meaningless. He always comes back to me, to our home.'

'But you don't have to put up with it. You have your daughters.'

'They belong to him.' She shrugs. 'I came up on the train with the girls today.'

'Meg?' My heart jumps. 'Meg is in London?'

'Once I guessed you were here, I thought it better she stayed in Suffolk.'

I drag my suitcase from under the bed and grasp the handle. 'I need to get out of here.'

Calista is still gazing down at the street; suddenly, she flinches from the glass. 'He's coming. Damn. I thought he'd go straight to meet the girls. He can't see me.'

I pick up my case and move towards the door, following her. 'I'm coming too.'

'No. Wait,' she says, turning back to me. 'Pretend everything is okay when he gets here. He's taking them to tea at Fortnum's, so he'll be out for a while. Go after he's left – that will give you a head start. There's a spare key hidden in the ice box.' She presses a scrap of paper into my hand. 'Call me at nine o'clock tomorrow morning to let me know you've got away.'

There isn't time to thank her. She slips out of the door. I drop my suitcase and go to the window, hoping Paul isn't going to run into Calista. He's moving purposefully down the street with long strides. I notice women turning to look at him, how people step out of his way.

I think of taking the stairs while he's in the lift. But Calista is right, I wouldn't have enough time – he'd come after me. I feel trapped and helpless, knowing he's coming back. Will be here any minute.

I run into the kitchen and grab a long knife from the metallic strip on the wall and dash back into the bedroom just as I hear Paul bang through the front door, calling out, 'Surprise!' The rustle of him throwing his jacket off. 'Forgot something. God, I'm parched.'

I push the knife under a pillow. I don't know what I'd do with it – but it makes me feel better to know it's nearby. I stand next to the bed, trying to erase fear from my face.

'I need to need to pop out again in a minute,' he's calling

from somewhere in the flat. The pipes rattle. The tap working in the kitchen.

He walks into the bedroom with a glass of water. 'It's like a furnace out there,' he says, gesturing towards the sealed window.

Then his gaze falls on my suitcase. I forgot to hide it. Terror pulses through me. He raises one eyebrow. 'Going somewhere, princess?'

Despite the casual delivery of his words, he's hyper alert, eyes narrowing, body tensing.

I can't pretend any more. 'Why did you tell me you wanted to leave your wife,' I say quietly. 'It's not true, is it?'

He cocks his head to one side. 'What?'

'I don't understand why you lied about it, why you made me believe you loved me.'

He laughs. 'Have you banged your head?'

'You gave me pills. You locked me in the flat.'

'Of course, I didn't lock you in,' he says dismissively. 'And they were migraine pills.'

'The telephone doesn't work.'

'You shouldn't be using the phone. And if it isn't working, maybe the line is down because of the roadworks.'

'I don't believe you.'

My four words change the atmosphere between us; it crackles as if an electric charge pulses through the air, sharp and dangerous.

'Believe what you like.' His gaze is cold. My heart flutters like a trapped bird. It's as if I can see another person appearing through a mask – a different set of features, a stranger – he's not bothering to put on an act any more. 'You were so much more appealing when you were taking your medication.'

'I don't know what they were – but they weren't migraine pills.'

'You're a fantasist, Irene.'

'What?'

'I read your notebook. All that stuff you made up about us.'

'I didn't make it up. It's true. You know it's true.'

'You've always been unstable,' he says. 'Neurotic.'

'No—' My words stutter into silence. The way he looks at me is terrifying. The colour has left his eyes. His pupils are pinpricks boring into me. 'You've drugged me,' I say. 'Kept me here against my will.' I take a step back. 'I'm going now.'

He laughs. 'I don't think so.' He sits on the edge of the bed and crosses his legs. 'I'll tell you what really happened, shall I? You followed me to Suffolk, married my wife's brother. You wouldn't leave me alone. Demanded that we have an affair. You threatened to kill yourself if I left you.' He shakes his head sorrowfully. 'You've made my life a living hell.'

The walls of the room edge closer, trapping me.

'So, your little story had to go,' he continues. 'It conflicted with mine.'

A shockwave hits, rage pushing through the safety net of reason. 'You've lied about everything,' I say. 'You told me you'd got Luke somewhere safe. But he would have found a way to contact me. I saw the news about the graveyard in Manchester – the executions.' I swallow. 'Please...' My voice breaks. 'Please tell me he isn't one of them.'

He watches me as he sips his glass of water.

'Well?' I clench my fists, bracing myself. 'Where is he? Tell me.'

'He was useful to me,' he says slowly. 'They wanted him. I got something in return. He was small fry. But they had to make an example of him. Can't have the staff stealing the silver. You know that, Irene.'

'You gave him up?' Air leaves my body. 'You knew you were going to hand him over to them when you came to get him from my flat?'

'Don't be so melodramatic.' He raises one eyebrow. 'He wasn't even your flesh and blood,' he says. 'Don't make a scene. It's boring.' He looks at his watch. 'I'm meeting my girls soon. I don't have time for this.'

'Bastard,' I hiss. 'I believed you. I thought you wanted us to be together. I've betrayed the people I love. I've left my child for you.' I rub my face. 'Did you ever love me? When the gang were after you, you rang me to tell me to get out of Manchester. You must have cared about me then?'

'I had to make you to leave. I'd mentioned my plans to you – to set up as an art dealer in Suffolk – a slip-up on my part. I needed to get you out of Manchester without coming back myself. Couldn't risk you blabbing.' He gives a short laugh. 'I was as surprised as you when you turned up in my life again.'

'But then, years later, you came for me again – began our affair. Why?'

'I don't like loose ends,' he says. 'You knew too much. It weighed on me. In the end, I needed to make sure you weren't a security risk. And I wanted you for myself. You belonged to me, not Robert.'

'I could tell everyone the truth – Calista, Robert. The police.' I swallow, glancing at the door. 'Let me go home now, Paul, and I promise I won't say anything.'

'Leave the blackmail to me,' he says, putting the empty glass on the bedside table as he stands up. 'I've got your daughter, Irene. So, you need to behave. And remember, you're a stalker, an obsessive. Nobody would believe you.'

Meg. She's at Deben Manor. The room spins before me, a blur of horror and regret. I grab the knife from under the pillow – I don't know what I intend – I want to kill him. I want to plunge the blade into my own heart. But he has me in an armlock before I can move, the knife falling from my fingers with a clatter.

'I told you before,' he whispers in my ear. 'Don't show the weapon. It needs to be in their ribs before they know about it.' A Mancunian accent shapes his words, the façade cracking.

He's ripped my wrist backwards, rotating it, wrenching my shoulder. I am limp in his grip. He's hurting me, twisting my arm high. 'I want to go home.' I wince. 'Let me go. I'll never mention any of this. I just want to go back to my family.'

'No, I don't think so,' he says, walking me out of the room in the armlock. 'You've burnt your bridges...'

'Why bring me here?' I pant, struggling to move my feet fast enough. 'Why did you ask me to run away with you?'

'Because you're mine.' His mouth is at my ear. 'Because I could.'

'I want to go back to my family,' I gasp. 'They love me.'

'Not any more, Irene. Not after you abandoned them.'

We're going down the corridor towards his office. I begin to dig my heels into the carpet, straining backwards. My feet slip and slide through the acrylic pile. I lean down to bite his hand, the one clamped on my shoulder. But he yanks my arm even higher up my back. Fire shoots through my shoulder. 'Nobody leaves me,' he says quietly. 'That's not how this works.'

We're in front of the empty container. The door is open, a blank mouth waiting. 'No,' I whimper. 'Please.'

'Just until you cool off,' he says, as if it's a reasonable idea. He propels me forwards and down, his hand on the top of my head like a policeman guiding a suspect into a car. I fall onto my knees. He's forced to release my arm to push my body into the tiny space, and I take the opportunity to twist around and flail at him, lashing his face with my nails, trying to get my foot free to kick. But he's grabbed my hands, crushing them in his fists. As I struggle to pull away, my opal ring slides off my finger. I'm bunched up, halfway into the crate, hanging onto the edges. His knuckles slam into my eye. Black floods my vision. Red blooms and sparks. The pain takes my breath. I let go of the sides, and I'm bundled inside like a doll. The door shuts.

20

I bang my head against the metal wall. The echo rebounds in my skull, a thud of pain. I keep doing it. He will kill me. I know too much. I'm a threat to his lifestyle, his business, his family, to everything he's built up. It's no good promising him my silence. He won't trust me to stay quiet.

I don't want Meg to know that I died in this metal box. That it was my own fault.

My mind is fragmenting, coming undone. I wish I'd had the chance to explain to Claire, to apologise to Robert. They'll never know that my last thoughts were of them, and Meg. Always Meg.

My brave girl, I'm sorry I won't be there to see you grow up – to be your friend – to cheer you on. I never deserved you, or your dad. I've been weak and stupid. But I loved you from the moment I felt you move in my belly. Live your life well. I know you will.

I think about the initials scratched on the wall, the blonde hairs, the knickers in his pocket. Where is 'K'? What happened to her? Was she locked in here before me? I have been a fool. The oldest kind.

When my body is eventually found – when people know how I ended up dead, nobody will weep for me. They'll think I deserved it. Perhaps there'll be a short piece in the papers. Woman found dead in container. A homewrecker, a cheater, a whore. She got what she deserved.

No. He won't leave me in here. He'll dump my body. He knows people. Someone else will do the cleaning up for him.

How will he kill me? It'll be something that won't make a mess. He doesn't need to do anything. They say you can go for weeks without food, but it's only three days without water. I don't know how long it's been. Impossible to tell whether it's day or night. My mouth is parched, my tongue sore.

I can't get out. I can't move. I can't breathe.

PART III

21

MEG

Then, 1993

My eyes opened into shadows. A tall shape stood over me. Lucian, back from London. 'Wake up.'

I blinked at him, confused. 'What time is it?'

'Time to get up. You're having your sailing lesson today.'

I pushed my feet out of the sheets. The room was dim as if it was still night. My windowpanes rattled as gusts of wind hit the glass.

'Weather's perfect for it,' he said from the threshold. 'You've got five minutes. See you downstairs.'

I wanted to tell him I'd changed my mind. But somehow it wasn't possible to contradict him. He had a kind of energy field that resonated in the air, making me nervous and clumsy. I stumbled into my shorts and T-shirt and followed him down into the hall.

I felt sick from the beer I'd drunk the night before. My mouth was sour and my stomach queasy. It might be better to eat something. Dry toast, maybe. That was what Mum used to recommend for a sore tummy, but it seemed breakfast wasn't part of the plan. Lucian was loading the Land Rover with sailing tackle, his hair and jacket whipped up by the blustery wind. There was no sign of the other girls. They must still be in bed. I climbed into the passenger seat, and we drove the short distance to the sailing club. I'd been longing to have him to myself. In my imagination, he was kind and funny, teasing me gently. But he drove with knuckles gripped white around the steering wheel, his mouth a hard line. He didn't speak to me. Something glinted on his little finger, a flash of colour triggering a memory that slipped away like a fish into darkness.

The club was deserted. I couldn't understand why we were there so early. I glanced at the horizon. A faint blood red curdled the navy blue. A cold wind whipped up waves, tore at the trees on the bank, making them bow and stretch.

Lucian showed me how to rig the sails in near-darkness. My fingers trembled, and I couldn't grasp the ropes. I helped him wheel the trailer down the launch slope and he ordered me to hold the prow of the boat as he dragged the trailer from under it. Freezing water lapped my knees.

The boat nudged me like an eager horse. 'Get in,' Lucian yelled, coming up behind me and taking hold of the side of the boat. 'Quick.'

The dinghy moved around, skittish and unstable; it was too much of a stretch for my short legs. I tried to pull myself in, but fell back into the water, grazing my elbow. Then Lucian had me around the waist, and I was tipped over the side like a bundle of washing. My calf slammed against an edge, a sharpness tearing at my skin. I pulled myself onto the narrow seat, muddy plimsols squelching. My leg stung and throbbed. As Lucian took the tiller, the sail billowed in my face; then, with a snap, it caught the wind, and we moved across the water. 'Damn,' he said. 'Forgot my blasted hat.'

Blood was flowing down my leg. I wanted to cry. I wanted to point out the wound to him, but I didn't dare. I clung to the seat, salt wind filling my nostrils, making my eyes stream. We were far from land in a matter of minutes, and Lucian motioned for me to sit next to him. I scooted along on my bottom, and he grabbed my hand and placed it on the tiller. 'Feel how she moves,' he shouted into the wind. 'It only takes a nudge to get her to go left or right, Irene. Remember, you're looking to keep the wind inside the sail.'

I gazed at him, bewildered. For a second, I thought he'd called me by my mum's name. The sailing lesson felt wrong. He was filled with a wild abandon, a kind of desperation I didn't understand. It was light enough to see him now, and I saw how his jacket strained at the buttons as if he'd grown a paunch overnight; there were several long, thin scratches down the side of his face, as if a cat had attacked him. He rubbed them absentmindedly.

'We're not wearing life jackets,' I said, suddenly realising.

'Life jackets are for sissies,' he said. 'You don't need one when you're with me.'

There were several big yachts moored in the middle of the river. I gasped, thinking we were going to smash into the nearest one. But he suddenly shouted, 'Ready about,' and grabbed the tiller from me, swinging the boat to the left so the boom lunged violently to the right, just missing my head. I clung to the side of the boat with both hands.

'I don't like it,' I blurted. 'Can we go back?'

'Don't be ridiculous,' he shouted. 'We've only just started.'

The boat was cutting though the water, leaning to the left,

the sail tugging to the right. 'Take the tiller,' Lucian said. 'Sit on this side,' he patted the seat on the other side of him.

I clambered over his knees. 'I don't know what to do,' I whispered, clutching the tiller, trying not to cry.

'Do what I tell you,' he snapped. 'Lean back. She's heeling.'

The rising disc of light cast shattered fragments of gold onto the river. My feet slipped, as I strained away from the left side of the boat, watching the water slap over the edge, puddling near the centre board. It sloshed around my plimsols. My skin tickled and stung where blood crept across it, a gaping hole of pain above. The sail was over to the right, and I felt the force of the wind in the tightened canvas, heard the creak as it resisted. We were in the widest part of the river, far from the distant banks. I knew the North Sea was around the next corner. 'We're not going out to sea, are we?' I yelled.

Lucian didn't reply. 'Ready about,' he shouted. 'Push the tiller away from you.'

I did as he told me, and the boom swung violently across again. I ducked in time, hearing the rustle and slap of the canvas, then a lull before the sail filled again.

The mouth of the river widened, the waves jumping just beyond; I stared at the wide-open spaces of the ocean, the boiling water where tide meets current in an explosion of opposing forces.

'Lucian,' I shouted in terror. 'Look! The sea!'

The dinghy was cutting a direct path out of the river. He grinned as the boat hit the first wave, leaping into the air. I let go of the tiller. 'I want to go back!'

'Hold the bloody tiller.' He put my hands back on the wooden handle. It quivered under my grasp, and it took all my strength to hold it steady.

'Ready about,' Lucian shouted again. 'Pull towards you.'

I pushed as hard as I could. As the boat bucked and rocked, I realised I'd misunderstood, but it was a moment before I realised that Lucian wasn't beside me. I let go of the tiller, and leant over the side, watching him bob up. 'Stupid girl,' he shouted. 'Quick, throw me a rope.'

The boat pitched wildly from side to side, the sail flapping in my face; the only ropes seemed attached to canvas. I picked an oar up instead and manoeuvred it over the side, pushing it towards Lucian. But the boat was moving further away, carried on the tide and waves, and the oar was heavy. The end of it fell short. I raised it high and tried again, shoving it towards him. The paddle fell with a splash. I tried again. The muscles in my shoulders screamed as I wielded it. I heaved it upright and threw it like a Scottish caber, letting go with as much force as I could.

He disappeared under the surface. I stood, trying to get a better look, desperate to see him re-emerge. I caught a glimpse of his hair. 'Lucian,' I yelled. 'Lucian!'

I grabbed the tiller and pulled it towards me. The boat lurched and I fell against something hard. My elbow flared with pain. I was on my hands and knees, sobbing in the water-filled bottom of the rocking boat. A flash of orange stuck out of the tiny hold, and I crawled towards it. A life jacket. With shaking hands, I put my arms through and fastened the belt around my middle. It was too big for me, rising over my chin when I sat down. I struggled to my feet again and shouted for help, just as the wind hit the side of the boat, catching the loose sail, knocking the boom into my waist. I stumbled to the side, canvas billowing against the back of my head and the world turned.

Black, green, bubbles. Water filling my eyes and mouth.

I didn't know which way was up, but the buoyancy of my

life jacket tugged me towards the surface. I broke through, gasping. The dinghy had capsized, the sail lying over the waves, limp as a broken wing. One of the sail ropes was floating next to me and I grabbed it, managing a kind of doggy paddle, fighting the flow of the current. Holding onto the curved side of the upside-down dinghy, I worked my legs beneath me.

Time made no sense, there was just the water and the sky. Waves washed over me. My fingers cramped and went numb. Seabirds circled above, and I longed for the power of flight. It was impossible to see anything from my low vantage point in the river. I hoped that Lucian was alright. He was a strong swimmer. Perhaps he'd already raised the alarm, got the rescue boat to come out to me. My eyes closed. I was so cold. Water seeped into me, pulled at my legs and arms. It wanted me to let go of the boat, to slip out of my life jacket, to give in and let myself be taken.

The roar and thud of an engine. A shout, muffled in the wind. My ears were full of water. Everything was indistinct, except the pump of my heart. Hands pulled at me; the river relinquished me reluctantly. I crumpled into a heap, the relief of being supported by a hard surface. I could smell fish. Someone tucked a blanket around me. I couldn't find any words, my teeth chattered, and my body shook. Everything went black.

* * *

A smiling nurse took my temperature. I'd been put into a bed in a ward where other patients coughed and moaned, and shoes squeaked across the floor. Dad perched on the plastic chair by my bed. He looked grey. 'I was so worried,' he said.

'When they called me. I don't know what Lucian was thinking. Out in a boat in that wind.'

I was bruised and shocked, not injured, except for the gash in my leg. They'd stitched it up and put me on an antibiotic drip. I was released a day later, with a fresh bandage around my calf and a bottle of pills. Dad came to pick me up.

'Where are we going?' I asked, sitting in the front seat of the Ford in the clothes Dad brought from the cottage, my river-stinking clothes in a plastic bag at my feet.

'Home,' he said.

'But what about my things?' I asked. 'All my stuff at Deben Manor.'

'Someone will send it. Or I'll pick it up on my way back from work.'

'I'm not going back?'

He shook his head, eyes on the road. 'I'm sorry,' he said. 'I should never have sent you to stay with them.'

'But you had to,' I said. 'You had to work.'

'I should have found another solution.' His mouth was a grim line. 'My sister said no at first. Then she called back, said she could have you, after all. I should have known she couldn't be trusted. She's selfish.'

'Is Lucian alright?' I asked, frightened of the answer. 'Did he make it to the shore?'

'Don't worry about him,' Dad said after a pause. 'We have our own lives to get on with. School starts soon.'

I thought about John and Fred the cat. I considered asking Dad to deliver a note to the summer house for me, but John had made me promise not to tell anyone about him. When we got back to our cottage, there was a 'For Sale' sign outside.

'It's for the best,' Dad said quietly. 'It'll be easier to manage if we live in town. I've found a flat.'

'What if she comes back?'

'She's not coming back, love,' he said. 'I'm sorry.'

It wasn't until a week later that Dad told me Lucian was dead. He stroked my forehead as he explained he hadn't been found after the sailing accident. 'I'm sure he didn't suffer.'

'Will we go to the funeral?' I asked.

He sighed. 'No,' he said. 'I think it would be best if we didn't. I'll send flowers.'

It was impossible to believe that anyone as big and powerful and full of life could be dead, that his strong legs and wide shoulders and heavy head could be inert and cold.

'It's my fault,' I said.

'No.' Dad shook his head. 'He should never have taken you out in a boat. He knew you were terrified of water and couldn't swim. I don't know what he was thinking.'

'But Dad, I—'

'It was an accident.' He turned to me. 'My sister didn't protect you. I was wrong to think she'd look after you. Leaving you without telling me. Going off to London. It could have been you that—' he bit down on a sob.

I reached for his fingers, and we sat for a long time, hand in hand, not speaking.

I remembered the weight of the oar, the way it twisted out of my grip. I saw Lucian's face again, his look of disbelief as it struck him, bright liquid blossoming above his eyes, his head sagging forwards. His limp shape, half submerged in the waves, drifting away.

22

MEG

Now, 2008

I drive back from Dad's slowly, peering through whirling white, thinking about Mum's postcards, her pleading words, her promises she'd see me again. Lies. She didn't want me. Her betrayal of me and Dad makes me feel sick.

As I park the Fiat next to Ophelia's Range Rover and Saul's BMW, I notice that Thea's business van is here too. The sleet has gathered momentum, becoming snow, settling on the ground. I breathe a sigh of relief that I made it back before it had a chance to cause drifts or freeze.

Inside, there are raised voices coming from the direction of the kitchen. It sounds as though Saul and Ophelia are arguing again. I'm about to creep upstairs when a figure comes out of the shadows of the hall. 'Awful weather,' Thea says.

'Yes,' I agree, with one foot on the stairs. 'Well. Goodnight.'

'Goodnight?' she echoes, eyebrows raised. 'Good grief, it's hardly bedtime yet. Join me for a drink. Those two are being very boring,' she gestures behind her to the sound of the row. 'And I hate to drink alone.'

I hesitate. I'm not in the mood for small talk.

'Please,' she says. 'I could do with the company. I can't drive home in this.'

'Okay.' I give in. 'Just for half an hour.'

'Great,' she turns towards the sitting room. 'Red wine, okay?'

'A small one, thanks.'

I follow her into the sitting room. She pours some wine into a heavy bottomed goblet and hands it to me as she sinks into a sofa, legs curled underneath her.

She pats the seat beside her. 'Come and sit down. I could probably find some crisps—' She glances towards the kitchen door. 'But I don't think either of us wants to interrupt.'

I take the opposite sofa, sitting to the left of her eyeline, and clasp my glass. The smell is sour, uninviting. I can't stop thinking about Mum. How long had she known this man she went off with? Who was he? How many weeks or months had she lied to us?

I realise that Thea is talking to me.

'Sorry.' I focus on her. 'What did you say?'

She casts a quizzical look at me. 'You were miles away.'

I give her an apologetic smile and take a sip of wine. The liquid slides down my throat. 'I'm all yours.'

'I was just saying that Ophelia is pleased with you – the kids really seem to like you. I hope you're happy, too?'

'They're great kids.'

She wrinkles her nose. 'I love them. But kids aren't my thing. I never wanted any of my own.' She shifts position on the cushions, and I notice that she's not wearing any make-up today. She seems tired, and her hair is tugged back into a messy ponytail. She looks more approachable, less composed.

'I suppose your work takes up all your time,' I say. 'It must be exciting. Being a fashion designer.'

She makes a non-committal noise in the back of her throat, pours herself more wine, leans over and tops up my glass too. 'It's hard work,' she says. 'And pretty stressful, to be honest.'

'I can't imagine being in that world.'

She gives me a keen look. 'Well, you could, if you wanted a change of career.'

I look at her. 'Sorry?'

'You could be a model.'

I force a laugh. 'Right,' I say, keeping the joke going. 'Of course. I'm a dead ringer for Cindy Crawford.'

'No,' she says with a straight face. 'I mean it. Take it from me, I work with models all the time. You have the height obviously, the boyish figure, and your face...' She waves a hand towards it. 'It's got clean lines. It's plain, but in the right way.'

I don't like her scrutinising me, and I can't stop suspecting she's making fun of me. 'Tell me about your show,' I say, taking a gulp of my drink. 'When is it?'

'Don't change the subject,' she says. 'You know, you remind me of someone,' she says slowly. 'But I can't think who.'

I struggle to hold her gaze, tightening my fingers around the stem of my glass. Then I look away.

'It'll come to me.' She sighs. 'I never forget a face. Anyway, to answer your question, the show is in a couple of weeks. I should be working tonight, but...' She trails off as she raises her gaze towards the window. The curtains aren't drawn, and beyond the black glass, the air is full of pale movement.

'What's the collection?' I ask. 'Winter coats?'

'Summer,' she laughs. 'Easy, breezy dresses, swimwear, culottes. Bubble gum colours.'

I laugh too. 'I don't envy the models.'

'Oh, those girls are tough,' she says. 'They have to pose in swimsuits on freezing December beaches and look as if they're having a wonderful time.' She takes a long drink from her glass. 'That's another reason I thought you could do it. I imagine you're tough, too. You seem self-reliant.'

I am uncertain how to respond. It makes me nervous to think that she's been observing me, making assessments about my character.

'But don't tell Ophelia I've said so.' She unfurls her legs and stands up, going over to the window, fingernails tapping her wine glass. 'She'd kill me if she thought I was even joking about asking you to leave.' She sighs and looks across to the closed kitchen door. 'Her life isn't easy now. Right,' she says, rubbing her hands together. 'I'm going to brave it for another bottle.'

I want to tell her that I've had enough to drink, that I must go to bed. But the truth is, her company and the warmth of the lit sitting room is a more pleasant prospect than being alone in my room. I don't want to consider Mum's betrayal any longer. I don't want to wallow in self-pity.

She comes back, brandishing another bottle of Burgundy. 'They've gone,' she says. 'They could be continuing the row upstairs, or having noisy, make-up sex; either way, you're better off down here with me.' She leans over and sloshes wine into my glass; she's a little unsteady on her feet, her hand wobbles spilling liquid onto the sofa. 'Whoops.' She giggles and slumps back into her seat. 'I've just come out of a long-term relationship,' she volunteers. 'We talked about getting married. But... this bloody career of mine. It's relentless, all-consuming. It doesn't give me time to have an actual life.' She laughs, but it sounds bitter. 'Although, looking at my sister's relationship makes me think I'm better off without a husband.'

'I'm sorry,' I say quietly.

'You're easy to talk to,' she says. 'You don't judge. In my world, there's a lot of criticism. Bitchiness. You have to watch your back.'

I don't tell her that it's part of my job to be detached and discreet, to keep my personal feelings to myself. Living in a family house, I see all sorts of things. But I remain on the outskirts of their lives, isolated by my position. I sink into the sofa, feeling a wave of exhaustion wash over me. The alcohol is hitting me. I have a floaty sensation, a softening of edges, a warmth in my belly, and my loneliness wells up, and with it, self-pity. I try not to acknowledge it. The truth is, I stay away from relationships. They're too dangerous. Letting anyone in is reckless. It will only lead to pain. Being abandoned by your mum isn't great for trust issues.

Thea moans. 'My sisters don't know how bad it is, but I'm in trouble with the bank. This new collection—' She shakes her head. 'It's my last chance.' She pushes her knuckles into her eyes. I pull a packet of tissues out of my back pocket and hand her one. She takes it. 'Thanks.' She blows her nose and sits up. 'Don't tell my sisters. I don't want them to worry.'

'Of course not.' I am touched by her confidences in me, her vulnerability.

We polish off the second bottle of wine. Then, before I say something I regret, or give myself away with a careless remark, I excuse myself and go to bed.

The mattress spins beneath me, the room tilting. My stomach twists and lurches as if I'm on a fairground ride. I'm not used to drinking so much. It means I can't think about

Mum. Can't think about anything before I tip over into oblivion.

* * *

I wake with a jolt, as if someone is in the room. I have a raging thirst and sit up to drink from my water glass. I had a dream. I swallow the dusty liquid in my glass, remembering. It was about the accident. A memory of being dragged from my bed, being forced into a dinghy. Lucian's face sinking beneath the waves. But something is missing – something I can't access. It's as if the wrong film is playing in my head.

Outside the thin curtains, there's a glow, and I get up and peer outside into the blue-white gleam of settled snow. It's layered over the outbuilding roofs and makes hunched shapes of the bushes. It's cold and I'm about to get back into bed when I hear a thump above my head.

I keep completely still. There are footsteps, careful foot-steps, moving slowly across the ceiling. My heart thunders. There's a kind of soft, dragging sound, and then, footsteps again. Someone is in the attic. As the minutes tick on, I strain to hear more noises, until I can't stand it any longer. I get out of bed and move through the darkened house, walking on bare feet along the chilly landing to the steep staircase. I hesitate for a second, looking up, then I mount the stairs, as if compelled by a hypnotist. At the top, I stop outside the door. A thin bright line glows in the gap beneath. I hear the strike of a match, smell the fug of smoke, the scent of cloves and leather.

When I wake the next morning, it comes back to me: the sound of someone walking around above my head. My climb up the dark staircase. The light showing under the door. But it was the shock of Mum's postcards and then consuming too much wine – considering the day I'd had and where I'm living, it's hardly surprising my mind dredged up another old memory, feeding it into my dreams.

I can't stay here. The house gives me nightmares. And the whole reason for this ridiculous subterfuge was to try and discover Mum's connection to the family, to see if it could help me find her. But it turns out she ran away with a lover, and she doesn't want to be found. And now I know what happened that morning at sea too: I did something stupid, and he saved me.

Thea is drinking coffee in the kitchen with Saul as I come in with the children to make their breakfast. Mrs Kerry is wiping down the surfaces. 'You got through the snow!' I say in surprise.

'I walked here,' she says. 'Over the fields. A bit of snow's not going to stop me doing my job.'

'Mrs K, you're a star,' Saul says. 'You're wasted here. You should be in the SAS.'

She flashes him a quick, pleased smile and scrubs even harder.

'How's your head?' Thea asks me.

I grimace. 'Not too good.'

'I hear you and Thea had quite a session last night.' Saul looks bemused, immaculate in his work suit and tie.

'Oh, we had a great time,' Thea says and winks at me. 'Anyway, I must run. Hopefully the roads are clear enough for me to get to the studio.'

Saul puts his cup on the side. 'I'd better get a move on too. Catching a later train this morning, but I need to get into the office today.'

Thea's phone rings and she answers, talking quickly. When she clicks it off, she yawns. 'That was Clem. She's coming over later. Says there's a book here she needs to study for a part.'

They leave, and I proceed around the kitchen slowly, opening cupboards, pouring cereal, trying to keep my skull steady on the stem of my neck. I am fragile. Made of sticks. Mrs Kerry puts down her cloth. 'I'll come back when you've all finished breakfast,' she says, picking up the hoover and disappearing into the hall. I wince at the noise the machine makes, dragging behind her.

* * *

I've promised Artemis and Kit that we'll build a snowman. But first, I pull on my coat and boots and make my way through the snow to the summer house. I've decided that as I'm going to leave, I'll come clean, confess my identity to Ophelia. Twice now, Thea has said she thinks she knows me from somewhere. It's only a matter of time before she remembers. I want to show Ophelia the Polaroid. She might know why Mum is wearing the pendant, might know what Mum's connection is to this family. It's my only hope of finding out the truth.

Snow crunches underfoot, virgin white and crisp. Sharpened air cuts through the fog in my head. My hangover is making me feel nauseous, fragmented, undone. I push open the door. Fred is curled up in his nest of old shawl, and I give him a pet and pour out some kibble. Then I get down on my hands and knees and pull up the floorboard. I reach into the gap, rummaging around the rough, narrow space. My fingers grasp cobwebs and dust. The envelope with the photo has gone. I sit back on my heels in shock. As far as I know, the only people that knew about the loose floorboard were me and John.

Standing in the open doorway, I stare out at the wintery scene, the rise towards the shrubbery and the roof of Deben

Manor, coated in silvery white. The tracks leading to the summer house are my own, so whoever took the envelope did so before the snow fell. Someone has been watching me from the moment I arrived. I shiver, realising they must have been spying on me through the summer house window as I hid the photo under the loose floorboard.

23

I stumble back through the snow to Deben Manor, aware of being in full view of the house. The hairs on the back of my neck prickle: am I being watched now? As soon as I'm through the door, Artemis and Kit rush to find me, excited by the snow, and the excuse to stay at home. 'You said we could build a snowman!' Artemis yells, Kit jumping up and down beside her. 'Please, Margaret!'

It takes ages to zip them into coats and boots, pull on hats and mittens. The air snaps with cold, the snow glitters, marked with animal tracks, the delicate shape of birds' feet and my own less delicate prints leading to and from the summer house. The three of us throw snowballs and make a snowman, and I want to centre myself in the moment, in their innocence, but my mind is elsewhere, thinking of each sister, Saul, Mrs Kerry, Mick, wondering, *is it you?* Or is there a stranger watching me? Someone with their own agenda.

Clem has made it over in her red Mini to find her book, and she and Ophelia have shut themselves in the living room with a bottle of wine. Clem has an overnight bag with her, so I'm guessing she'll be in her old room tonight.

Later, I lie awake in bed, anticipating movement over my head, footsteps, the dragging noises; I think over everything that's happened since I arrived at Deben Manor, and press the heels of my hands into my eyes until sparks fly. I can't make sense of any of it. Maybe I should stay, after all. If someone is so determined to drive me away, then it stands to reason they're afraid of me finding something out. Something important. My mind whirls. Sleep is impossible.

Years ago, Mum used to make me hot chocolate before bed, and the sweet drink always had a soporific affect. I wrap my dressing gown tightly around my pyjamas and creep downstairs. The light is on in Saul's office; the door is ajar, and he slumps at the desk, a glass of whisky in front of him. He raises his head as I pass. 'Margaret? Is that you?'

His words are thick and slow and my heart sinks. I hesitate in the doorway. 'Just going to make myself a hot drink.'

'Come in,' he gestures towards me. 'Shut the door.'

Reluctantly, I do as he says, remaining just inside the threshold.

'I'm fucked,' he says. He looks at me through heavy lidded eyes. 'Did you know that? Up to my neck in debt.' He flips a black notebook's pages, covered in numbers, prods at them with his finger. 'I'm a gambler. And I've been on a losing streak.'

Shock flickers through me. Nothing is as it appears in this household. Thea's fashion business is in trouble, and now Saul's telling me he's in debt. 'I'm sorry.' My hand hovers over the doorknob, anxious to get away from him. 'But there's not much I can do.'

'Don't be such a cold bitch,' he says, scowling at me. 'You sound like Ophelia's sisters.'

I begin to turn the handle. 'I'm leaving.'

'Alright,' he holds up his palms. 'I'm sorry. I'm just... very stressed. Just come in. I'm not going to bite.' He looks at me. 'Please.'

I edge across the carpet, a couple of steps, then a couple more.

'I saw you poking around in my wife's things.' His gaze narrows.

My heart bangs. 'You're mistaken,' I stutter. 'I was just—'

'Look, I don't care,' he cuts me off. 'I've got too much else to worry about. And you don't seem the criminal type.' He rakes his fingers through his hair. 'There's something wrong,' he says. 'In this house. Can't you feel it? Ophelia and her sisters, they're always whispering together.' He shakes his head. 'If I were you, I'd get out – leave while you can.'

I'm standing next to him. I clench my fingers. 'What do you mean?'

'Nannies never stay,' he says. 'It's this place. It freaks them out.'

My heartbeat quickens in my chest. 'Have you heard the noises, then?' I ask him. 'In the attic?'

He gives me an odd look. 'What, like rats?'

'Like a person.'

He shakes his head. 'But it's bloody strange the way Ophelia will never go up there, never open the door. She says it's sacred ground – something to do with her father. It's bullshit if you ask me. She's covering something up.' He grabs my hand. 'Just leave. The other nannies – they were scared... something frightened them—' His skin is hot and damp.

'What?' I ask. 'What frightened them?'

But he shakes his head. 'I'm lonely,' he says. 'That's the truth. I'm not in a relationship with my wife, I'm in a foursome with her and her bloody sisters.' I try and pull away, but he tugs me close as he stands up, swamping me in an awkward hug. He mumbles into my hair, 'They hate me, the two of them. They've turned Ophelia against me.'

Before I can pull away, his mouth is over mine, loose and wet. Our teeth clash. I struggle to free my arms, pinioned by his embrace. I put my hands flat against his chest, and push with all my strength. He unbalances and falls against the desk, crashes over his chair and slides onto the floor.

'I'm going now,' I tell him. 'Do not follow me.'

His slurred apologies are cut off as I shut the door firmly behind me. A figure materialises out of the darkness of the hall. Something human shaped. I gasp in fright. Pale skin gleams through the cover of night. The shape comes closer. It's Clem.

'What are you doing down here?' she asks sharply.

I think of telling her about Saul, about what just happened. But he's not a really a threat. He's drunk. I can deal with him myself; I don't want to start a row in the middle of the night. I don't think she saw me coming out of his study. 'Nothing,' I say. 'I came down for a hot drink. Couldn't sleep.'

In my room, I take the chair and ram it under the handle.

* * *

The next morning, I get up and draw the curtains. The snow is degraded, spoilt by people and animals, a maze of churned up slush and footprints. As I leave my room to go into the bathroom, there's the sound of childish chatter coming from the kitchen, a pop song drifting from the radio in Ophelia's room.

On the landing, Saul appears out of the guest room. He

looks terrible, unshaven, his skin grey. 'Sorry,' he says. 'About last night.'

'If you try anything like that again, I'll tell Ophelia.'

'Feisty.' He blinks at me, leaning close, breathing alcohol and the stink of nicotine. 'Good for you, Danby.'

Clem appears out of her old bedroom, making me startle and step away from Saul.

'Bit early for secret conversations, isn't it?' Her voice is ice.

She really does hate Saul, I think. I wait for him to contradict her, make a joke of it, but he gives her a slow smile. 'You should know better than anyone, Clem.'

She goes into the bathroom and slams the door.

When I reach the bottom of the staircase, something snags my attention. I pause and turn, wondering what's caught my eye. A familiar navy fisherman's cap is hanging on the newel post. I lift it from its perch with trembling fingers. It's well worn, exactly like Lucian's. He'd forgotten to wear it that last day on the river. I drop the cap, stepping back, then force myself to pick it up, replacing it on the post with a shudder.

* * *

It's my day off, but I don't want to drive into town in the snow. I call Dad instead to check he's okay. Seeing the hat has spooked me. It's still there, hanging on the newel post, as if Lucian's just back from a sail. It's a sign or a warning. Someone wants me to see it. I think they know what I did, what happened that morning.

After lunch, I go for a walk. I need to think. Fresh air might clear my head. I put on my warmest coat, a hat and scarf, and my boots and set off on foot. It's like stepping into a freezer: the air stabs at the tissue of my eyeballs, scours my nostrils.

Out of the gate, I turn left, walking carefully over icy patches, heading for the village along the lane. Except I've forgotten there's no pavement on this narrow, twisting stretch of road, and when cars come around the corner, I'm forced to press myself into the hedge to avoid being run over.

I hear another engine behind me, and step to the side, nearly slipping into a ditch. The car crawls past and stops. It's Saul's BMW. The passenger window lowers, and Saul leans across. 'Hey,' he calls. 'Get in. I'll drop you wherever you're going.'

I hesitate, not wanting to be stuck in a car with him.

'I'm not going to lunge at you,' he says, impatiently. 'I'm driving and I'm sober.'

I open the door and lower myself into the low-slung seat, pulling the door shut with a clunk. He drives on. The inside of the car smells of leather and a waft of pine air freshener.

'What I said before,' he says, as he changes gear around a corner. 'Forget it. I was drunk.'

'You mean, about me leaving?'

He shrugs. 'Whatever I said – I can't remember most of it.'

'And what about your gambling. Your debts. What are you going to do about them?'

His fingers tighten on the wheel. 'It's only a few rounds of poker. Nothing to frighten the horses.'

'That's not what you said last night.'

'Yeah, well, like I said. I was drunk.' He slows for a tractor to pass us going the other way in the narrow lane. 'Where shall I drop you?'

'In the village,' I say. 'Thanks.'

'So, you haven't been scared off?' he says as he pulls over by the shop.

I pause with my hand on the door handle. 'What?'

'You know,' he nods. 'Last night?'

'Oh,' I sit back. 'No.' My fingers pull the catch on the door as I slide to the edge of the seat, tensed to get out. I try the handle and push at the door. The car's central locking is on. I feel Saul's gaze on me.

'That's good, then,' he says slowly. 'Ophelia would kill me if you left because of me.' His hand brushes my thigh lightly. 'But she wouldn't be too happy to know you've been snooping around in her stuff either.' He lets his words sit in silence for a moment before he unlocks the mechanism with a flick of his finger.

'You don't need to blackmail me, Saul,' I tell him as I get out.

He laughs. 'I like you, Danby. I really do.'

I shut the passenger door, as another car drives past. I catch a glimpse of a red Mini. Clem. She must be on her way home. I watch as Saul's powerful saloon pulls away from the curb.

In the woods the light is odd, other-worldly, the sun already low in the sky, shadows falling long across the path. That summer, John and I built a tree-house here, hidden inside lush leaves. Today, tucked up in my jacket and hat, it's impossible to imagine how it felt then – every day a heatwave, the two of us in shorts and T-shirts. I was hoping for fresh air and space to clear my head, but it's colder than I'd anticipated; the tip of my nose is numb, and my breath makes white swirls. The place is deserted. Nobody except a dog walker would be mad enough to be out. The silence echoes around me, disturbed by quiet thumps as snow falls from the trees; I sense rather than hear the crackle of ice, the muffled movement of wings. I had a plan to circumnavigate the woods, but now I realise that it will be dark before I finish, and I've still got to hazard the lane, playing Russian roulette with passing cars. I turn around and retrace my footsteps.

The quiet makes my nerves tingle, every part of me alert. A soft claw-scratch to my right me makes me jump, and I turn to see a squirrel disappearing behind a trunk. I tense at the shuffle of an unseen creature scurrying between roots. Should I hand in my notice? It's creepy knowing someone is spying on me. I don't know what they're capable of – besides snooping in my room and stealing the Polaroid – would they harm me? I can't believe it, not if it's one of the girls. They were spiteful sometimes, but they wouldn't use violence.

A stick snaps like a pistol shot behind me. I spin around. There's a figure on the path, too far back to see properly, a dark shape glimpsed through a mesh of trees and branches. I can't tell if they're male or female. I walk on, expecting to hear a whistle, see a dog bounding through the snow. But there's no dog, just the figure following behind. I increase my pace, extending my stride, my breath coming fast.

I've reached the outskirts of the village. Feeling braver now there are people within shouting distance, I wait at the corner of the first house, watching the woods. The walker comes out after me. I can't see any details: I'm too far away and they're all in black with a hood over their face. They're slender, and something about the way they're moving makes me guess they're female. They walk quickly in the opposite direction. I breathe a sigh of relief. They can't have been following me, after all.

I need to get back to Deben Manor. The village street is deserted. I hurry along the pavement, anxious to beat the twilight. Suddenly, my foot is sliding away from me. It happens so fast, there's nothing I can do to stop myself falling backwards. I twist in mid-air and land heavily on my hip, pain shooting through bone. A metallic taste floods my tongue. I sit up on the snowy path and take off my glove to touch my mouth. My fingers come away slippery.

A shape looms out of the dusk, a hood pulled over their face. I shrink from their approaching shape. They stop and put out a hand. 'Are you alright?' A woman's voice. I realise she wants to help me up.

I take her hand. For such a slight person, she's surprisingly strong, and I'm yanked back onto my feet.

'I think so,' I say, taking a tentative step and wincing. Nothing broken. But my hip is smarting. 'Think I bit my tongue,' I add.

'You went down with a proper bang,' she says. 'You've had a shock. Come in for a moment. I live just here,' she gestures to a brick terraced house. 'We can check you in the light, make sure you haven't done yourself a real injury.'

'Oh, no,' I say. 'I don't want to put you to any trouble.'

'Don't be daft,' she says, taking my arm with a firm grip and guiding me through a small front garden, past a couple of lopsided plastic gnomes, a rusted motorbike, and a woodpile covered in a tarpaulin. Inside, the house is dazzling with electric light, and I realise that I've missed my opportunity to get back in daylight. Darkness already presses against the bare windows. Two children sit on a sofa watching cartoons on a large TV and eating crisps.

'Hello, you two,' she addresses the children. 'Hope you had a good day at school.' The kids grunt at her, not taking their gazes from the screen. 'You'll get square eyes,' she warns. 'Half an hour more, then homework.'

'Take your coat off,' she tells me, as she slips her anorak off and pulls her hood down. She draws the curtains. 'Come through,' she adds as she walks into a small kitchen.

I follow her. The woman is putting the kettle on. 'You need a cup of sweet tea,' she's saying. 'The bathroom's just there if you want to take a look at your mouth in the mirror.' She points to a narrow door.

Inside the tiny downstairs loo, I examine my mouth in the cabinet over the sink. My tongue is bleeding, but I know mouths bleed a lot and I don't think it's too bad. I bend over the tap and swill my mouth out, spitting scarlet. The sight of it swirling through water stirs something in me, and the edge of a memory skitters away. I stand up, wiping my mouth, frowning, trying to access another piece of memory. Something to do with Lucian's head injury? Nothing comes to me. I look in the cabinet for cotton wool, finding packets of plasters, digestion tablets and aspirins, but no cotton wool. I dab some loo roll on my tongue instead.

In the kitchen, the woman places a mug of steaming tea on the table. 'There you are,' she says. 'I put sugar in for the shock. And how's your hip?'

'A bit sore,' I admit, picking a piece of wet loo roll from my tongue. 'But it's just bruised, I think. Thanks.' She's familiar now that I can take a proper look at her. A thin woman, middle-aged, with deep lines cut into her forehead and around her mouth. Her eyes are wounded somehow.

'Where are you from, love?' she asks. 'You're not from around here, are you?'

'I'm a Suffolk girl originally,' I tell her. 'But I've moved around because of my job. I'm working at Deben Manor.'

I remember who she is – this thin, sad woman – the one putting up posters all those years ago. The one who lost her daughter. The woman who talked to Kit and me the other day.

She's looking at me more intently now. 'I met you in the shop, didn't I? With the little boy?'

I nod.

'The nanny,' she says. 'That's nice,' she goes on when I nod again. 'Nice to work with kids. And they're alright, are they, the parents? To work for, I mean.'

'The kids are lovely, and the parents are... fine,' I say.

She gives me a keen look. 'The Aldredge family have always kept themselves separate from the village,' she says. 'The kids were all sent to posh boarding schools. One of the daughters lives there now, I think. She must be your employer. There were three of them. Three daughters. I still see them sometimes, usually driving through the village too fast.'

I don't think I should mention her lost daughter. I don't want to cause her any distress.

'I'm Alison, by the way,' she says. 'Alison Greenwood.'

She smiles, and suddenly she reminds me of someone. I try to work out who, but nobody comes to mind.

'Well,' I put my half-finished tea on the table. 'You've been very kind. But I should get back.'

'What, walking all the way to the Manor?' she exclaims. 'The road is treacherous for walkers – even cyclists – too many blind corners and no pavement. Especially in the snow and the dark. No.' She shakes her head. 'I'll give you a lift.'

I begin to protest, but she holds up her hand. 'I'm a mum,' she says. 'And no mother would let their child walk that road in these conditions.'

I can see that she is determined.

'Damien, Lauren,' she tells the children. 'I'm giving this lady a lift. I won't be long. Your dad will be back soon, and he'll do your tea.'

They break their attention from the TV for a second to

acknowledge her – a straw-haired boy and girl, with round, ruddy faces, both about twelve – and then return their gaze to the screen. 'My step-children,' she explains. 'Their dad should be here by now,' she says, as if in apology. 'We try and make our shifts work so one of us is always here. But I think the weather's delayed him.'

We put our coats back on and I follow her onto the street. She knocks the snow off the windscreen of a small car, and I get into the passenger seat. It takes her a couple of goes to get the engine to turn over. I feel guilty for dragging her away from her warm home and children when she's obviously just got back from work.

She drives very slowly along the deserted road, turning into the lane that leads up to the Manor. 'How old are you?' she asks, as she changes gear, crunching the clutch.

'Twenty-six.'

'I have a daughter about your age.' I hold my breath, uncertain about revealing what I know. 'She got taken,' she says quietly. 'My Haley. She was just a baby when she disappeared. Sometimes I worry I wouldn't recognise her if I met her now.'

'I'm sorry,' I mutter.

'People were sympathetic at first,' she says. 'But then the gossip started. They made out I was a bad mum. But I couldn't have loved my little girl more.'

'I'm sorry,' I repeat, feeling inadequate.

'It's a terrible thing,' she says. 'Never knowing what happened to her.'

'You didn't want to move away?'

'I'm not leaving here,' she says. 'She might come back one day.'

I see the lights of Deben Manor ahead. I want to tell her about Mum – because of all people, she'd understand my agony, and all the unanswered questions I live with. Except, of course, Mum disappeared of her own accord. She wasn't stolen.

'What's your name, love? I don't think you told me.'

'Margaret Danby.'

'That's a good solid name.' She nods her head. 'My Haley is probably going under a different name – wherever she is. Everyone's given up on her, but I know she's out there, somewhere.' We pull up in front of the house. 'Never been up close before,' she says, peering up through the windscreen. 'Even bigger than it looks from the lane.'

I'm grateful she's changed the subject. 'Well,' I say, opening the door. 'Thank you so much.'

'You take care, love.' She leans across and gives my hand a squeeze.

As I come into the hall, shrugging off my coat and stamping the snow from my boots, the sailor cap is no longer hanging on the newel post.

24

The next morning, my hip is black and blue. My first waking thought is I was lucky I didn't break a bone. My second is John. I want to see him. I'll have to take the risk that he won't remember me or want to see me. He's the only person I could talk to about the summer at Deben Manor. He knows what it was like for me staying with my cousins, and he might help me make sense of that time.

My phone is an old Nokia. Ophelia's computer is sitting on her desk in the snug off the kitchen. It's not being used. She's making herself a cup of herbal tea.

'I wondered if I could borrow your computer,' I say. 'Just for five minutes?'

She turns. 'Can't you use your phone?'

I hold up my mobile in explanation.

'Okay,' she says. 'Just this once.'

'Of course,' I say quickly.

'Actually,' she says. 'I wanted to tell you how happy I am with your work here, Margaret.' She smiles. 'The kids love you.

I'm sorry if I'm a bit snappy sometimes. I've got a lot on my mind.'

I smile back, surprised and pleased. As I sit at her shiny glass table, she leans across me to put her password in, while I pretend to look politely the other way. Except, by squinting hard out of my left eye, I manage to catch the letters she puts in. Seeing out of the back of my head is a talent I've developed since caring for small children. It's her kids' names. Easy to remember. She retreats from the room, leaving the door open behind her. I hear her moving about in the kitchen. She clearly doesn't trust me not to pry. I wonder what's weighing so heavily on her mind. But from her comment just now, I don't think she knows Saul caught me in here looking through her stuff.

I open my Facebook page. I hardly ever bother to look at it, and never post anything, but now I enter John Catchpole into the search bar. Immediately, dozens of options come up. Heart sinking, I scan through them, flicking past those that are too old or too young, while Ophelia sighs heavily in the kitchen behind me. It feels hopeless. I'll have to stop before she runs out of patience. Her mobile rings. I've noticed it sometimes has a cheerful salsa tune, rather than the usual telephone chime. She speaks in a low, intimate voice; the one she uses when she answers that ring tone. It gives me a few more minutes to scroll through the John Catchpoles.

I think I've found him. My spine tingles. I click on his profile. My finger hovers over the Friend Request button. There's one photo of him. He's still dark-haired, although not as scruffy as I remember. His face is more defined, his nose larger. There's a landscape picture set as his profile photo – a shot of a steep hill with colourful houses, a pink and golden sky above – I stare at the image. San Francisco. He's living a glamorous life on the other side of the world. I click off Facebook with a jolt of disappointment. My hope that I might bump into him on one of my walks – imagining him appearing around a corner, our mutual pleasure in recognising each other – is not going to happen, and neither is an arranged meet-up. I chew the end of my thumbnail, quickly reopen the page and send him a Friend Request anyway, before I can change my mind. What the hell. It can't do any harm.

* * *

After I get the kids into bed, I remember, with a pang, that I haven't fed Fred today – he must be extra hungry in this weather. I slip on my coat again and make my way carefully over the patchy snow on the lawn, finding my way by moonlight. The children's snowman has collapsed sideways, his top half rolled over, his head squashed as if kicked in by a bunch of thugs. I push past laurel leaves, skidding down the slope to the summer house.

Fred is curled up in his nest of shawl; he gets up, purring loudly when I come in. There's no electricity in here, but I've brought my keyring torch with me. I shine it around, picking out his bowl, and the packet of hard cat food I keep on the table. I crouch beside him watching him tuck in, wondering if John will answer my Friend Request. As I stand up, there's a movement behind the cracked panes of glass. I stifle a scream with my hand, stepping back, hands clasping the edge of the table for support. But now that I look again, the face is no longer there. A trick of light and shadows maybe.

Fred didn't react. He's busy munching. But that doesn't mean anything; cats don't growl at strangers, not like dogs. And perhaps the person isn't a stranger to the cat. When I pluck up the courage to go outside, there are various footprints or animal prints in the remains of the snow. The snow is broken and dirty, the moonlight casting strange shapes. Here in the dip near the stream, the remaining snow is thicker and less disturbed than on the higher ground or on the lawn where the children have been playing. But I still can't tell for sure if I'm looking at recent footprints or old animal tracks. I shudder, not wanting to investigate further. Remembering the anonymous figure behind me in the woods, I hurry back, scrambling up the slope, past the shrubbery. As I cross the lawn, the windows of Deben Manor are blazing, sending alternate fingers of brilliance and darkness across the pitted landscape.

Approaching the front door, I hear raised voices, and my heart sinks. Saul's BMW is parked outside. Stepping into the hall, a missile just misses me: a bottle of cologne smashing at my feet, the powerful smell rising. Startled, I look up. Ophelia is standing at the top of the stairs. Around me, shirts and trousers and coils of bright ties lie in twisted shapes, and there is a smashed camera, shoes, a tennis racquet, a splayed open suitcase.

Saul steps forward and pulls me out of the way. 'Get out of here,' he hisses. 'She's gone mad.'

'I'm not mad, you bastard!' she screams. 'This is the sanest I've been for a long time!'

'For God's sake, Ophelia,' he calls up. 'Can we at least talk?'

'Get out!' she shouts. 'Get the fuck out of my house!'

He stoops to gather his belongings, getting onto his knees, arms full of crumpled clothes. I wonder if I should help him. He winces as his palm lands on some broken glass, and he sucks the edge, kneeling in the mess.

I realise that Thea and Clem are with Ophelia. 'She's run out of patience,' Thea tells him, coming down the stairs. 'And I don't blame her. Just get your stuff, Saul, and go.'

Clem follows and stands over him. 'You're a parasite. We never liked you.' She glances at me and then back at him. 'Men like you make me sick. You take what you want without thinking of the consequences.'

'Told you.' He shoots me a meaningful glance. 'They're like the bloody mafia.' He stands, having stuffed some of his things into the case. 'Alright,' he says. 'I'm going.' As he passes me, he grabs my arm. 'Watch your back.'

'Mummy.' I hear Artemis's wobbly voice. 'Where's Daddy going?'

She's clinging to her mother's leg. Ophelia is trying to unpeel her daughter's fingers. She casts a despairing glance at me. 'Margaret, can you help?'

I take the stairs two at a time, and squat down to Artemis's level. 'Come on, sweetheart,' I say. 'Back to bed.'

'Just take her away.' Ophelia lets out a sob. 'I can't deal with her now.'

She goes downstairs, and the other two rush forwards to embrace her. I throw one last glance in their direction before picking Artemis up. The sight of the three of them together reminds me of the huddles they used to get into with their father, how he held them tight, enclosing them all in an impenetrable fortress of love.

It takes me a while to calm Artemis down. I lie on her bed with her and read her countless stories. I tell her that sometimes grown-ups have disagreements. They don't always behave like grown-ups. But that both her parents love her and Kit. In the end, she falls asleep in my arms, her thumb in her mouth.

I'm exhausted when I get to bed myself. I open my door, and flick on the overhead light. It's become a habit to wedge the back of the chair under my door handle. It takes me a long time to get to sleep. I shiver under my blankets, wrapping them tightly around me. There are no noises from above, but I keep seeing the pale shape at the summer house window: the impression of a face, dark sockets, hollowed cheeks like a skull. It occurs to me that the person behind me in the woods might have veered off in the opposite direction just to throw me off the scent. Eventually, I fall asleep listening to the wind whining in the chimney and my own irregular heartbeat.

25

I'm yawning as I pour bowls of cereal for the kids, when Mrs Kerry pops her head around the kitchen door. 'Mrs Manners asked if you could pick up her dry-cleaning. She's left the ticket on the side.'

It's not my job. But I'm too tired to bother to make a big deal out of it. I scoop up the ticket on my way out. After I get Artemis to school, I drop Kit at another child's house for a play date, and then drive into Ipswich. In town, people are wrapped up against the cold, hurrying along, heads down. The pavements are gritted, the roads thick with black slush. As I walk back to the car with the dry-cleaning bags draped over my arm, I pass three down-and-outs in the bus shelter, huddled against the cold. They're passing a joint back and forth between them, beer cans in their hands. One of them glances up as I pass, and as we lock eyes I realise, with a start, that it's the homeless woman I've seen before. The one with the young-old face who'd been in the doorway of Dad's block of flats. She's all in black with a tarnished silver chain like a collar around her neck, and no coat. Her dyed hair is hard black, with paler roots. Despite her haggard look, I think she was once pretty. She notices me and scowls. 'What are you looking at?' I avert my gaze and walk quickly on.

Back at the house, as I hurry from the car to the front door, I notice a piece of rubbish on the gravel near the edge of the lawn. Ophelia won't like that. I pick it up. It's a piece of A4 lined paper covered in cramped writing, some it smudged from the damp. Looking closer, I realise it's a series of grouped numbers. I remember Saul's black notebook filled with numbers. Perhaps it fell out of his bag when he left the house. I fold it and put it my pocket.

I go upstairs and knock on Ophelia's door. She takes her clothes from me with a distracted smile. I remember the paper in my pocket, but she's already shut the door. I suppose I should leave it on the hall table in case it's important to someone. I look at it again, and this time I notice a pattern to the figures:

20.02.08 8.30 20.02.08 9.30.

It's a series of dates and times. With a start, I realise they all relate to me – it's a list of the times I leave to take the kids to school and when I return, and the occasional trips to go into Ipswich. I rush to the big landing window, expecting to see someone there, pen in hand, jotting down this latest journey. But the drive is empty, and the rain is falling hard.

* * *

The next morning, I don't hear my alarm. I wake with a jolt, grabbing my clock. I've overslept. I throw myself out of bed and hurry the kids through breakfast and into the car. 'Quick,' I tell Artemis. 'Here's your packed lunch. And Kit, hold still while I strap you in.' Whenever I'm with the children I feel almost normal, as if everything else is just a fantasy, a nightmare.

I couldn't sleep last night, listening for sounds above my head and thinking about the scrawled recording of my journeys. I can't even guess at the point of it – why on earth anyone would bother to write down when I drive away and when I return? This cat-and-mouse game is getting out of hand, and I'm the mouse.

When I get back, Mrs Kerry is in the kitchen again. I'm desperate for a coffee; I ask her if she doesn't mind if I make one. 'I'm stopping for a cuppa,' she says. 'You help yourself. I never touch coffee. Plays havoc with my insides.'

I have finally learned to tame the expresso machine and I make myself a cup. Mrs Kerry sits at the table stirring sugar into her tea. 'I hear Mr Manners has moved out,' she says. 'Are the kiddies alright? It can be a terrible blow for the little ones when they lose a parent.'

'It might be a temporary thing.'

'Hmmm.' She stares into her tea with a frown. 'Something tells me he won't be back. Mrs Manners doesn't need any more upset in her life. She and her sisters suffered a lot,' she says. 'In a few weeks, they were robbed of both parents. Imagine.' She sucks her teeth. 'You would have thought the mother would have stayed with her children, but some women are just selfish.'

'I wouldn't know,' I say, tightly. 'I'm sure she had her reasons.' I think of Calista packing her case, her vagueness worse than usual, the tremble in her arms when she hugged me goodbye.

'Anyway,' Mrs Kerry goes on. 'It caused a lot of gossip at the time, Mrs Aldredge going off like that.'

'Yes,' I agree, feeling sick. 'I suppose it must have.'

I remember Lucian's face as the oar hit him. It had been an accident – but if I believed in ghosts, I'd think he'd come back to haunt me for causing his death. I chew my nails and stare at the table, thinking of the sounds I'd heard coming from the attic, the whispering steps crossing my ceiling. The light on behind the door. The smell of smoke and nicotine. 'Do you believe in ghosts, Mrs Kerry?'

'Ah, now you're asking,' she says, lowering her voice. 'Just between us, sometimes I feel a presence in the house when I'm cleaning. Something watching me.' She shudders. 'I wouldn't be here at night on my own for all the tea in China.' I raise my head to stare at her and she lifts an eyebrow. 'I have a sense for these things. Always have.'

My heart is thumping. 'Have you heard noises, then?' I ask. 'You know, in the attic, behind the locked door?'

She's laughing. 'Bless you. Don't take me seriously, love. I'm having you on.' She gets to her feet. 'You looked so worried just now.' She shakes her head. 'Didn't expect you to take me seriously. Don't go having nightmares.' She gets up, hands on the small of her back, and stretches with a groan. 'I need to get on.'

In the hall, I shiver. Mum used to say that any kind of unexplained shiver meant someone was walking over your grave. But it's just that the atmosphere is icy, the temperature plummeting, even here in the main part of the house. I go upstairs, a breeze playing over my skin.

Clem is on the landing perched on the windowsill, the big window behind her thrown wide, a rollie between her fingers. She wafts smoke with a flapping hand towards the frigid air.

'I expect the other night was a shock for you,' she's saying before I can greet her. 'But I've been telling my sister to throw Saul out for months.' She gives me a quick, sharp glance. 'He's lied to her for years, saying his gambling was just a social thing, harmless poker with friends. But she found out exactly how much he's lost.'

She takes another drag on her cigarette. 'He kept promising her he'd stop. It's been very stressful for her.' She stubs her cigarette out on the windowsill and flicks the butt onto the gravel below. 'Thea and I are moving in for a bit, to give her support.' She stands and reaches up to pull the sash window closed. 'So, I'm afraid you won't be able to escape us.'

Is that a veiled threat? Or am I being paranoid? Clem is squinting at me. She gestures towards my face. 'I didn't know you wore glasses?'

I was in such a hurry this morning, I'd grabbed my glasses, not thinking straight. 'Must rush,' I say, ducking my head. 'Got to collect Kit.'

Did she notice my eyes are a different colour? Mrs Kerry didn't comment on my glasses or my change of eye shade. I nip into my room and take them off, putting the brown contacts in. My room smells ashy and stale. I sniff, looking around. Someone has been in here, someone with a lit cigarette.

Clem has gone from the landing. When I get into the hall, Mrs Kerry is standing next to the table doing up her coat, a rainproof headscarf on, and a basket at her feet. 'Filthy weather,' she says.

I try to shake off my unease. Why had Clem been in my room? Was it her who planted the diamonds, searched through my stuff before?

Mrs Kerry is giving me a curious look. I arrange my face into a smile. 'Do you want a lift?' I offer. 'I'm going to pick up Kit.'

'Bless you,' she says. 'My daughter, Mary, is coming to collect me.' She gestures towards the basket. 'I'm going to the post office if you want anything posting?'

I shake my head, noticing a package wrapped in paper sticking out of the basket. From what I can see, it's addressed to Calista in France.

My alarm goes off and I snake out an arm to silence it, my hairs rising in protest at the icy air. I get out of the covers reluctantly, strip off quickly, and go over to the chest of drawers to grab some clean underwear, opening the curtains to see what I'm doing. As I root through my clothes, something at the periphery of my vison snags my attention. A man gapes up at me from the garden. I let out a startled shriek and step back from the window. Mick Smith, the gardener. He hasn't stopped spying on women. Angry now the shock has subsided, I put on a dressing gown and look out again. I'm gazing down at the tops of sheds, a sprawl of bushes, a squirrel scurrying away.

The children are asleep, so I run myself a bath, shuddering as I remember the gardener's gaze on me. I can't let him bother me. Ophelia evidently doesn't feel he's enough of a menace to sack him. Perhaps she keeps him on for sentimental reasons. It was her father who'd employed him in the first place.

Yesterday, she told me she'd signed Artemis up for ballet lessons next term. When she mentioned it, I'd wondered if Mum's friend, the dance teacher, Claire Hockey, was still teaching at the dance academy in Ipswich. She used to come to our house and sit in the kitchen with Mum, the two of them chatting and drinking coffee. If Mum had confided in anyone, it would have been Claire.

As I go back to my room to get dressed, Kit comes out of his bedroom in his pyjamas, his face crumpled and blotched with tears. 'Margaret,' he says, 'I had a nightmare.'

'Did you, sweetheart? Let me put some clothes on and I'll get you dressed.' He follows me back to my room and sits on my bed while I get ready. 'We'll make a delicious breakfast, and you'll soon forget all about it.'

I take him to the loo on the way back to his room, and he shivers as I help him pull up his PJ bottoms. 'I haven't forgotten it yet,' he says.

'Shall we talk about something nice instead?' I say as I find his clothes. 'How about how many sausages you can eat?'

'There was a bad man,' he says in a wobbly voice. 'He wanted to take me away.'

'There are no bad men here,' I tell him, pulling a sock over his foot.

Artemis opens the door. She's managed to dress herself, and she swings on the handle. 'I'm ready before you,' she says in a sing-song voice. 'Bagsy Coco Pops for breakfast.'

We go downstairs, the children arguing about breakfast cereals. As we pass the hall table, I think about the package addressed to Calista. 'Do you ever see your granny?' I ask them.

'No,' Artemis says. 'She lives all the way away in France.'

I wonder why Calista hasn't been back to England to visit her grandchildren. It's not as if she lives in Australia, or something. Why would she ban her own children and grandchildren from visiting her?

'Does she send you cards or talk to you on the phone?'

'Yes,' Artemis says. 'But she's very busy. She's a painter.'

'Margaret.' Clem's stern voice comes from behind. 'Why aren't you giving the children their breakfast?' She looks at her wristwatch. 'Artemis can't be late for school.'

I bite my lip, feeling the sting of injustice. She's never been late with me, not once. Clem obviously wants to distract me from talking about Calista.

'Who's going to be first to the kitchen?' Clem grabs the children's hands and hurries them down the hall, making them laugh as she swings them off their feet. She turns to give me a pointed look, brows furrowing, before ushering them into the kitchen.

* * *

Saturday. My day off, and I'm hoping to see Claire at the dance academy later today. The house feels warm for once, and I give myself the luxury of a lie-in. As I leave my bedroom, I can hear the others downstairs. Clem and Thea have moved into their old bedrooms and I'm guessing one of them has adjusted the heating. It's strange hearing the sisters calling out to each other from their rooms, as though we've all been teleported back to that summer.

I head for the kitchen to make myself a coffee. Some French toast, I'm thinking. Or banana pancakes. I'm starving. The door to the sitting room stands partly open and Clem is speaking. Her voice is urgent and breathless. 'I've had enough,' she says. 'Something needs to be done about her.'

I stop still, standing just outside the entrance, hidden by the partially closed door. My heart thumps.

'She's going to ruin everything,' she goes on. 'I vote we get rid of her.'

'You mean kill her?' comes Thea's voice.

My hand clamps across my mouth.

'What else?' Clem says. 'And I know exactly how to do it.'

The ground moves beneath me, the corridor turning to putty. I sway, putting out a hand against the wall to steady myself. Something hits the back of my legs, and I shriek.

Kit clings to my knees, laughing up at me. The voices stop and the door opens. Clem stands there, looking annoyed, hands on her hips. 'Margaret,' she says. 'What's wrong?'

'Kit gave me a fright.' I can hardly speak.

'I'm in the middle of practising for my audition,' she says, turning away. 'You put me off my stride.'

An audition. My legs tremble as if they are going to collapse beneath me. I struggle to walk in a straight line as I continue to the kitchen, Kit hanging onto my hand. Clem's voice has started up again. 'We'll do it the way women can,' she's saying. 'With poison.'

I make myself a coffee, but my appetite has gone.

* * *

I park on the hill next to the park in Ipswich. Freezing rain falls from a pewter sky; there's hardly anyone about. I set off briskly down the hill, the park fence on my left. I'm aware of footsteps behind me, and they seem to slow when I do and speed up when I walk faster. I must be imagining it. I remind myself of the fear I'd felt when I heard Clem's words this morning, and how relieved and foolish I'd felt when I'd found the script abandoned on the sofa in the sitting room later.

On the other hand, someone *has* been spying on me at Deben Manor. I know because of the piece of paper with my comings and goings noted. And Clem has been snooping in my room. Perhaps my watcher has graduated to following me out of the house and grounds too. I stop and bend down on the pretext of doing up the lace on my ankle boot to let whoever it is overtake me. Instead, I catch a glimpse of a figure slipping through the park gates. I stand and wipe my glasses on the edge of my coat, and continue walking, hands in my pockets, head down. The scrape and tap of footsteps resume – further back, but still following. This time, I pick up my pace and cross the road, dodging between cars. The dance academy is just ahead, and I stride up the steps to the double front door, pausing under the porch.

I turn and stare into the street. There are a couple of people on the pavement across the road, bundled up against the cold, hats pulled low. Maybe I was mistaken.

I hurry into the dance academy, remembering Mum bringing me here for lessons. I wasn't very good, but Claire was always patient and encouraging. My favourite part of the lesson was at the end, when we got into pairs and did the polka around the room, hopping and skipping wildly round and round.

I find a corridor full of little girls in pale pink leotards sitting on benches putting on their ballet shoes or taking them off. There's a buzz of excited chatter, a smell of feet and chalk. Mothers chat together or help children get changed.

Through a half-glazed door, I see Claire teaching a class of older girls. Her hair is streaked with grey, but she's still slender and upright. She's wearing a long, dark green skirt, and her hair is swept off her face with a wide band. An older, plumper woman sits at an upright piano in the corner, banging out a familiar tune. The girls at the barre sway and bend and kick their legs up in front of them.

When the class ends, Claire's glance slides across me with no recognition. 'Claire,' I say. 'It's me. Meg. Irene's daughter.'

She stares at me, forehead creased, and then her face opens in amazement. 'Meg!' She gives a short laugh. 'My goodness, I'd never have recognised you. You've got so tall!' She comes close and clasps both my hands in hers. 'And your hair?' She touches one of my wet curls. 'You're soaking!'

Puddles are forming on the floor around my feet. My glasses are misting up and I take them off.

'Now I can see you properly,' she says softly. 'You have your mum's eyes.' She wrinkles her brow. 'What are you doing here?' She waves a hand. 'The last I heard; you were working in a different part of the country.'

'Yes.' I blink, polishing my lenses with a damp tissue I've found in my pocket. 'But I have a job closer to home now. I'm working at Deben Manor. It still belongs to the Aldredge family. Lucian and Calista's oldest daughter, Ophelia, lives there now, and has two kids of her own.'

Claire raises her eyebrows. 'You're working at Deben Manor?'

'I was hoping we could talk,' I add, as a crowd of young girls pushes past me into the studio.

'I'd love that,' she says. 'I have another lesson now. I'm free after that. Can you wait?' She smiles. 'I'm so glad to see you.' She bends down and picks something up. 'Here,' she says. 'Take this.' She presses a towel into my hands.

* * *

The last class drifts out of their lesson, chatting. Claire follows them, switching off the light. She opens a locker and takes out a pair of stout walking boots and sits to slip off her teaching shoes. She ties on a long, moss green cloak and puts her arm through mine. 'Right,' she says, 'I suggest we go and get a cup of tea. There's a cafe round the corner.'

Her cloak swirls behind her as we face into a sharp wind and walk uphill, making small talk until we reach a cafe, its windows opaque with condensation. We order a pot of tea and two muffins. She tells me that she's running the academy now. She's never married. Dance is her life. I nod and smile, and I mean to build up to asking the questions on my mind, but instead I find myself blurting out, 'Did Mum contact you, after she left?'

Claire plays with her teaspoon, clinking it against her cup. 'She sent me a postcard, from London,' she admits. 'It was an apology for running off without telling me.'

'Did she tell you why she'd left?'

Claire sighs. 'She was in love with someone else. She said she felt terrible about hurting Robert and you. But she seemed to think that she was coming back, that everything would work out.' Claire looks up, her eyes bruised. 'She said she'd known this man before she came to Suffolk. Someone from her past.'

My stomach clenches. 'And you never heard from her again?'

She shakes her head. 'I was worried. It was so unlike her.' She twists a ring around her finger. 'The Irene I knew wasn't selfish. She might have been a bit wild, but she never let people down. I went to see Robert, your dad, I mean. He said she'd made her choice, and we'd have to get on with life without her.' She leans forward. 'I contacted Robert again, to see if he'd heard from her. He said he'd tried to find her without any luck, and now he needed to focus on you and making a new life.'

I take a sip of the tea. 'And you don't know who he was? This man?'

Claire shakes her head again. 'In the note, she's careful not to mention his name or anything about him.'

'But she knew him before she met Dad?' I frown. 'The only clue I have to her disappearance is a photo of her wearing a pendant with the Aldredge crest on it.'

Claire looks puzzled.

'The Aldredges are old Suffolk,' I explain. 'Blue-blooded. She wasn't a relative. So why would she own a piece of jewellery with their crest on it?'

Claire tilts her head. 'And that's who you're working for? Ophelia Aldredge?' She narrows her eyes at me. 'I'm guessing that's not a coincidence?'

'She's Mrs Manners now.' I shrug. 'But you're right. I was hoping being in that house again might trigger a memory – help me make sense of all the questions I have about that summer – Mum disappearing – Lucian drowning.'

She wrinkles her brow. 'There was something in the paper about that.' She taps her teaspoon against her cup again, her frown deepening. 'I seem to remember it said something about him being badly injured. He didn't drown. I think he was taken to hospital.'

My body is rigid with shock. 'What? That can't be right.'

'Sorry, I can't remember the details,' she says. 'Maybe I got it wrong. Everything from that time is a bit of a blur. I was still in a state about Irene disappearing.'

'It's been fifteen years.' I curl my fingers into fists. 'She hasn't tried to contact me, not once.' I swallow a lump in my throat. 'She hasn't tried to contact any of us – the people who loved her the most.'

Claire's eyes are shiny with tears. She wipes them with one finger and turns her face away. 'Did she ever tell you how we became friends?' She stares into the middle distance. 'I told her my heart was set on becoming a dancer. She said she wanted to be a writer, but she loved dancing too. After that, we went bopping every Friday evening at the disco on the edge of town, letting our inhibitions go, letting the music take us. On the way home, we walked the streets, eating chips out of greasy paper and promising we'd be friends forever.' She glances at me. 'Oh, I'm sorry, Meg. I didn't mean to upset you.'

'No,' I say, blowing my nose. 'Don't apologise. It's a relief to talk about her. Dad doesn't like to.'

'Meg.' She leans forward, clasping my hand, her tone urgent. 'She could still turn up. We need to keep believing.'

I sneeze, the violence of it shaking my body.

'If I ever hear from her, I'll let you know immediately,' she goes on. 'And you'll do the same for me. Right?'

I nod, and we smile at each other, making a silent pact. One I doubt either of us will ever have to honour.

27

While Kit is at nursery, I drive into Ipswich to visit the library. I have a stinking cold. My head is thick, my throat inflamed and sore. I sneeze as I walk through the door to the reception desk, recognising the rows of book stacks and long, scratched tables. Even the elderly men, dozing over the papers in their laps look the same. Mum used to bring me here on rainy days, and we'd spend hours looking at the kids' books, sitting cross-legged on the green carpet.

I approach one of the librarians. Her short grey hair has a blue tinge. Her glasses hang on a plastic chain around her neck. I'm sure she was here when I was a child. 'Excuse me.' I clear my throat. 'How can I look at a back catalogue of old *East Anglian* newspapers?'

'Do you have a library card?' she counters.

I don't. But it only takes ten minutes to fill in a form and register.

'You can access an extensive archive of papers from around the world online,' she says as she takes me over to a large, square computer. She shows me how to set it up. 'Do you know what you're looking for?' She stares over her glasses at me.

'I'm particularly interested in looking at local papers.'

'Well, if you know what you're searching for, do a word search,' she tells me briskly. 'Call me if you need help.' She stalks off towards the front desk, telling a young couple to be quiet as she passes them.

After she's gone, I type in his name. One result comes up:

August 1993: The man rescued from the North Sea close to Bawdsey yesterday has been named as Lucian Aldredge, a local art dealer. He is in hospital with extensive injuries after being hit by a powerboat.

The words blur on the screen, and I blink at them. Claire was right. I reread the last sentence. *Extensive injuries.* Dad told me Lucian had drowned. He didn't mention anything about a powerboat. I shudder, imagining the damage propeller blades would do to a human body.

I feel sick and shaky. My instinct is to get up and leave, but I force myself to search for another piece – there must be an entry to do with his funeral. I put in *Lucian Aldredge, funeral. Lucian Aldredge, death.*

Nothing comes up.

My head is thick, as if it's filled with treacle. It's hard to think. I sit back in the chair, and fumble for my hanky, blowing my nose. I've been left with more questions than answers. I know Lucian is dead – his family certainly think so – and Dad told me he'd died. But why is there no record of it? There must be a mention of it somewhere. I do a wider search, putting in the name of the local village. Several things pop up: village

fêtes, a flood after the river wall breached, a fire in a council
house, and a piece about a missing child.

Suffolk Chronicle
July 1982

A little girl has gone missing from her home in the village of
Charsford. She is ten months old, with light-coloured hair
and blue/grey eyes. She disappeared at approximately
2 p.m. on the afternoon of 12 July. Her single mother, Alison
Greenwood, lives in a caravan at the edge of the village.
She says her child, Haley, was in her pram outside the caravan. Haley's father is out of the picture. 'He didn't even
know I was pregnant,' Alison says. She is desperate to get
her little girl back. When last seen, Haley was wearing a
blue jumper and pink trousers. Locals gathered last night to
search the area. Police say, 'We are increasingly concerned
for Haley's safety, and we are asking anyone with information to contact Ipswich station on this number.'

Alison. She'd been so kind to me. I remember how John
and I had stuffed her posters in the bin when we were children,
and I feel ashamed.

But there's no mention of Lucian's death.

I phone Dad as I leave the library. He answers at once, and I
ask him about Lucian, telling him about the report in the
paper. 'I'm sorry, love,' he says, sounding contrite. 'I didn't want
you to know about the speedboat injuries. You didn't need that
on top of everything else. He was dead, that was all that
mattered.'

'But I can't find a record of his death.'

'Can't you?' He sounds surprised. 'Calista told me he died of his injuries.'

I click off, a sense of unease brushing the nape of my neck like cold fingers.

* * *

On the way back, I notice Mrs Kerry waiting at the bus stop and pull over, winding down my window. 'Shall I drop you in the village or are you going to the Manor?'

'Bless you, I'm off home, dear.'

'I'll drop you on my way to get Kit.'

She settles into the passenger seat and snaps on the seat belt, her bag on her lap. I think about quizzing her about Lucian's funeral. But she'll wonder why I'm interested. It will seem ghoulish and strange.

'That's a nasty cold you've got there,' she says.

'Luckily nobody else seems to have caught it.'

'That's good.' She nods. 'The little ones seem very fond of you now.'

'I'm very fond of them too.'

'It's easy when they're small,' she says, sitting back. 'It's when they grow up it gets hard.'

'But your Mary is doing well, isn't she?' Mrs Kerry has shown me the photos of her daughter, plump and smiling, with her three children. 'Doesn't she live near you?'

'She does,' Mrs Kerry agrees. 'We're close as close can be. Mary's a good girl. It's my youngest I was thinking about.'

'I didn't know you had another child.'

'Another daughter, Karin.'

Then I remember, years ago in the kitchen, Lucian asking

after her daughters and Mrs Kerry proudly telling him that Karin wanted to be a film director.

Mrs Kerry's face clouds. 'She was fine until she was about fifteen. Her grades were good. She had nice friends. Then everything changed. It was after a school trip – she was away about ten days – when she got back, she was different, secretive. She stopped coming down for meals, stayed in her room smoking dope. I found empty spirit bottles hidden under her bed.' She stares through the windscreen. 'There were a lot of rows. Then she left home. Got in with a rough lot. Whenever she came back, it ended badly. She stole from us. When her dad was alive, he banned her from the house.' She clears her throat. 'I think it was the stress that killed him. Now it's just me, I'd have her back in a heartbeat, but she's feral. I never know where she is or what she's doing.'

'I'm so sorry.'

'Yes, well,' she grimaces. 'The last time she turned up at home, she'd been wandering around in the woods in the snow, and she was frozen to the bone. Haven't seen her for a while now. I don't like to dwell on it. I have Mary and the grandkids, only...' She blinks. 'Karin will always be my daughter. Whatever she does. That's blood for you.' She takes out the ubiquitous tube of mints from her handbag and puts one in her mouth as if in a trance. 'I took up smoking when she first went off the rails.'

'I didn't know you smoked.'

'Well, I'd never do it in the house when I was working,' she says, defensively. 'It wouldn't be professional.'

The atmosphere in the car has become awkward. Mrs Kerry stares out of the passenger window, her fingers gripping her bag. I wonder if she's regretting telling me.

We're driving through the village. 'Just here, please.' She

indicates towards a row of terraced houses. She heaves herself out of the car, lugging her shopping bag.

* * *

Ophelia is putting on her coat. 'I'm off for the evening,' she says. 'You don't mind babysitting again, do you?' She kisses both the children on the forehead. 'Be good,' she tells them.

I go to my bedroom to get my tissues and some painkillers – I have a thumping headache. Something slips beneath my foot. A piece of paper has been pushed under my door. I pick it up and unfold it. There's a short message written in wonky capitals:

LEAVE NOW. YOU ARE IN DANGER.

I catch my breath, and reread it, as if I can make the sentences say something different. The words scream at me.

'Margaret,' Artemis says, appearing in my doorway from the landing. 'What's for tea?'

I crumple the note in my fist. 'I don't know,' I tell her. 'You can watch TV while I sort something out.'

She grins and runs downstairs to tell Kit the good news. I leave the kids watching TV in the playroom and go into the kitchen, making their tea on automatic pilot. As the pasta boils, I uncrumple the paper and read the sentence again. Is it serious? A genuine warning, or someone playing a sick joke? Am I getting too close to a truth about Mum and this house? It doesn't feel as if I'm getting close to anything – all I've found is her cardigan. Unless this is about the stolen Polaroid? I stuff the note into my pocket. It's not addressed to anyone – so I don't know if the writer believes I'm Margaret or Meg.

My stomach churns with anxiety. I think of the smell of cigarette smoke in my room, Clem noticing my glasses, Saul finding me in Ophelia's study, my guilt as he'd confronted me, all the drawers open, her things scattered over her desk.

I'd registered as Margaret Danby with my agency, using my mother's surname. I'd wanted a clean start, and using a different name seemed a way to claim a new identity and stake a claim on my mother at the same time. But the agency knows my original name. I'd had to have a police check before I was taken on by them. If someone really wants to discover my identity, the information is available.

But Ophelia is trusting me with her children. If she thought I was dangerous or an imposter, she wouldn't leave me with them, would she? And if either of the other two suspects me, why hasn't she told her sisters?

* * *

My head is pounding. I feel attacked – by a virus, by an unknown watcher, by the house itself. Am I really in danger? After the kids are tucked up in bed, I wedge my chair under my door handle. I take a couple more painkillers, washed down with hot lemon, and crawl into my own bed, exhausted. I'm drifting off to sleep as familiar noises scratch at my consciousness: a soft scuttling sound, like mice behind walls. Then I hear it clearly, the whisper and scrape of feet moving across my ceiling. I sit up, holding my breath, and stare up towards the layer of plaster and wood between me and the unknown walker.

My heart bangs at my ribs. But I'm not frightened. I'm angry. I get out of bed. It's freezing but I don't bother with putting anything else on; I yank the chair away from my door and run up the stairs to the attic. Whoever's in there, switching the light on and off, making noises above my head in the middle of the night – whether they're real or a ghost – I am furious with them.

I bang on the door. 'Are you in there?' I push on the handle and rattle it violently, shoving my shoulder against the wood as hard as I can. 'Did you write the note?' I put my mouth close and hiss, 'If you're in there – why don't you show yourself? I'm not afraid of you.' Shouting provokes a fit of coughing. I bend over, struggling to catch my breath.

The room behind the door is silent. No light shows under it. I kneel, peering through the keyhole. Nothing. And then a flash of white, the glitter of a black pupil boring through me. I fall backwards with an exclamation, banging my knee and elbow, and scramble to my feet.

As I crash down the narrow attic stairs to the landing, Clem comes out of the bathroom. 'Jesus!' She puts a hand to her heart. 'Margaret! You nearly gave me a heart attack! What are you doing running about in the middle of the night?'

I stare at her, unable to speak. She touches my arm. 'You're shaking. What's the matter?'

'A noise woke me.' I press my fingers over my mouth, remembering the eye at the keyhole. 'I heard something,' I say. 'In the attic. Someone's in there.'

She steps closer through the gloom.

'Someone's in there,' I repeat.

'You must have been dreaming.' She's speaking slowly. I make out her features in the moonlight, her suspicious expression. 'The place has been shut up for years.' She sighs. 'I suppose there could be rats running riot in there for all we know.'

'Why doesn't Ophelia open it, then?'

'It was Pa's room,' Clem says. 'It's a bit like asking us to open a grave.' She shivers. 'It was out of bounds when we were kids and Ma wants us to keep it that way.'

'There's something alive up there,' I persist. 'Not rats. A... a person.'

Why will none of the girls believe me? Are they all hiding something? I back away from her, my throat tightening.

'I'll talk to Ophelia tomorrow.' She takes another step closer. 'See if I can persuade her to open the door. She must know where the key is.'

'Alright,' I say, my voice shaky with relief. 'Thank you. Goodnight, then.'

I sense that she's watching me as I go back to my room.

I lie in bed, shivering with cold and shock. My shoulder is bruised where I shoved it against the unforgiving wood; my knee and elbow hurt from landing on them. Did I really see an eye through the keyhole? I groan and press my face into my pillow. But Clem is going to talk to Ophelia. I'll get to look in the attic at last, and the sisters will have to believe me. I can't be imagining it.

28

The next day, after breakfast, Ophelia tells me that she's found the key and she'll open the attic door after I've dropped the kids at school. I drive home full of nervous anticipation. Thea has already gone to her studio, so it's three of us who troop up the steep stairs in single file. Ophelia fits the key in the lock. The door swings open into darkness. Ophelia fumbles around on the inside wall, and flicks on a light.

One bare bulb illuminates a small, empty room. Nothing in it, except a metal container. Shadows seep into corners. I feel an irrational disappointment, followed by relief. Then embarrassment. The girls don't say, *I told you so*, but I feel it anyway.

'No sign of any pests, thank God,' Ophelia says, staring up at the ceiling. 'Or damp.'

I walk around the metal container. It's about three foot by four with a keypad and sealed door. 'Looks like it's made of solid stainless steel.' There's something menacing about it. But maybe that's me being irrational again.

'Pa's art container,' Ophelia says, brushing the top of it with her fingers. 'We watched them carry it up here. Do you remember, Clem?'

Clem nods. 'He was so excited about it. State of the art, he called it.'

I squat in front of it and tug at the door. 'It's locked.'

'Well, there's obviously nothing alive in there,' Ophelia snaps, turning away from the room. 'Shall we go? I have somewhere I need to be.'

'There's nobody up here, Margaret,' Clem says. 'It's easy to mistake the creaks and taps of an old house if you have an active imagination.' She gestures around her. 'The Georgian part is built onto another much older house. There's even a bricked-up staircase somewhere. We tried to find it when we were kids. We were hoping we'd find a skeleton in it.' She gestures towards the front of the house. 'Before the river wall was built, the water came much closer to the house. And this place was used by smugglers.'

'All of that appeals to Clem's vivid imagination,' Ophelia says. 'As for me, I can do without thinking about secret staircases. And I definitely don't want to think about skeletons. Or smugglers.'

I take one last glance at the room before Ophelia flicks off the light and closes the door.

'But there was no art,' I say, as we go down the stairs. 'No paintings.'

'They must be in the container.' Clem is just behind me.

'Don't you want to see inside?' I ask.

'Whatever's in there belongs to Ma,' Clem says.

'She's asked that we keep the attic shut up,' Ophelia says over her shoulder. 'It's not up to us to question her request. While she's alive, this is her house.'

* * *

The next day, with the kids at school and nursery, I drive to Ipswich and park the Fiat. Outside the car, I do my jacket up against the wind. Gulls cry overhead. I glimpse the river over the tops of buildings. It looks uninviting and bleak. I shudder, remembering the time I'd spent clinging to the capsized dinghy, the terror of the water, how it had filled my mouth, weighing me down.

I never understood why he took me out before dawn had broken, when there was more darkness than light. He'd been manic, filled with a frightening, desperate energy. It had been irresponsible not to tell anyone where we were going, not to put us in life jackets. I was just a child. It seems unfair that the Aldredges blame me for the accident. Lucian had been the adult, the sailor. Did he really hold me up in the water after we capsized? I have no memory of it. I should speak to the sisters, explain that I hadn't wanted to go sailing that morning – it had been their father who'd forced me into the boat against my wishes. But I'd have to reveal who I am. And I can't do that until I know who's watching me.

I enter the library, flashing my membership card, and settle at one of the free computers. I open Facebook and my heart leaps when I see that John has accepted my friendship request.

He's written:

How the hell are you?

Our first contact after all these years.
I type back:

I'm okay. How are you?

Really? I couldn't think of anything more interesting? I chew my fingernail, wondering if I should erase it and try again. But my mind is empty of elegant or clever phrases. It will have to do. I'm about to log off when I see three little dots. He's typing back. A thrill of excitement runs through me.

> I'm in market research. Living in SF. I've got my dad over here with me, as he's ill. Where are you?

I reply immediately.

> In Suffolk. I'm working as a nanny at Deben Manor. I'm sorry about your dad.

> Whoa! That's weird. Who lives there now?

> Ophelia. She's married and has two kids.

There's a pause, and I think he's logged off. Then another message comes through.

> I think this deserves a conversation. Can I call you now?

My mouth is dry. I type 'yes'. And then I put in my mobile number.

I switch off the computer and get up. My hands are shaking, palms clammy. I wasn't expecting this. My phone is ringing as I walk past the reception desk. The librarian gives me a severe look.

'Hello?' I say, as I push out of the door into the street.

'Hi!'

God, it's good to hear his voice. A grin takes over my face. My nerves go.

I get in behind the wheel of the Fiat to escape the cold, holding the phone close. He has a faint American accent, and his voice is deeper, a man's voice, but it's unmistakably him.

'I don't understand why Ophelia is living in her parents' house,' he says. 'And you've ended up as her nanny?' He's launched into the conversation as if we saw each other fifteen minutes ago instead of fifteen years.

'Lucian is dead. And Calista lives in France. The house still belongs to the family, and I suppose because Ophelia is the married one with kids, she's living there. Although, a couple of days ago, her husband moved out and the other sisters moved in.'

'Alright,' he says slowly. 'But I don't get the bit about you being nanny to her kids. Why would you want to do that?'

'There's a reason for me taking the job,' I say. 'And they don't know it's me. I'm calling myself by a different name. They haven't recognised me.'

There's silence, and then a low whistle. 'Have you changed that much?'

'I shot up in my teens – grew inches overnight. And I've done something to my hair, bought myself some coloured contact lens.' I feel embarrassed describing the lengths I've gone to disguise myself.

'I'm all ears,' he says. 'What's going on? Why the anonymity? Sounds very cloak and dagger.'

'It's a bit of long story,' I hedge. Then I explain everything.

* * *

He listens without interrupting, but when I tell him about the warning note, he makes an exclamation.

'I don't like the sound of that,' he says. 'And you've no idea who sent it?'

'I didn't know whether to take it seriously,' I say. 'It seems unlikely. The girls aren't criminals. But the noises from the attic are... getting to me.'

I underplay this, not wanting him to know the extent of my unravelling.

'Are you sure you're safe?' he asks. 'I think you should do what the note says, and leave.'

I shake my head, even though he can't see me. 'It must mean there's something to discover, something someone doesn't want me to find. I can't leave until I know what it is.'

'Stubborn,' he says. 'I remember now.'

We both laugh, and it feels good.

'Keep me posted,' he says. 'I mean it. I need to know you're okay.'

'I will,' I say, feeling lighter than I have in weeks. 'By the way, what time is it there?'

'Early,' he says. 'Let's just say, very early. Or very late. Whichever way you want to look at it. You're eight hours ahead.'

'Oh my God! What are you doing up?'

'My dad's not well. I'm often awake with him.'

'I'm sorry about your dad.'

'So am I,' he says. 'But you've been a welcome distraction.' He laughs. 'That didn't come out right! You know what I mean.'

We say goodbye, and I click the phone off. Just to be able to share my experience, to talk to John about what's been happening, has made me feel better, and braver. Even though he's an ocean away, I don't feel alone.

* * *

Two days later, Ophelia takes the children to meet Saul for lunch. Thea is at her studio again, Clem has gone off to see a friend, and Mrs Kerry isn't here. I've tried to forget the attic. But I can't. I think Ophelia left it unlocked yesterday. I could have one more look; I might even find a way to open the metal box. But when I get to the door, it won't budge. Ophelia must have turned the key without me noticing, or she came back and locked it later. I consider searching her room again.

As I turn away, I notice an indentation running down the wall to my right. I squat to examine it more closely, running my fingers over the slight groove, tracing a rectangular-shaped panel. I've never noticed it before because it's so gloomy up here, and it's been painted over with a thick layer of colour, blending with the wall. I wonder what it gives access to; maybe I could get into the eaves, above the attic. I try to lift it away, but it's painted down and screwed on.

Mick Smith doesn't seem to be around today, so I slip out of the back door and hunt through the shed, looking past gardening paraphernalia, cobwebby plant pots and bags of fertiliser, until I find a substantial, rusting metal toolbox sitting on a table cluttered with cans of creosote, gardening tools and old rags. I open it, searching through the trays. As I grab the handle of a useful-looking screwdriver and close the lid, I notice something caught under the edge of the box: a torn scrap of lined paper. It's the same kind I found on the gravel. I frown at it. Is it Mick Smith who's been following me? But how could he possibly know who I really am, or have any interest in me? It doesn't make sense. I tuck it into the pocket of my jeans.

Back in the house, I kneel by the panel and fit the screwdriver into the head of a screw. It takes a while to loosen it. The

screws have obviously not been moved for a long time. I work
the next one free, placing it carefully together with the first on
the floor. I'll have to put them back afterwards. Flakes of paint
come off the heads as I unscrew them. I hope no one will notice
their new brassy glint.

When all four have been removed, the panel doesn't fall out
of its own accord, but needs teasing loose with my fingernails.
It's stuck down with paint. It comes eventually, and I lower it
onto the floor, leaning it against the wall. A dark hole looms
before me, stale and musty. I shine my mini keyring torch
inside. There are some plastic bags in the corner. They give
under my fingers, tacky with dust, bulky with something soft
stuffed inside. The tops are tied with twine.

I take them onto the dark landing and untie them. There
are some clothes in the first one, just old jumble by the looks of
it. I pick out a few items. It's all kids' stuff. I examine a yellowed
Babygro, a moth-eaten shawl, a pair of pink trousers, and a
little blue jumper with a stain on the front. There's a checked
dress, and a pair of scuffed leather shoes.

Perhaps Calista was saving these things for her girls to give
to their children? But Ophelia would never put Kit and Artemis
in anything like this – they seem badly made, mass market
things, and why put them away without washing them first?
Rooting further into the bag, my fingers discover a rustle of
paper. I pull it out and smooth it flat on my knees. It's a cutting
from a newspaper, yellowed around the edges. Using the torch,
I scan the beginning of a short article about Romanian orphan-
ages and remember the story when it broke. The pity and
scandal of it, pictures of babies tied to their cots.

I look in the second bag; it's full of junk as well. A tangle of
jewellery, necklaces and bangles, a hairclip made of fake
tortoiseshell, a couple of scarves. There's an envelope filled

with something soft. I recoil when I reach in. Human hair. Different colours and textures have been secured with pieces of ribbon or elastic bands. I sift through them: blonde, dark, red. Coarse and silky. I realise they must be cuttings from the girls' hair – people take locks of loved one's hair, don't they? Mementos from different ages. Though I can't think why they've been stuffed into an envelope and kept in the dark.

I push the bags and their contents into the hole. I don't like having my back to the attic door. I think I hear a noise and freeze for a moment, heart whirring erratically. I clutch the screwdriver tightly. When the blood stops pounding between my ears, I step through the gap, bending to squeeze through the small space. Surprisingly, once inside, I can stand easily. I feel across the walls, to see if there's another opening. It seems to be a bare, sealed space, until my fingers find a metal structure: a ladder. I squint upwards, shining my torch onto a cobwebby ceiling. There's a trapdoor.

Climbing the rungs, I shove the trapdoor hard, a rain of sooty dust falling into my eyes as it shifts. Pushing the door to the side, I haul myself through the gap. I'm right under the roof. The sloping sides are so low I'm forced to crawl but still bang my head a couple of times on struts. Above me, chinks of light come in where tiles have been dislodged. I scramble along, fingers and knees pressing into old dust and mouse droppings on the narrow joists. I stop to shine the torch around – it must be as wide as the house up here – I'm directly over the attic room. The space is empty, apart from some boxes piled in the far corner, and what look like a couple of old suitcases. Between the narrow wooden joists there's a layer of insulation: a thick, yellowy material.

I hear a furtive scurrying movement and shine the torch towards the sound; two green eyes blaze at me and then disap-

pear. A squirrel, or a rat. I shuffle slowly in the direction of the
eyes. Next to the joist, some of the yellowy substance has been
torn up. Perhaps the noises in the attic had been squirrels or
rats all along? I shove my hand into the torn-up remains,
pushing and scraping with my fingers. There's hardboard
underneath. A chink of light shines up between one piece of
board and the next. I push my fingers into the crack and press
hard, working some plaster free, making a tiny hole.

I lean down, putting my eye as close to the gap as I can, and
squint through.

Someone stares back at me. I gasp, nearly losing my
balance, and swing my torso upright, banging my skull on a
roof strut. I'm shivering with shock. Impossible. My heart
crashes against my ribs as I lean down again, forcing myself to
look through the gap. She's still there, her features calm and
composed. Calista.

She's not real. It's a painted impression of her. I try to see
more, but the tiny gap doesn't allow me to look beyond my
restricted view. I wish I'd brought the screwdriver with me; I
might have been able to use it to enlarge the hole. But I worry
that I've already been up here for too long. I shuffle backwards
the way I came, along the network of joists.

I'm dropping through the trapdoor, into the space behind
the panel, when I hear the distant slam of the front door
closing.

I scramble out, putting the panel back with shaking fingers.
I've managed to replace two screws when I hear Clem's voice
calling me. I slip the other two screws and the screwdriver into
my back pocket, and then saunter down the main stairs, hoping
my face isn't as flushed as it feels.

'Oh, there you are,' she says, taking off her boots in the hall.
'What have you been up to?'

'Reading in my room,' I say.

'Well, I should think Ophelia and the kids will be back soon, so prepare yourself for the onslaught.' She takes a closer look at me and leans forward, picking something out of my hair. It's a clump of dusty cobwebs. She gives me a questioning look. 'Looks like Mrs Kerry has been skimping on the dusting?' She arches an eyebrow.

I'm stuck for an answer. No excuse occurs to me. But luckily there's the sound of car wheels in the drive, the slam of a door. Artemis bursts in, her cheeks pink with cold and excitement. 'We saw Daddy,' she exclaims. 'We had ice cream.'

Relieved by the interruption, I lean down to help her off with her coat, but she shies away from me. 'Yuk! Your hands are all dirty.' She makes a face.

My palms are black with sooty dust. I wipe them over my jeans and glance around. Clem is walking away towards the kitchen, and Ophelia has just entered, shutting the door behind her with her foot, Kit clamped to her hip.

'God, you're too heavy to be carried now,' she says, unloading him. 'You're not a baby.' She looks at me. 'Can you take over? I've got to change and go out again.'

She's already halfway up the stairs, as I take Kit's hand. He doesn't complain about the dirt, and chatters on about something else. I've stopped listening. There's another part to the attic, another room. But where's the entrance? I wonder if there's a secret door in the first room, and if the girls knew about it all the time. I recall Clem's comment about a bricked-up staircase.

Seeing Calista's portrait in the attic has reminded me of the Oscar Wilde story: a portrait in an attic growing old and ugly, while its cruel subject stays young and beautiful.

29

The warning note replays in my head. I can't trust any of the girls. At least one of them is lying. Clem is suspicious of me. She's been in my room, so she could be the one who's following me, spying on me. When I wake in the early dawn hours with a full bladder, I stumble out of bed into an arctic atmosphere to go to the bathroom. There's a folded paper pushed under my door. I stare down at it. Not again. Shivering, I reach to pick it up. It's the same wonky writing in capitals, black ink smudged.

LEAVE – OR REGRET IT

I fling the note away from me with a shudder. It flutters onto the unmade bed. I wrench my door open, looking along the landing, hoping to catch someone disappearing into their room. All the doors are closed. The house is quiet.

I lock myself in the bathroom to have a shower. Under a blast of hot water, I try to clear my head. I can't go on like this. I'm going to confront Ophelia, tell her who I am and show her the notes.

When I get back to my room, the folded paper has gone. I look under the bed, in the wastepaper bin. It's as if it never existed. I open my drawer to look for the other note and the paper with the dates and times. I can't find them. I scoop out the contents of the drawer and throw them on the floor in a tangle of underwear and socks. On my knees, I search through the mess, then stand and run my fingers around the empty space of the drawer. I force myself to take deep breaths. I must believe myself. I am not mad. Someone is trying to make me think I am.

If I confront Ophelia with no proof, she'll deny it. And if she's not behind this, she won't believe me anyway, or she'll say she doesn't – just like she doesn't believe I've heard someone in the attic. I sink onto the floor and bury my face in my hands. I remember the scrap of torn paper I'd found under the toolbox. It's still in my back pocket and I take it out and smooth it between my fingers. It helps to centre me, to know I really did find it, but it won't prove anything to Ophelia – it's just a blank scrap.

I haven't slept properly since I started the job. I jump at every sound. My panic attacks had started after the accident. It was as if black holes opened under my feet. A sudden terror would freeze me into immobility, my heart thrashing and sweat prickling my forehead. I never knew when it was going to happen. It took years before they gradually stopped. I don't want them to start again, and I'm afraid they will if I stay at Deben Manor. My head tells me to pack up and hand in my notice. But my heart says, stay. There's something missing from my memory of that summer, and if I leave, I'll never have the whole picture.

* * *

Ophelia is out, Thea is at the studio and Clem went off last night to stay over at her friend's in London, as she has an audition first thing this morning. I get on with my normal duties, giving the kids breakfast, taking Artemis to school. I try to stay calm for the kids' sake as well as my own, but I'm all butter fingers, breaking a glass, burning the sausages, and dropping the car keys on the gravel. Even Artemis notices. 'Whoops a daisy,' she tells me, when I trip over my own feet on the way into the playground. Outside the school gates, the mum whose son is friends with Kit waves to me. 'Would Kit like to come for a play date after lunch?' she asks. 'Archie is much happier with a friend over. You'll be doing me a favour.'

'Actually,' I say, 'it's our turn to have Archie.'

She shakes her head regretfully. 'Archie is terribly allergic to several things. Peanuts and sesame for starters. I never let him have play dates in other people's houses.'

I nod, feeling bad about Archie's allergies, but relieved. 'Okay, thanks. I'll drop Kit at yours at about two o'clock, then.'

'Perfect,' she says, and then pauses. 'Are you alright? You look at bit... frazzled?'

I touch my hair, as if the cobwebs are still there.

* * *

At home, I'm peeling potatoes for lunch. It's not a nursery morning, and Kit plays with his cars on the kitchen table. Clem comes in and slumps down next to Kit. I didn't know she was home. I thought she was in London.

'Suppose it's too early for a proper drink,' she says, rolling her eyes.

I flip an egg over, the fat spitting. 'Is everything okay?'

'My audition was a nightmare,' she says. 'I was the first one they saw and they gave me about five minutes. All that travelling for nothing. I don't even know why I'm in this stupid business. It's like a form of torture, constant rejection followed by hope followed by rejection.'

'Shall I make you a cup of tea?' I ask.

'How very British of you.' She gives a snort of laughter. 'A nice cup of tea. Our answer to every problem.'

'I'll take that as a yes, then.' I take out a mug and switch the kettle on. 'When did you get back?' Could it have been Clem who left the note and then disposed of it when I was in the shower, along with the other pieces of proof? Maybe she's lying about when she got back from London. Her car has been in the drive all this time. 'Did you get a taxi from the station?' I ask.

'Do you have a boyfriend, Margaret?'

I look at her out of the corner of my eye. She hasn't answered my questions and now she's changing the subject. 'No,' I say. 'No time.'

'I guess the only men you meet are husbands and fathers,' she says. 'And they're all off limits.'

I place her cup of tea in front of her.

'We didn't have au pairs or nannies when we were kids,' she goes on. 'Our mother wasn't exactly hands-on, so we looked after ourselves. But Pa was a remarkable man,' she says. 'Everyone loved him. He was more than a successful art dealer. He helped people. Like our gardener, Mick.'

'How did he help him?'

'Mick needed a job when he came out of prison.' She sees my expression. 'I'm sure he wasn't in for anything violent,' she says quickly. 'But the point is, Pa gave him a job. Gave him a chance. He's been working for us for years.'

I'm poised to ask her another question about Mick, when Ophelia breezes in, trailing a hint of something musky, a whiff of basil. She's in a whirl as usual, dumping her handbag and phone on the table, shrugging off her coat. 'Dying for a pee,' she says, kissing Kit's head, and disappearing in the direction of the downstairs loo.

'Ophelia,' I call after her. 'Can we talk?'

'Not now,' she calls back. 'I need a shower.'

I cut up the eggs and put them on a plate with some mashed potatoes and peas for Kit. Clem leans over and picks up his fork to scrape up some potato from his plate and puts it in her mouth. 'Yum,' she says, making her eyes round. He laughs. Although if she takes any more, he won't think it's funny. Kit is possessive about his food. Then I notice that she only pretended to eat it and has slipped it back into his bowl. Of course. Not only do potatoes never pass her lips, she's also an actress. Faking it is natural to her.

She stands up. 'Right, I need to call my agent,' she says.

As she disappears, I hear the downstairs loo flush, a door opening and closing. Ophelia's mobile starts to vibrate on the table, ringing with the salsa tune. 'Grab my phone, will you?' she calls.

I pick it up. My glance sweeps the screen. The caller's name is PA. I hear Ophelia's footsteps returning.

The letters are in capitals and for a millisecond it doesn't register, and then it does. I nearly drop the phone, somehow managing to hand it to her as she comes in through the door. She answers, giving me a questioning glance. The shock must still be on my face. She's turned away, talking with her hand furtively cupped over the speaker as she leaves the room.

I stare unseeingly at the kitchen wall. Pa? Nobody I knew called their dad by that name except the girls. The room swims. I clasp my shaking fingers and squeeze. Get a grip, I tell myself.

I'm seeing things, hearing things that don't exist. Lucian is dead.

As soon as I'm alone, I text John.

MEG

> I got another anonymous note. Then Ophelia got a call and the caller ID came up as Pa.

JOHN

> Pa??

> As in their father? And another note?

> Go to the police. Show them the notes.

MEG

> I can't. Someone took them.

There's a pause, and I bite my lip, staring at my screen.

JOHN

> Get out of there fast.

His words leap at me from my screen, and it's as if I can hear his urgent voice in my head.

I am shaken by his vehemence.

MEG

> Alright. I'll hand in my notice.

JOHN

> Good! Now!

What I feel as I click the phone off, is relief. He's made the decision for me. It's over.

30

I feel almost cheerful as I pick Kit up from his friend's house and drive him back to Deben Manor. Thea collected Artemis from school, and is giving her tea at her studio, so it's just me and Kit this afternoon, which makes it easier.

Kit chats away from the back seat, and I make listening noises, but my mind is elsewhere. I've been trying to block out the sense of menace that surrounds me as soon as I set foot in the house. I've been kidding myself that this experience isn't damaging to my mental health, or that it could even be physically dangerous, insisting that I can handle it alone. It's a relief to acknowledge I can't. I want the nightmares to stop. I can't stand another night of hearing those footsteps treading softly across my ceiling – and I'm sick of suspecting everyone around me, anticipating being followed, thinking someone is watching my every move.

As I park the car, the sun is setting behind black silhouettes of trees. Rain begins to fall, a soft patter on the gravel and car bonnet. It's gloomy in the hall, as I help Kit off with his boots and coat before taking off my own. As we go through towards the kitchen, Lucian rears out of the shadows. For a second, I'd forgotten about the portrait. I step back, adrenaline thundering through my body. *Get out of there fast.* John's words repeat in my head. *Or regret it.* The last sentence in the note.

The rain splatters against the French windows; outside the sky has turned to night. I thought Lucian was dead. But now, I don't know. With no record of a funeral, could he be alive? I clench my hands. It can't be him, walking about in the attic, a disfigured horror caricature, hiding from the world, angry and resentful. Jesus. I try to laugh at myself. I'm not in a gothic novel.

Kit has wandered in to find me. He grabs the ball of my fist, unpeeling my fingers, one by one as if it's a game. Then he slips his hand inside mine.

I crouch down and pull him in for a hug, needing the solid certainty of his small body with its unequivocal earthy demands. I hold onto him as if he's an anchor that will stop my mind spiralling into madness. He struggles away from me, demanding, 'Sausages?'

We go into the kitchen, and I press the light switch, flooding the room with brilliance. Everything is revealed as ordinary and prosaic – clean surfaces, bottles of virgin olive oil, dried herbs and rustic ceramic bowls brought back from holidays – rain battering the glass, making the room feel safe and cosy. The fridge hums in the corner. I take out sausages and carrots and begin to prepare Kit's supper, but my chest is tight.

I sit at the table. Kit pushes his little metal cars across the surface, happily making *brroom brroom* noises. I must pull myself together. The sausages are burnt, the carrots under-done, but Kit doesn't mind, and eats his tea while running his small cars in and out of his bowl, through his food. I don't stop him or wipe his hands. I just need to get him into bed, then I can pack my case. I'll tell Ophelia I have to leave at once. Family emergency.

I help Kit down from his booster seat, his sticky fingers leaving greasy marks on my top. 'Time for a quick bath before bed,' I tell him.

He holds my hand to go upstairs. As I run the bath, checking the temperature, I feel a pang of guilt. I'll be abandoning the children. None of this is their fault.

Just as Kit is falling asleep, Artemis comes in, bouncing onto the bed, waking Kit, full of the excitement of an afternoon with her aunt. Thea stands in the doorway. 'She can go straight to bed,' she says, helpfully. 'I wouldn't bother with a bath or anything.'

She calls to Artemis, 'We had a cool girls' time, right?' She bends down, holding her hand up for Artemis to give her a high five.

Thea leaves, muttering something about getting a drink. Kit starts to whimper. It takes me half an hour to get him back to sleep, and persuade a fractious, overstimulated Artemis to get into her pyjamas and clean her teeth.

* * *

Downstairs, Thea is in the kitchen making an omelette, a glass of red wine on the side. It's such a normal, homely scene. I begin to doubt myself again. Do I need to run away? Am I being paranoid?

'Want some?' she gestures to the frying pan and the bottle.

I nod, too tired to think of making myself food.

'Guess what? Clem got a call back,' she grins at me over her shoulder. 'Just when she thought the audition had been a disaster. She's gone tearing off back to London.'

'That's good,' I say. 'I hope she gets it.'

We sit at the table together, and I take a gulp of wine. The omelette is good, perfectly cheesy.

'Pa taught me how to make a decent omelette,' she says. 'It's the only thing he could cook. I'm the same.' She picks up her glass. 'Life's too bloody short for boring tasks.' She gives me a long, assessing look. 'What's up with you?'

'Nothing.'

'Come on,' she says. 'You seem... depressed... I don't know... not yourself.'

'I'm going to hand my notice in,' I blurt, the relief of saying it making the tension in my spine release. 'I haven't told Ophelia yet. She's never around to talk to. But I will. Soon as I can.'

'Not you as well.' She gives her head a little shake. 'I thought you were different from the others. Don't tell me it's the noises in the attic that are driving you away?' She stares at me. 'You saw inside it. There's nothing there.'

'No,' I tell her. 'It's just... a family emergency has come up. My dad. He needs me.' It's a lie, kind of, but the best excuse I can think of. Dad does need me. 'Please don't say anything to Ophelia,' I add. 'I should be the one to tell her.'

She pours us both more wine. 'I think you're making a mistake. But I won't say anything to her. She'll be devastated, of course. She thinks you're great.'

Thea is the only sister who's really opened up to me. She's the one I trust the most. I shift in my chair, uncomfortably. 'How's the fashion show and your collection coming along?'

'Not good,' she says, toying with a forkful of omelette. 'I've run into an unexpected problem. The collection is finished, but a couple of my models have come down with flu, and it's not as if I can get hold of replacements at short notice. This isn't London.'

'I'm sorry,' I say, only half listening.

'Actually, you could help me out,' she says, leaning forward. 'Remember what I said the other day?'

'Sorry?' I gaze at her blankly.

'You could be one of my models,' she says. 'I'd pay you.'

'Oh,' I sit back in my chair. 'No. No, sorry. I couldn't.' The last thing I want to do is walk down a catwalk with strangers staring at me. All I want to do is to pack my bags and leave.

'Please, Margaret,' Thea blinks. 'I really need you.'

'I wouldn't know what to do,' I say, aware that I'm weakening. 'I'd probably be hopeless.'

'Nonsense,' she says briskly. 'All you need to do is walk to the end of the catwalk, pause, turn, and walk back. Anyone could do it.'

I put my fork down. Thea has the same talent as her father for making people want to please her, for making it impossible to say no. I know she won't stop until she's got her own way. And I do want to help her. I don't think she's my watcher – she's too busy with her business for a start. 'Alright.'

She claps her hands together. 'Fantastic. You've saved me. I'll need you to pop into my studio the day after tomorrow for a quick fitting. You can come after you've finished up here. The show is the following day.'

My stomach drops. 'So soon?'

Thea is regarding me through assessing eyes. 'Looks like you're almost the same size as one of the girls who's sick – so hopefully, I won't even need to do alterations. But we'll need to do the fitting to be certain.' She yawns. 'I'm exhausted. We both need some sleep before the weekend.'

I'll tell Ophelia I'm leaving on Saturday, straight after the show. I know I'm supposed to work out some notice, but I'll stick to my story of an emergency. Now that I've made the decision, I can't think why I didn't do this weeks ago.

* * *

As I'm getting ready for bed, I hear Ophelia come in. It's too late to talk to her now. My phone beeps. There's a message from John.

> JOHN
>
> Dad died today. I need to speak to you urgently. Text me when you are out of the house and can speak tomorrow. Doesn't matter what time.

I text back:

> MEG
>
> I'm so sorry about your dad. I could talk now?

> JOHN
>
> Can't. Got to deal with funeral director etc.

> MEG
>
> OK. I'll text you tomorrow soon as I can talk.

> JOHN
>
> Good. Hope you've handed in your notice.

> MEG
>
> Doing it tomorrow.

My body relaxes, knowing he's thinking of me, even after his father has died. I fall asleep with the chair wedged under my door and my mobile in my hand.

31

The next day, Ophelia is in the kitchen, slumped at the table sipping a coffee, her dressing gown gaping open, mascara smudged under her eyes. 'Hi,' she murmurs. 'Want a coffee?'

I wonder what time she got in last night, from her dishevelled appearance, I'm guessing the early hours. I only have a few minutes before I need to get the children ready for breakfast; I clear my throat. 'Ophelia,' I say. 'I need to talk to you.'

She glances up, her expression wary. 'Uh oh.'

'I'm afraid I need to hand my notice in,' I say quickly. 'Something has come up. A family matter.'

'No!' she cries, sitting up straight. 'Can't you deal with your... family matter and then come back? I can't lose you.'

I shake my head. 'Sorry. I couldn't agree to that. I have no idea how long it will take to sort things out at home.'

'It's not something we've done, is it?' She looks anxious. 'The kids love you. You make my life so much easier. God,' she exclaims. 'I can't face trying to find another nanny.'

'I'm sorry,' I repeat, feeling the familiar tug of guilt.

'Is there nothing I can do to persuade you to stay?' she gives me an appealing look. 'Money? More days off?'

'I'm really sorry.' I take a step back. 'There's nothing you can do. I'm afraid I'll be leaving on Saturday.'

'What about working out your notice?' She's frowning, her shoulders set. 'There's a contract.'

'I can't,' I tell her. 'I'm sure my agency will be able to find you an emergency replacement.' I glance towards the door. 'I'm sorry,' I repeat. I'm wearing the word out. I turn towards the door. 'I'm going to get the children ready.'

'Well, you can break it to them, then!' she calls out after me, her voice sharp with bitterness.

My guilt disappears. It's not as if you have a job, I fume to myself. You could just look after your own kids for a change. The thought strengthens my resolve, and I stride through the hall. In my room, I gaze up at my ceiling. 'You've won,' I say aloud. 'Whoever you are, I'm leaving. So, you can stop with the noises and the notes and things going bump in the night.'

* * *

I do the school drop with a grumpy Kit strapped in his car seat. It's not a morning for his nursery. He's asleep in his car seat as I begin the drive home. I pull over into a parking spot next to the woods and get out of the car, texting John to call now.

He rings immediately, even though it must be some awful-o'clock in the morning. I huddle into my coat, leaning against the side of the car. 'I'm so sorry about your dad.'

'Thanks. I knew it was imminent, but I suppose nothing really prepares you for it.' He sounds tired, his voice husky.

'You should be asleep, not talking on the phone.'

'I can't sleep. Not after what Dad told me.'

'Is that the something urgent?'

'Yeah.' He pauses. 'He told me—' his voice falters. 'It's... unbelievable. I need to tell you. You're the only one who'll understand.'

I hear the crackle of distance spinning between us and hold my mobile closer. 'What?' I prompt.

'Lucian was my father.' He pauses. 'Lucian Aldredge was my real father.'

'What?' I repeat, unable to process what he's telling me.

'Mum confessed to Dad that she'd had an affair with Lucian and got pregnant.' His voice is tight. 'When she'd told Lucian, he'd denied he was the father and ended their relationship. At the time, we were living in the village and Dad was working at Deben Manor as the gardener.' He clears his throat. 'She told Dad the strain of the lie was too much. She couldn't carry on pretending that I was his when I was really Lucian's. Dad confronted Lucian. But Lucian didn't blink an eye, said Mum was lying. Then he sacked Dad. My mother killed herself six months later.'

'My God.'

'It makes sense now,' he says in a dull voice. 'My parents didn't have any more children. They'd been trying for kids without any luck when she got pregnant with me.' I hear him swallow. 'It's so fucked up.'

'I'm sorry,' I say quietly.

'I asked Dad why he didn't demand a paternity test, kick up a fuss,' John goes on, his words wrung tight. 'He said he thought of me as his son. Always had, always would. Anyway, he didn't have any fight in him after Mum died. He said his main fear was that Lucian would come to claim me.'

'But he never did?'

John gives a short laugh. 'I get the feeling Lucian preferred daughters. A son would be too much like competition.'

I consider his words and realise he's right. For Lucian, his girls were a kind of extension of himself. Stars around his universe.

'Lucian seduced her before he bought Deben Manor. So, he offered Dad the job while he was sleeping with his wife.' John's voice is a growl. 'He must have got some weird kick out of that. When she told him she was pregnant, he twisted it around, said she'd been the one to come on to him and had tried to trap him by getting pregnant. He said he'd ruin her reputation if she didn't keep quiet.'

'Your poor mum. Lucian had incredible charisma, and if he wanted something, he didn't stop until he got it.' I wish I was with John. Wish I could put my arms around him. 'What was she like? Do you look like her?'

'I'll send you a picture on Facebook.'

I bend down, checking through the car window that Kit is still asleep in his seat. His cheeks are flushed, his thumb moving in his mouth.

John clears his throat. 'You know, after you left, I went back to the summer house several times. I thought you might come. I thought you might leave me a note.'

'I felt bad about leaving like that,' I say. 'I was taken straight to hospital after the accident. Then Dad wouldn't let me go back to Deben Manor. I didn't have any way of contacting you.'

'I understand,' he says quietly.

'I was ill for a couple of years afterwards. Panic attacks. Couldn't sleep. The doctors put me on anti-anxiety medication.'

'I'm sorry,' he says. 'You went through a lot. With your mum disappearing. And then the sailing accident.'

I swallow. 'What are you going to do?' I ask, thinking of the girls. 'You have three sisters – half-sisters. Are you going to tell them?'

'I don't know,' he says. 'I've got to deal with the funeral and paperwork. I can't get away yet. I need to think about it.'

'Okay. I'm here if you need to talk.'

'Thanks.' He pauses. 'Did you hand in your notice?'

'I'm leaving in a couple of days.'

'Why not immediately?'

'I've promised Thea I'll model in her show.' I clear my throat, embarrassed. 'Seems I'm the right size for the clothes.'

'You don't owe her anything – one of them is behind all this.'

'But I think it's Clem,' I say. 'Only I have no proof. I'm sure it's not Thea and I don't want to let her down. It gives Ophelia a chance to find a replacement for me, too. I'll leave straight afterwards.'

'I wish you were leaving right away,' he's saying, as I bend down to look through the misty window again. Kit is stirring in his car seat.

'I have to go,' I say. 'Kit's awake.'

'Take care,' he says.

I click the phone off and shove it into my pocket, blowing on my freezing fingers.

* * *

At home, I give in to Kit's demands for a video and stick a Disney tape in the machine in the playroom. He slumps against me, thumb in his mouth, as he watches Dumbo fly for the millionth time.

I remember that John said he'd send a photo of his mother

and sneak into Ophelia's study and put in the password. He's sent me a colour photo of a woman with dark hair and violet eyes. I'm trying to think where I've seen her face before. She seems familiar. I shut the computer down quickly before someone finds me using it.

'Margaret?' Ophelia's voice.

Closing the study door behind me, I step into the kitchen as she appears in the doorway. 'I'm going out this evening,' she says. 'I won't be back until morning. Clem's still in London and Thea will be at her studio all night.' She gives me a stern look. 'I'm trusting you with the kids until tomorrow.'

* * *

In the afternoon, I take Kit into the garden. The ground is muddy with all the rain we've had, and there's a brisk wind, but we both need fresh air. 'Kit,' I tell him, as we wander around under the beech trees. 'I'm going away. Soon you'll have a new nanny.'

'Why?' he asks, eyes round.

I don't want to lie to him. I think of something he'll understand. 'I don't sleep very well here,' I tell him, as we walk past the shrubbery towards the summer house.

'Do you have nightmares too?' he asks, looking up at me.

I nod. 'Yes.'

'The bad man?' His mouth quivers. He glances over his shoulder towards the house. 'He lives in our attic.' His words turn my spine to ice. I can't speak for a moment.

I sit down hard on a damp, fallen tree trunk. My legs are shaking. I don't want him to see my reaction, so I turn my head away while I try to collect myself. I'm torn between reassuring him and asking him questions. Lots of children think monsters or bad men are hiding under their beds or in cupboards, it's perfectly normal. A fearful fantasy. But the fact that his fear is the same as mine is too much of a coincidence. Kit's bedroom is also below the attic. I glance up at the house, visible above the top of the shrubbery. Blank windows flash in the brief winter sunshine.

'Don't worry about it. Nobody will hurt you,' I tell him. 'You're safe in your bed. In your house.'

Kit looks unconvinced, eyes wide, mouth strained.

There's a loud miaow, and Fred weaves through the grass to see us, pushing his bony head into my hand. Kit is afraid at first, then he wants to pet him, and I show him how to be gentle, explaining that he's almost wild. Fred. Another unresolved problem. When I leave, who will look after him?

There's something in the longer grass. As Kit strokes the cat, I reach through damp fronds to pick it up. It's hard and smooth in my hands. An empty vodka bottle, the glass glittering with fat raindrops.

32

After collecting Artemis from school, I take the kids back to Deben Manor in the Fiat. The other cars have gone from the drive. In the house, I find a note in the kitchen on the side. *I'm off now. Thea's left too. See you tomorrow. O.*

I get the children into bed, feeling sad that this is one of the last times I'll do the bedtime routine with them. I kiss them both goodnight, and go to my room, shutting the door. I pull my case from under the bed and open it, packing my things quickly, throwing clothes and books and shoes in and forcing the zip to close.

Restless and anxious, but with the rest of the evening to kill, I sit cross-legged on the sofa and spend an hour watching TV in the living room. My mind wanders from the programme. I flick through the other channels and switch it off. In the sudden silence, I'm aware of night pressing at the windows and get up to draw the curtains.

I think of Kit's worried face. *He lives in our attic.*

As I move through the hall towards the kitchen, the house feels bigger. Shadows jump in the corners. I check on the children. They are fast asleep. I didn't have a chance to feed Fred earlier. Remembering the empty vodka bottle, the last thing I want to do is venture out into the dark garden, but I can't leave him hungry in this weather. It'll only take five minutes. The bottle could have been lying in the grass for years. I grab my coat and set off for the summer house, my keyring torch clutched in my hand. As I walk across the lawn, I'm aware of a rustle in the bushes near me and my heart bangs against my ribs. I shine the torch around in swinging arcs, the pinprick light almost useless, showing tiny sections of leaves and branches. Stop it, I tell myself. You're scaring yourself. There's nothing there. Just a shadow, nothing more. But as I round the shrubbery, something human sized moves near the summer house, a figure slipping behind the building.

My instinct says run, but someone has been watching me, stealing from me, sending me threatening notes – this could be my only chance to find out who. I move softly around the side of the summer house, shining the beam before me. Its tiny light picks out two feet in boots, two legs. I stumble back, swallowing a cry of fear. As I raise the torch with shaking fingers, it blinks and goes out.

I try the switch again. It's dead. My heart leaps in my chest. 'Clem?' I force myself to say. 'Is that you?'

I squeeze the useless torch, my fingers welded tight around it. It can't be Clem. She's in London. The intruder doesn't move. I can hear them breathing. I think of Mick and his wall eye. I begin to back away.

'I know you're there,' I add, hoping it will make me sound brave. But my quivering voice gives me away. 'I've already called the police,' I lie.

A figure steps forward into the moonlight. Waxen skin glows in fragments, broken with jagged segments of darkness; a face stares at me from under a hood, a glint of silver at their throat. Her eyes are dark hollows. 'You,' I whisper. I can't move.

The homeless woman disappears into inky nothingness. I spin round and bolt back to the house, pushing past the shrubbery, stumbling over the muddy lawn. My breath is ragged, my chest tight. I imagine her behind me and run faster. I catch my elbow on the wall of the house in a painful scrape as I crash up against the front door, fumbling with the key. I skid into the hall, slam the door and turn the key in the lock.

My heart reels in my chest. Who is she – and why is she in the garden? What does she want from me? Trembling, I look out of the sitting room window, but there's no sign of her. She could be behind a tree or bush. She'll be invisible in the night. I walk around the house checking doors and windows, drawing every curtain. Everything is locked. She can't get in.

I wedge my chair under my door handle. As I lie in bed, I remember the ghost story about the man who bolts the door and window of his room and then a little voice from behind the curtain says, now we're locked in together. Something like that. I shiver. The person outside isn't a ghost. She's a sad woman, probably with a tragic past. But that doesn't explain why she's here, outside the house. Why she's watching me. Only... she can't be the person who left me the note, who planted the diamonds in my drawer and looked through my stuff. She's never been inside Deben Manor.

I am standing by my window. Below me, the shed and outhouses crouch in darkness. All my senses prickle. The night seethes with menace. It's not just one woman out there, more figures emerge from behind trees and buildings, coming towards the house, creeping, crawling on hands and knees. Oily dread fills me, but I can't move, can't cry out. Their eyes shine white and wet through the liquid air. Something bangs sharp and loud below me, and I know the back door has been forced open, slamming on its hinges. They're here. They've crossed the threshold. They're coming for me.

I wake, panting. A nightmare. I pull the covers over my head and lie in the dark, listening. Can I hear footsteps above me? I imagine the woman from the garden up there. Imagine her lying on the floor, her ear to the boards, listening to the sound of my frightened breathing below.

The house is locked up. She can't get in. Calm down.

I sit on the edge of the bed, pushing my fists into my eye sockets. I want to leave now, run away. But I'm responsible for the children. They're asleep in their beds, and I'm the only adult in the house. I pace my room. Are the children safe? I peer out of my window. Moonlight picks out the edges of the shed, the dustbins, and the trees beyond, pointed shapes etched against the sky.

I pull on my clothes, then search the room for a potential weapon. The best I can come up with is an empty vase. I take it from the chest of drawers and put it next to the bed. As quietly as possible, I remove the chair back from under my door handle and open the door a crack. My ears strain, listening for feet descending the attic stairs, the creak and groan of floorboards on the landing. The attic door opening. Nothing.

I hurry down the landing into Kit's room and sit on his bed, gathering him into my arms. 'Shhhhh,' I murmur into his hair. 'I'm going to take you to my room.'

He mutters and wraps his arms around my neck as I lift him up and carry him back along the landing. I tuck him into my bed, and then return for Artemis.

'What are you doing?' she protests when I try and lift her. 'Go 'way, Margaret. I'm asleep.'

'I'm taking you to my room,' I whisper. 'Hush. Go back to sleep.'

She's heavier than she looks. I stagger along the landing with her and tuck her up next to her brother. She complains in a drowsy voice and then nuzzles against him. They curl up together. Babes in the wood. I shove the back of my chair under the door handle again. I feel better, knowing the three of us are barricaded in.

There's no room for me in the bed. I take the spare blanket from the end and wrap myself in it, sitting on the floor, with my back to the chest of drawers, mobile in hand, and the vase nearby, just in case. I watch the door through the gloom, and the gradual lightening of dawn, my gaze fixed on the handle. I text John, telling him about the homeless woman and that I've barricaded myself into my room with the children. I feel better for sending the text, even if he's thousands of miles away. He texts back:

JOHN

Stay strong. Call the police if you hear her in the house.

I force myself to stay awake, pinching myself when my head droops. The gleam of sunlight grows brighter, shining blood red through the curtains, picking out objects in the room, the shapes of the sleeping children. Birds are singing, and rooks cry from the beech trees.

Thank God, it's morning. I get up off the floor, stiff and cold, and bend over the children. Kit murmurs and opens his eyes wide, surprised to see me. Artemis sits up, rubbing her eyes. 'Why are we in your bed?' she demands.

I don't want to frighten them. I consider telling her it's a game. But she's too sharp to fall for that.

'Kit had a nightmare,' I say.

She sighs and shakes her head. 'Such a baby.'

'Anyone can have a nightmare, Artemis,' I tell her.

'But I didn't. Did I?' She frowns. 'Why did you move me?'

'No,' I admit. 'You were fine. But I thought it would be nice for Kit to have his big sister with him.'

She looks pleased with this line of reasoning, then her eyes fall on my suitcase. 'I don't want you to leave, Margaret.' She sticks her bottom lip out. 'I don't want you to go.' She's revving up for a full-blown tantrum.

'Shall we get dressed and see if Mummy's home yet?' I say quickly. 'Maybe we could find clothes from the dressing up basket. What should you wear today? A cloak? A pair of riding boots? A golden crown?'

'Silly,' she laughs. 'I have to wear my school uniform.'

A squeaking noise makes me startle. The handle is turning to and fro. It's still wedged shut. The edge of the doorknob rattles against the chair. I pull the children to me, as the door bangs against the blockade with angry insistence.

'Who's there?' I manage, thinking of the homeless woman. Her desperate face. I tighten my grip on the children who wriggle in protest.

'Open this door!' Ophelia's voice.

I scramble up off the floor and remove the chair. She strides in, scowling. 'What on earth are you doing? Why are the children locked in here with you?' She puts her hands on her hips. 'I've been looking for them.'

'We slept here, Mummy,' Artemis pipes up. 'In Margaret's bed.'

Ophelia's eyebrows shoot up. She gives me a questioning glare.

'I just wanted to keep them safe,' I say.

'Safe from what?' Ophelia snaps.

'It was because of Kit's nightmare,' Artemis adds.

Ophelia's face relaxes. 'I see.' She holds out her hand to her daughter. 'Well, now I'm home. Let's go and get dressed in your room, sweet pea.'

Artemis beams and grasps her mother's hand. 'You sort Kit out,' Ophelia says over her shoulder to me. 'We'll talk about this later.' She adds in a hiss.

She leaves a trail of scent, musky cologne, a trace of basil and something else that makes my nose wrinkle – the briny tang of sex.

* * *

I wonder how it's taken me this long to work out that Ophelia has a lover. If I couldn't see what's right under my nose, no wonder I couldn't find any clues about Mum. I make porridge and squeeze some fresh oranges, put the espresso machine on. I need a fix of caffeine. My phone beeps in my pocket.

JOHN

Are you alright????

Guiltily, I text him back.

MEG

All okay. Nothing happened.

JOHN

Good. Just keep me in the loop.

Ophelia has gone to have a bath. The kids are eating their breakfast. Kit accidentally spills juice in Artemis's cereal. 'You did it on purpose!' she cries, pinching his arm.

Kit is sobbing and rubbing his arm as Ophelia comes in, the smell of sex I'd detected on her earlier has been replaced by a strong blast of Moroccan Rose. 'Mummy, Kit's crying about his nightmare again,' Artemis tells her quickly. Little minx.

'Are you, my darling?' she drops a kiss on his head. 'Poor Kit.'

Mrs Kerry comes in through the back door and takes her coat off. 'Filthy morning out there,' she says. 'I'll start in the living room, shall I?'

'Actually, could you take the children into the playroom, Mrs K?' Ophelia says. 'I need a quick word with Margaret.'

'Right you are.' Mrs Kerry holds out her hands. 'Come along, you two.'

Ophelia gets up and shuts the door.

'What's all this about keeping the children safe?'

'I saw someone in the garden last night,' I say. 'A homeless woman, I think.'

'Did you call the police?'

'No,' I admit. 'But – she kind of disappeared.'

'Disappeared?' Ophelia is giving me a strange look. 'And these noises you keep talking about in the attic? We've been up there, and you saw for yourself there's nobody in that room.'

'I know you don't believe me. But I think there's another part of the attic. A secret bit. Clem said there was a hidden staircase somewhere. And I really have heard footsteps and... and things being dragged or pushed around.'

'A secret room?' She sighs. 'Maybe it's just as well you're leaving, Margaret,' she says. 'It sounds as though you're under a lot of strain. Nervous exhaustion or something.'

I bite my lip. I want to tell her about the warning notes, the piece of paper with details of my comings and goings. But I can't without any evidence.

33

Kit is napping in his room. Clem is in the living room, reading a magazine. She looks up when I walk past to the kitchen to start lunch.

'How was the call back?' I ask.

She makes a face and shakes her head. 'I blew it.' Then she puts the book down and stands up. 'I hear you're going to model in Thea's show?' she says.

'Two of the models are ill,' I say. 'She thinks I'm the right size.'

She comes close and flicks one of my curls away from my face. 'I'm sure that's not the only reason Thea asked you.' Her fingers graze my cheek. 'You're not wearing your glasses. Do you have contacts, then?' Her gaze is thoughtful, knowing.

Embarrassed, I nod and give her a small smile. I can smell cigarettes on her. She must have had a sneaky fag outside.

'I hear you're leaving us?' Her blue eyes are locked on mine.

I clear my throat and nod, bracing myself for a tirade about neglecting my duty and letting Ophelia down.

'Just as well,' she says. 'Things could get awkward otherwise, couldn't they?'

I let out a breath. Adrenaline hums under my skin. I want to ask her what she means – but I'm afraid to. She's gone back to sit on the sofa and has picked up her magazine. She's ignoring me. It must be Clem who's behind the notes and the attempt to frame me. My head reels with confusion. I hurry away, up the stairs to get Kit. He's awake, but grumpy and tearful, sucking his thumb. He refuses to sit on his potty. He clings to me. 'Come on, Kit,' I try and set him on the ground. 'You're a big boy now. Big enough to walk.'

'No,' he cries, pressing his face into my knees. 'Don't want to.'

He's playing up because I'm leaving. Children hate change, but they're easier to understand than most grown-ups. I wish adults were as transparent.

* * *

Saul is having the kids for a sleepover tonight. Apparently, he's found himself a temporary flat in town. He arrives in a different car, a nondescript hatchback. He's already picked Artemis up from school and she's sitting in the back, a bag of sweets on her lap, her cheek bulging. She waves happily to me as I hand Kit over with his child seat, his overnight case and his teddy. Saul gets out of the car. He gives me a sheepish glance from under his brows, muttering hello. A scrap of tissue flutters from a crust of dried blood on his chin; he looks like he hasn't slept for a month, but he smiles as he tickles Kit under the chin. 'Hey, buddy. We're going to have so much fun together.' I can see the effort it's costing him, but he's a different man. He's lost his old bravado, his sarcasm. He's trying to engage with his kids. Clem told me he's in counselling to kick his gambling habit. It was Ophelia's main stipulation before he could have the children to stay.

* * *

Thea's studio is a converted barn. It's dusk as I park. There's a big sign outside that reads: Fashion by Thea. The only other vehicle in the drive is a black van with Thea's logo picked out in white and red. I press the buzzer. Thea opens the door, her hair pulled back into a ponytail, a white coat over her jeans, as if she's a doctor. Except there are needles and pins threaded through the top pocket. 'Come in,' she holds the door wide.

She turns the lock in the door after me. 'Don't want strangers wandering in,' she says, slipping the key into her pocket. 'Or the competition getting a look at my designs.'

It's an echoing space, double height, with a partial glass roof. There are rails of clothes on either side, a red sofa and chair around a low, glass coffee table. We go up a spiral staircase. On this atrium floor there are mannequins draped in cloth, a big cutting table with scissors and pins and paper shapes. It feels abandoned, as if everyone downed tools at the same time.

'Is there nobody else here?' I was expecting a hive of activity.

'I sent everyone home,' she says. 'The clothes are ready, except your outfits. And we have the big day tomorrow.'

She gestures to a screen. 'You can undress behind there.'

When I come out in a cotton robe, Thea is waiting with something draped over her arm. She slips the dress over my head. I stand silently, trying not to shiver, while she tugs fabric around me, adjusting and fiddling with the neckline. It reminds me of the afternoon the girls dressed me up in their clothes. Thea has the same expression of absorbed concentration on her face. She kneels at my feet and takes up the hemline, pins bristling in her mouth. Standing back, she makes me walk up and down. Fabric swishes around my ankles. I stand on a plinth while she re-pins the hem.

Next, I try on a pair of yellow drainpipe trousers and matching short jacket. She pinches some of the jacket fabric at my waist, frowns, and says they can cheat and use safety pins on the day, but the trousers will need taking up. Then she smiles for the first time. 'That's it. Put your own things on.'

I'm glad to be in my warm jumper and jeans. 'Stay and have a cup of tea with me,' she says. 'I'm going to be here for a little while yet, hemming the dress and trousers. And I need a break first. Camomile tea?' She slides a rueful glance towards me. 'I'd prefer a vodka, but I need steady hands.'

She leads the way down the spiral staircase, motions to me to sit on the sofa, and disappears. She reappears with two steaming cups, and places one in front of me. I sip tentatively. It's hot and there are bits of dried flower floating in the clear liquid. She leans back in her seat with a sigh. 'I'll be glad when this is all over,' she says, tilting her head towards the rails of clothes.

'I'm sure it will be a success.' I pick a bit of petal from between my front teeth.

'You're being polite,' she says, holding up a hand to stop me saying any more. 'I should have taken the business to London. Or Paris. I should have been braver, but...' She shrugs. 'None of us Aldredge girls has ever left Suffolk. We can't let go of Deben Manor.'

'But you've all done interesting things,' I protest.

'Ophelia married an idiot who's spent the last of her money

on gambling. Clem is an out of work actress who wastes her days worrying about her food intake. And I'm an average designer with a failing business.'

I stare at her, speechless. Not knowing what to say, I take another sip of tea. I appreciate her honesty, as much as it surprises me. I could never have imagined feeling close to Thea. She was always the most prickly and difficult of the sisters, so her trust in me seems even more precious.

'Well,' she says. 'I've told you the truth about us. And what about you? It's your turn to come clean.'

My throat tightens. 'What do you mean?'

'Okay,' she says. 'Here's another question. Where did you get that scar on your leg? The one on your calf?'

Startled, my hand automatically covers the place.

Before I can think of a reply, she's shaking her head. 'I've been wondering for a while,' she says. 'It's been nagging at me for weeks, how familiar you seemed. But when I saw the scar just now, I knew. You're Meg, aren't you?' She leans forwards, putting her cup down. 'Our cousin?'

Sweat breaks out under my arms. My mouth is suddenly parched. I tense, as if I'm going to spring up and make a run for it. 'How did you know?' I ask instead. 'About the scar?'

'I heard your dad talking to Ma that summer. He was angry. Said you'd ended up with a nasty gash on your left leg that turned septic.'

'I didn't know my dad visited your mum?'

'He didn't come in person. It was over the phone. I heard them on the extension.' She shrugs. 'Pa used to listen in when you spoke to your dad that summer you stayed.'

I remember the click. The faint sound of breathing.

She's staring at me, her brow creased. 'Why the pretence?'

she asks. 'What do you want?' She scoops her mobile off the table. 'I should call the police right now.'

'I think my mum had something to do with Deben Manor or your family,' I say quickly. 'Recently, I found a Polaroid of her wearing the Aldredge pendant.' I swallow. 'It looks identical to the ones you three have.'

She scowls. 'Impossible. There are only three.'

'I had the photo with me,' I say. 'I put it under a loose floorboard in the summer house.'

She raises her eyebrows. 'Why did you do that?'

'Because my room was searched. It didn't feel safe to leave it there. But then it was stolen. Someone's following me, spying on me.'

She's looking at me with concern. 'I heard you had panic attacks after the accident.'

'I'm not mad, Thea. I found my mum's cardigan in the dressing up box. There are noises in the attic. I've smelt cigar smoke in the middle of the night.' I bite the inside of my lip. It's clear she doesn't believe me. 'And there was a note,' I add. 'Two notes. They threatened me. Told me to leave.'

'And where are these notes?'

'They... they disappeared.'

Her eyes narrow. 'So, the only evidence you have of any of this is a cardigan you found in the dressing up box?' Her voice is gentler. 'Can you imagine how this looks from the outside?' She gets up. 'Lying to us. Pretending to be someone else. Claiming that your things have been searched. Stolen.' She folds her arms across her chest, looking down at me. 'Getting a job under false pretences must be a crime.'

I stare up at her; I can see why she thinks I'm deluded. 'I'll leave,' I tell her. 'I'll pack my stuff and go tonight.' I begin to get out of my seat.

'Stop,' she snaps, putting out her hand as if to push me back. 'You're not going anywhere.'

I catch my breath, remembering that I'm locked in with her. A prickle of fear runs across my scalp.

'I still need you,' she says wearily. 'So, I've decided I'm not going to tell Ophelia yet.'

I stare at her in surprise. 'What about Clem?'

'I won't tell her, either,' she says. 'She'll just blab to Ophelia. I'll tell them both after the show tomorrow. After you've gone.'

'Thanks,' I mutter.

'I need you to walk down the catwalk.' She scowls. 'I thought I could trust you. I liked you. We all did when you were Margaret.' She gives me a cold look. 'But you're a liar. You've never said what really happened that morning on the river. Our father would still be here if it wasn't for you.'

I want to explain how he'd dragged me out of bed that morning, insisting on taking me out in the boat – but in the face of her scorn, I bow my head.

'If you'd just talked to us back then... if you hadn't lied to us now, then maybe we could have forgiven you. But Pa said you were devious. He warned us. Said we couldn't trust you.'

My mouth drops open, confusion silencing me.

'And forget about this connection between your mother and our family,' she adds. 'There isn't one.'

I get up. Shame presses on me, and I shuffle towards the door.

'And Meg,' she says. 'After tomorrow, if I ever see you anywhere near Deben Manor, or any of my family again, I will call the police.'

PART IV

34

I drive home in shock, hands trembling on the steering wheel. One of the sisters was bound to recognise me in the end. But Thea's doubts about my sanity have made me see myself in a new light. I'm the one who looks dangerous now. She threatened to call the police, as if I'm a stalker. My chest feels as if it's about to explode. I pull over and stop the car, putting my head in my hands. Humiliation burns my cheeks. But I've promised to do the fashion show, and maybe that's the least I can do. I've done nothing but make mistakes since getting here – but the biggest was deceiving my cousins. I should text John, let him know the latest development. But I'm too embarrassed to tell him.

Ophelia is standing in the hall. 'You're here,' she exclaims. 'I was waiting for you. I'm on my way out, and I won't be back till morning.' She's at the bottom of the stairs, with an overnight bag in her hand, fresh lipstick on. 'Look, I need to tell you something. I've met someone,' she confides. 'I hope you won't judge me. But Saul and I aren't going to get back together. In fact, our relationship has been in tatters for a long time.' She gives me an anxious glance. 'Obviously, I don't want the kids to know. Not yet.'

'I'm glad you're happy,' I tell her. 'Of course, I won't say anything to the children.'

I'm relieved I'll be gone when Thea breaks the news tomorrow.

On the landing, Clem appears, with her coat over her arm. 'I'm off to Thea's studio,' she says. 'I promised to help with final preparations for the show. I'll probably crash at hers tonight, as it's closer to the venue for tomorrow.' As she passes me, she pauses. 'How did it go, by the way? The fitting?'

'Okay.' I nod. 'Just some minor alterations needed.'

'Margaret,' she says. 'I have to confess something.' She looks embarrassed. 'When you first arrived, I thought you were having an affair with Saul.'

I look at her in surprise.

'I saw you come out of his study late at night. You lied about getting a drink. And I saw you getting out of his car. You two seemed close, always whispering together.' She bites her thumbnail. 'Thing is, he did have a brief fling with one of the nannies before you. Ophelia was already in a state about his gambling. It would have been too humiliating for her to find out he was sleeping with you.'

I can't meet her gaze. I'm holding back a much bigger confession.

'Anyway,' she goes on. 'I've confronted Saul. He denied it and,' she sighs, 'it doesn't matter any more – they're getting a divorce. I'm sorry I suspected you – and I'm sorry I snooped in your bedroom. We three are very protective of each other, and I guess I overreacted. But there's something about you...' She tilts her head to the side, regarding me. 'It takes an actress to know an actress. I checked out some of your references. You really are a nanny. But there's something, isn't there? Something you're hiding?'

I swallow. It would be a relief to tell her, but Thea wants me to keep up the pretence until after the show. I owe it to her to stay quiet. I shake my head. They'll all know the truth about me by the end of tomorrow.

In my room, I push straggly curls out of my face and catch a glimpse of myself in the mirror on the opposite wall. A haggard, exhausted-looking woman stares back, dark bruises under her eyes.

I get up and draw the curtains closed, remembering Mick Smith peering up at me, the fragment of paper I found under the toolbox. I shudder. I wonder what he was imprisoned for. I know he's a peeping Tom – he used to spy on the girls, and he was spying on me through my bedroom window – but is he violent? I've never seen him in the house. But that doesn't mean he hasn't been inside. It's a big house with spaces for intruders to hide. He could have put the notes under my door. He could have looked through my stuff. I feel sick, thinking of his fingers rifling through my underwear and I have a sudden need to dump it all in my wastepaper bin. Unless – it suddenly occurs to me – he knows the homeless woman, and he somehow sneaked her into the house. But there my theory fails, because I can't think of a single reason why either of them would have any interest in me.

I walk around the house, checking that windows and doors are locked. I'm alone, without even the children for company. I wish Matisse was still alive. He was a comforting companion. He used to bark and growl at Mick Smith. I glance up at my ceiling. I should just try and forget about what's happened, put it behind me. I'll be gone soon. But this is my last chance to get inside the attic and look for the other room, find out if there really is someone up there. The thought terrifies me. But it consumes me too – I need to know the truth. I've been living with mysteries and cover-ups since Mum walked out.

I remember Dad picking our lock once when Mum left her key inside the cottage by mistake. He'd used a screwdriver, turning it until he could feel resistance. 'A-ha!' he'd said, and like magic, the door had opened. But I've put the screwdriver I borrowed back in the toolbox.

I don't want to venture out of the house again, but the shed is only a few feet from the back door, and I know exactly where the toolbox is. I'll grab the screwdriver, run back inside and lock the door. It'll take a minute or two.

Moonlight slants through the one window, picking out the box on the table. As I choose two screwdrivers, my senses are alive to a sensation moving on the back of my right hand. I look down at a black shape. A crouching spider, hairy legs spread. The shock makes me fling my fingers open, jerking my arm to get rid of it. The screwdrivers fall to the floor with a clatter, and I'm down on my hands and knees, cursing, to pick them up. The floor is covered in a layer of dust and dried mud. My kneecap lands on a hard object. I wince at the bite of pain, feeling for what it is, and grasp a heavy, round, metal ring. I tug at it, but it's attached to the ground.

A handle. There's a trapdoor here. I get to my feet and squat to pull at the ring, expecting resistance, but the trapdoor opens easily, making me think it's been used recently. I stare down into a dark void. It smells musty. There's a short flight of wooden steps. I don't have my house keys with me, so no useful mini torch. The sensible thing would be to go and get it, or find a proper torch in the house, but my curiosity gets the better of me. I tell myself I'll just go down the steps and see what's there.

At the bottom, I stoop to avoid crashing my head against the ceiling and can just make out an entrance into what looks like a tunnel leading in the direction of the house. It occurs to me that this is how the homeless woman could be getting into the house. The thought makes me shiver, but I need to see where the tunnel leads. I inch along slowly, shuffling one foot in front of the other, sliding my hand along a dank wall, gritty under my fingertips. Even going at a snail's pace, I still manage to walk straight into a hard surface. I exclaim in shock, putting my hand to my throbbing nose. I find a handle, and press. It opens. Inky darkness swells around me. I breathe through my mouth, filtering stale air, and push my foot along the ground until my toe meets a step, then I lean forward, crouching to check with my fingertips, realising I've discovered a narrow flight of steps leading up. I hesitate. I should go back for a torch. But I'm certain this will take me to the hidden attic room. I remember Clem mentioning a bricked-up staircase.

A sense of urgency propels me on, and I creep from one step to another, fumbling with my hands to check each one before I put my weight onto it. Blackness blinds me. I can't even see the glow of my skin in front of me. There's a sour smell of rot. Now I recall Clem saying something about hoping to find a skeleton, but she didn't elaborate. Did someone die in here? When a cobweb trails across my cheek, I scream. I touch the walls either side of me, running my fingers over rough bricks. I have the feeling they are closing in on me, narrowing to trap me. My lack of sight exaggerates my senses: the pump of my heart, the liquid roar of blood behind my eyes. I taste darkness on my tongue, acrid as smoke.

I'm at the top, dizzy and breathless. My fingertips are

exploring a door, trying to find a handle, when there's a rustle of movement behind me, an intake of breath. Before I can turn, a sharp crack explodes against the back of my skull. My head jerks forward, and I slump to my knees against the door.

I've been hit, I think, with a second's startled clarity.

* * *

I surface as if coming up out of water, blinking my eyelids apart. Except folds of fabric crush my lashes. I'm blindfolded, sitting up, legs straight out in front of me, hands tied behind my back. I touch a cold, hard surface with numb fingers. It's smooth and featureless. I seem to be leaning against a metal wall. My head aches. There's a twist of fabric in my mouth, pulling at the corners of my lips, giving off an oily smell.

I struggle to free myself, but the knots around my wrists are secure. My fingertips scrape against fibres of twine. I attempt to get up, swinging my upper body to the left and tucking my feet up, bending my knees, trying to get into a kneeling position. But my lack of sight is disorientating, and I don't have arms for balance. My ankles are secured. I'm stuck in a kind of half-raised foetal position. I haven't got the strength to get onto my knees, let alone my feet.

I slump back onto my bottom, breathing heavily from the exertion. The gag is suffocating me, making me panic. I lean my head against the metal surface behind me. *Think.* I need to know where I am. The blindfold is completely smothering. Not even a hint of light shows through the weave of fabric or the outer edges.

I must be in a darkened room, probably the attic, and I'm guessing I'm leaning against the container. The sisters will come back after Thea's fashion show. I'll find a way of attracting their attention. Except, fear fizzes inside me, what if I'm not in the first part of the attic, what if I'm in the secret back room? Will they be able to find me? Another thought, cold and sharp: did one of them do this to me?

35

I've lost track of time. I had strange, nightmarish dreams, so I must have fallen asleep. My shoulders ache. My arms crawl with pins and needles. Thea must know I'm missing because I haven't turned up at her show. She'll probably think I've done a bunk – just gone off. Nobody will think of looking for me, especially not here. Although, my packed case is still in my room. If they find that, at least they'll know I haven't left.

I need to make a noise. If I can strike the metal surface behind me, that would work. I struggle to twist my body around to face in the opposite direction, using the wall as purchase, squirming until my torso and legs are flat on the floor, head away from the wall and toes against the metal. My arms are squashed beneath me, blood pooling. I bend my bound legs, pulling them towards my belly and strike out with my heels. The impact jars my bones but makes a clanging thud. I pull up my knees again and hit the metal with the soles of my shoes. I keep going for as long as I can. My muscles are screaming. Everything hurts.

I stop, and listen, senses roaring. Is anyone coming? What if nobody hears? What if the person who did this comes back. What will they do to me? I give the metal one last, exhausted kick and lie back, wondering if I'm going to die here, alone.

The blackness of the blindfold seeps into my core, hopelessness dragging me under. I can't fight it. I drop down and down inside myself until I'm thrashing through grainy, green-black depths, falling through the cold river, a child once more. The spool of my mind unfurls and new images bob into view. I see it playing out again, how Lucian came for me, taking me from my bed before dawn. Behind the blindfold, my mind struggles towards flashes of light, flickers of knowledge dancing closer. When we were in the Land Rover driving to the river, I'd looked at his hand on the steering wheel. I'd noticed something. What? A glitter against his skin.

Her silver and opal ring on his little finger.

The ring I used to play with, turning it on her hand, while she explained the power of opals. *Hope*, she said. *Hope, clarity and truth.*

He'd noticed me looking. Lighting strikes of memory are exploding behind my eyes. In the boat, he'd called me Irene by mistake, or on purpose, I didn't know which. But I'd understood then that he knew where she was. 'Where's Mum?' I'd asked, as the dinghy sped across the river towards the sea. 'Where is she?'

'It doesn't matter – you'll never see her again,' he'd shouted, face lit by the red of the crowning sun. The cat scratches on his cheek were thin, raw lines. Fear crawled over my scalp.

'Where is she?' I'd repeated, clinging to the bucking tiller. He'd laughed and the boat leapt under us like a living thing. But he'd stopped laughing when he was in the water. He was angry. I saw the ridge of orange bobbing at his neck, the bulge of life jacket hidden under his jumper.

There were no good reasons why we were here so early, before anyone else was around. Why he'd lied to me about wearing a life jacket. And there could only be one reason he was wearing the ring she never took off. *You'll never see her again.* He'd done something to her, and now he was going to push me into the sea.

His arms sliced the water apart as he powered towards the boat, strong shoulders muscling waves aside, broad hands reaching for the edge of the dinghy. He grabbed it, knuckles shining. I staggered back. His upper body was already in the boat, one foot hooking up over the side. His breath rasped; face bunched with effort. He was dripping and spitting, tilting the dinghy precariously with his weight.

I fumbled in the bottom of the boat and found an oar. I grasped it with both hands for protection. He was nearly in the boat; he was coming for me. I drew back my arms and shoved the full force of my terror towards him, stumbling forward. The blunt end struck his forehead, the impact juddering up my arms to my shoulders. The blow split his skin: a spurt of scarlet, a rush of blood obscuring his startled expression, and then he fell back, swallowed by water.

The memory sits inside me, immovable, unknowable. Not a silly mistake, not just my fault, but my intention. I am rigid with shock. Beneath the blindfold, my mind is full of tumbling facts, falling into place, making a pattern, a terrible truth. That's who she went off with, and why she never wrote to me again, why she's never made contact. Lucian took Mum away from us and murdered her.

A pressure on my shoulder makes me startle. I flinch away from human touch, the scream in my throat stopped by the gag. Someone is here. Fear chokes me, and I move my head, trying to see who it is; I can't make anything out through the blindfold, but I detect a lightening at its edges, as if a switch has been flipped on in the room. Hands slip under my neck and lift my head from the floor. I try to pull away, but there's a tugging at the knot of the blindfold. It comes loose. Falls away. I look up through blurred, watery eyes.

'What the fuck?' a woman's voice is saying. 'What the actual fuck?'

I squint at a shape that becomes Ophelia. The light behind her is dazzling.

'Hang on.' She removes the gag, and I open my lips, probing the tender corners of my mouth with the tip of my tongue.

'Who did this?' she asks.

I shake my head, unable to speak as I blink around me, glimpsing my surroundings. I'm in the small, bare attic room. The one Clem, Ophelia and I looked inside. The one with the container.

'Let's untie your wrists.' She helps me sit up and struggles with the binding at my wrists. 'God, these are tight.'

I hold my breath, waiting for the moment of release. Then the bliss and agony of moving my shoulders and arms, shaking my hands. 'Someone hit me,' I tell her. I can hardly move my tongue. I lean forward and tug at the knots at my ankles.

She frowns. 'Who?'

'I didn't see them.'

'An intruder?' She helps untie the ropes I'm struggling with. She throws the gag and the lengths of twine on the floor, glancing behind her. 'There was no sign of a break-in. The front door was locked.'

'I found a trapdoor in the shed. A tunnel leading to the

house.' I remember the blow to the back of my head, the foot-steps behind me. 'How did you get in?'

'I have a key, remember?'

The door to the attic stairs stands open. It doesn't prove anything. She could have been the one to hit me. Does she know I'm Meg?

'Thea sent me to look for you,' she says. 'She thought you'd decided not to model in the show. I got back to the house and there was no sign of you.'

I rub at the indentations on my wrists and ankles where the rope has bitten. I'm parched, and my head aches. I don't know whether to believe her.

'Then I heard noises,' she's saying. 'Banging from the top of the house. You were lying on the floor. I thought you were dead.' She stops, frowning. 'What do you mean, a trapdoor? A tunnel?'

'In the gardening shed. I went through the tunnel and up the bricked-up staircase. Then someone hit me.'

The tunnel. The dark stairs that must have led to the other part of the attic. I get up, staggering on numb feet, legs full of pins and needles. I go over to the wall behind me and begin to examine it, feeling across it, looking for indentations, a catch, anything that might reveal a way through. I tap on the surface, discovering a hollow sound. It's a partition.

'What are you doing?' Ophelia is by my side. 'Shouldn't we leave now? Call the police?'

'I'm looking for a concealed door, an entrance. There's another room behind this one.' I press my ear to the wood. 'The tunnel must lead to the other side.'

Then she's next to me, feeling the surface too, arms and fingers spread.

'Oh my God,' she exclaims. 'You're right.'

A rasp of sound and movement, and I turn to see her disappearing through an open doorway. She must have found a catch that's operated a sliding door. It's rolled back inside the double partition, leaving an entrance. I follow her as she flicks on a light switch and the room blazes.

Faces stare at us. There are dozens of portraits of women, all painted by Calista by the look of them. This room is bigger. I notice an ashtray of squashed cigarette butts on a round, dark wood table placed in the middle of the floor, next to a high-backed green armchair. I look closer at the ashtray. There's a cigar butt. My insides clench.

Ophelia looks at the ashy remains. 'Someone's been here.' She prods the back of the chair. 'But who? Who could it be?'

'We should go,' I say.

But her attention has fixed on the portraits. I follow as she paces the contours of the room, staring at the framed paintings. Each woman has the Aldredge pendant around her neck. I recognise the self-portrait of Calista I saw when I looked down from the loft. 'It's Ma's work,' she says. 'When he talked about his collection, this isn't what I imagined. It's always been a mystery. This place.' She stares around her. 'Who are all these women? Apart from Ma, I don't recognise anyone.'

I rub my hands together, trying to force the life back into them. A cymbal is clanging inside my brain. I prod at my bruised skull, touching a matted texture. Dried blood. I gaze around me. There's a broom leaning against the wall in the corner of the room, a dustpan and brush next to it. A black thing sits on the seat of the chair. I go over and pick it up, turning it in my hands. 'A video recorder.'

She seems to come out of her trance and takes the machine from me. She frowns. 'This is all really weird,' she says. She gestures towards the portraits. 'They're named,' she says. 'Just their first names.' She peers at them, reading aloud. 'Louise, Sandra, Rebecca.'

I notice a dark-haired woman with violet eyes. With a jolt, I recognise John's mother from the photo he sent. 'Amy,' it says under her portrait. I think of the Polaroid of Mum. The gold glinting at her neck. My heart beats faster as I scan the portraits. Is there one of her?

'We've always been banned from coming up here,' Ophelia says, shaking her head. 'It was supposed to hold valuable artwork.' She glances at the paintings stacked on the floor against the far wall. 'Why are they hidden away? The thing is,' she goes on, 'you couldn't question Pa. Not about anything.' She's standing before a painting in the corner. 'It's me,' she exclaims, leaning close. 'As a child.'

The painting is of a toddler dressed in a grubby yellow and white gingham dress. Chubby knees. Old-fashioned shoes. She looks as though she's been crying. Her eyes are watery, her cheeks red.

'I remember,' she whispers. 'I remember this moment. Pa took my photo. I was frightened.'

'That dress you're wearing,' I say, gazing at the picture. 'I've seen it before.'

There's a painting of Clem as a chubby baby in pink trousers and a blue jumper. And a beautiful younger baby lying on her back, liquid, dark eyes staring out at us. I leave Ophelia looking at herself and bend over the stacked portraits, searching through them, checking each face, looking for Mum. There's a low, solid-looking door in the corner of the room near the stacked pictures. I go over and pull at it, then push. It doesn't budge. This must be where the hidden staircase comes out.

'We should go,' I say. 'Before the person who hit me comes back.'

But Ophelia is staring at the portrait of herself. I go into the first room and run my fingers over the large stainless steel container. Not a hint of dust. It was the metal wall I could feel with my shoulders and feet.

Ophelia joins me and squats down in front of the container. 'There's a keypad,' she says.

'We don't know the code.'

She ignores me and taps in six numbers. 'Our birthdays,' she says. 'He used it all the time.' There's a click, and a hiss of air. The door releases. She pulls it wide, peering inside. She's blocking my view. I try to look over her shoulder. When I manage to glimpse inside, I'm looking into a dark space lined with velvet, big enough to hold a crouching adult. A gilt-framed oil painting of Lucian takes up most of the space, positioned in the centre of the crate. He's wearing his sailor cap, and a confident smile.

Ophelia's crawled half inside. She wriggles out clutching a white envelope in one hand and a small red box. She rips the envelope open, sliding out an audio tape cassette. She holds it up, examining the handwritten label. 'It says, "For my girls".' She rattles it, as if it might reveal the contents. 'My sisters need to hear this too.' She tucks the tape back into the envelope. 'It must be from Pa. Except...' She frowns. 'It's Ma's handwriting.'

We sit cross-legged on the floor together as Ophelia stuffs the envelope in her pocket and flips the box open: a gold Aldredge pendant nestles on red silk. 'There's a fourth one,' I whisper.

She frowns, staring at the pendant. 'He told us there were only three.'

'We should leave,' I say, more urgently.

'Yes,' she says, blinking as if only just understanding the threat. 'I'm going back to the fashion show. Coming?' She shoves the jewellery box into her other pocket. 'We'll call the police on the way; report you being attacked.'

Before we can get up from the floor, there's a sound of hurried footsteps on the stairs, a fleeting shadow. The attic door slams shut.

36

'Fuck.' Ophelia grabs the door handle, rattling it hard. She hammers on the wood with her fists. 'They've locked us in. Come back!' she yells. 'Let us out!'

We try pushing together, heaving with our shoulders. It's hopeless. Ophelia paces the room. 'There are no windows,' she says. 'What about the other door?'

'Locked,' I say. 'Who shut us in?'

She shakes her head. 'I don't know.' Her eyes are stretched wide. 'A thief?' Her voice wavers. And in that moment, I know that Ophelia isn't behind this. 'It must be a robbery – mustn't it?' she asks, doubt leaching strength from her words.

'You have a key,' I remember. 'If they've removed theirs, we can get out.'

She puts the flat of her palm to her forehead. 'I left it in the door,' she says. 'They must have used it to lock us in.'

'What about your mobile?' I'm suddenly hopeful. 'We can call someone. The others. The police.'

Her mouth gapes. She pats hurriedly at the back pockets of her jeans, then frowns. 'Damn. I left it in my bag. On the hall table.' She bites one of her fingernails. 'What about you? Don't you have yours?'

'I did. But whoever hit me must have taken it.'

We slump onto the floor together, backs against the metal container. Behind us, in the other room, the painted women look on impassively. Mum is not one of them. She's not in this strange collection. I remember her silver and opal ring on Lucian's finger. What did he do to her?

'I don't think this is an ordinary robbery,' I say. 'Someone's been watching me and following me ever since I got here.' The time for lies and pretence has ended. 'Ophelia, I need to tell you something. I'm not Margaret,' I tell her. 'I'm Meg. Your cousin.'

'I know,' she says. 'Thea already told me. She said she was going to wait till after the show, but then you didn't turn up, and she wanted me to find you. I was going to have it out with you when I got here – but that seems like a million years ago.' She tears at her thumbnail with her teeth. 'Thea said some-one's been sending you anonymous notes. She says you believe your mother is an Aldredge.'

'I didn't say that,' I protest. 'But I did have a Polaroid of her wearing the Aldredge pendant, like all the women in the paintings.' I stretch out the back of my sore neck. 'The Polaroid was stolen. I'm sorry I lied to you. When I found out about the job, it seemed like fate or destiny. I've always had the feeling that something was off, that summer when Mum disappeared. Something wasn't right. I can't explain. I thought I might find a clue if I could be in the house again.' I rub my eyes. 'The thing is,' I say slowly, thinking of how to tell her that I'm responsible for Lucian's death. 'I have just remembered something—'

'Before now I wouldn't have believed you about the

pendant,' she cuts me off. 'I've always been told there are only three, and my sisters and I have them.'

'But there was a fourth all along.' I glance through the entrance at the portraits behind us. 'I know who one of the women is.' I take a breath. 'Amy is John's mother.'

'John?' She's frowning.

'The gardener's son. The gardener before Mick. Edward Catchpole. Your dad sacked him. John told me his mum had an affair with your dad.' I can't tell her that John is her half-brother. That's his story to tell, not mine. 'When Edward confronted your dad, your dad denied it. She killed herself.'

'I don't believe it,' Ophelia says, her face tight. 'She must have made it up. She was obviously unstable.'

I swallow my retort. Ophelia is scowling, her bony shoulder pressing against mine. What would she do if I told her what I did to her father? I knocked him unconscious – it's my fault he got run over by a powerboat. I sniff the faint tang of cigar smoke coming from the cold ashtray and remember the foot-steps criss-crossing my ceiling night after night, the cough behind the door.

'Your father—' I say, my words catching. 'Is he... still alive?'

She glances away, hands curling into fists, and then she nods. My stomach plummets. 'He's... he's been living here?' I glance up, expecting to see him coming through the partition door.

'What?' She frowns. 'No. He's not even in the country,' she says. 'He didn't do this.'

'Then where is he?'

'In France. Ma looks after him. He became a recluse, because of his injuries. He's disfigured. His face is ruined. He lost part of his left arm, his hand. He won't let anyone see him. Not even us.

'After he left hospital, he told us to think of him as dead – to tell everyone he was.' She buries her face in her hands. 'He wants people to believe he drowned. He's banned us from visiting him. He puts such store by beauty. Poor Pa. He's in hell.'

'Do you have any contact with him?'

'We write to each other. There are occasional phone calls. It's important to him that we keep the house on, keep it in the family. Protect his collection up here. Keep it locked up. When we went into the attic with you, I presumed his collection must be in the container. I didn't know about this room.'

'I think it's my fault,' I say quietly. 'About the powerboat accident. He fell in the river because of me, I think...' I correct myself. 'I'm sure, I'm to blame—'

'No.' She cuts me off again. She shakes her head. 'At the time, it was such a shock, our world was ripped away from us. Our dad was disfigured, and we never saw him again. You know how close we all were – how much we loved him. Then Ma left to look after him. We felt like orphans, and we needed someone to blame. You were the scapegoat.' Her arms go around her knees, hugging them. 'Only, how could it have been your fault? You were just a kid. It was the driver of the power-boat who did the damage. They disappeared without a trace. A hit and run. Maybe they didn't even know.'

Hearing her forgiveness, tears prickle the back of my eyes.

'I miss him,' she's whispering. 'The father I knew was good as dead. He was such a powerful force in our lives. I wear his cap sometimes. It helps me feel close to him, to the Pa I remember.'

The image of Mum's silver and opal ring on his finger flashes into my mind. He told me I'd never see her again. My chest is tight with questions. But how can I share any of this with Ophelia? Tell her what I know about her beloved Pa? All I have are fragmented memories newly surfaced in my mind.

'It was wonderful when we pleased him,' she's saying. 'But it wasn't all great.' She sighs. 'He expected perfection. I think we all felt the pressure... if we let him down by not coming first in an exam, or having dirty hair, or not reacting to something the right way, his disapproval was terrible. Like being cast out into the desert or something.' She takes my hand and squeezes it. 'We weren't very kind to you when you were here, were we?' She sighs again. 'I'm sorry. You'd just lost your mum.'

She twists her head to look at the paintings in the far corner. 'And the picture of me, as a child. It's so strange. It's brought back a sense of being frightened.' She pats the envelope in her lap. 'Maybe this tape will answer some questions. All my life, I've had weird memories that don't make sense.'

'Are you frightened now?' I nod towards the main door. 'Do you think – whoever they are – do you think, they'll come back?'

'I don't know.' Her eyes widen and she takes my hand again, threading her fingers through mine. 'And I am frightened,' she admits. 'I'm fucking terrified.'

'Me too,' I whisper.

'If someone's been following you,' she says slowly. 'They must have done this. Don't you have any idea of who they are?'

I shake my head. 'At first, I thought it might have been you or your sisters.' I shrug. 'It could be Mick. But I don't know why he'd want to tie me up – or lock us in.'

'Well, whoever it is. It's us against them now.' Her pulse ticks through our joined skin. 'We're in this together.'

* * *

The sound of feet on the stairs is like thunder: urgent footsteps coming closer. We stagger to our feet, hand in hand. Terror rips through my veins – is this a rescue, or the end? The door bursts open, slamming back on its hinges, and a woman stands on the threshold, her chest heaving as she pants.

'Thank God!' Ophelia lets out a half-laugh. 'Mrs K.'

Mrs Kerry doesn't respond, doesn't seem to hear. Her mouth is open, spittle shining at the edges of her lips. Her grey bun has come undone, wiry hair flying around her shoulders. Bright spots burn her cheeks.

It's then that I see the axe hanging heavy in her hand, curved blade touching the ground. I grip Ophelia's fingers and edge backwards, pulling her with me.

'Mrs K,' Ophelia says. 'What... what are you doing?'

Mrs Kerry stares right through us, her gaze glassy, unseeing. The tendons in her neck stand out like ropes. Her body blazes with power. She takes a step into the room and raises the axe with a noise halfway between a scream and a war cry. She runs towards us, the curved blade scything the air. I fall to my knees, dragging Ophelia with me behind the container, but Mrs Kerry continues straight on, through the partition doorway, where she brings the axe down on the painting of Calista. The canvas tears, the frame splintering.

Ophelia gasps. We turn, watching Mrs K move to the next canvas. The edge of the axe smashes and rips at the painting of John's mother. The blade flies and falls, dissecting paint and fabric and wood. Features are obliterated. Faces destroyed. Chunks of wall paster ricochet off.

'What are you doing?' Ophelia screams, pulling away from me, twisting towards the other room.

I grab her arm and wrench her back. 'Don't,' I hiss. 'We need to go.'

Mrs Kerry lets out another roar, raising the axe again. Veins bulge blue in her neck and shoulders. She is Viking-like, possessed by a super-power. She could turn on us any moment.

'Run.' I push Ophelia towards the open door to the stairs. 'Quick.'

Luckily, she seems to understand, and we make a dash for it, skidding down the narrow steps two at a time, hand in hand. As we turn the corner, my shoulder smashes into the wall and our sweaty palms slide apart. Along the landing, past the bathroom and bedrooms, and then we're running down the main run of carpeted stairs towards the hall, Ophelia just behind me, her panicked breathing loud. The car, I'm thinking. We need to get away from here and call for help on the way.

There's an obstacle blocking our path. We're not alone. A hooded figure stands below, positioned between us and the front door. They don't move. They're waiting for us. My steps falter, and I stagger to a stop, panting. Ophelia collides into me. I grab the banister for balance, staring at the person guarding the foot of the stairs.

She's still dressed in black with a silver chain at her throat. She looks up at us, her eyes shielded in shadow, her expression unreadable. The homeless woman. Fear washes through me.

She pushes her hood back and meets my eyes, her mouth curling into a sneer. She raises a palm, motioning us not to move, not to come any further.

Before I can edge back up the steps, Ophelia is pushing past me. 'Karin?' she says, stepping onto the floor. 'Your mother's gone mad.' She waves a hand towards the landing. 'She's destroying Pa's art.'

The woman doesn't move, just stares at us.

'Stop her!' Ophelia shouts, stepping closer to the homeless woman. 'Go and stop her.'

'No.' The woman shakes her head, greasy hair falling across her pale face. 'No,' she repeats in a rough voice. 'I told her what happened.' Her tone is flat, without emotion. 'What he did to me.'

'What?' Ophelia makes a strangled noise, pressing a hand to her heart. 'What are you talking about?'

'I was only fifteen,' Karin continues in that strange, dull voice.

The noise of the axe doing its work comes to us. The rip and smash of metal on canvas and wood setting my teeth on edge, making my heart gallop faster.

'I don't know what your problem is,' Ophelia growls, almost nose to nose with the woman. 'But you need to get out of our way.'

'He raped me,' Karin says. 'Your dad.'

'Liar.' Ophelia jerks back from her as if she's been scalded. 'I don't believe you.'

My body goes cold, remembering the violence in Lucian as he'd forced me into the dinghy. The terror I'd felt as he climbed back into the boat.

'I told Mum everything,' Karin says. 'She didn't say a word. Marched me straight here. Took the axe from the woodpile.' She turns and glances over her shoulder towards the sitting room, looking at something out of our view.

I step down into the hall and follow her line of sight. The portrait of Lucian is no longer on the wall. It lies in a wreck on the floor, hacked to pieces. Karin raises her eyes to the ceiling. 'She said there was a whole room full of portraits at the top of the house.'

'Oh my God,' Ophelia is bending over the smashed picture of her father. 'What have you done?'

'But why did she lock us in the attic?' I ask. 'Why did she hit me?'

'Dunno what you're talking about.' There's defiance in her gaze.

'Let's go.' Ophelia tugs at my arm.

'You calling the cops?' Karin turns, as we walk past her towards the front door. Her voice rises and she lifts her chin. 'Go ahead. I'm willing to talk to them now. Bet there's others like me, too. I won't be the only one.'

Ophelia jabs a finger towards Karin's chest. 'You're both going to prison for this.'

'It's the portraits,' Karin says. 'She said she had to get rid of them – she said they were evil.'

Ophelia is suddenly limp, her knees giving way. I link my arm with hers, taking her weight against me. 'She's lying, isn't she...' she murmurs into my shoulder. 'It's not right, is it? It's not true.'

Holding Ophelia up, I turn to Karin. 'Why now?' I ask. 'What made you tell your mum about Lucian?'

'A woman was giving out meals in the street. A charity thing,' Karin pauses. 'She sat down and talked to me like I was a human and not dirt under her shoe. I ended up telling her my life story and she said I couldn't go on living with the secret. It wasn't mine to carry. It wasn't my fault.' Tears shine on her cheeks. 'She said she'd been like me once. She'd got herself together. She said I could do it too.'

'I'm glad,' I tell her. 'It was brave to tell the truth.'

Ophelia pulls at my arm. She's choking back tears. 'I can't stay here.'

As we hurry out of the house, she stumbles. 'Oh, God. Oh, God,' she's whispering. 'Let it not be true.' It sounds like the fervent prayer of a condemned man.

She's scooped up her handbag from the hall table, and hands me her car keys with trembling fingers as I slip into the driver's seat. 'We have the audio tape,' she gasps, slamming the passenger door closed. 'We'll listen to it with my sisters.' She's taking out her mobile and jabbing at it. 'I'll call the others. Tell them what's happened. But the police.' Her voice rises. 'I need to call the police first. They need to go to the house and arrest Karin and her mother.'

I put the car into gear, and glance in the wing mirror as we roll away. Karin is standing in the doorway, watching us leave.

37

At the venue for Thea's fashion show, the audience has gone home, leaving empty bottles, bits of rubbish and abandoned programmes on the floor. The runway is deserted. The models, make-up artist and hair stylists are leaving by the front door in a flurry of hand waves, obviously curious about the drama unfolding between the four of us. After Ophelia had explained briefly what happened at Deben Manor, Thea borrowed a portable cassette player from the hair stylist and arranged four chairs in a circle around it. She's slotted the tape cassette from the attic into it.

When the last person leaves, the door banging shut behind them. Ophelia leans forward and presses play.

Calista's voice floats from the machine. I'd forgotten what my aunt had sounded like: her careful pronunciation, her quiet, breathy voice.

Girls, she says. *As I speak, your pa is in hospital with what the doctors are calling, 'life-altering injuries'. He's already asking that we go straight to France as soon as he can travel – I've never seen him so broken. He's utterly devastated by what's happened to his face. His poor arm. He doesn't want anyone to see him, not even you... I think especially not you. His beauties.*

This is not easy for me. I have only gone against your father's wishes twice in my life, but if you find this tape, it will mean that you've gone into the attic, and that will mean either Pa or I am dead. Perhaps both of us. I can't imagine living without him. I have wrestled with my conscience, but if we are no longer in the world, then you should know the truth. We are not your natural parents. I was unable to have children, but your father wanted them – especially daughters. Three beautiful daughters.

Ophelia gasps as Thea and Clem let out exclamations. We all stare at each other, but Thea puts her finger to her lips. Calista's voice is continuing.

...He took Ophelia from a poor area of Glasgow – just tucked her under his arm and brought her back to me. He rang me from a phone box and told me to buy nappies and milk. You were such a sweet little thing, Ophelia, although tearful at first. We were renting houses then, and we kept moving to avoid suspicion. Your father has his contacts, so getting false documents was never a problem. Thea, you are a Romanian orphan. He glimpsed your teenage mother when she was taking you to the orphanage and wanted her baby for himself. Money was exchanged. Clem, you come from closer to home. You are Alison Greenwood's daughter, the baby taken from outside her caravan. You have to believe me when I say, your pa was right when he told me it was better for you all to be brought up by us than your real parents – single mums struggling to cope.

When Lucian said we were moving to Deben Manor, I was scared. It was too close – but he said that was the point, nobody would suspect that you were the same child. He was right again, of course. Although, to be safe, we discouraged you from going into the village, and you went to boarding school miles away.

Please know that each of you have been loved and cherished as if you were our flesh and blood. Pa assured me that it was better for you to be brought up by us in lovely surroundings than to have been left where you were, in poverty and misery.

I have written down all that I know of your real identities, which isn't much, just the places and dates and times Lucian took you. I've hidden the paper in the back of your father's portrait in the crate. Goodbye, my darlings. I'm sorry for leaving you alone. But you are stronger than you know, and your pa needs me.

Her voice fades into silence.

Thea stands up suddenly, knocking her chair over backwards. 'Jesus Christ!' She slams her fist down on the top of the deserted runway. 'What the fuck!'

Ophelia sits motionless with her hands over her mouth, her face bleached of colour, and Clem is quietly crying, hugging herself.

I don't know what to do. I want to comfort them, but each one has coiled into themselves, the shock affecting them in different ways, all caught inside their own separate emotional turmoil.

The depths of Lucian and Calista's betrayal stuns me. But it was Lucian who'd taken the girls. He'd stolen three babies and got away with it. What else was he capable of? My fear that he murdered Mum seems even more likely now, even more horrifically real.

38

The bonfire blazes tall, a spitting, gleaming beacon in the cold night. All afternoon, the girls and I had gone up and down the stairs, dragging dismembered carcasses of paintings, heaping the smashed and splinted portraits together on the lawn. It was as I was carting one of them out that I'd trodden on my phone. It had been thrown or dropped in the grass. I'd picked it up and wiped the dirt and moisture away. It was out of battery, but not broken.

'Who are these women?' Thea had demanded, staring at the wrecks of shredded canvas at her feet. 'Now Mrs K has hacked the pictures to pieces, we can't even identify them.'

'Your mother painted them from Polaroids,' I'd remembered. 'Maybe they're still in her studio.'

We'd found the Polaroids in Calista's studio. Piles of them, discoloured with age, kept together with paper clips, each picture with a woman's first name on the back.

Now Thea stares into the heat, her scowl lit with gold. 'It's like a pyre.' She coughs as the wind blows the smoke in our direction. 'But we still don't know who we're burning. We only have first names.'

'But they're not dead,' Clem says, sounding shocked. 'I mean, some of them, perhaps. They were painted over fifteen years ago.'

'One of them is dead by suicide. And we know she was his lover,' Ophelia says. 'The gardener's wife.' She and Clem stand either side of Thea, their arms around her waist.

'What if they were all his lovers?' Clem says. 'It's weird the way they're wearing the pendant. Like it means something.'

'Who is he? I mean, who is he really?' Ophelia takes a shuddering breath. 'He stole us. He's lied to us all our lives. Only a psychopath would do that.'

Together we watch the flames, watch the remains of paint crackle and twist, disappearing into holes, blackening into smoke and ashes. The fire eats up Lucian's ruined collection of beauties. The only paintings Mrs Kerry's axe left untouched, were the ones of the girls as children. Why wasn't Mum in the collection? Maybe she wasn't his lover – maybe that's why he got rid of her, why she wasn't painted – because she refused him? I want that to be true. But she ran away with him. They must have been lovers.

'What now?' Clem is asking.

'We phone Ma,' Ophelia says. Her voice is hard. 'She'll know about the portraits – she painted them. She can tell us who they are – what they mean.'

'Tell her we're coming to France,' Thea adds. 'He's the one we need to question. Ma does whatever he says.'

'And what about Mrs Kerry?' Ophelia asks. 'What do we do about her?'

'Let's go and see her,' Clem says. 'The police let her go after we didn't press charges. We need to know more about what happened to Karin.'

'And how did Mrs K even know about the portraits?' Ophelia adds.

'I wanted to ask Mick to help with the bonfire,' Clem says. 'But he's disappeared. His mobile goes to voicemail. His things have gone from the shed.'

Ophelia shoots me a meaningful glance and I nod. Maybe it *was* him who knocked me out and locked us in the attic. I feel safer knowing he's gone.

'What about your real parents?' I ask, as the bonfire caves in, falling in on itself, a blackened, stinking mess of charcoal and ash. 'Will you try and find them?'

Clem swallows, hanging her head. 'I could walk to my real mother's house.'

'We can come with you, if you like?' Thea offers.

Clem kicks at the embers of the fire. 'Not yet,' she says. 'I'm not ready. Maybe I need to wait until we've been to France.' She looks up. 'It's a terrifying thought. Meeting her when I'm an adult – knowing she's been here all the time. We'll be strangers to each other.' She covers her face with her palms. 'What he did was so cruel.'

'Come here,' Ophelia says, wrapping her arms around Clem. They reach out to pull Thea into the huddle, and she grabs my hand and takes me with her. We stand together, arms entwined, heads touching. I feel the thump of their hearts, smell the cinders in their hair. But my secret keeps me apart. I need to tell them what I did to Lucian, and what I think Lucian did to Mum.

When my mobile is charged, I see five missed calls from John and nine text messages. I have no idea what time it is in San Francisco, but I call him. He answers immediately. 'Thank

God,' he says. 'I was just about to get on a plane. Are you alright?'

I explain what's happened and tell him what I've remembered about the sailing accident, but that Lucian is still alive, in France. 'And your mum?' His voice falters. 'You think he might have killed her?'

I grip the mobile closer. 'I don't know.'

'Go to the police,' he urges. 'You have to report it.'

'But there's nothing to report,' I say, wearily. 'Nothing except something I think I've remembered from fifteen years ago. And Ophelia has reported the break-in, and the attack on me.'

'Don't you think it was Mrs Kerry who did that to you?'

'No,' I say. 'I don't think it was her. The poor woman had just heard that Lucian had molested her daughter – raped her when she was fifteen. I can understand her anger. But it wasn't directed at me.'

* * *

The next day is brilliant and cold. I'm sitting at the kitchen table with my cousins. We're pale-faced, exhausted, clutching cups of coffee. Clem is smoking a rollie. For once, Ophelia doesn't complain. She'd phoned Calista last night to tell her we're coming to France. Calista hadn't denied any of it or tried to explain anything. Outside the window, the grass is seared with a scorched circle. None of us has any appetite. I sip my coffee, scalding my lip. I clutch the heat of my mug with rigid fingers. 'I need to tell you what happened,' I tell them. 'The morning of the accident. Lucian and me. Before the boat capsized.'

I feel the air coalesce around us, the breath held in their lungs, the intensity of their listening. I begin, and falter, and force myself on, telling the story as I've remembered it. My confession.

There is a stunned silence, and then they all talk at once. 'Jesus,' Thea says. 'So, you think your mother was with him when she disappeared?'

'He was going to drown you?' Ophelia stares at me. 'My God.'

'You were brave,' Clem is saying. 'You were just a little girl. Terrified of water. Terrified of him.'

'You don't hate me?' I ask.

'Fuck, no. Not now we know who he really is,' Thea says, her hands on the table curling into fists. 'I wish I could have hit him myself.'

My shoulders slump, fingers falling away from the mug, limp with relief.

'We'll tell the police he had her ring,' Clem says, her cheeks hectic with colour. 'That he told Meg she'd never see her mum again.' She scans our faces, nodding. 'They need to know what he might have done... that he might have...' She swallows, looking at me. 'I'm sorry, Meg. But he might have killed her.'

I nod. It's strange hearing her say it out loud: the thing I've been afraid of since Mum disappeared. She's not going to come back. I've been hoping to find her, but all this time she's been lying in a hidden grave, or burnt to ash, or rotting at the bottom of the sea. A hard sob stutters from my throat, and Thea puts her arm around me. 'First, we need to find out the truth from him,' she says. 'We make him confess. We could tape it. We need more evidence – otherwise the police will have nothing to go on.'

'He has to go to prison,' Clem says. 'He deserves to be locked up.'

'I've asked Saul to keep the kids for a few more days,' Ophelia says. 'Until we get back from France.'

'Ma never felt like a proper mother,' Clem says. 'She was always so distant. And then she chose him over us. She abandoned us.'

'Thank God he's not our real father.' Thea's voice breaks. 'He's a monster.' She looks at her sisters, tears in her eyes. 'But it means we're not real sisters.'

'We are,' Ophelia says fiercely. 'We'll always be that. He can't take that away from us.'

I'm not their real cousin, either, not related by even a drop of blood. But after the last couple of days, I've never felt closer to anyone than these three women, never felt such a sense of kinship.

I look down into the remains of my coffee. If the girls are right, and Lucian can be made to tell us where Mum's remains are, at least Dad and I can recover her body. She can have a proper burial, a memorial, at last.

39

Ophelia drives us to the village, Thea in the passenger seat, Clem and I in the back. As we pass the shop, Alison comes out holding a shopping bag. Clem notices me looking and turns her head. 'Is that her?' she asks in an urgent whisper. 'I've seen her around, but we've never spoken.'

I twist my head to keep Alison in my sights. 'She's a nice woman, Clem. A good person.'

'Oh, God, I feel sick.' Clem buries her face in her hands. She slams her palm against the seat in front. 'Stop the car!'

Ophelia pulls over, turning round with a look of concern. 'Do you need a moment?'

'Are you going to throw up?' Thea is asking.

Clem is reaching for the handle, flinging open the door. We tumble out after her, but she motions us back, eyes wild. 'I have to talk to her,' she says.

'Now?' Ophelia exclaims.

'I don't think that's a good idea...' Thea takes a half-step forward and hesitates. Clem is already running across the road, towards Alison, who's walking away along the pavement, unaware that her daughter is behind her.

'Alison!' Clem calls. A single, piercing shout.

The older woman stops and turns. When she sees Clem, she startles. We three wait by the car, not moving, hardly breathing. The world seems to shrink to this moment. Alison tilts her head to one side, as if listening to an invisible frequency, her eyes never leaving Clem. Then her shoulders snap back, and the bag falls from her fingers, tins of tomatoes clattering onto the pavement, apples rolling out into the road. She starts to walk towards the redheaded woman who'd called to her. Clem raises her arms, holding them out as if feeling her way in the dark. They meet on the pavement, Clem stumbling towards her mother, Alison's hands catching her daughter's. They clutch each other, staring into each other's faces.

'My God,' Thea says. 'They have the same body type – look how they mirror each other. They stand in the same way. The same Bambi legs. Narrow shoulders.'

'They have the same smile, too,' I say, remembering the moment I'd seen her smile in her kitchen. 'I knew Alison reminded me of someone. I just couldn't think who.'

'Have they said anything, yet?' Ophelia whispers.

'I don't think so,' Thea says.

Alison is touching Clem's face, her expression one of wonder. We can only see the back of Clem's head, her fiery hair. But her shoulders are shaking.

'They're talking now,' Ophelia murmurs. 'But I can't hear the words.'

'I think we should leave them.' Thea brushes her eyes with the back of her hands.

I turn away, opening the car door. I'm happy for Clem but I

can't help a lurching feeling of envy. I'll never have a reunion like that with my mum.

* * *

Ophelia flicks the indicator on, and we turn into a side street, and park outside a terraced house, the garden path guarded by plastic gnomes. The front door opens, and Mrs Kerry waits for us.

We go through into an immaculately tidy lounge with a red carpet and plastic-covered plush armchair and sofa. Porcelain figurines pirouette and grin from the mantelpiece. It smells of air freshener, artificially floral. 'Tea?' Mrs Kerry asks.

We shake our heads and sit on the sofa. Plastic crackles. Karin comes in and perches on the arm of the chair her mother sits in. I notice that she's washed her hair, and her clothes look clean.

We sit in silence, the atmosphere awkward. Karin chews her nails and gazes into the distance above our heads.

'We want you to know that we're not pressing charges,' Thea says. 'About the pictures.'

'They've already questioned me about the break-in,' Mrs Kerry says. 'Taken fingerprints and that. But I didn't hurt you, Meg.'

'I believe you,' I tell her.

'We would like to know the whole story, Mrs Kerry,' Thea goes on. 'You must have been up in the attic before. You knew about the portraits? None of us did.'

'It wasn't until after the accident that he asked me to take care of the paintings and do the videoing.' She sounds defensive.

'Sorry?' Ophelia queries. 'Videoing?'

'Why you?' I lean forward. 'Why did he ask you to do it?'

'I've been in his debt for a long time.' Her voice trembles. 'It started years ago.' She bites her bottom lip. 'He called me into his study and told me he had something serious to discuss. He said that my Karin had stolen a very valuable painting from him. He said it was worth half a million pounds.'

She falls silent and none of us speak. I'm holding my breath.

'I begged him not to go to the police – I said I'd ask her about it. I'd never normally have believed it of her, but the thing was, by then, Karin had started to behave out of character. She'd started skipping school. She'd become surly and secretive.' Mrs Kerry's voice wobbles and she straightens her skirt over her knees. Karin reaches down and squeezes her mother's shoulder. 'When I asked her about the painting, she slammed out of the house. I didn't see her for a couple of days. I searched her room. It was in her bag, under her bed. The bag she'd taken on a school trip.' She blows her nose on a cotton hanky and balls it in her fist. 'I took the painting back to Mr Aldredge, and he said because I'd been such a valuable employee for so long, he wouldn't report Karin to the police. I was that grateful, I'd have done anything for him.' She sniffs. 'Then he started to ask me to do things. Little jobs, he called them.' She blushes and looks away. 'I'm ashamed... but he asked me to start rumours about Alison, make her life difficult in the village. He wanted her gone for some reason.' She shrugs. 'Even when she got a stone through her caravan window, she wouldn't leave. It wasn't me that threw the stone,' she adds quickly. 'And I'd never have spread the rumours if I'd known what I know now.'

She shifts in her seat. 'After the accident, I hoped that would be the end of the jobs. But he's stayed in contact with me all these years from France. Said a lot of people believed he was dead, and he wanted to keep it that way and he told me the story I should tell if anyone asked, about him saving your cousin and dying in the effort. Then he said he had an important task for me – there were valuable portraits in the attic, and I should take care of them. It was top priority, secret work. He explained about the old smuggling tunnel that leads to the bricked-up servants' back staircase.'

'And the videoing?' Ophelia interrupts.

'He had the camera delivered to me. I had to video the portraits in a particular order and send him the tapes. It was creepy going down that tunnel and murder on my legs, but I made sure I went regularly, to dust and sweep, as well as doing the videoing. I went at night, mostly. He'd want me to switch the pictures around, put new ones up, change the order. They were all named. It was a code, you see. At least,' she finishes, shaking her head again. 'That was what he told me.'

We look at each other, our mouths open.

'A code for what?' Ophelia asks.

Mrs Kerry shrugs. 'I just did what he asked. I didn't want the police to come after Karin. She was already in such a bad place.'

'He was blackmailing you,' Thea says, in a dead voice.

'I believed that Karin had stolen that painting,' Mrs Kerry says. 'For years, I've been following orders. Reporting to him about who was in the house, and what you girls were up to. And when you came,' she looks at me, 'I told him about you, and he said to get rid of you as quickly as possible.'

'The earrings,' I say. 'The notes?'

She nods.

'But it wasn't you who hit me?' I sit up straighter, feeling the bruise on my head.

'No.' She frowns. 'I already told you. I'm not a violent woman.'

'She was with me when that happened,' Karin says.

'It must have been Mick,' Mrs Kerry says. 'He's got a nasty streak. And he was working for Mr Aldredge too.'

'Then Mick locked us in.' Ophelia looks at me.

'And I never took that painting,' Karin says. 'He planted it on me.'

'We believe you, Karin,' Thea says.

Mrs Kerry pats her daughter's knee. 'Tell them what you told me, love.'

Karin folds her lips, shakes her head.

'It's alright, love,' Mrs Kerry urges her quietly. 'You need to let it out. They need to know.'

Karin nods and wipes her nose on the edge of her sleeve. 'When I was a kid, Mr Aldredge was kind to me,' she says slowly, looking into her lap. 'One day, he saw me on my way back from school and gave me a lift. He said he knew I wanted to be a film director, and he could help me. He knew people.'

Mrs Kerry is sitting bolt upright, her expression fixed, fingers clasping and unclasping.

Karin keeps staring into her lap. 'He met me a few times, took me out for tea and cake, told me he believed in me. That I was a clever girl. Told me to keep our meetings secret because his family wouldn't want him helping the cleaner's daughter.'

Beside me, Thea growls at the back of her throat.

'Then he said he had a big opportunity for me – but I had to come to London. He said he was going to introduce me to an important film director. He told me to pretend to my parents I was going on a school trip because it was a secret – we couldn't tell anyone. It was exciting at first. He took me to his flat, gave me cakes to eat and let me drink champagne. When he kissed me, I liked it at first. I couldn't believe a grown-up like him would be interested in me, a schoolgirl. Then he left me alone in the flat for a couple of days, said he had meetings. I was lonely and bored; he'd locked me in. He said I'd get lost if I left the flat. I lay on the floor and scratched our initials into the paintwork, low down, so he wouldn't see.'

She stops and gazes at her bitten nails.

'I was so happy when he came back. But he was different. Told me I had to stop dressing like a child. He gave me stuff to wear. Slutty stuff. Then, he said I had to get used to pleasing a man, that I'd need to do that with the big film director, and he'd show me how to do it right—' She breaks off, swallowing a sob. 'I said I wanted to go home. But he... he made me do things... dirty things. He kept me in the flat for days. I think he drugged me because it was all a blur after that, but I was aware enough to know he had me whenever he wanted... however he wanted.'

Ophelia is crying. Thea holds my hand, squeezing it tight, her nails digging in.

'When he was finished with me, he drove me home. He said if I ever said a word someone would come and slit my throat, and then they'd come for my family. He said he had important friends in the police force and government. There'd always be someone watching me. He said nobody would believe my side of the story.'

'I didn't know,' Mrs Kerry says. 'I didn't know any of it. She changed from the moment she came home – started drinking and playing truant. I blame myself. I should have had an instinct for what was going on.'

'It's not your fault, Mum.'

Mrs Kerry blots her cheeks with a hanky. 'If Mr Kerry wasn't already dead, this would kill him. He never knew why

Karin went off the rails, never understood why our little girl changed —' She breaks off, pressing the hanky to her mouth.

'I'm going to give a statement to the police,' Karin says, tilting her chin. 'I need to tell them the truth. Mum has Mr Aldredge's address in France. He could still get prosecuted, couldn't he?'

Ophelia stands up. 'I don't know how it works when someone is abroad. We're going to see him ourselves, and we'll try to get a taped confession from him. We already have an audio tape my mother made – it's damning evidence – we'll go to the police as soon as we get back from seeing him.'

'There was a smell of cigars.' I stand up too. 'I kept smelling it in the house,' I say. 'Who was smoking them?'

'Mick,' Mrs Kerry says. 'He knew the way through the tunnel. He found a box of Mr Aldredge's cigars in the attic and he'd sit in that chair, looking at the portraits, a cigar in his mouth as if he was the boss. I told him he shouldn't do it, but he told me he was working for a powerful organisation, and he could do whatever he liked.'

As we leave, Thea tells Mrs K and Karin, 'Lucian's not our real father. We've just found out.'

We drive home in silence. None of us speak. Ophelia stares straight ahead through the windscreen, her fingers tight on the steering wheel.

'Should we pick Clem up?' I wonder.

'Let's leave her,' Thea says. 'She'll come back when she's ready.'

At home, Thea turns to Ophelia and me. 'Did you see Karin's portrait in the attic?' We shake our heads. 'I think what he did to her – he must have done it to the ones he didn't consider beautiful or special enough to put in his collection.' Her face is hard. 'I think his collection is a record of all the women he's seduced,' she goes on. 'He keeps the portraits like a butterfly collector keeps pinned specimens, to gloat over, as proof of his virility and power. And he has them all wearing the pendant like a mark of ownership or something.' She opens her hands. 'He'd been doing it all through our childhood. Pretending to be a great husband and father.'

'Don't,' Ophelia says, putting her head in her hands. 'And Ma painted them. So, she must have known. She was in on it.'

'At least we're not related to him,' Thea says. 'Bastard.' But her words are undermined by the sob in her throat.

40

The front doorbell rings, cutting through my dreams. I check my clock, yawning. It's gone ten, and my head is thick. We'd sat up drinking brandy last night, listening to Clem telling us about her afternoon with Alison, talking over what Mrs K and Karin had told us, discussing whether Ophelia and Thea would track down their real mothers. We'd gone into the attic and found the piece of paper with the details Calista had left for them. She was right. There wasn't much to go on for Ophelia and Thea. I'd texted John last night to tell him the news.

The doorbell goes again as I struggle into my clothes. I can hear voices from below, so one of the others must have answered. As I come onto the landing, still zipping up my jeans, Thea calls up the stairs, 'Meg, it's for you.'

I hurry down, with the sudden nervous, crazy hope that it's John, surprising me by flying in from America. But of course, it's not. Claire is on the doorstep, and I know at once from her expression that it's important. My heartbeat stutters. I put my hand to my throat. 'What?' I ask. 'What's wrong?'

'I told you I'd let you know,' she says. 'If I heard anything.'

Wings thrash inside my chest. 'About Mum?'

'Meg – I've spoken to her.'

'You've spoken to her?' My knees slump, and I stagger. Thea puts her arm around my waist, propping me up. 'But... she's dead.' I step away from Thea. 'You can't have heard from her.'

Claire holds my gaze. 'I know where she is.'

'She's alive?' I can hardly speak.

'Yes.' Claire smiles. 'Yes. She is. She'd like to see you. She's not far away.'

'Now?' I lick my lips. 'She's... here?'

'In Ipswich.' She gestures to her car parked on the gravel. 'I can take you to her?'

Thoughts whirl in a vortex – a hiss of white noise – cancelling each other out. I stare at Claire. I can't respond. Everything has slowed. Five minutes ago, I believed Mum was dead, and now, now I'll see her for the first time in fifteen years. My heart slams against my ribs, thunders between my ears.

Claire steps towards me. 'Trust me, Meg,' she says, as she folds my hand firmly inside her own.

I am in the car. Thea shuts the passenger door, puts her palm on the glass. I nod at her, and Claire starts the engine. She drives me down country lanes and onto the main road. 'Where is she?' my voice creaks through dry lips. 'How is she?'

She shakes her head as she changes gear. 'Better if it comes from her.' She's driving fast; we overtake a slower vehicle. 'But I have to admit something,' she says, staring through the wind-screen. 'Your mum contacted me a while ago. I knew where she was when you came to see me. But I'd been sworn to secrecy. I couldn't tell you anything then. I'm sorry.'

My stomach roils and clenches. 'I don't understand,' I whisper. 'What kind of trouble is she in? Has something terrible happened to her?'

'She's had a rough time,' Claire admits. 'But she's come through it. She'll explain.'

We arrive in Ipswich, and Claire parks on the street near the station. I follow as she leads the way to a building, a red brick church hall with pots of geraniums outside. My legs are trembling. A sign next to the open door says 'Free Hot Meals'. 'I can't do this,' I whisper.

Claire gestures for me to go in before her. 'It's alright,' she says.

There's an entrance with a large notice board covered in pinned cards and papers. I hear the rumble of voices, the clink of metal, feet shuffling over the floor. Inside the hall, people stand in line, waiting to get a plate. Helpers behind trestle tables are busy ladling out steaming food. I smell school-dinner gravy and behind that, unwashed clothes, unwashed bodies, the sour stink of alcohol fumes and cigarette smoke. My eyes scan stooped shapes, looking at tangles of dirty hair and the hunched shoulders of the people in the queue. Which one is she?

One of the helpers has put down her ladle. She's staring at me. A thin woman with a tired, kind face, her salt-and-pepper hair caught up in a chignon. She's taking off her apron as she steps around the trestle table. She doesn't take her eyes off me as she walks towards us. She catches Claire's wrist as she passes her. 'Thank you,' she whispers.

Claire dips her head and walks away.

It's just me and the woman. The noise in the room fades away.

'Mum,' I say. 'Mum.'

And then I'm crying, and she's holding me. She smells of

food. But under it, I think I detect something familiar, saline, minerally, a hint of patchouli. I let myself rest in her arms for a blissful moment before I struggle free to look at her again, trying to read in her face all the answers I've been waiting for. This is the woman who abandoned me – this is the woman who walked out on me and Dad – who's been missing and silent for fifteen long years. Anger flares, bright and righteous in my chest. She sees my expression, and colour drains from her cheeks.

* * *

We're wandering the streets, winter sunshine in our eyes. We walk side by side, not touching. 'I asked Claire to bring you,' she says. 'I contacted her when I came back to Suffolk. I've been staying in a hostel for a few weeks, working in the homeless shelter. When Claire said you'd come to see her to ask about me, I thought that must mean you'd be willing to see me. So, I plucked up the courage to face you.'

'Of course I wanted to see you,' I exclaim. 'How could you have thought otherwise?'

'Shame does strange things.' She hangs her head. 'I didn't feel I deserved anything but your anger. Your scorn.'

'I was a little girl when you left,' I tell her. 'For years I thought I must have done something wrong to make you leave us.'

'Oh, Meg...' Her voice clogs with tears. 'I'm so sorry.'

'But where the hell have you been?' A knot twists in my guts. 'Before now? Years, Mum. It's been years.' I frown. 'I thought you were dead.'

'I'm sorry,' she repeats. 'There are no words to make it right. Nothing to bring back that time.' She sits on a bench, and I sit next to her. 'I made a terrible decision. I ran away with a man. And then, it all went wrong, and I ended up homeless in London. Alone. I started to drink.' She clasps her fingers. 'I hated myself.'

'You were an alcoholic?'

She nods, her mouth grim. 'They were lost years. Terrible years. I was on the streets – ashamed and frightened. Drinking was my only escape.'

'It was Lucian Aldredge, wasn't it? The man you went off with?'

She gazes at the ground, and nods.

My body is cold, ice cold. I squeeze my hands together, fingernails biting into my palms. 'Did you know he was supposed to have drowned?' I ask. 'Did you know he took me out in their boat?'

She turns her head away, squeezing her hands together.

'But he didn't drown – he's alive,' I say. 'He was disfigured in an accident. A powerboat. He's been a recluse ever since.'

She lets out a long breath. 'What?' She looks startled. 'He's alive?'

'There's no portrait of you,' I say. 'In his attic collection. I thought Calista painted all his... women?'

She's biting her bottom lip, staring into space.

'Mum?'

'I knew he had a collection of portraits of women. But I never saw them.' She blinks and looks at me. 'Calista refused to paint me,' she says quietly. 'It was brave of her to defy him.'

'How could you have done it?' I move further away from her on the damp wooden slats. 'How could you have left me? And Dad?' Nausea overwhelms me. 'You chose him over us?'

'I know. I can never make it up to you.'

I can't speak. Words stick in my throat. I hold my body rigidly apart from her, my arms crossed.

'There is a story,' she says softly. 'And if you let me, I'll tell you.' She looks up at me. 'I don't ask for your forgiveness, Meg. I'm not expecting any of this to be an excuse for what I did. It's just the facts. And I owe you those.'

'Alright,' I nod. 'I want to hear it.' I pluck at my hair. It still has a faint smell of smoke. 'But first, explain something I don't understand. After you ran away, after it went wrong with... him, why didn't you try and come back? Couldn't you have asked me and Dad to forgive you?'

She looks at the litter of disintegrating cigarette butts and pigeon droppings at our feet.

'Did you come home?' I touch her arm, suddenly full of urgency. 'Mum?'

'He was very angry. I don't blame him. He told me not to come back.' She bites down on her lip. 'He said if I had any decency left, I'd leave you alone.'

I draw in a sharp breath. 'You saw Dad?'

'Don't blame him,' she says quickly. 'I don't.' She shivers. 'What I did was unforgiveable.'

I hunch into my coat. It's cold on the bench, but I don't want to move, not until I've heard her story. 'Start at the beginning,' I say.

* * *

When she gets to the end, my hand is in hers, our intertwined fingers squeezing painfully tight. 'What happened?' I whisper. 'How did you get out of the crate?'

'It was Calista,' she says. 'When I didn't call, she realised something was wrong and came back to the flat. She let me out. I don't think I would have lasted much longer in there.'

My tears come fast; she's crying too. We hug each other. She feels fragile in my arms. I'm bigger than her now, stronger. It's too cold to go on sitting outside. As we walk slowly back to the church hall, I tell her what I've been doing at Deben Manor, and what we've discovered about Lucian. 'None of it surprises me,' she says quietly. 'What terrifies me is how I fell for his lies, how manipulated I was by him.' She rubs her forehead. 'I knew him as Paul in Manchester. He worked for a gang. He was in with dangerous people, but he was charming and funny, and I didn't think he was violent. I was naive. He reinvented himself in Suffolk. Became Lucian Aldredge. He'd always wanted to be considered cultured, artistic. I think he used the gang to make money – a lot of money – but he planned to start again, turn himself into someone else.'

Out of the corner of my eye, I glimpse a figure scurrying across the street behind us and the familiar feeling of being followed makes my skin prickle. But that's all over now, I remind myself as I glance at a heavily wrapped man shuffling into a doorway. I push my uneasiness away.

'It's overwhelming, isn't it?' she says with a sad smile. 'We can take this slowly. I don't want to swamp you.'

In the church hall, there are just a few people left eating at the long tables. Mum goes into the kitchen and pours us mugs of strong tea from an urn. As she gives me my cup, I notice how rough and red her hand is, the joints of her fingers swollen. Those lost years on the streets have aged her, and I know she won't be the same woman I remember, not after what she's been through.

'I was told I wasn't good enough all the time, when I was a child,' Mum says quietly. 'I've never really explained my upbringing to you. My mother abandoned me when I was a baby. I was alone in the world, and people took advantage of me. I met Paul – I mean, Lucian – when I was in Manchester. For the first time, I felt someone recognised me, valued me. But none of it was real.' We're sitting side by side on a bench at an otherwise empty refectory table, wiped clean and smelling of Dettol. 'I believed it was love. But that's what he did – he groomed people, manipulated them – I think having control was the thing he wanted, more than anything, to be the puppet master. And of course, vulnerable people, people with low self-esteem, are easier targets.'

'What will you do now? What about Dad?' I ask, swallowing my tears. 'Will you tell him you're here?'

'I'd like to see him more than anything,' she says. 'But he might not want to see me.'

As I leave the hall, I peer up and down the street in both directions and wonder when I'm going to stop expecting someone to be behind me, to think I hear footsteps, glimpse a watcher in the shadows.

11

IRENE

Fifteen Years Ago

The crate opens. Light stabs my eyes. I can't see, can't move. I force myself to crawl onto the carpet where I collapse, flexing cramping muscles, trying to unstick my frozen joints and welded bones. 'You stink,' he says.

I cower, expecting a blow to the back of my head, but I'd rather die in the open than in the box. I sense him squatting beside me, peering into the container. 'For fuck's sake,' he growls. 'Couldn't you have waited?'

I feel his toe in my ribs, nudging me. 'Get up,' he says.

I fumble onto my hands and knees, groaning. Then, holding my breath, I manage to straighten, afraid the bones in my spine will snap with each tiny movement I make to uncurl. I stand, dizzy, disorientated.

He hands me a glass of water and I gulp it down. I can only see out of my left eye. He leads me into the bathroom and stands guard while I use the loo. There's no room for pride any more – he's stripped any dignity away. I splash my face afterwards, drinking from the tap. I avoid the mirror, not wanting to witness my bruised face but more than that, I'm frightened the glass will be empty, as if I'm already a ghost. My clothes are damp with urine. He won't let me get changed.

'I'm still deciding what to do with you,' he says, his voice unemotional, practical, as if he's discussing an old car. 'The problem is, unlike the others, you know about my past.'

I open my mouth to speak, but he grabs my hair in his fist, twisting tight. The pressure at my scalp jerks my head back so that I'm looking into his face. He's a stranger. I do not recognise him, this man I thought I loved, this man I've known for years. His eyes are cold, unblinking. A trace of disgust twists his mouth. 'I have an appointment this afternoon,' he says. 'I'll be back this evening.'

I realise he's leading me towards the container, his grasp corkscrewing my hair from my head, the pain electrifying. 'No,' I manage. 'No. Please.' I don't have the strength to fight him. He pushes me onto my knees, kicking and shoving, forcing me into the container again. Tears of frustration and terror blur my eyes. Salt in my mouth. Darkness.

* * *

I don't know how many hours pass before there's a sudden rush of air, and the slab of darkness turns into a square of dazzling brilliance. My heart flips. He's back. But if he wanted to kill me, wouldn't he just leave me in here? I edge out, head down, hand, knee, hand, knee. Everything aches.

'Irene.' A woman's voice.

Shocked, I force myself to sit upright and rest on my heels, blinking up. My right eye is still partly closed. A shape stands over me. Light and dark flickers across my vision. 'You didn't phone,' Calista says. She grabs me under the arms and helps me to my feet. 'Where is he?'

I move parched lips with difficulty. 'He said... going out...' My voice cracks with each word. 'Back this evening.' I touch my right eye, wincing at swollen skin.

'Alright.' She sounds relieved. She points me in the direction of the bathroom. 'Have a shower. I'll get some clean clothes for you.'

I should ask her why she's doing this, but I don't have the energy. I want that shower with every fibre of my being. I step out of my clothes and stand under it, turning it up to full. It feels incredible. Each tiny jet of clean water bouncing against my skin is a blessing. I begin to feel human – to feel like myself.

After I'm dressed, she hands me a cup of tea. My hands tremble around the hot cup as I watch her pacing the kitchen. She wheels around, biting her fingernails, her eyes wild. 'We should go. When he gets back and finds the container empty, he'll know it was me.'

'What will you do?'

'I don't know.' Her voice is tight. Breathless with panic. 'I've never gone against him before.'

'Leave him.' I touch her hand. 'Calista, you're a talented painter. He's mad – and dangerous.'

'I can't leave him. I don't know who I am without him.' She pulls away from my touch. 'You don't understand,' she says. 'I belong to him.'

'I do understand,' I say quietly.

She's parked the car a couple of streets away. We stop on the outskirts of London to buy sandwiches in a garage. I gobble down stale egg and cress on white, the curling slices the most delicious thing I've ever tasted. 'I'll drop you at the cottage,' she says.

I think of Robert. How can he possibly forgive me? I've lost him. My chest contracts. Shame and self-loathing crawl through me. 'I need to see Meg,' I tell her. 'Can we go to Deben Manor?'

She frowns. 'Too dangerous.'

'Please.' I put my hand on her arm. 'I need to get her away from your house, from him.'

'Alright.' She shrugs me off. 'But let's get going. He'll head for home as soon as he realises you've escaped.'

We drive in silence as night falls, both of us lost in our own thoughts. She puts her foot down; hedges and fields blur past as the light fades. A fierce wind buffets the car, whipping the scrubby trees backwards. On the A12, the car stutters and hiccups. Smoke comes from the front, clouding the windscreen. Calista slams her hand on the steering wheel. 'No, no, no.' She steers onto a hard shoulder. We get out and she pops the bonnet. She gazes into the tangle of metal below and spreads her hands towards it. 'Oh my God. It's a sign. I should never have let you out.' Her voice is high, hysterical.

I stand next to her, my hair whipping into my face as I stare at the smoking engine. 'It's just an electrical fault or… or the fan belt or something. It's a coincidence it's happened now.' I touch her elbow. 'Calista, you did the right thing – you saved my life.'

We walk along the verge to an emergency phone, stumbling in the windy dark, cars flashing past. Then we trudge back to the car, and sit on the prickly grass to wait, a drift of rubbish at our feet. Calista shivers, her teeth chattering, more with fear I think than cold, although the weather has changed. The summer stillness and heat has blown away, the wind ushering in a drop in temperature. I am sick with frustration at the delay. I think of hitching, but I can't leave Calista. Not after what she's done for me, what she's risked. Vehicles rush past, headlights on, tyres roaring. Eventually, an AA tow truck arrives, and a man gets out. After fiddling with the engine, he says he can't fix it by the side of the road. He agrees to tow us to the nearest garage. From there, we get a taxi. 'It's too late to take you to Deben Manor,' Calista says, her voice tight. 'He'll know you've escaped by now. He could even have driven past us – he could already be at the house.'

'Let's ask the driver to take us to a police station,' I suggest.

'No,' she grips my hand. 'Not that.' Her nails dig into my skin. 'I released you because I owe it to my brother – but I'm not going to let you send my husband to prison.'

I think of Meg in that house – Lucian could be with her at this moment. My chest constricts. But even if I manage to get to a phone box without Calista knowing, and the police arrive at Deben Manor, I know she'll deny finding me in the crate, and side with Lucian. And why should the police believe me? I left home of my own free will – sent Robert a note telling him I'd met someone else.

'Okay,' I agree. 'But please, Calista. I must find Meg.'

The taxi drops us at the bottom of the drive. It's nearing dawn. There's a faint milky light on the horizon, inky darkness diluted. The wind is just as fierce here, pushing at us as we walk along the edge of the gravel. Rooks caw from the thrashing trees. 'His car is here,' she grabs my arm, fingers digging in.

'I'm going inside,' I tell her, wriggling out of her clutch. 'Where's Meg's room?'

Calista waits outside. I creep through the dark hall and a large dog rises from the floor, a low growl in its throat. 'Matisse.' I remember his name. 'Here, boy.' He pads over and I pat his head. Every creaking floorboard makes me wince. I expect Lucian to appear from a doorway, grabbing my neck, twisting my arm behind my back. There's another crate here, I remember, in the attic.

Upstairs, I find the back bedroom, the door flung wide. Her bed is still faintly warm, the covers thrown back as if she left in a hurry. I pick up her pillow and press my face into it, searching for a trace of her breath, the scent of her skin. Panic flails inside me. Where is she? I creep along the landing. She could be in a bathroom. But I don't know the layout of the house.

There's no sign of waking life in the rest of the house, apart from the dog. I slip out of the front door. Calista gestures behind her. 'The Land Rover's gone,' she says. 'That might mean he's at the river.'

Terror squeezes the breath from my lungs. 'He's got Meg with him,' I gasp.

We get into his car; the keys are in the ignition. 'This has tipped him over the edge,' Calista says as she starts the engine 'He has to be the one in control.'

'I can go alone,' I tell her. 'You've already done so much.'

But she shakes her head. 'I want Meg to be safe, too.'

And she doesn't want me to call the police, I think. She's keeping an eye on me. In the car, the smell of warm leather and pine air freshener makes me remember the morning I left home, my naiveté and stupidity as I sat next to him, thinking we were starting a new life together.

At the river, there's no sign of them, or anyone else. The river is empty of sails or activity. 'He's taken the dinghy,' Calista says, scanning the boat park.

The wind tugs at my clothes, plucks at the wires on the masts of boats, making an odd metallic sound, like ghostly instruments. I stare at the expanse of dark water, the beating waves. 'She can't swim,' I whisper. 'She's terrified of water.' I turn to Calista. 'He knows that. He's doing this to punish me.'

'No,' she says. 'Meg kept asking him for a sailing lesson.' But her face reflects my fear. We both know he hasn't taken her for a sailing lesson. A sleek white speedboat is moored close to the jetty, jibing against its rope.

'If only I could use that,' I mutter. 'I want to get out there. Look for them.'

'That's Bill's boat,' Calista says. 'I know where he keeps the key.' She touches my arm. 'Have you driven one before?'

I nod. But it's a lie.

She takes me out in the Aldredge rowing boat and waits while I clamber into the speedboat. The key is where she said it would be. I take the cover off the huge outboard engine and find a lever that lowers the propellers into the water. I have no idea what I'm doing, but it's just a floating car, I tell myself. And I'm a good driver.

I slot in the key into the ignition and the engine starts with one turn. My fingers tremble on the wheel as I turn it, swinging the boat around. I push a knob on the controls and the boat rears up. I'm thrown backwards, smashing my shoulder as I land on my back.

The boat veers to the left as I'm scrambling to my feet. I grab the wheel. I'm heading straight for a large, moored cruiser. I manage to swerve at the last moment, pulling the throttle back. The boat slows. I steady myself at the wheel, swiping my hair from my eyes and take a deep breath. I have to do this for Meg.

I push the throttle forward again more gradually to increase the speed. The prow lifts as the craft surges ahead. I look behind at the spreading trail of wake, lit by a red glow coming up over the horizon. Calista is standing on the quay.

The river has become wider, the banks distant. I'm nearly at the bend in the river before it opens into the sea. I've got the hang of the controls now and I slow the boat so that I can scan my surroundings, looking for a sail, for my child. She's in danger. I feel it in my core. An urgent, swelling terror. There's something in the water, a dark shape. I approach carefully, my heart thumping. I think at first, it's a seal, then I see the pale of human flesh, the bloated movement of fabric. Meg! But when I'm nearly on top of it I recognise Lucian. He's floating on his back, a flash of orange life jacket just visible under his top. He opens his eyes as I edge the side of the craft next to him, cutting the engine.

'Thank fuck,' he says between chattering teeth. 'Get me out of here.' He lifts an arm, not knowing who he's talking to. 'I'm freezing.'

'It's me,' I say, ignoring his hand. 'Irene.'

'You,' he exclaims. 'Of course, it's bloody you.' He frowns. 'It was Calista who let you out, wasn't it?' He gives an odd grunting laugh. 'Who would have thought she had it in her?' Dark liquid seeps across his forehead, leaking from a gash near the hairline.

'Where's Meg?' I ask.

'When I saw the empty crate, I knew you'd come to get her.' He coughs. 'Stupid girl had us over.' He rights himself, treading water. 'Help me in.'

'You mean you capsized?' My flesh prickles with fear. 'Oh my God. Where is she?' I stand up, turning to stare over the steering wheel down the river towards the sea, the boat rocking beneath my feet. 'Where's my daughter?'

'She won't have made it. She didn't have a life jacket on,' he says. 'Quickly, Irene. Take my hand.' He reaches for me again. 'Help me out.'

'What do you mean?' I lean over the side, staring into his

face. Waves slap the hull. 'You know she can't swim.' Hysteria bubbles inside me. 'You took her out without a life jacket?'

'But Irene.' His face creases into a smile. 'That's what you're supposed to do – drown the runts of the litter, the ones nobody wants.'

My vision implodes into nothingness. Red bursts through. My mind snaps shut as if I'm locked in the box again. The memory of his fist cracking my cheekbone, the grip of his fingers as he pushed me into the container. I shudder and open my eyes.

He frowns up at me from the water. 'Irene,' he says. 'Concentrate. You need to help me into the boat.' He reaches his hand towards me again. 'Remember the story I told you in the flat?' he says. 'The one about you being a stalker, how you followed me here to Suffolk and married my brother-in-law, just to get close to me?' His lips are blue. 'If you don't want everyone to hear that version of our history, take my hand.'

I shake my head. 'I'll tell them the real story.'

'There's no such thing,' he says. 'The strongest lie wins. Nobody will believe you.' His voice, despite his chattering teeth, is full of confidence. 'Calista will come to heel. She'll regret her little rebellion. You're on your own, Irene.'

My fingers move towards his; then I snatch them away.

A wave washes over his face. He splutters. 'For God's sake. Get me out.'

But I'm already restarting the engine and turning the wheel. I hear him calling as I set the prow towards the mouth of the river. My hands on the wheel are shaking. It's not enough to abandon him. Someone will find him. A sob sticks in my throat as I remember his words. Where is Meg? He's done this on purpose to hurt me. He can't have drowned my daughter. He can't. But I know him now – and I know he could.

Anger burns through me, the flames of my rage scouring me with something pure at last – clean and sharp – it allows my body to act independently from thought. I sweep the boat around, turning it in a wide half circle, spray curving behind in an arc and point the speedboat directly at the figure bobbing in the water. I squeeze my fingers around the steering wheel, gripping the throttle. The engine revs and roars as the boat leaps forwards.

I don't hear him shout a warning or protest; I don't even know if he sees me coming. The world narrows to this point – to this moment, stretching and slowing – as blood rages between my ears, and the distance between me and Lucian closes, the wheel steady in my hands. I shut my eyes as the keel bumps against him; a thump and the wheel twists in my grip, the blades of the propeller meeting an obstacle, tearing into it, slicing through it, churning on. My knuckles whiten as I grip the juddering plastic. It's over in seconds.

I stop the boat behind a moored yacht, gasping for breath. I don't look back at what I've done. There was no human scream, nothing to signal my crime, just the sound of the wind and the lap of water, seabirds calling. I'm trembling, nauseous. I lean over the side and retch. There's no time for this. I need to find Meg. The horizon is light now, the world waking up. I wipe my mouth on the back of my hand and start the engine, continuing downriver, straining my eyes for the lost dinghy, for Meg's body in the water.

There's another engine, loud in the stillness. A bigger craft is coming in from the North Sea, it looks like a fishing boat in from a night's fishing. I steer behind a tall, moored yacht; I don't want the fishermen to see me. Ahead, lit by the rising sun, I can make out the swell of waves where the current meets the ocean. Dawn picks out something bobbing on the white horses:

the upturned dinghy. My hand flies to my mouth. But the fishing boat is slowing; they've seen it too. They've stopped, and they're hauling something out of the water. I can't breathe, can't take my eyes away. I see the outline of a child caught in a man's arms. Her arm twitches, her dangling legs move. She's alive. I let out a gulp of joy, tears blinding me. She's alive.

I cut the engine and slip into the bottom of the boat, shivering as I hug my knees to my chest. Tears choke me. Nothing matters except she is alive.

On the wind, the voices of the fishermen reach me. I need to get to shore before them. Lucian's remains could be found at any minute and people will be looking for the culprit driving a speedboat. I need to get the boat back before anyone sees me. Sailors will be arriving at the river soon.

* * *

I moor the boat to its buoy, cover the engine, and put the key back, pulling my sleeve down to wipe the places I've touched. I don't examine the dripping blades of the propeller, not wanting to see fragments of flesh, hair, strips of caught fabric, though I'm hoping the river has washed the blades clean. I slip over the side and swim the short distance to shore in my clothes as there's no Calista waiting with the rowing boat. The water is silty and freezing. I trudge up the slipway, sodden, exhausted. Lucian's car has gone.

As I get onto the quay, I hear a siren approaching. The fishing boat must have contacted emergency services with their radio. An ambulance rounds the corner, flashing lights scissoring blue beams. The vehicle pulls onto the quay, just as the fishing boat arrives, its thumping engine loud. The tide is high enough for the boat to come right alongside the quay. There's a smell of fish competing with diesel fumes. Hiding in the shadow of the bus shelter at the side of the quay, I watch the paramedics go on board. I can hardly breathe as they carry Meg off on a stretcher and put her into the back of the ambulance.

I want to rush forward and claim my daughter, every part of me longs to go to her, but how to explain that I'm fully dressed and soaking wet? Someone might have seen me mooring the boat or swimming to shore. I can't risk giving my name here, not yet. Lucian's remains will be discovered soon; the first sails have already unfurled; I can see a couple of triangles of white out there, dinghies heeling in the wind as they skim the river. Questions will be asked. There will be a murder hunt.

I walk out of the village and keep walking down country roads until I can hitch a ride, striking it lucky when a lorry driver picks me up. I explain that there's been an accident on the river, and my daughter's been taken to the local hospital. He insists on going out of his way to drop me at the gates of the hospital. The morning has broken, bright and flawless. I apologise for making his seat wet. 'Don't you worry about that. You go and see your daughter,' he says. His kindness stings my throat.

I ask for Meg at the reception desk, explaining that I'm her mother. Eventually, I'm directed to a ward on the second floor. My clothes have dried to an uncomfortable dampness, but my shoes squelch, leaving wet footprints. A nurse explains that the main problem is the wound in Meg's leg. 'A nasty gash, and infected, but it's been caught early, so she'll be just fine.' They let me see her. She's asleep, hooked up to an antibiotic drip. She looks fragile, her freckles bleached by pallor, her left hand wrapped in a bandage with a canula. I bend down and kiss her forehead.

A creak of feet on the floor behind me, stopping close by. I turn. Robert stands at the foot of Meg's bed. His anxious face is stretched wide at the sight of me.

'She's okay,' I tell him quickly. 'She's asleep.'

His mouth hardens, and he beckons over his shoulder as he strides out of the ward. I follow. He stops in the corridor and swings round to face me. 'This is your fault,' he hisses. 'You did this.' He holds himself stiffly from me. 'Who is he,' he asks. 'Who's the man?'

'Lucian,' I whisper.

Robert's already pale face turns dishcloth grey. He takes a step back, reeling as if from a punch.

'I'm sorry,' I say. 'So sorry. It's over now. I made a mistake.'

He blinks and swallows, setting his shoulders straighter. 'Well, don't think you can come crawling back,' he says. 'We don't need you. We don't want you. You disgust me.' His voice breaks and his chin wobbles. When he can speak, his voice is icy. 'If you have any decency, you'll leave us alone. Go far away. You've already damaged Meg. She's better off without you.'

I lift one hand towards him and let it fall.

I notice him staring at my bruised eye. But he hardens his expression, swallows again, his Adam's apple bobbing in his throat. 'Excuse me,' he says with rigid formality. 'I'm going to see my daughter now.' He gives me a wide berth, avoiding contact with the air around me, as if I'm untouchable, as if I pollute the environment.

I hobble down the stairs and collapse into a seat in the waiting area in the reception. The hospital entrance is busy with people, but I'm alone, isolated. I've locked myself into a different kind of box. One of my own making. I've killed a rapist, a criminal, a murderer. But I've killed Paul, too, the man I once believed I loved and who loved me, the one I'd given my

heart to when I was hardly more than a child. Worse, I've abandoned and hurt my child. She nearly died because of me. My
teeth are chattering. I hunch over the hollowed remains of
myself until I can find the strength to get up.

I have no idea where I'm going. I leave through the
revolving door, putting one foot in front of the other, my mind
wiped by shame and grief. I remember Robert's words. I need
to get away from Suffolk, far from Robert and Meg. As I walk
the dusty pavements, I feel myself disappearing from the real
world, entering a place of shadows. It's as if I'm stepping into
the other side of a mirror, where things are warped and barren,
and I am invisible.

42

Early morning. The rooks are making a racket in the trees outside my window. I couldn't sleep last night. It feels incredible to have Mum back, although I know there's still a lot to talk about, and we need to find a new way of being together. I've promised her I'll talk to Dad when I find the right moment. I heard the hope in her voice. I think of the photo he keeps by his bed and let a flicker of hope enter me too.

The rest of the house is quiet and I'm guessing the others are still in bed. Emotional exhaustion has hit us hard. I'm grateful that Saul has kept the children with him. I pull on my clothes, thinking I'll slip down to the summer house before breakfast to feed Fred – I don't want to abandon the cat in all this excitement. It's not raining, although the grass is muddy from the battering it's taken over the winter, and my trainers are soaked. I go up the steps and open the door. Before I can step inside, a hand shoves me hard on the small of my back sending me sprawling into the room, landing on my hands and knees on the wooden boards. I struggle up, gasping for breath, kneecaps and palms stinging, bones jarred.

A man stands in the entrance; he hooks the door closed behind him with his foot. His face is distorted by a brown mesh mask, squashing his nose, blanking out expression. A woman's stocking has been squeezed over his head. One gloved hand is pointing a revolver at my chest.

'Thought you'd got away with it, didn't you?' he says. His accent is nasal with flattened vowels.

I recognise his stocky frame, the battered old jacket. My heart lunges in my ribcage, fear thickening my throat. I smell a familiar scent of leather and cloves as I edge behind the table. 'Mick?' I'm trying to keep my voice calm.

'Shut up.'

Having the gun pointed at me saps my strength. That small black eye is hypnotising. My body is heavy with dread, numb with the anticipation of death. I struggle to kick-start my mind, to remember things I've read in books and seen on TV; I need to make him see me as an individual, a human being. 'I'm Meg. The Aldredge's cousin.' He doesn't react. 'You're working for Lucian, aren't you?' I'm making a guess, but it seems more than likely. 'Whatever he's told you, he's lying.'

He gives a short, gruff laugh. 'That's what you would say.'

'It's true,' I say. 'Ask Mrs Kerry. Ask her daughter, Karin.'

He steps closer, floorboards creaking under his weight. He motions with the gun for me to sit down. I sink into the chair, keeping my gaze on him. My mind is racing, trying to think of things to say. But if he's been in Lucian's employ for years, he'll have been brainwashed into believing whatever lies Lucian's spun him.

'Lucian manipulates people,' I try. 'He makes up stories.'

'Be quiet,' he says, kicking the table leg, making it jump and rattle. Then he pushes it closer to me with his foot. It scrapes against the floor until the edge of the table is next to my right elbow. 'I've known the Guvnor for years. He trusts me, and I trust him.'

I think he's Mancunian. Mum said she met Lucian in Manchester. Was Mick part of the gang Lucian worked for? He must have been the one to hit me and tie me up, acting on Lucian's orders. His was the face I saw through the summer house window that night. My heartbeat reverberates in my ears. Talking is the only thing that might save me. Will the others notice I've gone? They're probably still in bed, and even if they're up and wondering where I am, they won't think to look here. I'm on my own. 'He asked you to log my comings and goings, didn't he?' I'm gabbling, trying to buy time. 'I found a page on the gravel. Look, I was just taking the kids to school. You could see that, couldn't you?'

'I said shut up.' He raises the revolver and motions with it towards my heart. 'I'm the one asking the questions.' I flinch as he steps closer. I can smell him, under the fusty stink of his clothes and the trace of cigar smoke, a chemical scent of adrenaline comes from his skin, spiking the air. He flexes the gloved fingers of his free hand and takes a small hammer out of his pocket, a pair of unhooked pliers, and puts them on the table neatly, like a surgeon preparing his tools.

'I'm Meg,' I say, desperately. 'I'm the little girl that used to play here in the summer house.'

'If you don't shut up,' he says, 'I'll make you.'

I can't see his face, can't read the emotion. It's chilling, like trying to communicate with a robot, a Halloween mask. 'Put your hands behind your back,' he says, pulling a length of twine from his other pocket. I shrink back as I move my arms a fraction, unable to think of how to resist.

He steps towards me, and I see the shape of his mouth under the stretch of nylon, the way the fabric pulses with his breath. Out of the corner of my eye, I sense movement above our heads. As my brain catches up, a black streak drops, a bundle of hair with whiskers and tail. Fred lands on Mick's back with a thump. Mick gives a startled shout and wheels around, the cat clinging to his shoulders. He's dropped the gun, and it skids across the floor. I fling myself towards it, landing hard on my knees.

I have it, but don't have time to get to my feet. I raise the gun, pointing the muzzle towards him. It's heavy and cold. My fingers tremble around the trigger.

Fred leaps down from Mick's back with a yowl, tail electrified. Mick straightens, aiming a kick at the cat, and turns towards me, the mesh of the stocking sucking in and out of his mouth. 'You're not going to use that.' His voice rasps. 'Give it to me.'

I remember John at my side, how he'd steadied my arm holding the catapult. He'd explained how to breathe into the shot. I hear him speaking into my ear. *Visualise it hitting the mark.*

Mick's black-leather-clad fingers reach for the gun. I fill my lungs, exhale, and squeeze the trigger. The noise is ear-splitting, a crack of metal dissecting air. The window explodes behind him, shattering into fragments.

Mick staggers backwards. With my other hand, I fumble for the mobile in my pocket. 'Don't move.' My voice sounds stronger than I feel. I gesture to Mick to keep still as I haul myself onto my feet, keeping the gun trained on him.

I'm in the middle of making a call to the police when Clem and Thea burst into the room. 'We heard a gunshot,' Thea is saying.

They stop when they see the scene before them – the

revolver beginning to droop in my grasp, and a man wearing a stocking on his head standing in a puddle of broken glass.

'You've got a gun.' Clem's hand goes to her mouth.

'What the hell?' Thea says.

I gaze at it in my hand. Black and metal and terrible. I can't move.

'What's going on?' Thea asks. She turns to the figure in the mask. 'Mick?'

There's a woman on the other end of the line asking me questions, and I keep talking into the phone, explaining to the police, giving our address. Thea takes the weapon from me and points it at Mick herself. 'Sit down,' she tells him. He slumps into the chair, ripping the stocking from his head.

'Did he hurt you?' Clem asks.

I shake my head, as I finish the call. I can't stop trembling.

* * *

A couple of uniformed policemen turn up twenty minutes later, the siren screaming. One of them talks to me, while the other snaps handcuffs on Mick. I explain it all again, and he jots it down in a notebook. Then they take Mick into custody, bagging the gun and taking that too. We'll have to go into the station later to give witness statements.

The three of us walk up to the house, following the policemen with Mick between them, and watch him be put into the car. They drive away. 'I think we all need a cup of tea,' Thea says.

'Yup.' Clem laughs shakily. 'That will make everything alright.'

Ophelia arrives in the hall wrapped in her dressing gown, a

towel twisted around her head, fresh from a bath. 'What have I missed?' she asks, eyes round. 'Did I hear a siren?'

Clem and Thea are talking at the same time, trying to explain. I'm suddenly worried about the cat. What if Mick hurt him? What if he's run away, terrified? Or if somehow the bullet found him?

'I need to go and check on Fred,' I tell the girls.

'Who?' Thea asks.

'A cat.'

'The scruffy black cat I sometimes see in the garden?' Ophelia asks.

'He lives in your summer house.'

'I'll go,' Clem says. 'You should stay here,' she tells me. 'You're in shock.'

I let the other two lead me, hobbling, into the kitchen. I ache all over. They sit me down at the table. Ophelia puts the kettle on. 'Did you mean to hit the window?' Thea asks, as she sits next to me. 'Or were you aiming at Mick?'

'The window,' I say. 'I just wanted to scare him. Warn him away.'

As I'm sipping sweet, hot tea, Clem comes back with Fred in her arms. 'He was sitting on the table looking pleased with himself,' she says.

I explain who he is, and how John and I looked after him in the summer house.

'One of Lola's kittens?' Clem is grinning.

'Who's John?' Ophelia asks.

'That boy who was always hanging around,' Clem says. 'You remember.' She looks at her sisters. 'He ran away when he saw us.'

'The gardener's son.' Thea nods as she pours boiling water

into a teapot. 'As in, the nice gardener who was here before Mick.'

'The one whose mother had an affair with... with *him*,' Ophelia adds.

Fred jumps up on my lap, purring. Clem finds a tin of tuna to feed him and puts out water in a bowl, and he leaps down and crouches over the fish, tail twitching.

'Well, I suppose he can stay,' Ophelia says, looking at him eating. 'Seeing as he was the hero of the hour.'

43

I didn't know what the shock of seeing Mum might do to Dad. I worried about his heart. When I'd told him she was back, he'd collapsed in tears. 'I never meant for her to disappear,' he'd said. 'You'd just been fished out of the river and were in hospital. I was angry. Hurt and humiliated. It was a reaction. I regretted it almost immediately. But by then she'd vanished.' He'd curled his fists against his temples. 'I tried to find her.' He'd given me an agonised look. 'I went to London. Walked the streets.'

I escorted her to the front door of the flat and stood back as Dad opened it. They didn't move. They were staring at each other as I crept away; I heard Dad's exhalation, his muffled cry, and Mum's answering sob. I went for a walk and rang John to tell him. After we'd talked about it, he said he'd booked his flight. 'Can we meet?' he asked.

'What do you think?' I said, and he laughed.

'Will you tell the girls?' I asked. 'About him being your father?'

'No,' he said. 'Because he's not. He was just, I don't know, a strike of a biological match. It was my dad who brought me up, taught me to ride a bike and shoot a catapult. It was Edward Catchpole who read me stories, and looked after me when Mum died, even when his own heart was broken. He was the dad I loved.'

'Okay,' I said. 'I get it.'

'I know you do,' he said.

* * *

The five of us get a connecting train from Paris to a tiny country station. A taxi takes the sisters, me and Mum down a straight road lined with poplars. The fields are brown and wintery. A light drizzle mists the windscreen, making everything ghostly. I sit close to Mum in the back seat. Ophelia is on the other side of me, leaning forward. 'We haven't been here for so long,' she says, staring through the glass. 'It was always summer then.'

'All the holidays here were happy ones,' Clem says. 'If only we'd known.'

'What you know now doesn't detract from what you felt then,' Mum says. 'The happiness was real. So are your memories.'

'What are we going to say to them?' Thea asks. 'I keep going over it. Their lies. Deceit. I don't know where to start.'

'We'll know what to do when we get there,' Clem says. 'We'll let instinct guide us.'

The taxi pulls up outside a stone-coloured villa. Before we reach the front door, it opens, and Calista holds it wide. She's dressed in a cream twinset and navy skirt to her knees, navy brogues with gold chains across the tongues. Her hair has been chopped brutally short; the brown peppered with grey.

The girls don't touch or hug her. The atmosphere is tense.

But Mum steps forward and embraces her. 'I'm sorry,' Mum says. 'For everything you've been through.'

'But she knew,' Ophelia says, her voice hurt and angry. 'She knew Pa stole us.'

'She was under his control,' Mum says quietly. 'And a long time ago, she rescued me. She risked everything for a woman who'd been having an affair with her husband.'

Calista looks at her daughters. 'I know I failed you.'

'Can we see him?' Thea asks. 'Where is he?'

'He's in there,' Calista says, gesturing towards the back of the house. She looks at her watch. 'But first, come into the sitting room.'

She guides us into a cold, stone-floored room. It's spartan, just an old sofa, one wooden chair, a dark wood sideboard; there's no fire in the yawning space under the chimney breast. I'm guessing the money has run out. 'You've come for answers,' she tells us, as we squash onto the threadbare sofa. 'And I'll try and give them to you.' She glances towards the back of the house. 'You won't get any from him.'

She takes an envelope from the sideboard and hands it to me. 'This is yours, Meg. I didn't want you to stay, that summer,' she adds. 'I was afraid Lucian might use you for some purpose of his own – that somehow, you'd be damaged by him.'

I slit the sealed flap with my thumb and extract the missing Polaroid.

'Mick Smith sent it to Lucian.' She answers my puzzled expression. 'He'd been following you, on Lucian's orders. After the accident, Lucian had short-term memory loss. He still can't remember the sailing accident, the speedboat, or that I let Irene out of the crate. He believes she died in there.'

'He thinks I'm dead?' Mum asks.

'I told him you were coming this morning – he's in a state of shock.' Calista sits down on the wooden chair and presses her hands over her knees. 'I let him go on believing you'd died in the crate – that way he didn't know I'd let you out, so he wasn't angry with me. Then Mrs Kerry reported a new nanny starting at Deben Manor and when Mick sent the Polaroid, Lucian guessed who Meg was and thought she was onto him for murdering Irene.' She leans across and picks a silver ring up from the dresser and hands it to Mum. 'He was wearing this when he was fished out of the river.'

Mum slips it on her finger, turning it around and around.

Calista leans forward, staring at Mum. 'It was you, wasn't it?' she asks in a low voice.

Mum looks up and the two women hold each other's gazes, the air between them alive with the unspoken. Mum gives a small nod, and in answer, Calista nods too and presses one finger to her lips. I stare between the two of them, puzzled; whatever has passed between them is private.

'So, you knew that Mrs K and Mick were working for Pa?' Clem asks Calista. 'That he'd tricked them into believing his lies?'

'Not for years,' Calista shakes her head. 'But after the accident, yes. I was the one opening the mail. He had to tell me what was going on.' She opens her hands. 'I tried to persuade him to put an end to it, but he wouldn't.'

'What did he tell Mick?' I ask.

'Mick knew Lucian before when they'd worked for the same people in Manchester. When Lucian contacted Mick on his release from prison, he told him he was an MI5 agent. That he'd been working undercover in Manchester. Then Lucian "recruited" him,' she says. 'Mick believed the Russians tried to kill Lucian when he had the accident.'

'You could have reported Pa to the police,' Thea says. 'But you've helped him deceive and hurt people.'

Calista looks down. An eyelid twitches. 'I stayed silent when I knew what he'd done. But he was my husband.'

'You make me sick,' Ophelia says, her voice shaking. 'You were the only mother we had, and you lied to us and deserted us.'

'I know why you're angry,' Mum tells Ophelia, turning her head to look earnestly from her to the other two. 'But Calista is a victim, too. Your father was more than a very persuasive man. He knew how to draw you in, and then how to destroy you and make you dependant on him.'

'Where did the pendants come from?' Clem asks. 'Were they really made for three Aldredge sisters years ago?'

Calista shakes her head. 'He commissioned them to be made. He wanted something to showcase the family crest he'd brought in an auction – it's real, the crest, but it belonged to another family. Not the Aldredges. He chose that name because it's an old Suffolk one.'

'My God, everything about our life is a lie,' Thea whispers.

'I want to know why you painted the portraits,' Ophelia says, looking at Calista. 'Why you agreed to do it?'

Calista licks her lips. 'After art school, I was hungry to change my life, to find success. I'd done well at college. But it wasn't easy, especially for me, a woman from my background. I didn't have any confidence. Then we met at a gallery showing... and everything changed.'

'Not much of an excuse for what you did,' Thea mutters.

'Lucian made me feel as if I could conquer the world,' Calista continues in a steady, quiet voice. 'He gave me a different identity, told me how to dress, sent me for elocution lessons. He had complete confidence in himself, and it seemed to transfer to me when I was with him. When he asked me to marry him, he promised we'd have a beautiful home filled with art and colour. He gave me a way to escape my past. Then soon after we'd moved into the Manor, he asked me to paint a woman's portrait from a Polaroid – he said it was payment for my new lifestyle. That was the start. I realised quickly that the women were his lovers. But also, once he gave me a Polaroid, the liaison was over.'

'But he used you,' Mum says. 'He saw your talent and he wanted it for himself. You could have become a successful painter if your work had ever been shown outside Deben Manor. Instead, it's been locked in an attic with Lucian as the sole viewer.' She frowns. 'He collected you, too. Calista. Kept you prisoner.'

'There were other women,' Ophelia says. 'The ones he didn't get you to paint because they weren't important enough to go in his collection. He kidnapped girls – raped them. Did you know that?'

Calista's face drains of colour, she presses her temples with her fingers.

'We need to see him,' Clem says, standing up. 'We need to talk to him.'

'Wait.' Calista stands up too. 'I'm ready to face the consequences of my actions. When I told him the portraits had been destroyed, all my work gone, I was glad. It's given me new strength. I'm going to hand myself in to the police.' She looks towards the back room. 'I'll tell them everything. You must understand there's no guarantee he'll be successfully extradited to the UK. It will be a long process. He may never get to trial.' She shakes her head at her daughters. 'But the last fifteen years have been his punishment.' She gestures towards us. 'And now, his daughters seeing him for who he really is, his lies found out; his collection destroyed. When I take you in, you'll understand.' She pats her chest, on the left-hand side. 'I'm not sure if his heart is up to this. He's very weak. He can't talk much.' She walks to the doorway. 'Come.'

She leads us into a smaller back room. A figure lies on the bed. Even though I know about the injuries, I recoil. One of his cheeks sags where the mouth pulls it, distorted by scar tissue. There's an empty sunken cavity where his left eye should be. Scars criss-cross his whole face, puckering the skin like old material. His fiery hair has gone. Just grey wisps remain.

The girls approach the bed. 'My beauties,' he whispers.

In answer, each girl drops something onto the sheet. A sheen of metal slipping through the air onto Lucian's hollow chest. The pendants. They clink together, gold and glistening.

'I gave you a beautiful life,' he says, turning his face on the pillow to use his eye. 'You've had everything you could have wanted.'

'Except the truth,' Thea says.

'Except our real parents,' Ophelia says.

'I only wanted the best for you.' His voice is weak.

'We don't forgive you,' Clem says. 'It's not about us any more. It's what you did to other women, like Karin.'

'But—' he wheezes.

'Don't,' Ophelia says. 'There's nothing to say. No excuses.'

The girls stand for a moment, staring down at him, and then they turn away. As we leave the room, Mum slips back and goes to Lucian's side.

44

IRENE

'It was me,' I whisper, my mouth at his ear. 'I was the one driving the boat.'

I hear his startled intake of breath, the crackle of air wheezing from his gaping mouth. His one good eye regards me with disbelief. I nod, watching as his expression changes to understanding.

'Goodbye, Paul.' I touch his shoulder, and he flinches.

I don't look back.

EPILOGUE

John and I sit on the rotten step of the summer house, looking out into a bright March morning. The bank of shrubbery shields us from the house and the gaze of other people. He'd arrived from America straight after we got back from France. When I found him on the doorstep of Deben Manor, he was both the boy I remembered and the man I'd imagined – sinewy and tall with a nose bent from an injury sustained in a hockey match, and the same broad, mischievous smile he'd always had – I knew it was me that had changed the most, but he'd swept me into his arms, and lifted me off my size eight feet as if I was still a child.

Now, we're wrapped up in coats and scarves, our breath visible in the clear air. Fred is settled in my lap, a living hot water bottle pressed against my belly. His purr rattles, loud as a lawnmower. 'He's a true survivor, isn't he?' John leans over to scratch under the cat's chin.

'Lucky he's forgiven us,' I say. 'For deserting him.'

'He kind of set the example there,' John says. 'With your

mum and dad getting back together. I guess there was a lot of forgiveness needed, on both sides.'

'They're taking it slowly. Mum's staying on Claire's sofa,' I say. 'But she sees Dad every day.' I wipe Fred's dribble on my jeans. 'They're working things out.'

'How's it going with Clem and her real mum?'

'They're waiting for the DNA tests to come through. But they're together all the time – they just seem to have clicked. Alison says she knew Clem straight away. The moment she turned to face her on the pavement – she knew.'

'And the others?'

'Ophelia has decided not to track her parents down. Not yet, anyway. Says she can't cope with any more change. But Thea is in Romania. She's determined to find her real mother.'

'And what's going on with Calista?'

'Janet. She's calling herself Janet again.' Fred gets down from my lap and stalks away into the grass, his moth-eaten tail a banner in the air. 'She's waiting for her trial. They've let her out on bail. She's packing up the French villa ready to sell it.' I brush some of the cat hair off my jeans. 'Mum talks to her on the phone. Hopefully, the jury will be lenient when they know the whole story.'

'It's horrible to think he's my father,' John's voice tightens. 'I wake up in a cold sweat sometimes. I don't want to be like him.'

'You're nothing like him.' I take his hand impulsively.

John twines his fingers with mine, keeping hold of my hand. We watch Fred prowling through the long grass, emerald eyes glinting. 'So, what now? Are you going to apply to a modelling agency?' he asks, giving me a sideways glance.

I laugh. 'God. No.' His skin is warm against mine. 'I like looking after children. But Ophelia's uncomfortable with me being her nanny. She says I'm part of the family now. So I'll look for another job. A local one. But I'll still visit the kids, and my cousins.'

'What's going on with Mick Smith?' he asks. I've already explained the odd, meticulous way Mick had recorded my comings and goings in the car, how he'd intended to question me, possibly even torture me.

'He's in jail. I've given my statement. There'll be a trial.'

'Sounds like he thought he had you under surveillance. He must have believed you were a spy or something.' John nods at the cat. 'And what about him?'

'He's been adopted by Ophelia. The kids love him.'

'I'm glad he gets his happy ever after.'

We're silent. And then he says softly. 'Hey, come here.' I lean my forehead against his shoulder, and he puts his arm around me. It feels right, I think. We fit. 'I can almost hear spring coming,' he says softly. 'Buds pushing through bark, the first green shoots making their way through the earth.'

'You sound like a gardener.'

'Maybe it seeped into me, osmosis or something.'

'Your dad would have liked that.'

'You won't consider coming to San Francisco for a visit?' he asks. 'I know I've already asked. But I'm going back in a week, and I'm going to miss you.'

'I don't want to leave just yet,' I tell him. 'Not when I've only just got Mum back.'

'I understand.' He gives me a squeeze. 'But that means,' he says slowly, 'that you will consider it, in the future?'

'Yes,' I sit up and look at him. 'I will.'

Deben Manor is to be sold. The girls are moving out. Clem is going to stay with Alison. After Romania, Thea is planning to travel, having closed her business, and Ophelia is buying a little cottage in the village for her and the kids. The rhythm of a hammer striking wood comes to us; the estate agents are banging a 'For Sale' sign in at the end of the drive.

John did tell the girls he was Lucian's biological son, and therefore a kind of stepbrother to them. But Lucian doesn't know any of this. Because he is dead. He died of a heart attack just minutes after we visited him, so he never faced trial. But as Calista said, he'd been punished. As far as I know, there are no more secrets to uncover, and even if there are, I'd rather leave them buried. I think of the silent agreement that had passed between Mum and Calista. But some things are better left alone. What I have is enough, more than enough.

* * *

MORE FROM SASKIA SARGINSON

Another book from Saskia Sarginson, *Identical*, is available to order now here:

www.mybook.to/IdenticalBackAd

ACKNOWLEDGEMENTS

I am very grateful to my editor, Isobel Akenhead, for her guidance, keen eye and brilliant suggestions. My thanks also go to Nia Beynon, Niamh Wallace and Claire Fenby, and the whole Boldwood team, for their support and hard work.

A huge thank you to my agent, Eve White, for her unwavering belief in my writing and good council.

Thanks, too, to Sara Sarre and Alex Marengo, for excellent ideas and advice after reading early drafts. Also, to my sister, Ana Sarginson, for reading a later version and giving thoughtful comments. And to fellow writers, Mary Chamberlain, Viv Graveson, Cecilia Ekback and Laura McClelland for work-shopping excerpts and providing encouraging feedback.

ABOUT THE AUTHOR

Saskia Sarginson is a bestselling author whose debut novel, *The Twins*, was a Richard and Judy Book Club pick. Saskia started her career as a Health and Beauty editor on women's magazines, and then became a freelance journalist. Saskia grew up in a Suffolk pine forest but now lives in London with her husband.

Sign up to Saskia Sarginson's mailing list here for news, competitions and updates on future books.

Visit Saskia's Website: www.saskiasarginson.co.uk

Follow Saskia on social media:

instagram.com/saskiasarginson
x.com/SaskiaSarginson
facebook.com/SaskiaSarginsonBooks

ALSO BY SASKIA SARGINSON

Identical

One Dark Summer

THE
Murder
LIST

**THE MURDER LIST IS A NEWSLETTER
DEDICATED TO SPINE-CHILLING FICTION
AND GRIPPING PAGE-TURNERS!**

**SIGN UP TO MAKE SURE YOU'RE ON OUR
HIT LIST FOR EXCLUSIVE DEALS, AUTHOR
CONTENT, AND COMPETITIONS.**

SIGN UP TO OUR
NEWSLETTER

BIT.LY/THEMURDERLISTNEWS

Boldwood

Boldwood Books is an award-winning fiction publishing company seeking out the best stories from around the world.

Find out more at www.boldwoodbooks.com

Join our reader community for brilliant books, competitions and offers!

Follow us
@BoldwoodBooks
@TheBoldBookClub

Sign up to our weekly deals newsletter

https://bit.ly/BoldwoodBNewsletter